CRAWFORD SMITH

Fester Descent

SWEET WEASEL WORDS
PORTLAND, OREGON, USA
sweetweaselwords.com

First published by Sweet Weasel Words 2026

Copyright © 2026 by Crawford Smith

All rights reserved. No part of this publication may be reproduced, stored, or transmitted in any form or by any means, electronic, mechanical, photocopying, recording, scanning, or otherwise without written permission from the publisher. It is illegal to copy this book, post it to a website, or distribute it by any other means without permission.

This novel is entirely a work of fiction. The names, characters, and incidents portrayed in it are the work of the author's imagination. Any resemblance to actual persons, living or dead, events, or localities is entirely coincidental.

The words and thoughts of the characters are not meant to be offensive to readers; they're merely characterizations, meant to convey the attitudes and worldview of certain characters. Please don't get your shorts all in a bunch over it.

First edition

ISBN: 978-1-7332699-8-8

This book was professionally typeset on Reedsy. Find out more at reedsy.com for NancyAnne

Acknowledgments

Special thanks to Kim Smith and Jess Truhan for helping me bring this project from concept to completion with their patience and valuable suggestions.

Also, many thanks to Rob Padovano, who helped straighten out some of the legal and procedural issues in the book. Any errors or outright BS are mine, not his.

Thanks to my aunt, Claudia Pattison, for helping me proofread and generally clean up the text.

It was great to have Paula Guran back to edit this work. I always love working with her, and always grow as a writer when I do.

Above all else, super-extra-special thanks to my wife NancyAnne, for putting up with all of my foolishness.

I

Part One

September 1995

Chapter 1

"Where the hell's my money?" snarled Cecilia Schmidt.

She lounged behind the enormous mahogany desk that would be in her possession for another few minutes. On the other side of the desk were her two most hated in-laws: Ophelia Schmidt and her husband Herkimer. Ophelia was the aunt of Cecilia's late husband, Emile. When Emile died and left everything—including control of the family business—to Cecilia, Ophelia had become her *bête noire* and opposed her at every turn.

Most of the family disliked Cecilia; to them, she was a gold-digger, an interloper, a pretender. She'd made no friends when she cleaned house on the Schmidt Pretzel Bakery board of directors, thus depriving a half-dozen Schmidts of well-paying sinecures. She'd always played defense—on the lookout for whatever rotten scheme her in-laws were going to try next—and never allowed them to score. The fact Cecilia had overseen a 20 percent increase in profitability made them resent her even more.

After the Night of the Mill Fire last year, Cecilia had been at a disadvantage. She'd been arrested after waving a gun around in Mill Park that night. Okay, sure—she'd also shot that redneck Merle Totenkopf, but it was only a flesh wound and he hadn't pressed charges. Relatively minor compared to the other events of that strange evening, but Cecilia had still left the park in handcuffs in the back of a Pennsylvania State Police cruiser.

The charges had been dropped, of course. She was a Schmidt—albeit by marriage—but that still made her a Top Hat, and in Fester the Top Hats did pretty much as they pleased. *Accountability* wasn't a word frequently used by or about the town's leading families. Members of Fester's other Top Hat families acted out in much more destructive ways and never got much more than a scolding. Compared to them, Cecilia was a shining star of virtue.

However, the incident had provided an excuse for Ophelia to rally the family to get rid of Cecilia. Her solution was simple: buy Cecilia out. Ophelia had browbeaten the rest of the family into putting up the considerable sum needed. Many of the family members had balked at the idea of paying out money to the loathed Cecilia, but Ophelia had exercised her iron will and the rest of the family eventually fell in line.

Cecilia had squeezed her odious in-laws for as much as she could. They'd been surprisingly accommodating. Cecilia felt she had earned every penny. The Schmidt family was getting a bargain, in her opinion.

The time had come to pay up. The office in the family mansion where they met was already stripped of anything Cecilia wanted to keep. She intended to make a clean exit.

"Your *money* ... is right here," said Ophelia with a perfectly timed pause to convey her contempt. She nodded at Herkimer. He stepped to the mahogany desk and placed a small aluminum suitcase on the polished surface. After flipping the case open, he swiveled it around to show Cecilia the contents: bundles of tightly bound hundred-dollar bills.

"It's all there," said Ophelia.

Of course you'd say that, thought Cecilia. She dug down to the bottom of the suitcase and extracted one of the packs of money. She thumbed through the stack while Ophelia and Herkimer watched, frowning.

"Okay, looks good," said Cecilia. She'd expected them to pull something shitty.

"I hope you realize how difficult it was to gather this much cash," sniffed Ophelia. "I don't understand why you couldn't have chosen a more conventional method of payment."

"Because I don't trust you any further than I can throw you," said Cecilia. "You're lucky I didn't demand payment in Krugerrands. I seriously considered it."

CHAPTER 1

"I've no doubt of it," said Ophelia. "Now, I believe you have something for us."

Cecilia reached into an otherwise empty desk drawer, pulled out a thick manila envelope and shoved it across the bare desktop. Ophelia and Herkimer, settling into the guest chairs uninvited, opened it and began carefully reviewing the contents.

"Everything's in order," said Cecilia. "All reviewed and signed by Messieurs Nasté, Brutus, and Shore."

The Schmidts nodded and continued thumbing through the documents.

Cecilia was impatient. She intended to leave Fester forever as soon as this transaction was concluded. She had put a down payment on a large ranch in an exclusive community outside of Taos and was looking forward to putting the better part of a continent between herself and south-central Pennsylvania. Her flight left from Baltimore the next morning.

"It's all yours now," said Cecilia with a trace of bitterness. "The company, the house, all of the properties. Your dream realized at last. Although where you scraped the money up to buy me out, I'll never know."

"That's very true," agreed Ophelia. "The family has resources your *nouveau riche* mind can't begin to grasp." She looked at Herkimer, who gave her a quick nod. "Well, I believe this is all in order. Our business will be concluded just as soon as you hand over the keys."

Cecilia pulled an enormous ring of keys from her purse. It was tempting to just fling them at Ophelia's head, but she figured she might as well exit the scene with a bit of grace. She stood, walked around the desk, and handed the keys to Ophelia.

"Very good," said Ophelia. Cecilia closed the suitcase, flipped the latches closed, and sat back down in the leather executive chair. She took a minute to set the two combination locks before standing again.

"Leaving so soon?" asked Herkimer.

"Absolutely. I can't wait to shake the dust of this town off my boots."

Ophelia sighed. "I know things have always been difficult," she said. "I would be lying if I said I was sorry to see you go. Now that it is almost behind us, though, there's no reason why we can't be civilized about it. I think we should have a drink to seal the deal."

"I couldn't agree more," said Cecilia. She'd been wanting a stiff drink all afternoon. "Unfortunately, the liquor cabinet has been packed up."

"Not a problem," said Ophelia. She reached into her voluminous purse and pulled out a very dusty—but sealed—bottle of cognac and three chunky glasses. She poured out three hefty drinks and slid one over the desk. Cecilia reached for it, hoping she wouldn't strain the seam on her Armani. It was nifty black-and-white houndstooth-patterned virgin wool tube dress she'd bought for the occasion. She was going to blow this popsicle stand in style.

Ophelia hoisted her glass. "Here's to a rewarding—if not quite happy—ending."

"I'll drink to that," Cecilia said and downed her drink in one go.

II

Part Two

June 2014

Chapter 2

The flatbed semi-truck lumbered down Route 23, just south of Mellonville, the WIDE LOAD banner flapping in the evening breeze. Dave, the driver, proceeded cautiously, looking for the correct turnoff. It was getting late, and he hoped to deliver his load and be back home in Shippensburg before dinnertime. He found the turnoff, a narrow two-lane called Dockstock Mountain Road, then made the turn and headed up into the hills.

Dave was nervous. He had been told the address he was delivering to had the space to unload the items under the tarpaulin on the back of the truck, but there was no sign of even small industrial facilities out here. The last one he'd seen was the old P-Rite factory about ten miles back, and that place looked like it had been unoccupied for thirty years.

He was also nervous about the area in general—Kerian County had a bad reputation in central Pennsylvania. Weird things happened there frequently. The farther he went, the more nervous he became. The trees encroached closely on the road, which became narrower and more winding the farther he went. He slowed down and took a look at the clipboard on the seat beside him. The address was 20256 Dockstock Mountain Road, with instructions reading: *exactly 3 mi. past Rte. 23, on right, look for mailbox*. He had pretty much gone that far already, and he certainly didn't want to overshoot the mark; turning the rig around on this road would be almost impossible. He kicked on the high beams and proceeded at a crawl. Ahead on the right he could see a faded gray mailbox with stick-on numbers *20256* and the name *W. Snyder*. Above the name was a hand-lettered wooden sign reading

Military Antiques. He looked up the driveway—it was narrow and the trees grew together overhead to form what appeared to be a leafy, green tunnel. It seemed unlikely he would be able to get the truck through it. He stopped and put on his four-ways.

Dave pulled out his phone, consulted the clipboard, and dialed the number listed for the recipient.

"What?"

"Uh, hello. I've got a shipment here from the Shippensburg DOD logistics depot for a William Snyder. Is that you?"

"'Bout fuckin' time! Where are you?"

"At the end of your driveway. I was told there would be space to turn my rig around at the facility, but it doesn't look like the driveway's big enough to get up, much less turn around."

"Don't be such a wuss. The driveway widens out after the first fifty feet and there's plenty of space to turn around at the shop. Now get it in gear, Rubber Duck. You got a crane on that rig, right?"

"Yes."

"Good. Get going. I've got shit to do."

The call ended and Dave stared at the phone. He didn't like being here, and he definitely didn't like being called a wuss. All of the bad things he'd heard about Kerian County seemed like an understatement.

A Ford F-150 rolled up behind him, flashing its high beams and honking. Dave waved him around. The guy in the F-150 rolled slowly by, flipping him off. Dave shook his head, put it in gear and turned into the driveway.

Billy Snyder watched the flatbed make its way up the driveway. He was well past sixty now, almost completely bald and with an ever-growing paunch he couldn't seem to get rid of. His doctor had said it was just what happened as the body aged. Billy thought that was bullshit. The quack also told Billy he should exercise more and cut back on the beer. Billy *knew* that was bullshit. He still ran five miles a day, rain or shine, and there was no way he was giving up his beer. Maybe Billy had a few (or more than a few) cans every evening, but the last two decades had been hard on him. He needed to be

CHAPTER 2

able to unwind.

No time to grouse about it now—there was work to do. He waved the truck over to the front of the workshop, went through the insanely complicated paperwork that came with the military surplus shipment, and instructed the truck driver to unload the cargo onto a nearby concrete pad.

Dave got busy, removing the canvas tarp from the flatbed. It revealed a strange object that looked like a giant metal spider. In the center was a flat disc with a hatch in the back. On either side of the disc was a stout metal arm that supported three long metal tubes with various flanges, brackets and geegaws arranged along the length.

"What the hell *is* that thing?" asked Dave. "I've been delivering military surplus for damn near a decade, but I *never* seen anything like that."

"It's an FU-69 Mind Your Own Fuckin' Business."

Dave pursed his lips to respond, but the grim look on Billy's face changed his mind. "Fine," he said quietly and hopped up on the flatbed to work the crane. In short order, he had unloaded the strange object, given Billy's paperwork a quick once-over, and took off. Fortunately, it was easy enough to turn around and get his rig back on the road. He drove a little fast but managed to make it back to Shippensburg in time for dinner.

Billy checked his watch. His best client would be here soon, but the client was also a little nosey. Billy wanted to have his new acquisition under cover before he showed up. He dragged a huge blue tarp from the workshop and draped it over the object, then weighed it down with cinderblocks. He was just putting the last one into place when he heard a car turn off the road and onto the driveway.

Billy waited at the top of the driveway, standing at parade rest. Even though he had been drummed out of the Constabulary twenty years ago, he still wore a dark blue uniform shirt (without insignia, naturally) and khaki trousers. He watched as a red Maserati Merak approached. A man with sandy hair sat behind the wheel. The passenger seat was occupied by a medium-sized monkey. In the tiny back seat, there were at least two more monkeys. Billy could see their heads popping up and down like critters in a

Whac-A-Mole game. They actually seemed pretty well-behaved, but Billy didn't care. The monkeys stayed in the car whenever this client came to visit. The car stopped; the engine revved and shut off. Billy waited while the driver addressed the monkeys individually, then emerged. He was six foot six and wore a pair of glasses so ugly they must have cost thousands. He was dressed in plain-looking khakis and a blue-and-white button-down shirt, both from Brooks Brothers.

Billy stepped forward and extended his hand. "Mr. Schmidt," he said. "Very good to see you again."

"Oh, for Christ's sake, Billy. I've told you a hundred times: call me Ronald."

"Yes, of course—Ronald. Old habits die hard. I spent my career being deferential to the Top H … er, the top members of our community."

Ronald Schmidt hated the name "Top Hats," mainly because most of Fester's upper crust had turned on the Schmidt family. They no longer had the social status they'd long enjoyed. Ronald was now second in line to the family fortune, after his aunt Ophelia. Ronald's younger sister Thelma Louise was the family's sole saving grace. She was active in the local arts scene and gave generously to Fester's charitable organizations.

These three were the last of the once-great Schmidt dynasty in Fester. Shortly after the events of the Night of the Mill Fire, Ophelia had engineered the buyout of Cecilia Schmidt. Rumor had it that there had been a duffel bag full of cash, and possibly an incriminating sex tape involved. Regardless of the details, Cecilia had taken the money and quickly disappeared into the desert Southwest, which had bothered absolutely no one in town.

What *had* bothered many people was Ophelia's eventual decision to sell the entire Schmidt Pretzel Bakery to one of their hated rivals in Hanover. Some of the other Schmidts had put up a determined resistance, and an intra-family war had ensued. In the end, Ophelia prevailed—aided by some convenient hunting accidents, heart attacks, and one flat-out disappearance. The rest of the Schmidts, seeing the writing on the wall, backed Ophelia's plan. Certainly, they were enticed by the huge payoff promised by the Zut Brands, Inc. buyout. In the end, Zut had bought the company, modernized the bakery—and laid off half the workforce.

CHAPTER 2

The Schmidt name had been dirt after that. The bakery had been the largest employer in town, and many folks now blamed the Schmidts for selling out their livelihoods. As a result, most of the Top Hat Schmidts had taken their checks and headed off to sunnier climes. There were still dozens if not hundreds of shirt-tail Schmidts still around, but nobody cared about them. The last of the Top Hat Schmidts in Fester were Ophelia, Ronald, and Thelma Louise who spent most of their time ensconced in the mansion at the top of Morningwood Promenade.

And they still had plenty of money. Or at least Ronald threw it around like he had an unlimited supply. Billy was hoping to relieve Ronald of some tonight.

"Well, come on in," said Billy. "I have some prime merchandise I've been holding back especially for you." Billy led Ronald into the front room of his house.

Billy's house was threadbare but neatly kept. His military and police sense of orderliness had not left him—even though his wife Rose had done so as soon as he had been removed as chief constable. The place was modest, but better than the dump he'd rented in Kugels after the divorce.

"Have a seat," said Billy. "Can I interest you in some Glenlivet?" He kept a bottle of the top-shelf stuff for special clients—and Ronald was pretty much the most special of all the clients he had.

"No thank you, Billy. Think I'll pass tonight."

Billy breathed an inward sigh of relief. He'd seen Ronald Schmidt drunk, and it wasn't pretty. He was nice enough to deal with when sober, but after even a single drink, the man could turn arrogant and angry. Billy really wanted a beer but decided it could wait. It was time for his show, and he wanted to keep a clear head.

"Okay, Ronald," said Billy. "Our first item is in amazing shape. Like new, really." He reached into a large leather case on the coffee table and pulled out an ornate helmet with a wicked-looking spike on the top. "A genuine Prussian *pickelhaube,* circa 1870. See this insignia right here?" He pointed to an emblem on the visor consisting of four arrows arranged with their points touching so they formed a cross. "These indicate the helmet's owner was a member of the *Johanniterorden*, the personal guard of Otto von Bismarck."

Ronald stared raptly at the helmet. "May I touch it?" he asked.

"Of course," said Billy, and he carefully handed it over.

Ronald handled it as if it were a baby, stroking the cross emblem with his thumb. "Do you think…" he said. "Do you think this might have *belonged* to von Bismarck?"

"Unlikely, sir," said Billy. "I'm sure I would know if it belonged to him. It was, however, worn by a member of his personal guard, so I think it's safe to say this helmet was in the presence of the great man himself, although not actually on his head."

"Wonderful, wonderful," said Ronald. "How much?"

"Well, I could probably go online tonight and sell this for ten thousand dollars. Maybe even fifteen—it's in such wonderful condition. For you, Mr. Schmidt, I'll let it go for eight thousand dollars." Billy knew it was a fake—he'd paid $450 for it and buried it in his backyard for a week to make it look aged.

Ronald scrunched up his face. "Hmmm, no. Four thousand."

"Oh, I don't know," said Billy skeptically. "I couldn't see taking less than six for this priceless piece of history."

"Okay, then—five thousand."

"Done," said Billy. Ronald smiled and placed the helmet next to him on the sofa. Billy continued. "Next, I have a collection of Civil War bayonets, both Union and Confederate. Admittedly, some are a little corroded, but they're all in good shape. And they have a certificate of authenticity from Sotheby's."

So the one-man auction went. Billy paraded an array of military antiques—some genuine, some bogus—to his best client. He knew better than to completely rook the man. There was a chance, albeit a small one, that Ronald would have these items appraised. More likely, Ronald might know some other rich, eccentric collector who would be able to spot the fakes. Billy wasn't too concerned. Ronald, like his aunt and sister, was a recluse. As far as he knew, Billy was the only other person in the area who had personal interaction with the man, excepting perhaps the odd delivery

CHAPTER 2

or repair person.

By the end of the evening, Billy had sold the Prussian helmet, the bayonets, a British cavalry sword from the Crimean War, and a rusted metal gauntlet said to have been worn by a French knight at the Battle of Agincourt.

"Well, all together that comes to..." Billy made show of totting up the numbers in his head. "Twelve thousand, three hundred dollars. Let's just call it an even twelve thousand, shall we?"

"Very good," said Ronald. He pulled a huge roll of hundred-dollar bills from his pocket and began counting them out. "Oh, and one more thing," he said. "I want a gun."

"Certainly," said Billy. "I have an amazing replica of a Mannlicher-Carcano just like the one used by Lee..."

"No," said Ronald. "A *real* gun. No replicas."

"Ah," said Billy carefully. "Mr. Schmidt, I do hope you realize the local authorities are aware of my business enterprise. Not two months ago a deputy came by to check up on me. I don't *have* any functioning firearms available. Too much liability."

Ronald's face darkened. "Oh, bullshit!" he exclaimed. "You must have *something*. You are hardly the only dealer around here, you know." He made a show of returning the bills to his roll and moving to put it back in his pocket.

Billy was torn. On one hand, Ronald was by far and away his wealthiest and most gullible client. The money he was preparing to hand over was going to go a long way towards underwriting the special project Billy had going in the workshop. And Billy *did* have a number of functioning firearms—not all of them legal.

Sensing he was about to alienate a major cash cow, Billy thought fast. He didn't want to provide Ronald Schmidt with a functioning firearm, but he also didn't want him to leave with his entire bankroll. "Well, Mr. Schmidt," said Billy slowly. "I *do* have an item that might be of interest to you. I had promised it to a Japanese businessman who has a particular interest in its time period. But . . . Wait here, please."

Billy disappeared into his back room and returned with a wooden box.

He laid it on the coffee table and reverently opened it to reveal a tarnished revolver. "This," he said somberly, "is a British Webley .455 Mark VI. It was used in the assassination of Reinhard Heydrich." Only the first half of the statement was true.

Ronald's mouth opened slightly. "Operation Anthropoid?" He gave Billy a sly look. "So, this pistol killed the Butcher of Prague?"

"No, of course not," said Billy. "It was a grenade that took out Heydrich. The Czech commandos had a Sten gun, but it jammed. The grenade wounded Heydrich and his driver, but at first, they were able to fight back. This revolver was used to kill the driver. It's a top-break revolver. You open it by pressing this flange and folding the barrel and cylinder down." He picked up the revolver and opened the frame. "Solid piece of hardware. It kicks like a mule, though." He closed the revolver and handed it Ronald.

"Wow," said Ronald softly, his eyes running up and down the gun like he was eyeing a pinup model. He opened the revolver again and held his eye up to the barrel. "Yes. I must have it. How much?"

"Welllll," said Billy with feigned reluctance. "Mr. Sakimoto is going to be *very* disappointed that I won't be able to deliver this as promised. But who would I be to put the interests of some Jap over those of a respected member of my community? The price is steep, however. I couldn't part with it for less than ten grand. I suppose Sakimoto won't want to do business with me after this." He shook his head at the thought of losing the patronage of the imaginary Japanese businessman.

"Tell you what," said Ronald, gesturing at the pile of quasi-authentic memorabilia with the Webley. "I'll give you twenty thousand for the whole shootin' match."

Billy chuckled politely. "Whew, you drive a hard bargain, Ronald," he said, figuring the stuff was worth three thousand dollars, tops. "But since you're such a good customer—and a local—I'll accept."

"Great! Great!" Ronald pulled out his dog-choking roll of bills and began counting them out. "Do you have any ammo for this?"

"Afraid not." This was the only reason Billy deigned to sell Ronald the pistol. He knew .455 ammunition was hard to come by. He hoped Ronald

CHAPTER 2

would get distracted before he could get his mitts on the ammo. At this point, Billy didn't particularly care—twenty grand was going to go a long way towards financing his special project. He just wanted to get the cash in hand and see Ronald Schmidt on his way.

"Shooty's Gun World down on Fifth might be able to order it for you," said Billy. "If not, I know a place in Las Vegas that would be able to get it. That place has *everything*." This was absolutely true, which is why the BATF had raided the place and shut it down two years ago. He got out his address book and scrawled down the address and phone number.

"Here you go," said Billy, handing over the contact info as Ronald gave him a thick stack of bills. "Let me get you a duffel to carry your treasures."

Out in the driveway, Billy watched as Ronald carted his loot back to the Maserati. The monkeys, seeing him coming, went nuts. The big one in the front seat began thwacking the dashboard with its meaty hands, producing loud thumps. One of the little ones in the back seat tried to climb into the front, but the big one shoved him back. A fight ensued, and Ronald yelled, "Knock it off, you guys!"

And they did.

He stowed the duffel in the tiny trunk, climbed in, and spent some time talking to the monkeys before starting up the sports car and driving away.

Billy watched the taillights disappear into the trees, then headed back into the house. He wanted to get online and start spending the cash he had just received. The only major parts he needed now were an engine and a transmission. The engine should be easy to find, the transmission less so. Billy wasn't particularly worried; he knew people who knew people.

Chapter 3

Martin Prieboy didn't want to go home. He'd been dreading this day—and this evening—for weeks. At least during the day, he could lose himself in his work. That was easy enough to do. As chief constable of Fester, there was always plenty of work.

He'd put off coming home for as long as possible. If it had been any other night, Martin could easily have stayed in the office past midnight. But he had an appointment this evening and he needed to come home to change out of his uniform. If he'd thought about it, he could have brought a change of clothes to the office and put off this whole sad scene.

But he couldn't put it off forever. Might as well suck it up and deal with it now. He unlocked the door to his modest Cape Cod-style house and dragged himself over the threshold. He fetched a large sigh as he dropped his heavily laden briefcase to the floor of the entry foyer. Turning to his left, he marched into the living room and removed a framed photograph from the mantelpiece.

The photo was nearly twenty years old. It showed a smiling Martin Prieboy looking very sharp in a white tuxedo. With him is another white-tuxedoed man, also smiling deliriously. He had a shy grin, wire-rimmed specs and a small, brown mustache that curled up at the ends. His name was Sam Bolton, and he had been Martin's life partner for almost two decades.

Martin had come out of the closet shortly after he'd met Sam; up until then he hadn't even known he'd been *in* the closet. The strict upbringing in the orphanage and the corporal punishment favored by Father McJaggar there had resulted in his stuffing his sexuality deep into the recesses of his mind. Martin knew he liked boys; he also knew liking boys was bad. The list of things that were hell-bound sinful at the Holy Jesus Christ Almighty School for Unfortunate Boys was a long one, and Martin ended up thinking about liking boys in the same way he did about swearing or eating meat on Friday—perhaps you wanted to do it but just didn't. It brought too much grief. Martin's pubescence had been a lonely and difficult one.

Once he got out of the orphanage, he'd buried his desires in his work. No longer under the strictures of the guilt- and punishment-heavy orphanage, Martin had been free to explore his sexuality. He hadn't. He knew his sexual orientation was not bad or evil, yet he still didn't care to indulge it. The monks at HJCASfUB had essentially stripped away that part of Martin Prieboy's personality.

That had changed in 1994. It had been a strange time for him. After chief constable Billy Snyder had been hospitalized following an assassination attempt, his temporary replacement had suspended Martin. Still obsessed with a case, he'd continued the investigation on his own, including an extremely short stint as a costumed crime-fighter known as the Fliedermaus. No doubt that DC Comics' lawyers would have been all over Martin had they seen the cringe-worthy Batman knockoff costume he'd concocted.

Even more cringe-worthy was the get-up Martin had put together to go undercover in Fester's sole gay bar, The Embers. Martin had tarted himself up to a degree that would have alarmed the most flamboyant participant in a San Francisco Pride Parade. The proprietor, a kind and patient man named Sam, had tried to help Martin understand the gay community did not generally behave like a cheap stereotype from TV.

This had been a revelation to Martin. He'd noticed most of the patrons of The Embers were regular guys in regular-guy outfits who just wanted to have a good time. No big deal. He'd struck up a friendship with Sam and was thankful to have someone he could talk to outside of work.

The friendship with Sam had deepened, and Martin eventually realized they were flirting. In retrospect, he was certain Sam knew what was going on between them much sooner than Martin did. Yet Sam was a man of deep kindness and infinite patience, and hadn't pushed, knowing Martin had a lot of baggage from his upbringing. Like a persevering gardener, Sam had slowly nurtured their relationship, let it grow at its own pace and supported it when needed.

Martin's love for Sam allowed him a dimension of happiness and freedom he'd never thought possible. It took nearly two years for Martin to completely come out of his shell and allow the physical component of their relationship to develop. Again, Sam's patience and "go at your own pace" approach had been worth the effort. When the dam had finally burst Martin had gone at it with enthusiasm—he was making up for decades of physical self-deprivation. It was a lot of fun, at least at first, but it soon began to wear Sam down a little. Nonetheless, he'd maintained the same patience and grace with which he'd always treated Martin.

One of the things that had initially made Martin reluctant to engage with Sam and in their relationship was the fact that Martin had been promoted to chief constable. He had been extremely wary of mixing his personal and professional lives, especially since he was involved in times of intense transition in both. He and Sam had done a lot of sneaking around—not appearing in public together and generally behaving like a "we've got to stop meeting like this" movie cliché.

It wasn't just the constabulary's disapproval that Martin had to worry about. Fester wasn't the most enlightened place on the map. Sam had told stories about the abuse he and his patrons had had to endure at the hands of the constables, local church leaders, and the general populace. Reverend Georg Eyler of the Calvary Reformed Lutheran Church was a hell-and-fire homophobe who was still preaching jaw-droppingly intolerant sermons at the age of ninety-one. Calvary was the largest and most influential church in town, and Eyler still wielded a lot of influence.

Things had come to a head when Martin and Sam took the plunge and moved in together. Martin had not made a big deal of the situation; there was no grand coming out party or announcement. Martin didn't want one and Sam had been through all of that when he was much younger. They simply bought a small house and lived there together. As far as Martin was concerned, this was simply who he was. If anyone had an issue with it, that was their own problem to deal with, not Martin's or Sam's.

People *did* have a problem with it, of course. This was Fester—a town that was mean and proud of it. Martin couldn't do anything about it except demonstrate being gay was only one part of his life. If people decided to judge him based on that one part, then so be it. He continued to do his job with the same skill, intelligence, and integrity that he always had, and hoped it would be enough.

It almost wasn't. There had been a concerted campaign—led by the scabrous Reverend Eyler—to have Martin removed as chief constable, and, ideally, run out of town on a rail. Fortunately, Mayor Augenblick, who was in charge of appointments for the position of chief constable, had a skeleton or two in his own closet, and was sympathetic to Martin's cause. There was also a lot of general support for Martin from the town. People had long memories and did not miss the police corruption and brutality that had been the hallmark of Billy Snyder's regime. Martin was a good cop. With the exception of Reverend Eyler and his hateful ilk, people didn't want to get rid of him.

Martin had also had a struggle within the ranks of the constabulary. There had been enough trouble with the remnants of Snyder's reign as chief constable—crooked, incompetent constables whom Martin had purged as soon as he'd taken over the Big Chair. He put the entire force on notice that corruption and brutality would not be tolerated and had fired the worst of the bad eggs. It hadn't gone as smoothly as he'd hoped, but not nearly as badly as he had feared.

Most of these bad eggs were long gone before Martin's sexual preference became common knowledge. Nonetheless, there were still resentful constables on the force. Martin had heard plenty of whispered references to "Chief Tinkerbell." It would be a lie to say this didn't hurt his feelings, but he was, after all, a professional.

He had dealt with the situation with a mild form of collective punishment. Whenever he'd heard whispers about "Chief Tinkerbell" or any other slur, Martin would schedule a mandatory sensitivity training seminar for the entire force. Personally, he thought most of these things were ridiculous, but he forced himself to sit through every one he scheduled. They may have been ridiculous, but they served their purpose. Eventually, the constables figured out the connection between ill-chosen remarks that reached Martin's ears and the frequency of the sensitivity seminars. Both tailed off quite rapidly after that.

Also, America seemed to be a more tolerant place, at least a little. The proliferation of same-sex marriage laws had swept the country at the beginning of the century. Even stone-hearted Fester had inaugurated its own annual pride parade three years ago. Martin made sure he was visible to the parade participants and the spectators as he paced up and down the parade route. There would be no harassment of those wishing to march, and the Fester Pride Parade continued to flourish and grow.

Even the stodgy Commonwealth of Pennsylvania had seen fit to legalize same-sex marriage a few months ago. Martin wished Sam had been alive to see it; they had often talked about officially tying the knot themselves. They had even considered going up to Massachusetts to do the deed, but the conservative Pennsylvania legislature had opposed recognizing same-sex marriage from other jurisdictions. In the end, Martin and Sam had been content to leave well enough alone. They were together, they were happy; that's all that really mattered. They'd talked about getting married eventually, but the opportunity never came.

What came first was Sam's diagnosis. A year and a half ago, Sam had developed a cold that just wouldn't go away. Martin had nagged Sam to get checked out, fearing he might have developed bronchitis. When Sam finally relented and got examined, it turned out to be much worse than bronchitis: he had been diagnosed with stage-four pancreatic cancer. True to form, the disease burned through Martin's partner in record time.

Martin still had trouble internalizing the monstrous injustice of it all. Barely two years ago, Sam had been happy, healthy, and full of fun. After the diagnosis, he deteriorated quickly. Martin sometimes wondered if getting the diagnosis had somehow sped up the course of the disease. If Sam had remained in blissful ignorance, perhaps he would he have survived longer.

CHAPTER 3

Martin's life had been filled with such "what-ifs" in the twelve months since Sam had died. It didn't matter—the love of his life was gone.

Martin had been devastated. He responded to the soul-wrenching tragedy by doing the only thing he could think of—working. It was his only solace. Even his life-long obsession with Batman didn't help. Sure, Bruce Wayne had lost his parents, but that was just some cheap plot twist a couple of funny-book writers had dreamt up seventy-five years before. Martin's pain was *real* and it was of a previously unimaginable intensity. So he got up every morning and he went to work. When he came home at night, he ate a meager dinner and worked some more. Often, he fell asleep at his desk. It was the only way he knew to block the pain.

One of Martin's first acts as chief constable had been to shut down the Pine Room—a bar on the edge of town that served as a prostitution front. To his mind, the notion of women (and a few men) selling their bodies for money was entirely unacceptable. Less than a week after he had been promoted to chief, he'd taken a hand-picked flying squad of constables to the Pine Room and shut it down for good.

The results of the closing of the Pine Room had been immediate and dramatic. The frequency of domestic violence and rape—already high in Fester—had increased substantially. Martin had wracked his brain trying to figure out how to counter this spike in violent crime. At first, he'd tried tactics similar to those that had been successful in blunting problems associated with youth crime and gang activity. It turned out that Midnight Basketball wasn't going to cut it.

Realizing the problem wasn't going to be one his iron-rod orphanage upbringing could address, he'd had to do some serious recalibration of his moral compass. He'd backed way off his involvement in the prosecutions, letting the DA in Weaverville make all the calls. Fortunately, the internet was becoming more widespread, and between the dating sites and the avalanche of online pornography the frustrated men of Fester soon found outlets other than brutalizing their wives and girlfriends.

When he heard Solheim had served his sentence and opened another bar on the east side of the river, Martin had taken a much more low-key approach. He'd first visited Solheim and informed him he'd better keep his nose clean, and that any public complaints would be dealt with immediately and forcefully. He'd also cultivated one of the "waitresses" at the new joint—called Mike's Place—an attractive young woman named Renee. Martin paid her a modest sum each month to report on the doings at Mike's Place. She'd initially indicated a willingness to provide more than information—"I just go gooey for a man in uniform," she'd said—but Martin had politely rebuffed her. All he wanted was info. As long as there was no violence or coercion at Mike's Place, he was uncomfortably willing to let things slide.

As always, there were many other things to occupy his attention. None, however, came close to filling the huge aching void in his life that had opened up exactly one year ago when Sam had left this earthly realm.

A year with the love of his life gone. It seemed like only a day; it seemed like a hundred eternities.

Martin checked his watch. He really needed to get going. He took another hard look at the photograph, and a tear rolled down his cheek. They were so young then, and so happy. How quickly it had all changed.

He pulled a handkerchief from his pants pocket and wiped away the tear. He replaced the photograph on the mantel and turned to go upstairs to get ready.

Chapter 4

Inside Bollinger Automotive, Michael "Bolly" Bollinger was just finishing up working on a Honda. In the past, Bolly's old man had refused to work on anything other than American cars, but Phil Bollinger no longer ran the business. He now spent his days watching game shows in a retirement home in Weaverville. Bolly had taken over the business ten years ago and had known immediately he was going to have to be more flexible than his old man if he wanted to keep it afloat. Times were tough.

At least that's what people said, although Bolly thought things were now cooking along pretty well compared to the last ten years or so. People in Fester also tended to blame President Obama for anything bad that happened. A bad harvest, any increase in the price of food or gasoline, *any* weirdness with healthcare, the bottom tearing out of a trash bag while dragging it to the curb—it was all Obama's fault. Bolly knew this was bullshit, but there were plenty of people in town who absolutely could not stand the thought of a Black president.

Bolly drove the Honda out of the bay and pulled in his own car. It was a 1975 Chevy Nova he had owned for nearly twenty-five years. His old man had helped him buy it when he was fourteen, allowing Bolly to work off his debt at the shop. It had been a real beater, but Bolly put a lot of elbow grease into it, first getting the engine purring, then getting the body pristine. The car had been road-worthy well before Bolly was old enough for a learner's permit. Of course, he had taken it out on his own but had never been caught. Phil Bollinger had been wise in allowing his son to hone his mechanical aptitude on the car—Bolly had been instrumental in the shop's continued success, and Phil had been able to retire knowing the business was in good hands.

It was now full dark, and the other mechanics had gone home. Bolly was going to dink around with the carb a little bit, to see if he could get a little more bang out of the 350 engine. The phone rang, and Bolly put his wrench aside to answer the extension on the shop wall. It was Janie.

"Bolly, where are you?" she asked. "Your dinner's getting cold."

"Gotta pay the rent tonight, babe. I thought I told you this morning." Actually, he distinctly remembered telling her this morning.

"Oh, yeah, I guess so. I'm kinda high. I guess I forgot."

"No worries. Just wrap it up and put it in the fridge. I'll nuke it when I get home."

"Okay, sure," said Janie. "I hate it when rent night rolls around. It's so creepy."

"Yeah, I know," said Bolly. "It's just how they do business."

"Well, maybe you should look for another place to rent."

"Babe, the shop has been here forty years. The old man would blow a gasket if I moved it. Plus, I'm in hock up to my eyebrows since I bought that frame straightener. Once the body work picks up and I get the thing paid off, maybe I can look at buying a place." Probably not, though. The shop felt like home, and he really didn't want to leave, even if buying his own place made more financial sense in the long run. "Look, Janie, relax a bit. I'll be home in two hours, tops."

"Okay, Bolly. Oh, I almost forgot! I heard from Paul today. He bought a new house!"

"Hey, that's great! So, you talked to him?"

"No, I just saw a post he made on Facebook."

"Oh. Still, that's pretty cool. Good for him."

Paul Plummer had been Bolly's best friend in high school. The Plummer family had moved to Baltimore after the Night of the Mill Fire, and Paul and Bolly had drifted apart. Paul ended up moving to the Southwest and starting his own computer security firm. He was Facebook friends with

CHAPTER 4

Janie, but Bolly detested social media. He hadn't had direct contact with Paul in years. Sometimes it made him wistful, but usually he didn't think much about it. Paul had busted out of the gravity well of Fester, but Bolly remained in the tight orbit that had been ordained for him.

He put a Quiet Twisted Iron Goat CD into the boombox and resumed tinkering with the carb. He worked until quarter to ten, then spent some time putting away his tools and cleaning up. At ten o'clock on the dot, a 1959 Cadillac Sedan de Ville rolled into the lot. It was obsidian black, with heavily tinted windows. Bolly loved the car, with its Batmobile fins and bullet taillights, but he wasn't especially fond of its occupants. He stood respectfully off to the side and waited.

Eventually, the rear door opened and out stepped Thelma Louise Schmidt. She was in her mid-fifties and dressed in the latest fashion, or so Bolly assumed. He knew little about *haute couture* and cared even less; all he knew was that her clothes looked like those on the TV fashion ads Janie watched so avidly.

"Good evening, Ms. Schmidt," he said politely. Thelma Louise had never married, but it was rumored she had once had a passionate fling with an Italian count. "I trust this evening finds you well."

"Well enough, Mr. Bollinger. I believe you have something for me."

Bolly reached into his coveralls and pulled out an envelope. He handed it over and watched as Thelma Louise counted the cash inside. This always frosted Bolly's shorts; he had stayed late every single month for ten years to hand over the rent in the dead of night, and not once had he been light.

Thelma Louise finished her counting and tucked the envelope into her Birkin bag. "I am afraid I have some bad news to impart. Starting next month, the rent is going up to $3000. Inflation, you know. I'm really very sorry."

"Three grand!" exclaimed Bolly. "Jesus Christ! That's almost a twenty percent increase!"

"I will thank you not to take our Lord's name in vain in my presence, Mr. Bollinger," she said. "I am sorry, but that is just the way it will have to be. It was not my decision."

Bolly huffed impotently. He didn't care whose decision it had been. The Schmidts had jacked up the rent a little over a year ago, but nothing like this huge bump. They owned all the commercial property on this and the two adjacent blocks on Jackson Street. Half of the properties were vacant. If they needed the income that badly, they should put some effort into fixing them up and renting them out rather than putting the squeeze on the remaining tenants.

He almost said so, but then he cut his eyes to the Caddy, and the darkened figure sitting behind the wheel. He couldn't be sure, but it was almost certainly Ronald Schmidt. The man had a bad reputation, and Bolly did not want to end up on his shit list. He was rumored to enjoy starting brawls at dive bars in town.

"Okay, I guess I don't have much choice," said Bolly.

"Very good," replied Thelma Louise. "I knew you'd understand." She disappeared into the Cadillac, which backed slowly off the lot and cruised slowly and silently down Jackson Street.

Fuming, Bolly turned to close up the shop and go home to his dinner of reheated mac and cheese. This rent raise was really going to put a crimp in his ledger book. As he walked back to the office, he muttered to himself, "Fuckin' Obama."

Chapter 5

Martin Prieboy's "date night" was the first Monday of the month. He hadn't been on a *real* date since the last millennium, and probably wouldn't know what to do on one, anyhow. Just the *idea* of dating was intimidating. It didn't really matter; this was business.

It wasn't *uniformed* business, however, and Martin took a little extra time picking out his wardrobe. He was going for a specific look, namely "not an off-duty cop." In this he was only partially successful, but he was pleased with the way the turtleneck concealed his jowls.

After a moment's hesitation, he picked up an ancient bottle of Canoe cologne and sprayed the tiniest of spritzes on each wrist. Then he grabbed his nicest nylon windbreaker—the gray one—and headed out the door.

Fifteen minutes later, he walked into the Wise Owl Café on the edge of downtown. It stood between a row of sagging wooden apartment buildings and a defunct electroplating company. Behind the counter, a middle-aged man with greasy gray hair and a paper cap nodded at Martin. Martin nodded back.

He slid into a booth and glanced around the café. Other than an elderly couple huddled together at the far end of the counter, the place was empty. The bell over the front door tinkled. A woman in her early thirties walked in, removing a pair of large sunglasses. She wore tight jeans, open-toed leather sandals, and a baggy Penn State sweatshirt. Platinum-blond hair framed a pretty face that bore a lot of makeup. A massive amount of mascara set off hazel eyes shining with wicked humor and wickeder intelligence.

"How are ya, Marty?" she asked.

Martin hated the nickname "Marty," and she knew it. He also knew complaining about it would just make her lean into it, so he always let it slide. "Good evening, Charlene," he said. "You are looking quite well."

"Thank you, sweetheart," she said. "You look pretty sharp yourself. That turtleneck really shows off your cheekbones."

Martin chuckled. Was that a slight flush he felt creeping up his face? He turned to the man behind the counter and twirled his hand over his head. The man nodded and turned to the grill.

"How are things at … your work?" asked Martin.

"Ya mean how's things at the whorehouse?" asked Charlene brightly.

Martin disliked that term even more than being called Marty. "If you insist," he said with a sigh. "Let's just call it 'Mike's Place' and leave it at that, shall we?"

"We shall," said Charlene. "Things at *Mike's Place* are doing just fine. There was a convention downtown that brought in a lot of customers. Accountants or CPAs or something like that. Addin' up numbers must make guys horny, because they flooded the place the whole time they were in town. I made a lot of bank, but *whew* was I sore afterwards! Walked funny for about a week!"

Martin cringed and Charlene laughed. "Hey, relax, Marty—it was nothing I couldn't handle. I can refuse any customer at any time for any reason. You know that. Solheim's house rules."

"I do know that," said Martin. "Otherwise, I'd have shut him down straight away."

"Well, I'm sure glad you haven't. Otherwise I'd be out of a good-paying job. Lotta other girls, too."

"I learned my lesson," said Martin. "I don't approve of what goes on there, but I learned to tolerate it."

Renee, his original informant, had married a trucker and moved to Ashtabula, Ohio. Martin had then recruited Charlene Troutman—professional name "Candy Floss"—to replace her. Charlene was sharp, personable and pretty. It confounded him that such a nice, *intelligent* young woman would voluntarily have sex with strangers at a dingy bar. He shook his head.

CHAPTER 5

"Whatsa matter, Marty?" Charlene asked. "Oh no—not that old shtick again—'what's a nice girl like you doing screwing accountants for money?'"

Martin shook his head. "I just want you to be well, Charlene. You tell me you're well, so I'll believe you. It's hard because it's antithetical to my strict Catholic upbringing."

"Is that so? Well, if I'm the antithesis of a strict Catholic upbringing, I'm okay with it. No corporal punishment, either—unless you pay extra."

Martin winced, and Charlene laughed, but reached out and touched his forearm. "Don't get all George C. Scott *Hardcore* on me, Marty. I'm just kidding, anyway. I don't go for that whip-me-beat-me-call-me-Edna stuff. I don't have to do anything—or anyone—I don't want to."

"That's what I like to hear."

The man with the paper hat materialized with platters of cheeseburgers and fries, and tall, frosted glasses of Pepsi. Without a word, he put them on the table and disappeared back into the kitchen. Martin and Charlene dug in.

After they had chowed down, Martin asked, "So, any new girls?"

"Yeah, we got a new one," said Charlene, with a laugh. "Name's Jane. She's a real piece of work."

"How so?"

"Well, she's from Noo Yawk City, and she doesn't mind reminding you of the fact. Like, every five minutes."

"Is she new to the, um, trade?"

Charlene laughed again. "Oh, *hell* no! This isn't her first rodeo, and she enjoys pointing *that* out every damn chance she gets as well. Thinks were a bunch of rubes, amateurs. I guess she knows what she's talkin' about, though—she gets a lot of repeat business."

"Anyone else new?" asked Martin. "Any young Asian girls?"

"No. C'mon, Marty, have you been watching *Inside Edition* or something? One of those shows that always runs stories designed to frighten old people?"

"No, this was from a state police bulletin," said Martin, who didn't like the implication he was an easily frightened old person.

"Well, there are no underage Asian sex slaves, okay?" said Charlene. "Even if Mike's Place isn't entirely legal, it *is* legit, okay? If anyone messes with one of the girls—even a little—they get tossed out on their ass. Mike makes that clear to all of the clients, and he's big enough to back it up. And if *he's* not big enough, Klep and Jerry—the bouncers—sure are."

Martin sighed and looked around the café. "Uh oh," said Charlene. "Feels like a lecture is headin' my way."

"Well, no," said Martin. "It's just ... I wonder how long you expect to be able to, um, keep up this sort of lifestyle."

"What are you saying?" said Charlene, scrunching up her face in mock anger. "That I'm losing my looks? That nobody will want to *fuck* me?"

"No, no," said Martin. "I just, oh, I don't know—I don't want to . . . *worry* about you. It just seems like you might be able to contribute more to society than providing accountants with the occasional *fuck*." Martin's mouth puckered as he forced out this last syllable. Charlene laughed again.

"Oh, my Marty," said Charlene. She reached out and touched his arm again. "We've already established I work there by my own choice. I've got a high school diploma—that's it. Where else would I be able to earn this kind of money without a friggin' master's degree? Nowhere! Besides, I *like* it. I like sex, and I get paid well to do what I like. How many people can say that? You? Do you like *your* job?"

"As a matter of fact, I do," said Martin. He'd wanted to be a crimefighter ever since he'd found a Batman comic book in the orphanage bathroom.

"Well, we should start a club, then," said Charlene. "I think it would be pretty small—all of the people in Fester who like their jobs. It'd be you, me, and the special-needs kid who bags groceries at the Food Ape."

Martin chuckled. "Well, you're probably right. We are fortunate in that respect."

"Besides, I'm no dummy," said Charlene. "I know jobs like this have a limited shelf life. So you'll be pleased to know, *Dad,* that I've signed up for night courses at Prosser College."

Martin's face lit up. "Really?" he said. "That's wonderful! I am very pleased to hear it."

CHAPTER 5

"That CPA convention really helped with my credit card bills. I am *so close* to paying off my monster credit card debt. I want to be out from under these bastards so bad. Eight years. Eight fuckin' years I been paying off that shit. Last week, I sat down and figured it all out. I'll end up paying about $94,000 on $17,000 worth of debt; $77,000 in interest—for *nothing!* Does that seem right to you?"

"No, of course not."

"Yet those bankers and credit-card company guys walk around scot-free. Get buildings and roads named after them, while I run the risk of jail time for giving some accountant a blowie."

"You don't have to worry about me," said Martin. He reached into his pocket and slid an unmarked business envelope across the table. Inside were two twenties and a ten—the reward for Charlene's information.

"Thanks," she said. "Every bit helps pay off those damn credit cards."

"I'm glad to help," said Martin. "I'd like to think of it as a contribution to your college fund. What are you going to study?"

"I want to get into the nursing program. For now, I'm just going to take a few night courses to make up for some of the holes in my high school transcript. Soon, I'll be banking all of the money I've been paying to those crooks at Visa and Discover. In two years, I'll say goodbye to Mike's Place and go to school full-time. Provided I get accepted."

"Oh, I have little doubt you will be," said Martin. "You've got a good head on your shoulders, Charlene. I'm pleased to hear you'll be using it for more than, um, servicing accountants."

"Thank you," said Charlene. She slapped the envelope on the edge of the table. "You know, I was talking to Doris the other night. She's a veteran—been working for Solheim for ages. She told me that back in the day, the constabulary wasn't so … nice. Said things were the other way around." She waved the envelope. "That the constables took money from the girls rather than handing it out. Took more than money, too. Said there was a cop named Roscoe who was a real bag of crap."

"Yes, he was," said Martin. At one point, Roscoe Dirkschneider had suspended Martin for not going along with a cover-up to the state police.

The state police had bagged Roscoe anyway, and he had gone down for a long stretch at Camp Hill. He'd died of a heart attack after serving less than a year, much to the disappointment of the other inmates, who wanted to do the job themselves.

"Fester is better off without the likes of Roscoe Dirkschneider," said Martin.

"No doubt," said Charlene. "And I certainly appreciate the money, Marty. And I want you to know that I appreciate *you*. You're a good-looking man, Marty. And you're *nice*. That's an unusual combination in this town." She reached out, touched his arm, and looked him in the eye with a smile.

"I appreciate you saying so," Martin said. "It's been a difficult day for me—today is the first anniversary of when I lost my partner, and, uh..."

Charlene's hands flew to her mouth. "Omigod," she said. "I am so, so sorry for your loss."

"No, no—it's okay. I really appreciate the thought. It's just been very, um, difficult for me." Martin could feel tears welling up in the back of his eye sockets and willed them to go away. He didn't want to lose control of his emotions—especially in front of Charlene.

"Look, do you want to go somewhere and get a drink?" asked Charlene. "Maybe talk it out?"

"I'm not much of a drinker," said Martin. "And I really do need to get back to the office."

"Are you kidding? It's like quarter to ten!"

"I know. There's always police work that needs to be attended to in Fester."

"Okay, fine," said Charlene. "I'll take a raincheck. But it *is* going to be a raincheck, understand? It's going to happen, okay, Marty?"

"Thank you, Charlene. I appreciate your concern." And he did. He really didn't have anyone to talk to about what he had been suffering, not since Sam had died. Martin wanted to pour his heart out; he wanted to share his burden with someone. He had grown closer to Charlene in the time since Sam had died, but he still wasn't ready to share with her the things he'd been able to talk about with Sam. At least not yet.

CHAPTER 5

Martin pulled out his wallet and dropped a twenty on the table. "Same time next month?" he asked.

"Oh, I'd better hear from you *long* before then. Seriously, Martin, I want you to call me anytime you want to talk … about anything. Okay?"

"Okay, I sure will."

"Good. You'd better." She turned and walked to the door with an exaggerated sway to her hips. He'd never been drawn to the female form, but the way Charlene made her derriere twitch was somehow hypnotic. She reached the door, looked over her shoulder to see Martin staring at her and smiled. Then she gave a quick wave and was out the door and into the night.

Martin sat awhile. He was glad Charlene had charted a path from her life of moral turpitude. She was a good kid and deserved better than whoring for Mike Solheim. He smiled, slurped up the last half-inch of his Pepsi and left.

Chapter 6

Harold Todd hunched over his desk and scrutinized the spreadsheet on his computer. He didn't like what he saw. The business was going to break even this month—but only barely. If it got even a little worse, Harold would have to dip into the cushion. After that, who knew? Begging the banks for loan extensions? Bankruptcy? Anything was possible.

Harold dove further into the spreadsheet, checking to see if there was something he might have overlooked. A sign things weren't as dire as he had feared. No luck. Barring a sudden and miraculous reversal in fortunes, the Hickory Acres Mall would soon be in the red.

The trouble had started six months ago when Fashion Bitch had failed to renew their lease. Fashion Bitch was a mega-hip clothing store for women ages sixteen-to-twenty-four. It was cutting-edgy and frequently embroiled in culture-war controversy. Their Cum Dumpster sweatshirt line had attracted a great deal of negative attention in the media. Fashion Bitch had pulled the sweatshirts, but their overall sales rose 30 percent in the same quarter.

Fashion Bitch wasn't the largest store in the mall, but it was the most popular. Young women came from all over the region to visit the Hickory Acres Mall in order to shop there. When Fashion Bitch left, Harold worried there would be a domino effect of other stores losing revenue and eventually pulling out, too. Unfortunately, the data seemed to be bearing this prediction out.

When Harold had first floated the idea of using the family's property to develop a shopping mall, most of them had been against it. He had put together a proposal showing a new mall could do well in Fester. It hadn't swayed many of the family members, but it *had* convinced his father, and his father was the final arbiter of all decisions in the family.

It had been good news at first. Harold's aptitude for real estate and property development had really blossomed. He had managed to get the mall built and the retail spaces leased with a minimum of difficulty. The family had, as he promised, done well. Harold himself had done even better.

Now it was all in danger. Malls were a relic of the previous century; their popularity had been in decline for years, competing against online retail giants like Amazon. Harold had managed to keep the wolves at bay for a long time, but things were starting to look a little hinky.

The Fashion Bitch pullout was unfortunate, but there was nothing Harold could have done to prevent it. Two other small retailers—a women's plus-size clothing store and a hobby shop—had also announced recently their intention not to renew their leases. Harold had polled the reps from the two anchor stores—Sears and the Bon-Ton—and they seemed solid enough, but Harold was still nervous. If one of them pulled out, the mall would fold quickly.

There were also some other minor problems. An uptick in loss reports for instance. Nothing like the problems the old Spendmor Mall had, but concerning all the same. Likewise, there were also reports of minor vandalism. Strange stuff, too, like stores reporting merchandise displays had been tampered with after hours. Harold figured disgruntled employees were responsible and it was, therefore, the stores' problem.

The shoplifting and vandalism issues could wait. Harold needed to get his vacant spaces re-rented quickly, before the blight could spread further. He had to demonstrate to his anchor stores, to prospective tenants, and to the shoppers in Kerian County that the Hickory Acres Mall was a fun and exciting place to spend time—and money.

The Fourth of July was coming up, and it fell on a Friday this year. It would be an ideal time to get people to the mall. But how to attract them? "A carnival!" Harold said aloud. There was no one else to hear him—the rest of the management staff had long since gone home—but when he got really excited about something, Harold would frequently vocalize to himself.

"Yes, a carnival—YES! We can set up some rides in the parking lot! And ponies! Kids love ponies! We'll get a buttload of ponies! And balloons, tons of balloons. And free ice cream! Yeah, gotta have some free shit—rubes'll fall all over themselves for free shit. Maybe clowns? Nah, fuck clowns. But ponies!"

He grabbed a legal pad and began jotting down notes as fast as he could. The ideas came tumbling out, and he worked maniacally. Two hours passed with Harold barely noticing. He would have kept at it even longer if he hadn't been interrupted by a tap at the door.

"Yez still in there, Mr. Todd?" came a voice. It was Jacob, the night watchman.

"Huh?" said Harold. "Yeah. Come in."

Jacob Zook had been a friend of Harold's family since before Harold was born. He seemed old when Harold was a kid; he appeared positively *ancient* now. Still, he stood straight at six foot one and didn't seem to get tired doing laps of the mall every night. Plus, he worked cheap.

"It's almost ten, Mr. Todd," said Jacob through the door he'd just opened. "I was getting ready to do a sweep of the parking lot and saw the light comin' out from under the door. I was gonna shut it off if there weren't anyone in here. 'Lectricity ain't free."

"No, it's not. Thanks, Jacob. I was just getting ready to go home. I'll be sure to turn out the light before I lock up."

"Thank yez, Mr. Todd," said Jacob. "Heh. Still cain't get used to yez new name."

Harold frowned. "You know we don't talk about that, right?"

"Oh, yes sir, yes sir. I forgot, 'sall."

"Right. Good night, Jacob." He turned and began stuffing his notes for the carnival into his briefcase. Jacob nodded, closed the door, and left.

Harold turned off the light, locked the office door, and headed out to his car. He could have gone out the office entrance that opened directly on the employee parking lot, but he preferred to walk to the far end of the mall

CHAPTER 6

and circle back.

Harold got a great deal of satisfaction walking around the mall when it was busy, bustling with people, families out having fun and spending money. Christmas was the best for that. January was always dreadful—a dull hangover after the excitement of the Grand Shopping Season.

But he also liked to walk around when the place was vacant. *All this is because of me,* he thought as he strolled through the empty mall. He felt a swelling of pride. It was like he was a Roman emperor striding out a passageway in the Colosseum while the lions were sleeping off their meal.

He took huge strides, enjoying the way his footsteps echoed off the faux tile and plate glass. *Gotta keep this all going,* he thought. *The fair will turn things around.*

Something hard hit him on the back of the head. A small object rattled across the floor. Harold jumped.

"What the fuck!" he exclaimed, turning on his heel. A few feet away a small blue stone rolled to a stop next to a trash bin. He took a few steps closer and leaned over. It appeared to be a piece of turquoise.

Suddenly, there was more rattling, and more stones were zipping through the air and bouncing off the floor. "What the *fuck?!*" said Harold, now thoroughly alarmed. "Jacob?"

It *had* to be Jacob. Who else could it be? Maybe he was sore Harold had upbraided him about his name. It was only a mild rebuke—and this sort of sneak attack wasn't Jacob's style. If you made Jacob sore, he'd let you know about it directly.

"Who's there?" Harold demanded. He stood stock still, heart pounding, trying to look in ten directions at once. "Security is right outside!" he announced. "All I have to do is make a call!" He pulled his phone out and held it up to demonstrate his imminent willingness to call mall security.

The mall was dead quiet.

Harold stood in his dramatic phone-brandishing pose for a solid minute. Then he put the phone away. It just seemed a lot easier to not make a big deal about this. He looked around the floor at his feet. Seven or eight turquoise pebbles were scattered around close by. He looked up and down the mall promenade but could see no other blue stones. Harold scooped up the pebbles and dumped them into the trash.

His heart rate came down from the stratosphere, but there was a hefty surplus of adrenaline racing through his system. Harold quick-walked to the mall entrance and let himself out. At the far side of the parking lot, by the woods, he could see Jacob's flashlight bobbing along as the night watchman patrolled the perimeter. So, it couldn't have been Jacob—there was no way he could have gotten from a hiding spot in the mall to the edge of the parking lot in such a short amount of time. The old man was spry—but not *that* spry. Besides, Harold would have seen him bolt.

For some reason, this made Harold feel a little better. He considered calling Jacob over and telling him what had happened but decided it could wait until tomorrow. Or even later. Harold got into his Lexus and headed home.

"Overwork," he said to himself as he drove. He'd just been too worried and working too hard. Had imagined the whole thing. Happens all the time. By the time he'd gotten back to his condo, he'd almost talked himself into believing it was all a figment of an overtaxed mind. Four fingers of Maker's Mark erased any remaining doubts.

Chapter 7

Bolly couldn't sleep.

Beside him, Janie was out cold and snoring heartily. She had a light, musical snore Bolly usually found amusing. But tonight, it was just annoying. He sat up abruptly, half-hoping he would wake her. He was jealous of her ability to take a few tokes off a joint and conk right out. She didn't stir, and Bolly stomped out into the living room.

He'd slept like shit ever since the Schmidt bitch had laid that rotten rent hike on him. He wasn't sure how he was going to make ends meet now. Janie's job as an admin at Prosser College had decent bennies—it was how they both had health insurance—but the pay was mediocre, and her skimpy raises didn't come close to keeping up with the increased cost of just about everything.

There was only one thing for it—Bolly was just going to have to take on more work and spend more time at the shop. He hated to do this, because he had done exactly that for the first five years after he had taken over from his old man. He'd routinely worked seventy- or eighty-hour weeks to build up business and demonstrate Bollinger Automotive was still the same—or better—under new management.

It had sucked, and Janie had complained about how much time Bolly spent at the shop. But he hadn't felt like he'd had a choice. After making it through those shaky first years, he was finally at the point where he felt he didn't have to work so hard, those rotten Schmidts had yanked the rug out from under him. Now he'd have to go back to working long hours.

He stalked into the kitchen, grabbed a bottle of Yuengling from the fridge and plopped down on the couch to consider his options. There were always his "special projects"—the remains of old beaters he kept out behind the shop. If fixed up, they would be collector's items. There was a '69 Firebird convertible he could probably get thirty or forty grand for with a little elbow grease. He'd stay late tomorrow night and start working on it.

Maybe it *was* time to look for a cheaper place. The idea was unwelcome, but things were tight and Bolly felt he should consider his options. The thought of relocating all of the tools and inventory—stuff that had been accumulating for nearly half a century—was daunting in the extreme. Plus, his old man would have a conniption if he moved the shop. Well, fuck it—if the old man didn't like it, he could kick in a few bucks to cover the rent increase. Of course, that wouldn't happen—Phil Bollinger had no income: all of his Social Security went to cover the expense of his retirement home in Weaverville. Bolly just prayed *they* wouldn't jack up the rent. If that happened, the old man might very well end up moving in with them. Bolly shuddered at the idea.

He looked down and spied the corner of the antique tin serving tray Janie used to clean her marijuana. A thought popped into Bolly's head as if radioed in from Planet Bad Idea: *zoo run.*

Bolly snorted. He couldn't even remember the last time he'd done a zoo run—probably when Bill Clinton was president. Did kids even do zoo runs anymore? Bolly didn't think so. *Kids these days.*

The concept behind a zoo run was simple: slowly drive to the top of Morningwood Heights, then come hauling ass back down the hill as fast and as loud as possible. Nobody remembered how it got the name *zoo run*. That's just what it was called.

The ride up was spent making sure there were no cops on the road— and getting loaded as quickly as possible. There was a story about a kid named Webby Schultz, who supposedly chugged an entire fifth of Southern Comfort while cruising his Olds 442 to the top of the hill. Webby had been so wasted he'd grossly misjudged the sharp turn by the country club. His car had slammed into an oak tree at nearly seventy miles an hour and exploded spectacularly. What had remained of Webby Schultz after the fire had been put out could have been held in a tuna-fish can. Of course, the turn by the country club was thereafter known as Dead Man's Curve.

A zoo run was a dangerous idea. Back in high school, Bolly and his buddies had played cat and mouse with the constables, who were forever finding new places to lay in wait for the zoo runners. Usually, this was the gated driveway of some Top Hat family who hated the noise and audacity of proletarian kids running their noisy beaters past their manicured lawns. And the rotten Schmidts—the richest and assholiest of the Top Hats—lived at the very top of the hill.

Pissing off the Top Hats was only half the fun. The other half was adrenaline. The street was called Highland Avenue close to town but switched to Morningwood Promenade as it got up into the rich properties. It was like a rollercoaster in places—plenty of opportunities to catch air and plenty of curves on which to screech the tires. Bolly had a semi-distinct memory of two or three or fifteen nights when he was a teenager, screaming down the promenade in the dark, Guns N' Roses or Motörhead blasting from the Rockford-Fosgate speakers, his shoulder-length hair blowing back in the slipstream. He usually had one or two friends with him, all of them buzzed, laughing like loons and convinced they were indestructible. Good times. Maybe the best times.

"Yeah," said Bolly. "Zoo run." He toed Janie's weed tray out from under the coffee table, rolled a bomber joint and tucked it behind his ear. He stuck his head in the bedroom where Janie was still snoring away. "Hey, babe," he said softly.

"Snwhxxt?"

"I'm headin' out for a bit," he said. "Be back before too long."

"Mrfftsz."

"Great. See you later."

Bolly strolled to the garage but did a U-turn and fished a couple of CDs from the pile by the stereo before returning to the garage and firing up the Nova. He cruised smoothly through the streets of Krump Acres, where their modest ranch house was located. Along the way, he passed the house where Paul Plummer used to live, but Bolly didn't give it a second glance. They'd had some high times there in high school, but that was ancient history now.

Bolly made the turn out of Krump Acres and was soon ascending Highland Avenue. He popped the joint in his mouth and lit it with the car's cigarette lighter. Bolly tried to keep the Nova pristine. Someone had once asked him why he hadn't given his beloved car a name—something feminine like "Lucille" or intimidating like "The Crushinator." Bolly had replied that it had seemed juvenile, and that "the Nova" was a good enough name for him.

He popped one of the CDs into the stereo: Quiet Twisted Iron Goat's *Whiplash Farm*. When he'd bought the car, it had had its factory-original AM/FM radio with an aftermarket 8-track player. He'd quickly replaced it with a cassette deck, which was grudgingly swapped out for a CD player ten years later. His nephews ragged him about the CDs, asking why he didn't just plug in his phone and listen to MP3s. Bolly scowled. He didn't want to use the cigarette lighter jack to charge the phone; he still had some use for the thing.

He took another hit off the joint and continued climbing the heights, the nighttime city of Fester unfolding below him like jewels on a dark cloth. The Goat was pumping, the windows were down, and Bolly finally felt himself relaxing. He'd figure out a way to get out of this mess. He just needed to get some perspective.

He cruised slowly up Highland Avenue, past the entrance to the country club. He took another hit from the joint, then stubbed it out. He didn't want to end up wrapped around a tree like the legendary Webby Schultz. The shit Janie got these days was *strong*—much more potent than the weed Bolly had smoked during his blazing days in high school. He hardly ever smoked weed now. Just a beer or two was good enough for him.

Janie, on the other hand, smoked nearly every night. She claimed it was impossible to get to sleep without it. Bolly could well believe it—she was out like a light most nights, snoring and muttering like she had as he'd left. They'd gotten into a fight over it shortly before they were married. Since then, Bolly had just let the subject drop. He loved Janie too much to spend a lot of effort hassling her about something she clearly enjoyed and that helped her rest.

CHAPTER 7

The Nova passed between the stone pylons marking the official boundary of Morningwood Heights. This was big-bucks country, and if there were any cops lurking around, they'd be up here. Bolly downshifted, slowed down, and lowered the volume of the stereo. His head swiveled back and forth, looking for cruisers hidden in cul-de-sacs or clumps of trees. He could see none. Maybe doing zoo runs wasn't a thing in Fester anymore.

He was near the very top now, where the really big houses were. Most of the remaining Top Hat families lived up here. The very last house on the street was the Schmidt mansion. The road ended in a small turnout just past the gate to the driveway. Bolly cruised by slowly, peering through the bars of the gate to see if he could catch a glimpse of that freaky Caddy. All he could see was the bulk of the house behind the fence and a few lights way back in the trees.

He got to the turnout, turned his car around, and put it in neutral. The Quiet Twisted Iron Goat disc was replaced by Black Sabbath. Bolly punched up a track number and sat idling. Guttural synth tones burbled ominously from the speakers. He pushed in the clutch and shifted to first, then goosed the gas pedal slightly. The engine revved and plumes of exhaust drifted from the dual tailpipes. The guttural tones were replaced by a series of tinkling keyboard notes, then a fast, heavy guitar riff. Ronnie James Dio screamed, "OHHHH! COME ONNN!"

Bolly popped the clutch and floored it.

The Nova peeled out, leaving twin thirty-foot-long streaks of smoking rubber in front of the gate to the Schmidt mansion. "The Mob Rules" blasted from the stereo as he rocketed down the street.

His shoulders hunched, as he worried about the cops or misjudging a turn and rolling the car. He forced himself to think like an eighteen-year-old, not a thirty-eight-year-old. *You got this,* he thought. *No one can touch you.*

"Fuck, *yeah!*" he hollered, and turned up the stereo. He laughed as he worked the Nova through turns where the rear end broke loose—but only a little. He had it in control. He hit a slight rise at speed and the Nova became airborne. Probably only an inch or two, but it felt to Bolly like he could fly all the way to the moon.

He shot past the stone pylons like a bullet leaving a gun barrel. He reached under the dash and pulled a small knob. He wasn't sure if it would even work; he hadn't tried the exhaust cutout in years. There was a brief pause, then the Nova shot forward as the cutouts bypassed the exhaust system. The car roared like a hungry dragon.

As he approached the country club, he flicked his eyes towards the speedometer: just a tit-hair above seventy miles per hour. The Nova topped another slight rise and got air again. Black Sabbath continued to rage. Bolly felt awesome.

The iron fence of the country club was zipping by on the right. Dead Man's Curve was only a few seconds away. For the briefest moment, adult-Bolly's reflexes slid his foot off the accelerator and towards the brake. Then teenage-Bolly regained control and his foot pushed down on the gas.

He entered Dead Man's Curve at speed, then suddenly yanked on the parking brake and cut the steering wheel hard to the left. The Nova slewed sideways around the curve in a modified bootlegger's turn that would have impressed a professional stuntman. When the nose of the car was pointed more or less down the center of the street, Bolly released the parking brake, spun the wheel back to the right and gave the gas a little goose. The Nova straightened right out and zoomed down the hill toward the lights of Fester.

"The Mob Rules" ended and the CD rolled to the next track. It was "Country Girl" and Bolly thought it sucked. He turned off the stereo and reached for the exhaust cutout knob. He paused, then downshifted to produce a final almighty roar. Then he closed the cutout and took his foot off the gas. There were more side streets closer to the city, thus more opportunities for unwary drivers or—worse—cops to intersect his path. The Nova slowed to a speed within spitting distance of legality.

"Holy shit!' said Bolly aloud, and he shook his head. He couldn't believe the move he had pulled on Dead Man's Curve. He'd never even *thought* of trying something like that when he was younger. *Wait 'til I tell Paul*, he thought—then shook his head again. He hadn't spoken to Paul in ages, and he sure wasn't going to call him up out of the blue to tell him about some suicidally dumb-ass stunt he'd just pulled. He'd have to settle for telling the regulars at the Buck and Wing, a pub close to the shop.

After he'd tucked the Nova away in the garage, he headed to the fridge. His pulse was still racing, and he figured all of the adrenaline he'd just dumped into his system would keep him up late. He grabbed a couple of bottles of beer intending to down them in front of ESPN but found himself yawning after the first one. That zoo run really had opened his pressure valve. He put the second beer back in the fridge, went to bed, and was soon snoring louder than Janie.

Chapter 8

Harold Todd swung his Lexus off Route 23 and onto a narrow gravel track. It ended at a small clearing a couple hundred yards from the highway. The only thing there was a decrepit shack that was almost completely overgrown with vines. Harold pulled a remote from the glovebox and hit the button. A row of bushes swung aside, revealing the track went further into the woods. He drove through and the bushes swung back into place behind him.

Another hundred yards farther down, the woods opened up to a large clear area of churned-up dirt. It was on a mild slope that flattened out at the bottom, where a small pond stood. About a half-dozen small houses and trailers were scattered around the pond, with others on the periphery of the clearing. Overlooking it all was a large wooden farmhouse, painted white. A crew was on top, working on the roof.

Harold bumped the car across the clearing towards where a man was walking with a small child. He recognized the man as his cousin Vince. Harold had over eighty cousins in the area. He rolled down the window and pulled up next to Vince.

"Howdy, Vince."

"Well, if it ain't the Fancy Man," said Vince. "How ya doin', Mr. Fancy Man?"

Harold expected this sort of treatment. A lot of the family had been unhappy when he'd changed his name. "Doing great, Vince. Thanks for asking. You know where my pap is at?"

"Ain't my turn to watch him," said Vince. "Though if I hadda guess, I'd say he was up to the Big House."

"Thanks, Vince. See ya around."

Vince just nodded. As Harold pulled away, he heard the little boy ask, "Daddy, is that the one who thinks he's too good to be a Totenkopf?"

Harold gunned the engine so he wouldn't have to hear Vince's reply.

He pulled the car to the front of the house and mounted the steps. Half of the floorboards had been removed. A sign by the front door read, *Contruction in Progres—Mind You Step*. He walked gingerly to the front door and went in.

The interior of the place had changed a lot over the years. In his mind's eye, Harold saw it as it was when he was a boy: dark and crowded, crammed to the ceilings in some places with junk, furniture, and boxes of bric-a-brac. Now it was uncluttered—a bit dusty, perhaps, but otherwise presentable. And there was more natural light, since there were no longer mounds of junk crammed up against the windows.

The hallway was clear enough for Harold to see all the way to the kitchen. A skinny woman in her mid-twenties was stirring a huge pot on the stove. It was his sister Sassafras. She looked up at him and squealed, dropped the ladle into the pot, and ran to give him a hug.

"Harry! Where the hell you been?"

"Hey, Sassy. Good to see you. How's my favorite sister?"

"Can't complain, big brother. Got a job at the new Target out in Weaverville."

"Weaverville?" asked Harry. "That's a long drive. I could get you a good job at the mall, no problem. Only take fifteen minutes to get to work."

Sassy shrugged. "I dunno. Pay at Target's pretty good, and if I stay on for more'n six months, the bennies start to kick in. Better than anything I'd get at the mall. Besides, the mall is pretty creepy."

"What? What do you mean—'creepy'?"

"I don't know, it gives me a weird vibe. It's probably nothing. Just me being flaky. Hey, are you going to stay for dinner? I'm making chicken and dumplings. It's Uncle Cody's birthday."

"I don't know," said Harold. "I didn't really come to socialize. I need to talk to Pap. Is he here?"

Sassy pouted, but said, "Yes, he's upstairs. He turned Grandpap Jeff's old room into an office. I really hope you can stay for dinner, Harry."

"We'll see. Business first, okay?"

"Okay."

He went upstairs, marveling at how much better the house looked now. He tapped at the door at the top of the stairs. "Pap, you in there? It's Harry."

There was a pause, then the door flew open and Harold was engulfed in a bear hug. "Harry!" cried Merle Totenkopf. "So good to see you home! Come on in. You're looking well."

"You're looking pretty good, too, Pap—for an old man."

"Old man! Why, I could kick your youthful ass any day of the week." He threw a few air punches at Harold's face, coming close but not connecting.

"Okay! Okay!" Harold held up his hands and took a step back. "I take it back, okay?" He didn't doubt his father could whup his ass—or pretty much anyone else in the family. Merle Totenkopf had enlisted in the Army on his eighteenth birthday and had ended up in the 75th Ranger Regiment—special forces badasses. Merle had seen combat during Operation Desert Storm and still retained his military bearing. He was still lean and fit as he'd been in his twenties, even though he was nearing his fiftieth birthday. His buzzcut was a little grayer and his chiseled face had a few more wrinkles, but he was still large and in charge. He had to be, to keep the Totenkopf clan under control.

"So good to see you, boy!" Merle repeated. He pulled a ceramic jug from a shelf behind him and wagged it in Harold's face. "Wanna snort? Just uncorked this batch—some of the best we've ever made, I think."

"No thanks, Pap. I got work to do later."

"Your loss," said Merle. He took a hit from the jug then replaced it. "Ah, good stuff."

"The place is looking good, Pap. You've really spruced up the homestead."

"Yep—it's amazing what a coat of paint can do. But you already know that, dontcha, Mr. Real Estate Wiz? We got some boys finishing up the roof." He jerked his thumb towards the ceiling, where hammering could be

CHAPTER 8

heard from above. "And we'll have the porch squared away soon, too. Me and Vince are doin' that ourselfs."

"Yeah, I talked to Vince on my way in," said Harold.

"Was he an asshole to ya?"

"Yeah, kinda. His boy said something about me thinking I was too good to be a Totenkopf."

"Ah, that's too bad," said Merle. "You know Vince has always been a bit of a jackass."

"I know. But a lot of folks up here thought I was puttin' on airs by having my name changed."

Merle shook his head. "Well, we knowed that to make it in this town, you can't use the name 'Totenkopf.' Hell, ever'body in Fester knows who you are and where you from, but bein' 'Todd' instead of 'Totenkopf' helps open a lot of doors. We couldn't let your gift or your ideas go to waste. It's made the family a lot of money. Ever'one up here knows that, too. If they flip you shit because of the name, they're just jealous. They orta be more thankful. Hell, I might just go kick Vince's ass for him to teach him a little gratitude. Might just do it 'cause it's a good idea."

"Yeah, okay. Thanks, Pap." Harold thought about what his father had said about his gift. It was a strange thing, his almost uncanny ability at real estate. He thought it was a weird thing to have a knack for.

It had started twenty years ago, when Pap had found a man from the city snooping around down by the highway. Pap had brought him back to the Big House to talk to Grandpap Jeff. Turned out the man was a real estate agent who claimed he could prove the Totenkopfs were rightful owners of a big parcel of land down by the river. The real estate man claimed he could help the Totenkopfs sell it for a lot of money.

When Pap had explained it to him, Harold was puzzled. How could somebody *own* land? It just seemed stupid. It wasn't as if you could pick up a piece of land and carry it away with you if you wanted to go somewhere else.

Harold pestered Pap fiercely, asking about real estate and selling land. Merle's extremely limited knowledge of the subject was quickly exhausted, as was his patience. After he hollered at Harold to "shut up about it forever," and gave him a spanking to seal the lesson, Harold had indeed shut up about it—at least around the house.

But the concept and its magnetic weirdness had lodged in his brain like a fishhook. Especially after he began to realize the absolutely staggering sums of money people would pay to "own" land. He'd had a history teacher in high school who'd helped him get a handle on it.

The teacher's name was Mr. Goyer. A lot of the kids said Goyer was a pinko, but Harold thought he was all right. Mr. Goyer had explained ownership of land was essentially a social contract that everybody bought into. Basically, one entity was paying for the right to do whatever the hell they wanted on a certain part of the planet. The cost of that right was driven by the collective perceived value of that particular hunk of terra firma. Could it be used to generate money, by building a farm or a factory? Did it have value because it had a view that made it desirable to build a home there? It was all just a mutually agreed-upon delusion at the bottom of it.

Despite Mr. Goyer's college-league words, Harold grasped the concept immediately. It was all bullshit, Harold thought—but very *lucrative* bullshit. If the value of this entirely immaterial agreement was driven by perception, it should be possible to manipulate the perception and make bank.

Harold hated school, but he was not in the least bit stupid. He formulated a plan and put it into action. First, he dropped out of school. This was not a big deal; very few Totenkopfs had high school diplomas—although it seemed like more of the youngsters were making it all the way through. To hedge his bet, he checked out a bunch of books from the library about passing the GED. He crammed for a week and got his equivalency diploma on his first try.

He then secured a job at the Dairy Ferret in town and took every shift they would give him (pretty much anything shy of thirty-two hours a week, after which they'd have to pay bennies). Prosser College offered extension courses towards getting a real estate license, and Harold signed up. Ironically, these were night classes held at his old high school. Harold was soon applying himself in a way he never had when he was a student there.

He'd aced the real estate exam on the first go. He pimped himself out to a variety of real estate firms, sucking up what specialized knowledge he could from one firm before moving on to the next. After he had run the gamut of Fester's limited real estate community, he was ready to hang out his own shingle. Then a plum had dropped right in his lap.

The chunk of land the real estate agent had come to see Grandpap Jeff about turned out to belong to the Totenkopf family. It had taken nearly a decade of tortuous—and expensive—legal wrangling for this to be well and truly settled. At last, the Totenkopfs had one-hundred-sixty acres of prime real estate to do with as they pleased.

Most of the family had wanted to sell it immediately and bank—or, most likely, spend—the cash. Harold had a better idea. Rather than just cash out, he knew the parcel of land could be used to generate income that would keep flowing into the Totenkopf family coffers. A steady income would benefit the family much more than a one-time real estate deal.

He put together a prospectus and gave the family a presentation. He showed that by developing the land commercially, they could bring in much more money than by simply selling the land outright. Most of the family thought he was nuts—they just wanted to get their hot little hands on a pile of quick cash. Some of the family, though, had seen the wisdom of Harold's plan and supported it. Merle had been one of those—and his support swung the family. Merle was the *jefe,* and what he said was what happened.

Harold plunged into action implementing his plan. First, he legally changed his last name to *Todd*. It had been a tough decision, but he knew that the Totenkopf name had bad associations around Fester. Again, his father had backed up his choice.

The newly minted Harold Todd then threw himself into the project, schmoozing with bankers, hiring an architect, wrangling with the planning department. It was incredibly exhausting but awesomely exhilarating. The land was cleared and buildings rose from the ground. The spaces were rented, the mall opened, and it was an all-around success. The money had come flowing in.

At least until now.

"Earth to Harry, Earth to Harry," said Merle. "You still with me, boy?"

"Sorry, Pap. Just wool-gathering."

"So, as I was asking, Harry-boy—how's business down at the mall? You still bringin' in the big bucks?"

"For now, Pap, for now."

"'For now'? What the hell's that supposed to mean?"

"Things are a little shaky, is what I mean. We had a store pull out. Called Fashion Bitch. You heard of it?"

Merle shrugged. "Dumb name."

"Yes, but it was a big draw. I practically had to tie myself in knots to get them to commit. That one store attracted people from four counties. Now the parent company's closing a lot of locations—including the one at Hickory. I'm worried other dominoes will start to fall."

"They damn well better not," said Merle. "This family's countin' on that income." He gestured at the ceiling where the noise of the roofing crew could still be heard. "These repairs ain't free, y'know. Plus, I've contracted to replace all the trailers down by the pond with sturdier pre-fabs. Already made the down payment."

"I see."

"And tuition! Did you know we got two young'uns wantin' to go to college this fall? It's true! And I promised 'em the family'd cover tuition as long as they kept their grades up. We need that money, Harry."

"Okay, Pap—I got it."

"Okay, just so's you know," said Merle. "You're a sharp fella. You figger something out. I have faith in you, boy."

"Thanks, Pap. I have some ideas. I'm planning a Fourth of July carnival—bring a bunch of people to the mall and show 'em a good time. Pony rides, free ice cream, balloons—all that sort of stuff."

"There ya go!" said Merle. "I knew you'd stay on top of it. And if you need any help from the family, you just ask. We're all proud of you, Harry—even assholes like Vince. We all appreciate what you've done for us."

"Thanks, Pap. I'm glad I can help, you know?"

"Sure do. Now, you gonna stay to dinner? Sassy's got a mess of chicken an' dumplings on the stove. Might help your standing with the family if you showed up more at family events."

Harold wasn't sure of that. He'd intended to go right back to his office to do some more work on the carnival. On the other hand, it wouldn't hurt to seem less stand-offish. Besides, Sassy made some damn good chicken and dumplings. "Sure, Pap," he said. "I'll stay to dinner. And since I'm staying, I might as well take you up on that snort."

"That's my boy," said Merle, and he reached for the jug.

Chapter 9

"What do you mean you can't find it?" demanded Ronald Schmidt. "I don't know!" said Ophelia. "It's in my room *somewhere*—it has to be."

"Fine. Then go get it."

"I've already looked. I can't find it anywhere."

"Then look again!" snarled Ronald. "You said it's in your room. So go find it!"

Thelma Louise, who was listening from down the hall, shrank back into her room. Ronald was in a very bad mood, and it made her nervous. She knew from experience he was on half-cock today, and anything could set him off. The fuss about their mother's ring was just an excuse—Ronald wanted to lash out. She briefly considered going down the hall to try to defuse the situation but suspected that butting in would only make things worse.

It was difficult for Thelma Louise to watch her brother push Aunt Ophelia around like this. Ever since Cecilia Schmidt had taken off, Ophelia had been the head of the Schmidt family. But Ophelia had aged noticeably in the last five years and was no longer the firebrand she once was.

"Okay," said Ronald. "I'm going out to work in the garden. You better have found that ring by the time I come back in."

"I will, Ronald," said Ophelia. "Don't worry."

Thelma Louise breathed a sigh of relief. Beside spending time with his monkeys, gardening was one of the few things that really seemed to calm Ronald down when he was in one of his moods. Maybe he would vent his

CHAPTER 9

anger on the weeds and not cause any more trouble. She left the doorway and went back to the desk in her bedroom. She was putting together the program for a gala fundraiser for the Arts Council of Kerian County. Thelma Louise has been the council's chair for over a decade, and the annual gala was her signature event. She wanted it to be perfect—she had a reputation to uphold.

Unfortunately, other than Thelma Louise's work with the local arts and charity scene, little positive reputation remained for the once-proud Schmidts. There weren't even that many Schmidts left in the county. Those with the means to do so had hauled stakes after the new owners of the former family business laid off most of the workforce. Prestige had turned to animosity.

Thelma Louise lost herself in the planning of the gala: entertainment, decorations, caterers, guest list. And a thousand other seemingly endless details that went with them. It seemed like an impossible task, but every year she managed not only to pull it off, but to make it a spectacular success.

At one point, Thelma Louise heard Ophelia emerge from her room and descend the stairs. *Must have found the ring,* she thought, then went back to the guest list. She was debating whether to invite that bitch Margie Strickler. Margie had given Thelma Louise the cold shoulder at a gallery opening last month, and Thelma Louise hadn't forgotten. She decided she would be the bigger person and—reluctantly—added Margie's name to the list.

She became vaguely aware of some noise from the front of the house—raised voices. *Uh oh,* she thought. She poked her head out into the hallway. The grand staircase was at the far end of the hall; her room was at the opposite end. She watched as Ophelia came clattering up the stairs, with Ronald right behind her.

"I'll find it, Ronald, I'll find it!" Ophelia cried.

"You won't find it in the damn refrigerator!" yelled Ronald. He was driving Ophelia along by slapping her lightly on the back and shoulders, like he was herding livestock. He drove her halfway up the hall until they were outside of Ophelia's bedroom.

"I was thirsty!" said Ophelia. "I hadn't stopped looking! I just wanted to get a drink of milk!"

"You can have a drink of milk when you've found my mother's damn ring!" shouted Ronald. "You know she wanted Thelma Louise to have it. She gave it to you for safekeeping—*and now you've lost it!*" Ronald's voice rose nearly to a scream.

Thelma Louise stepped halfway into the hall. "It's okay, Ronald," she said. "Really." *I don't even* like *the darn thing,* she almost said. This was true—the ring was a monstrosity. A twelve-carat blue diamond surrounded by smaller rubies and emeralds. Thelma Louise thought it looked like a pimp's Christmas tree ornament but knew better than to say this to Ronald. Their mother had loved that ring, and anything beloved by Mother was sacred to Ronald.

"No, Thel, it's *not* okay," said Ronald. "It's *not.* That was Mother's favorite ring, and she meant for *you* to have it and now Auntie Ophelia's gone and lost it. And she's going to find it *right fucking now!*"

"Okay, okay," said Ophelia, and she ducked into her room and quickly closed the door.

"And you're not coming out until you've found it!" declared Ronald. He pulled a brass skeleton key from his pocket and locked the door. The doorknob rattled and there was a pounding on the door.

"You can't do this!" shouted Ophelia. "Let me out right now!"

"No," said Ronald. His voice was eerily calm, which was even scarier than when he'd been shouting. "You had your chance, Ophelia. I'm afraid you leave me little choice. Now *find it!*"

Thelma Louise stood in the hallway, hand at her mouth. Seeing Ronald herding their aunt like a cow in a chute was deeply disturbing, as was the fact he had locked her in her room.

Even more disturbing was that Ophelia had let it happen. She had been the hard-headed matriarch of the Schmidt family, the one who had engineered the removal of the usurper Cecilia, and the sale of the company at a massive profit. But now, she seemed less sure of herself, she moved much more slowly, and her memory was increasingly spotty. Now she let her nephew

CHAPTER 9

push her around—literally.

"Ronald," said Thelma Louise. *"Really."*

"Do you have a problem with what I'm doing?" asked Ronald. "Maybe you should go in there and help her. Yes, I'm sure the search will go much more quickly with *two* people looking." He began stalking down the hall towards his sister.

Thelma Louise ducked back into her room, pulled the door shut and turned the lock. "Ronald, you're being *very* unreasonable."

"Not at all," came Ronald's voice. *"Someone* has to be the voice of reason in this family—and it certainly isn't going to be one of you flibbertigibbet women. That pretty much leaves me." He chuckled, then Thelma Louise heard his footsteps receding down the hallway.

She sat down at her desk but couldn't concentrate. The exchange between Ronald and Ophelia had been too disturbing. It felt like there had been a fundamental shift in the family dynamic, one that had been slowly building and had suddenly come to a head. Aunt Ophelia was no longer in charge; Ronald was.

Thelma Louise couldn't work. She struck that bitch Margie Strickler's name from the guest list, then put the cover back on her typewriter. It occurred to her that Ronald's skeleton key could unlock the door to her room. She didn't think that Ronald would barge in and press-gang her into helping Ophelia find the ugly ring, but there was no telling. He had become so unpredictable lately.

She carefully unlocked the door, eased it open and peeked out. The coast was clear. She carefully went down the hall to Ophelia's room. She could hear her aunt shuffling around—it also sounded like she was sobbing. Thelma Louise's heart went out to Ophelia, but she wasn't going to intervene on her behalf and run the risk of incurring the wrath of Ronald. She decided to keep her head down until this ugly spat blew over.

She retreated down the hall to the servants' stairs in the back corner of the house—she didn't want to run into her brother. She went down to the basement. Normally, she avoided the basement. It was creepy and cluttered except for a well-lit, pleasant sewing nook her mother had maintained.

Thelma Louise liked to retreat there whenever things in the household got tense. It seemed to be happening a lot more lately.

She descended to the bottom of the stairs and made her way through the labyrinth of boxes and junk, carefully avoiding the corner of the basement where the appliances were. For some reason, the area by the washer/dryer, refrigerator, and chest freezer seemed extra creepy.

Of course, the rest of the basement was plenty creepy as well. It was lit mostly by bare 40-watt bulbs hanging from the ceiling—many of which were burned out. Random tables were scattered throughout the basement, each heaped with debris and boxes of junk. Ronald had always been a packrat, and it had gotten worse after their parents passed away. Thelma Louise had wanted to give most of the clothes and such to charity, but Ronald had refused, saying that all of it had sentimental value. She supposed that same sentiment was driving her brother's insistence Ophelia find their mother's ring.

Less obvious was the sentimental value of the endless stacks of the *Fester Daily Dispatch* that were heaped all over the basement. She glanced down at the nearest stack—the paper on the top was from April 1966 and had a headline about a nuclear test in Nevada. Thelma Louise shuddered. It was getting harder to ignore the fact the basement resembled a hoarder house.

She hustled to the sewing nook and turned on the warm overheads—banishing the gloom from that corner of the basement. The walls were painted sky blue with sunny yellow highlights. There were two sewing machines (one a foot-operated antique), a dressmaker's dummy, and cabinets full of sewing paraphernalia. The space was warm, safe, and provided Thelma Louise with fond memories of spending time here with her mother as a child. It was her happy place. She sighed and took up a blouse that needed mending. Soon she was happily sewing a missing button on the blouse, grateful for the relaxing, simple task to take her mind off her worries.

Those worries came rocketing back soon enough. She hadn't even finished the button when she heard a commotion in the front yard. Even down in the basement, the muffled voices seemed angry. The front of the

CHAPTER 9

house was where the vegetable garden was located—where Ronald was working.

"Oh Lord," she said, dropping the blouse. The last thing she wanted to do was interfere with Ronald when he was in one of his moods, but she had to do *something*. Squabbling in the house was one thing, but doing so in the yard was a lot more serious. Someone might *see!*

As it turned out, a neighbor was already involved. Thelma Louise stepped out onto the front porch to confront a strange tableau. Aunt Ophelia was hanging out of her bedroom window, shrieking for help. Ronald was at the edge of the lawn by the road, waving a hardpan rake. He was waving it at Alexander Fitch, their next-door neighbor.

The Fitches weren't exactly Top Hats, but they were just as rich. The Fitch family had moved to Fester from Massachusetts in the early nineteenth century, which made them newbies as far as the Top Hats were concerned. The Fitches resented their reduced social status in Fester, and Alexander Fitch had proven to be an unneighborly neighbor. Of course, the same complaint could be made against Ronald.

"Look here," said Fitch. "This woman says she's being held against her will! She says she's been kidnapped!"

"I have!" shouted Ophelia. "He's locked me in!"

Ronald twisted to shout at her, "Knock it off and keep looking for that ring! Leave this to me!"

"Look, this is highly irregular," said Fitch. "I'm calling the police!"

"You'd better just butt out, buster!" said Ronald. He stepped towards Fitch, brandishing the rake.

Fitch shrunk back. "See here now, Schmidt—watch it with that rake! This is menacing! I could have you arrested!"

"No, it's not," said Ronald. "You're trespassing. I have a right to defend my home!"

"I'm not trespassing," said Fitch. "I'm on the public right-of-way, and I'm calling the police!"

"*Mind your own business, you* nouveau riche *meddler!*" yelled Ronald. He raised the rake and ran at Alexander Fitch.

"Ronald! No!" shouted Thelma Louise. She jumped off the porch and went after her brother.

"Get away from me, you maniac!" yelled Fitch. Seeing the face of lunacy bearing down on him, he turned and ran.

Ronald pursued in gangling, awkward strides. Thelma Louise was much faster, but he had a big lead on her. Fitch cowered back into the street, and Ronald took a running swing with the rake. At the last moment, Fitch turned to run again, but he was too slow. Ronald connected with the rake, but he was off-balance and struck a glancing blow to Fitch's right calf. Fitch went down, bawling.

"Ronald! Stop it at once!" Thelma Louise caught up with her brother and grabbed for the rake. Ronald, perhaps sensing he had let things go too far, let it go without a struggle.

"You crippled me!" shouted Fitch, who was curled up on the pavement.

"I'm so sorry Mr. Fitch," said Thelma Louise. "Ronald shouldn't have done that—it was very wrong. But you're hardly *crippled*. Look, the rake didn't even tear your trouser leg, much less break the skin.

"It's still assault!" said Fitch. "Believe me, I'll be making a report."

"You do what you need to do," said Ronald, not looking him in the eye.

"I think the less said of the matter, the better," said Thelma Louise. Fitch just shook his head and muttered.

Thelma Louise looked back at the house. She hoped Ophelia wouldn't stir the pot and make things worse than they already were. Fortunately, Ophelia had closed her window and was out of sight.

"Let's get inside," said Ronald. He put his arm around Thelma Louise and began escorting her to the front door. Alexander Fitch made his way back towards his house, with an exaggerated limp, casting dark looks over his shoulder.

"Let's go, let's go…" said Ronald. "I'm going to close the front gate and lock the doors. You call the lawyers."

Chapter 10

The intercom on Martin Prieboy's desk buzzed. He pressed the button. "What can I do for you?"

"Hi, boss." It was Chief Inspector Daniel Blount, a man Prieboy trusted with delicate situations. Dan Blount was one of the hires Prieboy had made shortly after he had cleaned the constabulary of the bad apples after his succession to chief constable. "Got some trouble up on Snob Knob."

Prieboy sighed. "Snob Knob" was local slang for Morningwood Heights. Blount, being one of the most trustworthy men on the force, was tasked with dealing with any and all problems in that neighborhood. For serious problems, Blount had been instructed to report them immediately to the chief constable. "Better come in, Dan," said Martin.

Immediately, Blount appeared in Martin's office. He was a tall man, in his late forties. The other constables called him "Bull," due to his passing resemblance to an actor named Richard Moll, who played a character called Bull on an old sitcom about a wacky court that convened at night.

"Trouble on the hill?' asked Martin.

"Schmidts," said Blount.

"Better sit down, Dan." All of the Top Hat families had rococo rivalries that resulted in various acts of petty atrocity. Traditionally, the legal structure in Fester looked the other way when these acts occurred, even to the detriment of the safety and well-being of regular citizens. Martin had come into office vowing to tamp down on the extra-legal excesses of the Top Hat families.

Following the chaos of the Night of the Mill Fire, the Schmidts had been the top dogs of the Top Hats—at least for a while. Of the high-caste

Schmidts, only Ophelia and her niece and nephew remained in the mansion at the top of Morningwood Heights. Ophelia was rarely seen in town these days, and when she appeared, she seemed frail and easily confused. Frequently, she was in a wheelchair, although some of the local wags figured she did it to garner sympathy and deflect criticism of her sale of the pretzel bakery.

The niece, Thelma Louise, was a throwback to the more civilized age when the family was respected and honored. She was active in a large number of charities and arts organizations, both in Fester and in the county seat of Weaverville. Friendly and outgoing, she was a constant fixture at any high-profile event in the county. Thelma Louise was a delight.

That left the nephew, Ronald. If any family had ever had a black sheep, Ronald was it. Frequently truant during his school years, he'd been picked up for vandalism multiple times as a teen. Each time, he'd gotten away with a slap on the wrist, if that.

The Schmidts had gotten Ronald into Penn, but he left the first semester of his sophomore year under a cloud. Rumors swirled he had been accused of sexual assault, but they were only rumors. Ronald returned to Fester to take up the role of the wastrel son of a declining family—a role he fulfilled admirably. He had apparently learned to be more discreet in his indiscretions as he got older, and he had fewer run-ins with the law. They still occurred, usually drunk and disorderly conduct from fighting in bars. He was never prosecuted or even charged, to the surprise of no one.

"Is this about Ronald?" asked Martin.

"Of course," said Blount. He slid a case folder across the desk.

"Give me a quick rundown," said Martin.

"Their next-door neighbor, Alexander Fitch, claims Ronald Schmidt assaulted him with a rake. Fitch claims he was taking a walk when he heard Ophelia Schmidt crying for help from a second-story window. He said Ophelia claimed to have been held against her will—that Ronald locked her in her room. When Fitch confronted Ronald, he claims Ronald ran at him and took a swipe at him with a rake he was using to work the garden."

"And Fitch reported this?" asked Martin.

CHAPTER 10

"Yes, and immediately upon receiving the report, I went to the Schmidt residence."

"And what happened then?"

"I was met at the front door by one Pierre Nasté, attorney at law."

"Oh, for goodness sake," said Martin. "What then?"

"He said he was on the phone with Mayor Lincoln, and that I should wait until that had been resolved. Which I did. I wasn't about to make a potentially, um, difficult move against the Schmidts without getting clearance from you."

"Did you interview Fitch?"

"I went to his house, but he wasn't home."

"Oh boy," said Martin. "Another fine Top Hat mess, huh, Dan?"

"Yes, sir, it sure seems like it. I hope I didn't do anything wrong."

"No, of course not. Sometimes it seems like there isn't a *right* way to handle things when the Top Hats start acting up."

"What do we do next?" asked Blount.

"*You* go back to doing real police work; *I* will go referee this silly mess."

Blount left—with an air of relief, Martin thought. He called the law office of Nasté, Brutus, and Shore, and learned Pierre Nasté was in court in Weaverville this morning but was expected back in the office any time now. Martin said he would be by shortly.

Martin had learned to tread lightly around Pierre Nasté. The man had been practicing law since John Marshall was chief justice. He swung a lot of weight with the local politicos and in the county seat. Martin had found that with Nasté, a little respect went a long way. Nasté was experienced and wily, but at heart he respected the principles of the law. He'd bend the law as much as he could to serve a client, but not so far as to break it. The Schmidts had been clients of the firm when it was just Pierre's grandfather Armand handling the cases.

Martin gave the case folder that Blount had given him a quick read. There was nothing in it they hadn't covered in their conversation. Then he took some time to tidy himself, making sure his hair was combed, his tie was on straight and that he generally looked the part of the head of Fester's law enforcement.

Martin timed his arrival at the law office well; he had just introduced his visit to the receptionist when Nasté stepped in the door behind him. The man was of average height and slender, dressed to the nines in a coal-black three-piece with light gray pinstriping. He looked amazingly youthful, although Martin suspected the man was seventy if he were a day. His face was largely free of wrinkles, and his hair was suspiciously dark and lush. He reminded Martin of Christopher Lee in the old Hammer Dracula films—but with a more expensive wardrobe.

Nasté brightened as he noticed Martin in the reception area. "Ah!" he said. "Inspector ... no, *Chief Constable* Prieboy. Please forgive my lapse ... when you get to my age, the memory sometimes slips."

Martin doubted that. Even well past retirement age, Pierre Nasté was sharp as a scalpel. He suspected Nasté was just playing a mind game with him, reminding him that he was a relative newcomer to the legal arena in Fester, while Nasté himself had been around since nearly the dawn of time. "No problem, counselor," said Martin.

"Please, let's repair to my office," said Nasté. He turned to the receptionist and said, "Hold my calls, Myra."

"I won't take much of your time, Pierre," said Martin. "Just a few things I need to have explained to me."

"Certainly. Please follow me."

They took the elevator to the top floor of the building and were soon ensconced in Nasté's office. It was enormous—forty feet to a side—and furnished with thick wine-colored carpeting and enough mahogany to denude a small tropical forest. Nasté sat down behind a desk the size of a ping-pong table and indicated Martin should have a seat.

"What can I do for you, Chief Constable?"

"I understand there was an, um, incident at the Schmidt house the other day."

Nasté sighed and effected a look of sadness. "Ah, yes. Unfortunate incident, that. Merely a misunderstanding."

"Is that so?" asked Martin. "My understanding is that Ronald Schmidt assaulted his neighbor Alexander Fitch with a gardening tool."

"No, no, sir," said Nasté. "Not at all. Fitch was trespassing and being quite aggressive. My clients say he was drunk. Mr. Schmidt was well within his rights to defend himself, his family, and his home. And I'd be careful about using incendiary language such as 'assault' if I were you. Mr. Schmidt may have brandished his rake during what was a rather heated discussion, but *assaulted?* Utter nonsense."

"All the same, I would feel better if I could interview your clients. And, since Mr. Fitch filed a report, protocol would be to speak to him."

Nasté tented his fingers and smiled a thin, vulpine smile. "There's absolutely no need for that, Insp… Chief Constable. There will be no charges pressed. Mr. Fitch has agreed the entire thing was a regrettable misunderstanding."

You paid him off, in other words, thought Martin. That's how it usually went with cases involving Ronald Schmidt. Nasté or one of his minions handed a fat envelope to the aggrieved party. Martin wondered how much it had taken to silence Fitch. It was probably not a small amount. Fitch himself was worth quite a bit, and the enmity between him and the Schmidts was well-known. It must have been a hefty sum to buy his silence.

"I see," said Martin. "Well, I'm glad it was cleared up without any need to involve the legal system. Again."

"Yes, of course," said Nasté. "There's no need to sully anyone's reputation. My clients are good people. And they have good legal representation."

"Indeed," said Martin. "I suppose there's no reason to bother your clients. All the same, I do need to have a chat with Mr. Fitch."

"That is certainly your prerogative," said Nasté. "Although I think you would be wasting your time."

"Why is that, counselor?"

"I was visiting my clients earlier on an unrelated matter. I noticed there was a *For Sale* sign on Mr. Fitch's lawn and a large moving truck in the driveway."

"Well, I guess you saved me a trip, then. Thank you. I will not take up any more of your day, Pierre. I appreciate you're taking the time to speak with me." He rose to leave. As he got to the door, he looked back over his shoulder at the lawyer. He was regarding Martin with that same thin, wolf-like grin.

"Until we meet again, Chief Constable."

"Good day."

Once back in his car, Martin lost no time making his way to the top of Morningwood Promenade. He was always puzzled by the psychological workings of the uber-wealthy Top Hats. A long career in police work in Fester had taught him that the very rich behaved quite differently from most folks. Their immense wealth provided a force field of unaccountability that permitted behavior most people would find unimaginable. Martin was worried it was only a matter of time before Ronald did something really dangerous. He intended to start handling anything involving the Schmidt family personally.

When he arrived at the Fitch residence, he found Nasté had been correct: there was an ornate *For Sale* sign on the front gate. The house was being listed by an out-of-town realtor who specialized in luxury properties. He rang the bell, but there was no answer. There was also a realtor's lockbox on the gate. The house looked deserted.

Alexander Fitch and family must have flown the coop. It seemed unlikely that Nasté had paid him off to such an extent as moving would be part of the deal. Unlikely, but not impossible. Maybe Nasté and the Schmidts had some leverage over Fitch they decided to exercise. More concerning was the thought that the Schmidts were hiding something so bad they would shell out a huge sum of money to make any legal complications go away. Most likely, however, was that Fitch had tired of living next to the Schmidts and that this incident was the last straw. Well, Alexander Fitch may no longer be in residence, but he was certainly not out of reach. Martin would have to get in touch with him soon, for no other reason than to try to gauge Ronald's behavior. The part of the story about Ophelia being locked in her room was worrisome. Maybe there was a way to approach Thelma Louise and talk to her. She seemed reasonable.

As he drove back down the hill to headquarters, he reflected on something

CHAPTER 10

Nasté had said about his clients, and how their reputation must remain unsullied. There was a big difference between keeping the family name out of the police reports section of the paper and having an unsullied reputation. Fester was a small town—and word travels fast in small towns. Especially if it has anything to do with rich toffs who nobody much likes in the first place. Martin didn't know Alexander Fitch very well, but he made it a point to know a little bit about all the residents of Morningwood Heights. Fitch wasn't afraid to shoot his mouth off and had already aired grievances about the difficulty of living next door to the Schmidt family. Even if he'd shuffled off to Buffalo, it seemed unlikely he hadn't told at least a few of his acquaintances about his dust up with Ronald Schmidt before Pierre Nasté had bought his silence. Martin had little doubt the local taverns and diners would be abuzz with the latest evidence of Schmidt weirdness.

Constantly amazed by the unceasing variety of weirdness his job encountered, he shook his head and headed back to headquarters.

Chapter 11

Billy Snyder shifted into first gear and roared up the hill, his strange cargo lashed tightly to the Land Rover. His destination was the farthest, most isolated section of his property.

Billy's property was wedge shaped, with the narrowest part ending where the driveway met Dockstock Mountain Road. The lot widened the farther up the hill you went. Up past the house and the workshop, it broadened to over one hundred acres of rugged Allegheny foothill country.

The hill behind the house rose steeply, eventually flattening out at the top of the ridge. This area had been logged early in the previous century and was partially accessible via a network of overgrown logging roads. These roads could only be accessed from the other side of the ridge—some twelve miles away.

To provide more direct access, Billy had hacked and chainsawed a crude path in the woods up the side of the ridge. Billy's civil engineering skills were limited, and he had avoided such fancy features such as switchbacks, opting instead to carve his path directly up the hill. As a result, it was only navigable with a heavy-duty four-wheel-drive vehicle. Fortunately, Billy had a powerful Land Rover, a 1972 Mark III. It was a real workhorse, not one of those latter-day plush yuppie status symbols.

The top of the truck had been removed, and the windshield had been folded down to accommodate a long, crenelated tube that was slightly longer than the Land Rover itself. This was held down with a series of ropes, heavy-duty bungee cords, and tarps. Equally trussed was a tall wooden box in the back stenciled with the legend *Ejercito de Republica Dominicana*. It was

CHAPTER 11

padded with a thick layer of straw. The final item on the manifest was a cracked toilet that had been indifferently tied down with nylon line.

Billy roared and jounced up his rough path, which sometimes seemed to cut a 45-degree slope. The old Land Rover was up for it—it was made of cast iron and plate steel and ground gamely up the ridge in first gear.

From time to time, Billy cast a glance over his shoulder at the wooden box in back. It was tied securely and the straw kept it from moving around too much. Billy didn't think there would be a problem, but the contents of the box were forty years old at least, and perhaps not very stable. Or maybe dead as dinosaur shit. The whole purpose of this trip was for Billy to find out if his special project would have full live fire capability.

He reached the top of the ridge. He shut off the engine and sat for a few minutes, listening. Birds called, the light wind soughed through the trees. Other than that, nothing. Satisfied there were no dorks on four-wheelers trespassing on his property, he started the engine again and moved out.

Up here, it was flatter and the trees were widely spaced enough he could maneuver the Land Rover without difficulty. He headed south, to the remotest part of the property—the farthest away from the logging roads connecting the upland part of his land to the county-maintained road. This was where he had built his firing range.

He pulled up to a tree where a specialized wooden bracket had been bolted. There was a similar bracket on an adjacent tree. The one on the adjacent tree had a mechanism to raise and lower it. Billy had made it from an old car jack.

Billy unstrapped the long tube from the Land Rover and, with difficulty, hefted it into the brackets on the trees. The thing weighed a ton; he'd have to bring a winch next time. He tightened the clamps and took a sighting down the tube. It was aimed towards a clearing about one hundred yards away. Behind the clearing, the land rose steeply, forming a natural backstop.

Billy climbed back into the Land Rover and drove it to the clearing. He unloaded the toilet and placed it where it would be in line with the tube. Then he returned to the firing point and began unstrapping the wooden box. Once freed, Billy muscled the box—the sumbitch was heavy—over to the base of the tree. He retrieved a large flathead screwdriver and carefully pried open the lid.

Inside the box were what looked like three giant bullets. They were rounds for the M40 106mm recoilless rifle that Billy had just strapped to the tree. He had gone to great lengths to obtain this ammo. He'd worked his entire military surplus network and called in a number of favors. Finally, he had been put in touch with a quartermaster in the Dominican army who, for an outrageous fee, provided the requested rounds. Billy had another half-dozen boxes hidden in the woods by the house. He was concerned about their stability, and he didn't want to store them anywhere in proximity to things he didn't want to explode.

Billy carefully took one of the shells from the box. It looked clean and new. "Goddamn," he muttered to himself. It had been nearly forty years since he had handled one of these things. Back in Vietnam, doing so had been all too commonplace.

For a long time, Billy avoided anything that reminded him of his service in Vietnam. In the last five years or so, those memories—horrible though they were—had started to take on a distant, sepia-toned quality. He could think about them without having to worry about waking up hollering in the middle of the night.

Right now, he had plenty of other things to worry about. Hell, hadn't he spent the last twenty years stewing about his fall from grace—reduced from the powerful head of local law enforcement to someone on the margins of society, someone who eked out a living selling bogus military antiques to rich jerks who couldn't get it up without strapping on a broadsword or a Luger.

He'd had plenty of time to cast blame and assign fault. None, of course, was ever assigned to Billy himself—that would be ridiculous. He was just a guy trying to make it in a tough world. People had been jealous of his power and had screwed him royally. And who could have mustered the juice to do that? Why, the Top Hats, of course—specifically, the Schmidts, and especially specifically that bitch Cecilia Schmidt. He didn't care she was only a Schmidt by marriage—a Schmidt was Schmidt and a fink was a

CHAPTER 11

fink.

In the last few years, he spent more time stewing over his own descent, and those who had caused it. Oddly, his recollections of his time in Vietnam—dark and troubling though they often were—also seemed to provide Billy Snyder with a sense of relief, a sense of control. That sense of relief was why Billy had started his special project. Now it was time for a functional test.

He stood up, pressing his hands into the base of his back. Hauling the rifle had given his spine an unwanted workout. He'd have to do some extra stretches before he went on his run this evening. He sighted the M40 on the toilet, using the car jack to make minute adjustments to the rifle's elevation.

Satisfied, he loaded the shell into the breach. He pulled a small box and a spool of wire from his pocket and attached the wire to the firing mechanism. Unspooling the wire behind him, Billy went to the far side of the Land Rover, hunkered down behind the front wheel, and plugged the wires into the control box. A small LED lit up red.

When Billy was about twelve, he and the neighborhood urchins would have bottle rocket fights, running around the neighborhood shooting airborne explosives at each other. The preferred delivery system was a sawed-off wiffle ball bat. It was highly portable and easy to aim. A recoilless rifle was much the same: basically, a tube open at both ends. The projectile flew out one end, and the propulsive gases flew out the other.

Billy silently counted backwards from three, then hit the button on the control box. From the M40 there came the sound of *mrr-CHUNK* as the firing pin hit home.

Then nothing.

"Hangfire," muttered Billy. "Dammit!" It was a dud. Hardly unheard of even when he used this weapon in the Marines. He waited a few seconds, then went to the firing stand and carefully removed the round. The firing pin had hit clean; it should have fired. He gingerly carried the round about forty yards into the woods, then propped it up behind a tree.

The second round looked just as pristine as the first. He loaded and locked it and returned to his shelter behind the Land Rover. Another quick countdown, another *mrr-CHUNK*—then nothing. Another dud.

"God*dammit!*" shouted Billy. He had gone to a great deal of trouble and expense to obtain this ammo. He knew there were going to be a few bad rounds, but if none of these damn things were good . . . well, Billy just might have to fly to Santo Domingo and have a serious conversation with a certain Master Sergeant Lopez.

He removed the second dud and hauled it off into the woods—in the opposite direction from the first—then loaded the third round into the M40. He went back to the Land Rover but didn't bother squatting down behind the fender. He glanced over his shoulder—one hundred yards away, the toilet sat in the clearing. It seemed to be mocking him.

"Fuck that," Billy said. He pressed the button on the remote.

For a quarter-second, Billy thought, *Damn that master sarg—* There was a loud *whoosh* from the M40, followed by a tremendous explosion. The toilet disappeared in a cloud of gray smoke. Every bird within a half-mile radius took to the sky, complaining raucously.

Billy waited for a moment, listening. The woods went dead silent. The nearest neighbors were at least eight miles away. Anyone close enough to have heard the explosion would have to be trespassing on Billy's property.

He walked over to the target area. It was a direct hit. The commode had been pulverized. There was a fan-shaped spray of tiny porcelain fragments spreading out from the impact site and into the hill behind. Satisfied, Billy walked back to the Land Rover and began packing up. He removed the M40 from its tree mount and strapped it back on the truck. Then he took a folding spade and buried the two dud rounds. He policed up the rest of the area and prepared to head on home.

Driving back down the hill was a bit tricky. It was so steep in places that the prudent thing would have been to turn the Land Rover around and back down in reverse. Instead, Billy downshifted to first and punched the accelerator, laughing wildly as the Land Rover slewed down the muddy, steep hillside, barely in control.

When he got to the bottom, he parked it behind the house. He sat for a moment, enjoying the feeling of his heart hammering in his chest—of

CHAPTER 11

feeling *alive*. It seemed like it had been a long time since he had felt like this—simply alive. He had felt that way more often when he was younger—and in charge of the town's constabulary. That had certainly changed. Time was a cruel mistress.

"Time wounds all heels," Billy said to himself. "Now quit woolgathering and get back to work." He unstrapped the M40 and stowed it in the workshop, then headed to the kitchen to heat up a can of Dinty Moore beef stew.

Chapter 12

Bolly debated getting a third beer. He was watching TV with Janie, and they'd had a large dinner. He wasn't worried about going to sleep; he hadn't been sleeping for shit lately. Rent on the shop was coming due. He had enough in the bank to cover the next month's rent, and maybe one more after that. Afterwards ... who knew? Bolly knew he wasn't getting the Firebird restored quickly enough. In fact, he felt a little guilty about not working on it right now.

Fuck it, he thought, and retrieved another beer from the kitchen.

"Another beer?" asked Janie. "You're gonna put yourself to sleep."

"Look who's talking," said Bolly, nodding at the joint she'd just sparked up—her second since dinner.

"You want some of this?" she asked, holding out the joint.

"Naw, I'm good, babe. Thanks." He plopped back down on the couch.

"I can't believe they put Tyrion in prison for Joffrey's murder!" exclaimed Janie. Her eyes looked redder than normal and she seemed genuinely upset. It was tempting to chalk this up to the weed, but Bolly knew Janie got genuinely attached to characters in shows and movies she liked—and she *really* liked *Game of Thrones.*

"I'm sure Tyrion will be okay, babe," said Bolly. Truth be told, he thought Tyrion Lannister was annoying. Then again, he thought most of the characters on the show were annoying, but Janie loved them, so he kept his mouth shut. He found the politics on the show to be boring as hell, but there were dragons and full-frontal nudity, so it wasn't a total loss.

Bolly sipped his beer and half-watched the show. He was starting to feel

CHAPTER 12

the effects of the brew. Strange how it seemed to hit him harder as he got older. It kicked his ass harder the next day, too. He'd be lucky to get away with just a slight headache the morning after three beers.

He looked over at Janie. After fifteen years of marriage, she still looked great. She was fastidious about what she ate (although she served Bolly whatever garbage he wanted) and made regular use of the gym at Prosser College.

Five years ago, they had gone to their year high school reunion, and Bolly had been amazed at how many of his classmates had bloated up. He'd gotten noticeably thicker around the middle himself. Janie had looked spectacular in a brand-new black cocktail dress and had basked in the avalanche of compliments she'd received. Bolly knew there had been any number of catty comments behind her back. He was pretty certain that he'd heard Heather Zeidel make a snarky comment about a "coke habit." Heather, who'd been head cheerleader their senior year, weighed two-twenty if she weighed a pound, and now bore an unfortunate resemblance to Ron Jeremy.

Yes, Janie still looked great. She was wearing an old polo shirt that was a little too tight on her. It accentuated her breasts and Bolly eyed the nipples attempting to poke through the thin fabric. He felt a bit of stirring south of his beltline. Sometimes beer had that effect on him. He tried to remember the last time they'd had sex. A couple of weeks at least.

He slid over and put his arm around her. She snuggled up to him, her eyes never leaving the TV screen. He began rubbing her arm. She snuggled up closer and he kissed her head. Bolly checked the time on the show: only seven minutes left in the episode. Timing was everything—he didn't want to wait too long.

"Hey, babe," he said.

"Mmmm?"

"Maybe after the show, we could, um, rock the Casbah. It's been a while."

"Oh, I dunno, Bolly. I'm pretty tired. Plus, I have to get up early tomorrow for a meeting. Sorry."

Damn, thought Bolly. *Skunked again.* "It's okay babe. The Casbah will still be there when we're ready to rock. Maybe this weekend."

"Yeah, maybe."

When Bolly and Janie had married, they'd both wanted to have kids—a girl and a boy. They'd decided to wait until things with the garage were going sufficiently well before they would try for a family. That had taken about five years, and afterwards they'd had a lot of fun trying to bring little Arlene or Michael into the world. Despite their frequent and vigorous efforts, nothing came of it.

Bolly secretly suspected the fault was with Janie—a lot of women in her family had difficulty conceiving. He also suspected that *she* suspected he was the one at fault. As it turned out, they both were. Janie proved to be infertile, and as Bolly's doctor had told him, "Your swimmers are few and far between."

That had put the matter to rest, but ever since then Janie's interest in sex had diminished markedly. This was especially frustrating for Bolly since Janie was still very attractive. Bolly wasn't happy about the situation, but hell—that's what porn was for, right? He had amassed an impressive collection of triple-X DVDs he kept in an old toolbox in the garage. The porn sometimes made him feel guilty, but he was only human. A guy had to blow off steam somehow.

He also still loved Janie like mad, and he was sure she felt the same way about him. He'd tried talking with her about the disparity in their desire for sex, but every time he tried, she'd become sullen and uncommunicative, answering his questions with one-word answers. Bolly decided the situation was what it was, and that he had little choice but to accept it. It could always be worse—he knew plenty of guys in absolutely loveless marriages.

"I think I'm goin' to bed, babe," said Janie when the episode wrapped up. "You coming?"

Seems unlikely, thought Bolly. "Nah," he said. "I'm gonna stay up for a bit."

"Okay. Don't stay up too late—it always makes you cranky in the morning."

So does the demon jism build-up, thought Bolly. "I won't be late," he said. "Probably just go for a drive to clear my head. This rent hike is drivin' me nuts."

CHAPTER 12

"I'm sorry, sweetheart," said Janie. "We'll get through it. We always do." She circled back from the bedroom door to give Bolly a quick peck on the cheek. "Night."

"Good night, Hot Pants."

She disappeared into the bedroom. Bolly grabbed his jacket and his keys. It was time for another zoo run to let off some of his pent-up tension.

Except it wasn't very satisfying. He managed to leave an epic strip of burned rubber in front of the Schmidt house but had eased off on the stunts on the rest of the way down. He was aware of the three beers in his system and didn't entirely trust his reflexes. The rear tires broke loose around Dead Man's Curve, and for a split-second Bolly thought he was going to high-side it. He managed to get the Nova under control and drove back into town at a more sedate speed. His heart hammered—he had gotten a good scare.

He still didn't feel like going home, yet. The near-miss on Dead Man's Curve had wound him up again. Abruptly, he decided to check out a potential new site for the shop on the east side of town. He'd been over there last week and thought the place was too small and too isolated to be a good replacement for the current shop. Nevertheless, he decided to go have another look at it.

He cruised through town and over the Iron Bridge, past the ex-Schmidt pretzel bakery, and up through the industrial east side. He cruised up Slocum Avenue, past the warehouses and siding factories and upholstery shops. They were all closed and dark. The only place that wasn't dark was up ahead. It was a riot of neon and bright halogen pole lights illuminating a surprisingly full parking lot. Bolly slowed down as he passed by. In red neon script the establishment announced itself as Mike's Place.

Of course, Bolly had heard of it; the place was notorious, just like the Pine Room before it. He'd never been to either—had never even thought about it. Simply not on his radar. He eyed a Budweiser sign in the window and thought that he *could* go for a beer after his hairy moment on Dead Man's Curve. Then he shook his head and kept driving.

The shop was another quarter mile along Slocum. The only light was from a small mercury halide lamp bolted to the corner of the building. Bolly slewed around in the parking lot and hit the high beams, but it didn't help much.

Even in the dark it was still too small and too distant from the rest of town. Bolly shook his head. Why'd he bother coming back when it was so evidently unacceptable the first time he'd seen it? He got back in the car and pulled out.

As he passed by Mike's Place, his left hand reached out and hit the turn signal. *What the fuck you doing?* he thought as he pulled into the parking lot. "Just gettin' a beer," he said as he cruised through the lot. "That's all."

He found a discrete parking spot in the back, locked up the Nova, and went inside.

Chapter 13

HICKORY ACRES MALL FOURTH OF JULY FAIR! Fun for the Whole Family! Face Painting! Pony Rides! FOOD! FUN! PRIZES!

Harold Todd was again spending the evening in his office. He'd been going over the promotional material for the big fair.

He marked up the rough draft of the poster the advertising firm's graphics department had put together. He put a heavy red X through the clown that was prominently featured. Clowns hadn't been very popular in Fester ever since semi-retired TV clown "Cowboy Bob" Warnke had gone berserk at the Calvary Reformed Lutheran Church.

At the bottom of the page, he scrawled *Huge Savings Mall-wide!* in large letters. This was only partially true. Most of the merchants in the mall were more than happy to throw their full support behind the fair. They knew it was sink or swim. Some of the smaller stores had claimed their profit margins were too thin to offer any special sales. Harold had made a half-hearted attempt to change their minds but didn't push too hard. He knew what tight margins were like.

He'd managed to get the anchor stores to kick in some money to help defray the expenses. He was also committing most of the mall's financial cushion to this endeavor. He knew that if he didn't somehow reverse the slide, the cushion wouldn't make much of a difference in the long run. He'd even thrown in eight thousand dollars of his own money. This was a Hail Mary pass, and he wanted to give it everything he could. He'd even considered going to his father and asking for money but decided it would not be productive. He might get the money, but it would definitely set the family to grumbling about his stewardship of the Totenkopf golden goose.

Harold had enough to deal with as it was. He didn't need the family pestering him as well. Earlier that day, the entertainment company that had promised to provide the pony ride had backed out, saying the ponies had contracted African Horse Sickness and were unavailable for the foreseeable future. After an hour of frantic calls, he had finally been referred to a local outfit called Tony's Ponies. He dialed the number.

Five rings, and a gruff voice answered, "Greasy Tony. Waddaya want?"

"Um, yes," said Harold. "I'm calling for Tony Vaginello. About the ponies."

"Yeah, look," said Greasy Tony. "If this is about another one of them movie deals, forget it. Last time, some asshole gave them ponies a buncha blow, tryin' to keep them hard longer or somethin', totally fucked 'em up. I still owe my vet for that one."

"Uh, no" said Harold, wondering what kind of movies Greasy Tony was talking about, then deciding he'd rather not know. "I'm talking about a pony ride. You know, for kids."

"Oh, yeah, yeah, yeah, yeah," said Greasy Tony. "Of course. Never mind the thing about the movie. Just funnin' ya. So ya want a pony ride for the kiddies, correct?"

"Yes, that's right." The fourth was a week from Friday. He needed to get the pony ride squared away, along with a long list of lesser needs. He gave Greasy Tony a rundown of the fair and what he wanted.

"How many ponies ya need?" asked Greasy Tony.

"Uh, I don't know," said Harold. "How many do you have?"

"Hey, Tony's Ponies got ponies out the wazoo. However many ponies ya need, I can get."

"Um, six ought to be fine. You have the corral and people to help guide ponies when the kids are on them, right?"

"Yeah, yeah, sure, sure, sure," said Greasy Tony. "I got ya covered, pal."

Harold was a little doubtful about that, but there was no time to dicker. He concluded his business with Greasy Tony Vaginello and got off the phone.

After dealing with a myriad other details, he looked at the computer and was surprised to see how late it was. Time seemed to be slipping away very

CHAPTER 13

quickly lately. He scanned the flyer and emailed it to the graphic designer, then packed up.

Jacob was sick tonight. One of the day-shift security guys had worked four hours of overtime, but by now the mall was empty. Harold was the only one who was supposed to be there, so he decided to a quick circuit of the mall to make sure there was no bullshit going on. Fortunately, there had been no more reports of vandalism or weirdness—at least not since the night the blue pebbles had rained down.

The Hickory Acres Mall was shaped like a wide V. The main entrance to the mall was at the notch of the V, with smaller entrances at the end of either wing. There was a large triangular courtyard just outside the main entrance At the center of the courtyard was a large sculpture of a hand sitting in a triangular patch of grass. It seemed to be half-finished. Part of it was very clearly a hand with the index finger extended, while the rest was unfinished stone that just sort of looked like a hand.

The rock had been there for a very long time, longer than the mall. It was so massive the decision had been made early on to leave it in place. The problem was that from certain angles, the original rock looked like it was flipping the bird. Harold brought in a sculptor to reshape it. The first sculptor had done most of the work getting the rock to look like the "we're number one" gesture rather than the obscene one. Then he dropped dead from a heart attack.

After a great deal of searching, Harold had located another sculptor who lived farther away and charged more for his services. Fortunately, Harold hadn't had to pay the new sculptor very much because he walked off the job after one day. The second sculptor had said something vague about how the rock "didn't want to change" and that it was more than the job was worth to keep working on it. After that, Harold had given up on sculptors. At least the rock no longer looked like it was giving the finger to the town.

Harold's pap, despite his support of the idea of the mall, had been surprisingly resistant to building it near the hand-shaped stone. He said the rock had a "bad history," but wouldn't go into detail. The geotechnical report for the property had indicated the area immediately around the rock was the only area suitable for the construction project. The rest of the area was too swampy and unstable. It was either build by the hand-shaped rock or not at all. So that's where they built.

The mall office where Harold worked was at the end of one of the wings. Harold gathered his belongings, locked up the office, and made a sweep of the premises. He walked slowly through the mall, stopping from time to time to peer in the windows of some of the stores. No vandalism, nothing out of place. Good. Harold continued his tour, sometimes just stopping in his tracks and listening. Other than the subtle hiss of the HVAC, there was nothing. He realized he was listening for the *tak* of falling stones. Fortunately, there was no sound, no inexplicable rains of stones, no inventory being mysteriously shifted around in the stores after hours. All seemed clear.

Relieved, Harold headed back towards his office—his car was parked right outside it. As he passed the main entrance, he thought he saw movement from the corner of his eye. He turned and stared. There it was again—a flicker of bluish light right by the hand sculpture.

"Goddammit!" muttered Harold. Someone was fucking around out there again. Probably kids screwing around or people digging for treasure. Teenagers sometimes used the mall parking lot as an after-hours make-out spot. It was isolated and not as far from town as Redskin Lake, the traditional site of teenage hanky-panky in Fester.

Teens were easy to run off. More persistent were the treasure hunters. When the mall was under construction, workers had found two or three old coffee cans stuffed with moldering dollar bills. The few bills that hadn't completely decomposed indicated they were from the early twentieth century. It was known that a German witchdoctor, or "powwower" called Professor Schmuck had lived nearby. His house had burned down sometime around 1930, and the professor perished in the flames. The man had been reputed to be very rich, although he had no bank accounts or any other valuable goods, so it seemed a good bet that the coffee cans contained what remained of Professor Schmuck's wealth.

The main problem was that after the story had circulated around town for a bit, the cans no longer contained wads of rotting paper but solid gold Eagle coins. (There had been a handful of corroded coins found in one of the cans, but they were pennies, nickels, and dimes.) After the story of the gold coins had circulated, treasure hunters descended on the construction site with metal detectors and shovels. The construction company brought on extra security and that had put a damper on the treasure hunting, at least for a while.

The treasure-hunting hadn't gone away entirely. From time to time some optimistic or desperate citizen would show up in search of Professor Schmuck's legendary gold. It was a safe bet that was what was happening now. "Goddammit," Harold repeated, and began fast walking back to his office to get a flashlight. He kept a big six-cell police flashlight in his desk—it threw a bright beam and, in a pinch, could be used to smash heads if the situation turned combative.

Harold grabbed the flashlight and exited the mall through the employee entrance on the side of the plaza. It was an overcast night, and sticky—it would probably rain later. The parking lot lights glimmered through the humid haze. Keeping the flashlight off, Harold approached the hand rock carefully. He saw nothing. As he got closer, he switched on the flashlight and swept the area, in case someone was hunkered down in the dark or hiding behind one of the benches lining the plaza. Nothing.

He was just about to turn back when the blue glow he had seen earlier reappeared. It seemed to be coming from the opposite side of the hand statue.

"Hey!" Harold Shouted. "Who's th-there?" His voice cracked, and his mouth was suddenly devoid of moisture. "Show yourself!" He felt the hairs on his forearms and the back of his neck standing up. What the hell was going on here?

"Come on, I can see you there," he said loudly. *Fuck this*, he thought. It was just some punk. He he was the owner and operator of the biggest retail establishment in western Kerian County, and a goddamn *Totenkopf* to boot. Totenkopfs didn't take shit from anyone. "Damn you, come out!"

He raised the flashlight over his head and was working up the nerve to charge around the statue when the figure emerged from around the other side. Harold froze. It appeared to be some sort of punk/hippie hybrid: a tall man, shirtless, who was wearing fringed pants. On one side of his head, the hair hung down past his shoulders; the other side was shaved to the skull.

"Who are you?" Harold croaked. His voice had all but fled; he could barely hear himself. "You-you shouldn't be here."

This last statement made the man look at him sharply. Harold was glad he had gone to the bathroom half an hour earlier, because he was certain he would have pissed himself if he hadn't. His breath momentarily froze as he got a good look at the hippie punk.

The blue glow seemed to be coming from *inside* the man. His hands were empty; he was carrying no flashlight or light source. Also, it appeared as if the man's feet weren't touching the ground. Harold could see a good three inches of space between the top of the grass and the bottom of the man's moccasin-type shoes. Then Harold noticed he could actually *see through* the man! The contours of the hand statue were faint but clearly visible through the man's torso and legs.

"Ya ... ya ..." Harold sputtered. "Ya ... ya ..." He made the monumental effort of clearing his throat and finally managed to weakly spit out, "You're trespassing."

The man's eyes blazed at this statement—literally. His eyes were filled with an intense flame that pulsed and flickered like the blue blazes of hell. A tiny bit of urine squirted into Harold's undershorts.

The man moved towards Harold—*without moving his legs*. Then he pointed directly at Harold and shook his head. Harold raised the flashlight again, preparing to defend himself from whatever the hell he was facing.

Then the man was gone.

Harold fought the urge to simply turn and run. Something had happened, someone was *fucking* with him, and he needed to get to the bottom of it. He flicked on the flashlight and cautiously circled the hand statue. Nothing. He swept the beam farther around the plaza, but nothing was in sight. Where had that punk hippie gone? The plaza was fairly open, other than the hand

CHAPTER 13

statue, some benches, and some low-lying shrubbery, there was really no place for concealment. He circled the plaza, checking behind the benches and shrubs, but found nothing.

Harold came back to the hand statue and played the light around the ground, looking for footprints in the grass. *There are no footprints,* his mind said. *The dude was floating.* "Bullshit," he said out loud. "That's impossible." *Yet it happened. He was also transparent—you could see right through him. And where was that blue glow coming from?* "I don't know," he said, not liking the whine in his voice. "I don't fucking *know.*"

He was starting to give himself the whim-whams. Staggering over to the nearest bench, he collapsed onto it. His heart jackhammered madly; was he having a heart attack? He took a few deep breaths, willing himself to think of nothing but becoming calm.

"It's just stress," he told himself. "You're working too hard, worrying too much about the mall." This was true, and it helped calm him down—a little. This fair was a big deal—the future of the mall and his family's finances could very well hinge on its success. He hadn't been sleeping well, and his diet lately largely consisted of what he bought from the mall's food court. He was in rough shape. After a few minutes, his pulse had dropped down out of the danger zone.

He reached for his cell phone, then stopped. Who was he going to call? The constables? And say what? *I was menaced by a hippie punk who floated. He was glowing blue and his eyes were like blue fire. Also, he was transparent.* Yeah, they'd bundle him off to the psych wing of Kerian Memorial in a heartbeat.

He got up and walked back towards his office to replace the flashlight but balked. For some reason, he really didn't want to go back into the mall. Plus, the flashlight felt good and solid in his hand; a form of protection that made him felt a little bit better.

He locked the entrance to the mall, set the security system, then drove slowly home. He washed down two Ambien with a highball glass half full of scotch. Eventually, Harold was able to fall asleep.

Chapter 14

Bolly stood just inside the door of Mike's Place, uncertain of why he was there or what he should do.

"Welcome to Mike's Place, sir," came a voice from his elbow, causing him to jump. "May I please see your ID?"

Bolly whipped his head around to see what looked like a professional football linebacker. He was six-three and weighed at least 275—all of it muscle. He had on a headset and dark glasses, despite the dimness of the room.

"Oh, uh, sure." Bolly fumbled out his wallet and handed his driver's license to the bouncer. The bouncer gave it a cursory glance and handed it back. Bolly stood there, not moving.

"First time here, sir?" asked the bouncer.

"Uh, yeah. I'm just here for a beer, okay?"

"That's just fine, we've got over sixty taps at Mike's Place. Find a comfortable place to sit. One of our hostesses will be by shortly to see to your needs."

"Yeah, great, thanks."

With some difficulty, Bolly replaced the license in his wallet and the wallet in his jeans. He looked around. He was pretty sure the building used to be a carpet warehouse. This bar area had evidently been the showroom. It was a large open rectangle, with a massive bar running down one of the long sides. Big-screen TVs were arrayed along the walls, all of them showing sports. The TVs and the bar glowed brightly, in contrast with the open area in the middle of the space. This was dimly lit, with small, widely spaced tables. Small lamps on the tabletops provided the only illumination, to help keep the patrons' identities discreet. Despite it being a Thursday night, the place was nearly full.

Amongst the tables circulated at least a dozen hostesses. A few hostesses toted menus or trays of food and drinks; most didn't. The standard hostess uniform was a very tight midriff-baring white polo shirt, red satin short-shorts and six-inch red heels.

Bolly cautiously made his way towards the back wall, which was the darkest part of the room. *What are you doing here?* he asked himself again. "Just stopping in for a beer," he muttered.

Was that true? He had managed to locate himself in Fester's most infamous cathouse. There were more bars per capita in Fester than any other city in Pennsylvania except Pittsburgh. He must have passed a dozen between the end of the zoo run and this neighborhood, so why stop in *here* for a beer? *You know why,* said a voice in his head. *You're horny, the wife won't put out, and the porn collection is getting a little stale. A man needs what he needs, and tonight this is the only place to get it.*

A menu appeared in front of him. Bolly jumped. "You doing okay, darling?" asked the hostess who had stolen up on him. She looked to be in her mid-forties and was pretty good-looking, too.

"Oh, um yeah," said Bolly. "I've just got a lot on my mind."

"You look like a man who could use a drink."

"Um, yeah. I just came in here for a beer. Waddaya have on tap?"

The hostess laughed and gestured at the bar. "This is the longest bar this side of Albuquerque," she said. "We got over sixty beers on tap. Why don't you tell me what you like, and I'll tell you if we got it. And we probably have what you want—it's our specialty."

"Yuengling porter?"

"Coming right up, darling."

The hostess disappeared and Bolly's inner dialogue continued. *Are you really going to cheat on Janie? With a prostitute? What kind of man does that?* Bolly thought of the old Warner Brothers cartoons he'd watched when he was a kid—the ones where a small angel and devil appeared on Porky Pig's shoulder and debated some questionable course of action. Now it was the devil's turn to argue: *The type of man who's not getting what he needs at home. Women just don't understand the male sex drive. If they did, places like this wouldn't even exist.*

"I just came here for a beer," he muttered again.

"And here you go," said the hostess as she placed a big mug of brown beer in front of him. "That'll be eight-fifty."

"Holy God!" exclaimed Bolly. "Eight and a half bucks for a draft?"

The waitress shrugged, then smiled. "Darling, if you really just came in for a beer, then you picked the wrong place. But I don't think you did. We've got great food and drinks at Mike's Place, but that's not why guys come here, y'know?"

"Oh, hell," said Bolly as he fished a ten from his wallet. "I don't know what the hell I want or what I'm doing."

The hostess reached down and touched his shoulder. Bolly felt an electric thrill shoot down his shoulder, across his torso and down to his groin. *That's why you came here,* said the devil.

"This your first time here, darling?" asked the hostess.

Bolly nodded. *It ought to be your last,* said the angel. *Just leave. Right now.*

"Well, look, there's no pressure, okay?" said the hostess. "Maybe just talk to one of the girls, see how you feel after that. Sound good?"

Hell yes! said the devil

Certainly not! said the angel.

"I guess so," said Bolly. He handed her the ten. "Keep the change."

"Thanks darling. Tell you what—you just relax a bit and enjoy your porter. I'll send Candy over to talk with you in a little bit. She's super-friendly and good with newcomers." She put an extra emphasis on *comers*.

See, this is a filthy place, said the angel.

Nonsense, said the devil. *That's why guys are here. That's why we're here. It's certainly not for the overpriced beer.*

Bolly was getting tired of this argument. *You can end it right now by getting up and going home,* the angel said. Bolly picked up his mug and drained half of it in one go. *That's the spirit, kiddo,* said the devil.

CHAPTER 14

The porter settled in on top of the three beers he'd had at home, and his anxiety began to drain away. His eyes had adjusted to the dark room, and he could take in his surroundings better. Most of the tables had only one customer. Hostesses—the non-serving kind—circulated amongst the tables. From time to time, one of the hostesses would join one of the men at a table. They would chat for a bit, usually not for very long. Sometimes, the hostess got up and circulated some more. More frequently, the hostess and the customer would get up and make their way to a door on the wall opposite of the entrance. Occasionally, a guy would emerge from the door and head straight for the bar. *One for the road after he's blown his load.* Bolly was pretty sure that the devil said that.

He noticed the hostess who had served his beer talking with another woman. The beer hostess nodded in Bolly's direction. The other hostess looked at him, smiled, and gave him a little wave. Bolly, paralyzed, didn't wave back.

The beer hostess disappeared towards the kitchen and the new girl smiled wider and began walking to Bolly's table. *You really should leave right now,* said the angel. *Hey, at least get a good look at her first,* said the devil. *You don't want to be rude.* "I might be many things," said Bolly to himself. "But rude is not one of them." *No, but you're about to become a whoremonger,* said the angel. *Is that what you want?*

Don't listen to that wussbag, said the devil. *Have another drink.* Bolly took another big swig as the girl approached his table. She looked to be a few years younger than Bolly's thirty-eight, but she wore it well. Platinum blond hair was done up in a seventies Farrah Fawcett do. The tight shirt showed off her boobs to maximum advantage. Her stomach was flat and bore the slightest hint of a six-pack. Her legs were long, lean, and tanned.

She stopped by the table and extended her hand. "Hi, I'm Candy," she said.

Unbidden, Bolly said. "I bet you are—you sure look sweet." Where the hell did that come from? *Good one, dude,* said the devil. Bolly took her hand and gave it a shake—it felt warm and soft. *Wonder what it'd feel like wrapped around your tool?* said the devil.

"Got a name, handsome?" asked Candy.

"Oh, uh, my name's Mike." Bolly had been called Bolly since he was a baby. When he was thirteen, he'd experimented with trying to have people call him Mike. It hadn't taken, and he'd given up and resigned himself to being Bolly forever.

"Well, Mike, I guess you're in the right place," said Candy with a laugh. It was a nice laugh, light and musical. "Mind if I sit down?"

"Oh, please," said Bolly. Automatically, he jumped up and pulled out the other chair for her.

"Well, a gentleman," giggled Candy. "I'm always glad to meet a gentleman."

"Uh, yeah, well my mom raised me right," he said. *And what would she say if she knew where you were right now?* asked the angel.

"I can tell," said Candy. She leaned over and gave Bolly an intense stare. Her eyes were an amazing hazel color, reflected in the light of the small lamp on the table. "So what do you do for a living, Mike?"

"I'm a mechanic."

She leaned back and regarded him with a grin. "You know, for most of the guys who come in here, if any of them told me that, I'd be apt to say something like 'Oh, maybe you can help buff out my bumpers' or 'Maybe you could help me get my front end aligned.' You seem like you're a little too smart for that."

"Oh, I don't know. I'm not that smart."

"Oooooh!" she squealed. "Maybe you could stick your nozzle in my tank and fill me up!"

"Um, okay, let's stick with smart then," said Bolly. "Besides, I'm a mechanic, not a gas station attendant."

"See—too smart for me," said Candy. She leaned over and lightly rested her hand on Bolly's. This time the thrill went straight to his cock, which responded immediately. *Game over,* said the devil. *I win.*

"So, Mike, Ingrid told me that this is your first time here."

Bolly nodded.

"Well, maybe we can get straight to the point. What is it that brings you to Mike's place tonight?"

CHAPTER 14

"Well, there's this place up the street that I was thinking about renting. You know for a shop."

"Uh-huh."

"And I was getting thirsty and saw this place, so I just pulled in to grab a beer."

She cocked her head and gave him a quizzical half smile. "Is that really it, Mike?"

"What do you mean?"

"Well, I figure that a guy as smart as you probably wouldn't be doing any sort of in-depth real estate analysis in the dark like this."

"Well, uh, I had actually taken a look at it last week, but, um, sorta forgot some stuff about it, so I just drove back out to, y'know, refresh my memory."

Candy laughed lightly. "Well, you are both smart *and* thorough." She looked pointedly at his left hand. "Your wife is a lucky woman."

"Yeah she is ... I mean, we both are."

She laughed again. "Well, Mike, I know a lot of guys, when they come here for the first time, might feel a little nervous or ashamed. There's no reason for that. We're here to make you happy. There's nothing wrong with that, is there?"

"No, I guess not."

"Of course not. We provide a service for guys, mostly—but not always. Whether that service is just a beer and a burger or something ... more involved. Well, it's all part of the same spectrum, wouldn't you say?"

"Yeah, I guess so."

"Good, good," said Candy. "I'm not surprised we'd see eye to eye on this. I knew two intelligent people like us would." She paused and stroked his hand. "So," she said in a lower voice, "are things not quite all right on the home front then? You seem like a really nice guy, Mike. I'm sure you wouldn't have turned up here unless certain parts of your life weren't a little lacking." She leaned over, letting her breasts push against the fabric of her cropped top. Bolly's eyes instinctively followed, and Candy laughed again. "What's going on, Mike? What's missing in your life?"

Bolly spilled everything. He told Candy all about the situation with Janie, the lack of success in conceiving, and her subsequent drop-off in sexual interest. Candy listened carefully, nodding and making sympathetic noises, all the while stroking Bolly's hand.

"That's tough," said Candy. "A lot of women really don't respect sexual impulses in that regard. There are so many factors leading into that—upbringing, religious beliefs, experiences in adolescence. Our culture is very confused about sex, don't you think?"

"Oh, yeah," said Bolly, thinking of some of the kak-headed advice he'd received as a kid. "But it still feels wrong, y'know. Society thinks it's wrong."

"Society thinks a lot of things are wrong that probably aren't wrong. More confusion, right?"

"But sex . . . like this . . . it's also illegal," said Bolly. *That's right,* said the angel. *It is.*

"Just more confusion," said Candy. "For example, it's not illegal *everywhere*. And in places where it *is* legal—well, the Earth hasn't opened up and swallowed those places for their sinful allowances. Nevada is still with us; so is Amsterdam."

"But the constables … " said Bolly. "Couldn't they just bust this place any time and haul everybody off?"

"Certainly. But they won't."

"Mike's paying them off?"

"No, at least I don't think so. They recognize that as long as no one is being coerced or getting hurt that it is much easier to let things be."

"I can't believe the constables would go along with that."

Candy laughed. "Oh, Chief Constable Prieboy is a little more broad-minded than you give him credit for, I think," she said. "Remember: he shut down the Pine Room. Domestic violence spiked. When Mike's Place opened, it dropped again. Prieboy is smart enough to see the writing on the wall. There will be no legal trouble here, I think."

Bolly sighed. Candy made a lot of good points. She was very persuasive. "Okay," said Bolly. "That sounds legit. I just don't know … I love my wife. Cheating on her—it just seems wrong. I'm not a super-religious guy, but I made vows at my wedding. It wouldn't feel right." *Good man,* said the angel.

CHAPTER 14

Candy let go of Bolly's hand and leaned back. "I respect that, Mike. You are clearly a man of integrity. I guess the question is how you define 'cheating.' I mean, in one sense, it can be defined as upholding the bargain of marriage. It sounds to me like your wife may be falling a little short in that area."

"Yeah, well, maybe," said Bolly. "But also, maybe not."

"My point is that it's not black and white," said Candy. *"Nothing's* black and white in this world, although there are plenty of simple-minded people who would like you to think so." She gave him that quizzical half-smile again. "Let me ask you a personal question, Mike: do you masturbate?"

"Uhhh, yeah, sure," said Bolly, caught completely off-guard by this question.

"Oh, my—you're *blushing!*" said Candy. "Oh, you are a rare gem, Mike. My point is this: you get hand jobs from someone who isn't your wife, correct?"

"Yes, I guess so." *Listen to the woman,* said the devil. *She makes a great point. She's also got great tits.*

"Let me ask you another personal question," said Candy. "If you could, would you suck your own dick?"

Bolly's mouth dropped open. He stammered and huffed. "Well, I ... I don't ... never thought ..."

"Oh, my goodness, you're *really* blushing now!"

Bolly though about a half-remembered comedy routine where the comic told the women in the audience that if men could suck their own dicks, the women would be sitting in the audience alone ... watching an empty stage. "Yeah, well, I guess if that was possible, I'd at least give it a try," he admitted.

"I appreciate your honesty," said Candy. "A lot of guys wouldn't have the balls to admit that."

She turned Bolly's hand over and slowly stroked the palm of his hand and his wrist. Immediately, his cock sprang to full attention. "I guess the question you have to answer, Mike, is this: where do *you* draw the line?"

Bolly drained his beer. He was thoroughly confused now. On one hand, he loved Janie and would never do anything that would hurt her. On the other hand, there was a beautiful woman stroking him—literally and figuratively.

And she made a lot of good points. Maybe Janie *wasn't* holding up her end of the bargain. If that was so, why should he? *Damn straight,* said the devil.

"Well, that's convincing," admitted Bolly. "Still, I have some questions. Like how much does it co—"

Candy reached out and held her index finger to Bolly's lips. Bolly felt another electric surge blast into his pants. "Ah, ah, ah," she said. "We don't discuss business down here," she said. "If you want to move this to the next level, we'll go upstairs to my room to discuss services and payment. Cash is always welcome, but if you want to use a credit card, it will appear on your bill as 'Stehle's Pipes and Fittings.'"

The devolution of the discussion to such stark business made up Bolly's mind. His hard-on crashed like the Hindenburg. "Uh, I'm still not sure," he stammered. "I really … I really think I should just go home now."

"I see," said Candy. "Well, I respect your decision, Mike. Like I said, I can tell you're a man of integrity."

"Yeah, um, thanks. There's something else I wanted to ask you …" This wasn't entirely true; Bolly just didn't want the conversation to end.

Candy stood up. "Sorry, Mike, but I must be moving on," she said. "Time is money, and I have to make a living." She moved off, leaving Bolly feeling confused and light-headed. He watched as she stopped at a nearby table, exchanged a few words with the man sitting there, then sat down. By God—was that a flash of *jealousy* he felt?

Time to go home, said the angel.

Bolly drained the dregs of his porter, rose unsteadily from the table and stuck to the darkened edges of the room as he made his way to the door. He'd have to be extra-careful driving home. He pushed his way into the parking lot with a sense of relief.

You're a good man, Michael Bollinger, said the angel.

This isn't over, said the devil.

Chapter 15

"Hiya, Pap," said Harold as he mounted the porch to the Big House. "Harry m'boy!' cried Merle, who was relaxing in his favorite chair—an ancient papasan held together with baling wire and faith. "Good to see you. That's twice in one month you've graced us with your presence. Folks'll start thinking you're part of the family."

Harry winced, and Merle walked his comment back. "Sorry, son—that wasn't a wise thing to say. I just meant you coming around more often is a good thing. We're always glad to see you, y'know. It's just that it's better for others to see you more often, too."

"Yeah, I guess so, Pap. I passed Vince on my way in, and he didn't flip me off or anything."

Merle stared at him for a moment and then they both burst out laughing. "Seriously, Pap," said Harold. "I got some stuff I need to talk to you about."

"Okay, let's talk about it."

Harold looked around. Various Totenkopfs were about their business on the homestead. Occasionally one would amble by and wave a greeting. "I thought we might go up to your study," said Harold. "I was hoping you might have some more of that hooch."

"Woo-ee, sounds serious," said Merle. "Yeah, sure I got more of that hooch. Let us retire to my inner sanctimony."

They went inside and stumped up the stairs to Merle's study. After a few pleasantries, Merle said, "Okay, m'boy, let's cut to the chase. What's on your mind?"

"Well, Pap, it's about the mall."

"Yeah, well, I seen ads for that fair you're puttin' together. Looks like a good idea."

"I sure hope so, Pap. I'm worried that if the fair don't work out the mall might not be around too much longer."

"What?" exclaimed Merle. He swallowed hard, twice. "What are you talking about, Harry?"

"I told you about that Fashion Bitch store pullin' out? Well, I've been slicing and dicing the numbers the best I can. If we lose even one or two more stores, even the small ones, things will get bad quick. And if one of the anchors decides to pull out, it's game over."

"Harry, you can't let that happen. You know how much the family depends on the income. We'd be in rough shape, for sure."

And I'd get all the blame, thought Harold. Hell, the worst that could happen was that things would go back to the way they were before the mall was built. Harry had *made* that mall—it was his idea, and he'd worked exceptionally hard to have it come to fruition. Harold's real estate acumen and hard work had provided the entire family with a steady income for years. They'd never see it that way, of course. They'd accuse him of being the sell-out who killed the goose that laid the golden eggs.

Merle must have sensed what he was thinking. "Harry, I don't think you get enough credit," he said. "You took a marshy old piece of land and built it into something that has done good for this family. A lot of the folks here can't really see how hard you worked, but I can. I'm impressed, Harry. *Proud.* I just want you to know that."

Harry felt himself choking up and could feel tears a millimeter behind his eyelids. "Thanks, Pap," he said thickly. "That really means a lot to me."

"Good deal," said Merle. "Now that we got the sentimental mush outta the way, how about that drink?"

"Sounds great, Pap."

Merle reached around to the shelf behind him and pulled out an earthenware jug and a pair of mismatched jelly-jar glasses. He poured out two hefty knocks, and they both sipped in silence for a while.

"Well," said Merle eventually. "I sure am sorry to hear the mall ain't doin'

CHAPTER 15

so well. That money's been a real boon to the family. Had some big plans."

"You said you had contracted for some work around the homestead. How much of a stretch is that gonna be for you?"

"Well, I ain't the spendthrift that some of the family are," said Merle. "And since I control the disbursement of the mall income, I been able to lay some aside while still being able to keep up feeding time at the zoo. Woo, some of them folks get rid of their money so fast, you'd think it was radioactive."

"Look, Pap," said Harold. "It's not like the mall is goin' tits-up tomorrow. If anything, it'll be like the Spendmor: Things will decay slow, then one of the anchors will bail and then it'll go downhill fast. We might be able to limp it along for a few more years, but we'd barely be keeping it in the black. I got a few rough ideas what we might be able to do with the property if worse comes to worst."

"Like what?"

"Nothing I want to talk about now. Like I said, they're just rough ideas. What I'm interested in right now is not having to exercise those options. The patient ain't dead yet, Pap. I just want to get the sumbitch out of his hospital bed. That's what this fair is all about. Get a resurgence of interest in the mall, keep those anchor stores happy."

"How's all that comin'?"

"I been bustin' heavies making sure it's just right. It's got everything: rides, games, ponies, face-painting for the kids."

"It ain't got no clowns, does it?"

"Hell no!" said Harold. "I know better than that."

"Good."

"I just had to get the pony ride swapped out at the last minute. Pap, you ever heard of a guy named Tony Vaginello?"

"Greasy Tony? Yep, I know of him."

"Is he okay to do business with? He was talkin' some weird shit about what he rents those ponies out for."

"You need to keep a close eye on that one," said Merle. "They don't call him Greasy Tony because he owns a bunch of oil wells."

"Will do, Pap. I know the family will back me if he causes trouble."

"Yep. Speakin' of which, is there anything the family can do to help you with this fair?"

"Yes—tell everybody you know about it. Call all of the kinfolk—even the ones out of county. Tell 'em there'll be free stuff—that should bring 'em. I got some flyers people could put up if they've a mind to."

"Hell, yes," said Merle. "Gimme all the flyers you got. When's this fair—Friday, right?"

"Right. Fourth of July."

"Well, tell ya what: I'll get up a couple of truckloads of folks, and we'll take all them flyers and just blanket the town. Every telephone pole, bulletin board, and windshield wiper will get a flyer. How's that sound?"

"Perfect. I got about five hundred in the car now. I'll run up a thousand more before Thursday."

"We'll get 'em handed out, Harry—don't worry about that. Wanna 'nother snort?" Merle hefted the jug.

"Yeah, Pap, hit me up." Harry lifted his glass. He was going to need a stiff drink to turn the conversation to the topic he had in mind. He emptied his glass in one go.

"Damn, son!" said Merle. "Things really as bad as all that?"

"I dunno, Pap. There's other stuff goin' on around the mall. *Weird* stuff."

"What kinda weird stuff?"

"Well, at first it just seemed like minor vandalism. Merchandise in the stores getting moved around after hours. Displays tossed around. Stuff like that."

"Probably employees pissed off at having to work overtime."

"That's what I thought at first. Then..." Harry paused, not wanting to go on. The story was ridiculous. But if he couldn't tell his old man, who could he tell? Sassy, maybe—but she'd broadcast it far and wide. That wouldn't do. He took a deep breath then took the plunge.

"I've been working a lot of late hours, y'know. Haven't been getting as much sleep as I should, either. So maybe it's just the stress, or I was tired and my imagination ..."

"Just get on with tellin' what happened," prompted Merle.

CHAPTER 15

"Okay, so one night I was workin' late. Me and Jacob were the only ones in the mall. I was giving the place a quick walkthrough before locking up. And I get hit in the head with a little blue pebble. Next thing I know, they're falling all around me. From outta nowhere."

"Must've been Jacob pullin' a prank on you."

"Heh, the last time Jacob did something crazy like pullin' a prank, Herbert Hoover was president. Besides, he couldn't have done it. I went outside a few minutes later, and I could see him patrolling the edge of the parking lot. There's no way he coulda thrown those rocks and run out there that fast. Old man like him? No way."

"What did you do then?"

"I cleaned up the rocks, went home and had a stiff drink."

"Good call. I'da done the same. Any other weird stuff?"

"Yeah, and this happened just last night." Harold went on to describe his encounter with the glowing figure by the hand statue. "I dunno, Pap," he said. "It's like the place is, uh, haunted or something." He sat back, expecting his father's ridicule.

"Huh," said Merle at last. "Well, that's what you get for building it on a haunted place, I guess."

"What?" exclaimed Merle. "What are you talking about, Pap?"

"I told you not to build on that spot," said Merle.

"I thought that was because you thought it was too far from the highway! You didn't say anything about it being *haunted!*"

"Of course not!" shouted Merle. "You'd a thought I was crazy. 'Let's not do this project that could make the family a fortune because of an ancient ghostie story!' Yeah, that'd make it sound like I was ready for the rubber room."

"Well, doesn't matter, anyway," said Harold. "That site was the only place we could build. The rest of the property was too swampy. It would have cost a fortune to shore it up." He held out his glass for more booze. Merle obligingly topped him off.

"What do you know?" asked Harold after a healthy knock of his drink. "Do you know why it's haunted?"

"All right," said Merle. "I'm gonna pass on some of the secret history of Fester. Grandpap Jeff passed it on to me, now it's time for me to pass it on to you. Maybe if I'da done it earlier, we wouldn't have all this mess."

"Maybe."

"Okay, here's what I know: back when Fester was first settled, there was a buncha Indians livin' on the north shore of Redskin Lake. I guess that's why they moved there—they liked the name!" Merle burst out laughing, but Harold wasn't in a humorous mood.

"Anyway," Merle continued. "Even though them Indians weren't causing any problems and were friendly, the leader of the town, Wolfgang Ziffer, decided they had to go. He invited them to a feast, then had the townfolk lie in ambush in the woods south of the town. When the Indians got to the hand-shaped rock, they got blown to bits.

"Only one of them got away, and that's because of our great-great-great-great-great-whatever-granddaddy, Poppi Totenkopf. He'd been kept in the dark about the ambush, and when he finally figured out what was going on, he tried to stop it. He beaned Wolfgang with a shovel, allowing a pregnant Indian girl to get away. Her and her baby were the last of the tribe.

"All of the people of the town swore to never mention it again. But Poppi was wracked with guilt. He eventually dictated the story to his grandson who wrote it down. It got lost in the Big House for many years, but Grandpap Jeff turned it up. The rest of the Top Hats weren't too happy about that. But that don't make no nevermind.

"That place has always been trouble. Back in the thirties, there was a powwower lived out there, name of Schmuck. He was killed after he crossed some of the Top Hat families. I don't know if it was right by the rock or not, but his house was somewhere out there close to where the mall is now. That's why they call it the Wizard's Woods.

"There was a mental hospital that was built out there after our family donated the land. But it burned down in the sixties. The land shoulda reverted back to us, but it didn't. You know the rest of the story.

"Also, there was some hanky-panky out around there when the Old Mill fire happened. Some local kid was havin' visions or hallucinations. They ended diggin' up some of the bones of them massacred Indians because of that kid. Lotta weird shit went on around that piece of land, especially by that damn rock hand."

"Well, what the hell am I supposed to do?" asked Harold. "What *can* I do?"

"Nothing. Not a damn thing you can do, except keep your head down and keep workin' on that fair. You got the family behind you."

"That's good to know, Pap."

"You bet. Now you gonna stay for supper? Sassy's making fried chicken."

"You bet."

Chapter 16

Bolly was up to his elbows in the engine compartment of the Firebird. The damn thing was driving him nuts. "C'mon, you lousy motherfuck!" he hollered as he hammered on the distributor housing with the handle of a screwdriver. Finally, the cap came loose, but when he'd finally wrenched it off, he noticed that it was cracked. "Son of a bitch!" he yelled and threw the distributor cap to the floor.

He was extremely short-tempered tonight. He didn't want to be here right now. Usually, he enjoyed working on the Firebird. It was really coming along nicely—the interior was in great shape and had cleaned up nicely. The problem was that he felt like he had to rush the project. It wasn't for fun—it was for money. He needed to finish the Firebird and get it sold so he could move on to the next project. The need for extra income loomed large in Bolly's mind.

The rent was also due tonight, and that was another reason Bolly was in a shitty mood. He'd gotten sick of the Schmidts and their greedy highhandedness. Those bastards had more money than Fort Knox but were squeezing him on the rent. Absolutely unbelievable. Or maybe not—greed was a hallmark of the Top Hat class.

There was yet another reason for Bolly's incredibly foul mood: he'd had a big fight with Janie. There had been some sort of interaction between her, her boss, and another employee. It had gotten complicated. Janie had come home upset and wanted to unburden herself, but Bolly'd had no interest in listening. Usually, he was willing to hear his wife's tales of workplace woe, even though they tended to be byzantine and overly detailed. Bolly

CHAPTER 16

had made the mistake of telling her to "save the drama for the afternoon soaps." This had touched off a huge argument that had stopped just short of throwing things at each other. In the end, he'd stormed out of the house—without dinner—and come back to the shop to work on the Firebird.

He regretted how he'd treated Janie but wasn't ready to apologize. He suspected she wasn't, either. It would probably be tomorrow before either had cooled down enough to have a rational conversation.

Bolly skinned his knuckles while cranking on a ratchet wrench. "Dammit!" he yelled. He was hungry, he was angry, and he was horny. "Hangrorny?" he said out loud, then managed a small laugh. Laughs had been few and far between lately. He hadn't done a zoo run since the night he'd almost lost it going around Dead Man's Curve. It felt like he didn't really have a good way to blow off steam anymore.

He put some Metallica on the battered boom box in the corner and went back to working on the Firebird. He was almost done with *Master of Puppets* when the giant, pointy Cadillac pulled into the lot. Bolly retrieved the rent money and went out to greet the landlords.

As usual, the car kept running as Thelma Louise stepped out. He caught a momentary glimpse of someone else in the back—old Ophelia, who looked like Nosferatu wrapped in a shawl. They began their courtly exchange that always reminded Bolly of a scene from *Downton Abbey*—another of Janie's favorite TV shows.

"Good evening, Mr. Bollinger," said Thelma Louise. "I trust you are well."

"I am, ma'am," said Bolly. "I trust you are the same."

"Indeed, I am—thank you for inquiring. I believe you have something for me."

Bolly nodded slightly as he held out the envelope. *For you, your worshipfulness,* he thought.

Thelma Louise reached out for the envelop, then paused. "I presume you haven't forgotten about the rent increase."

"No, I haven't." *It worries me every fucking day, your majesty,* he thought.

"Very good," said Thelma Louise after she finished counting. She turned to the car, then turned back. "Oh, yes, I almost forgot that I had a question to ask you."

"What?" Bolly snapped. He didn't feel very deferential this evening.

Thelma Louise must have sensed this and drew back a bit. "Mr. Bollinger, do you drive a Chevrolet Nova?"

Bolly started, but only a little bit. He'd been half-expecting this question. After his third zoo run, it occurred to him that the rich bastards had security cameras around their mansion and had probably gotten video of him peeling out in front of their house. He guessed they hadn't gotten a clear shot of his license plate, otherwise he'd already been questioned by the constables by now.

"That's my car right there," he said, waving towards the cherry-red Firebird in the open bay.

"Well, that's very interesting," said Thelma Louise. "You see, there is someone who persists in driving up by our house and performing what you automotive types would call, I understand, 'burning rubber.' It appears to be a dark-colored Chevrolet Nova. My brother believes he has seen such a car at this shop." She nodded towards the driver's side door. The smudged image of a pale face floated just behind the tinted glass. A little chill went down Bolly's spine.

"Well, Ms. Schmidt—this is a *car* repair shop. We get all kinds of cars, every day." He gestured at the four cars that were parked haphazardly around the lot, waiting their turn in one of the bays. "The Nova was a popular model. Sturdy, too. There are a lot of them still on the road."

"I see. Well thank you for your time, Mr. Bollinger. Until next month." She turned and climbed back into the Caddy. Once again, there was a brief flash of the beshawled Nosferatu. *Creepy-ass car full of weirdos,* thought Bolly. It reminded him of the old reruns of *The Munsters* he'd watched when he was a kid.

He watched the Schmidtmobile drive off and went back into the garage. His Nova was tucked away in the far bay with the garage door pulled down. He replaced the Metallica CD with Quiet Twisted Iron Goat and resumed working on the Firebird, but it was no use. He was too pissed and distracted and hungry and angry to focus. "Fuck it!" he almost yelled and began

CHAPTER 16

putting the tools away.

You're such a fuckin' idiot, he thought. Of course, the Schmidt bastards would see who was burning up the street in front of their house. But what was the worst thing he could be charged with? In his hell-raising youth, the most common charge for doing burnouts was VDP, or "vulgar display of power." Bolly wasn't sure if that was really the name of the law or just slang. He'd never gotten busted for it (although he'd done smokin' burnies plenty of times). He had friends who'd been popped for VDP, but it was only a misdemeanor and a fine.

Then again, there was no telling what the Schmidts might be able to do if their hackles were up. They were still tied tightly to the local power structure, even the cops. Chief Constable Prieboy seemed like he was too aboveboard to take a bribe, but there were plenty of other constables who could be induced to throw the book at him. Trespassing? Noise pollution? Felony menacing? None of those were out of the realm of possibility.

Bolly had been driving the Nova since he was sixteen—over twenty years now. Everybody knew it was his car. The only consolation was that Top Hats like the Schmidts wouldn't know anyone who knew or cared what kind of beater Bolly drove.

Maybe he should drive the Firebird; it was road-worthy. But—ah shit—he'd just cracked the distributor cap. That could be easily replaced tomorrow. Tonight, he'd just have to keep a low profile in the Nova.

He went into the office and checked the mini-fridge—sometimes the guys stashed beer there. Sure enough, there were three cans of Keystone Ice tucked behind the aging remains of a Subway sandwich. He sipped a beer and paged idly through a new Bust-Out Tools calendar that had landed in his in-box that day. Mechanics everywhere loved the Bust-Out Tools calendar, which featured curvy, scantily clad young women posing with various pieces of Bust-Out hardware. Bolly really liked Miss Bust-Out October—she reminded him of a girl from high school named Sandy. Bolly had had an enormous crush on Sandy his freshman and sophomore years, but she was two years ahead in school. For her, Bolly didn't exist.

Now, here was her doppelganger, ripe as a peach, wearing a tiny halter top and bent over the hood of a Corvette fingering a large torque wrench. *Damn,* thought Bolly. *Why can't I have ever gotten a girl like that?* Bolly flipped through the remaining months, but those girls weren't as hot. He checked the time: the Schmidts had been gone for nearly an hour. It didn't seem likely they'd waste a lot of time lurking around in order to follow him.

He drained the Keystone and threw the can in the trash. The beer had really made him hungry. He hadn't had dinner and it was almost eleven o'clock. He'd go down the street to the Buck and Wing for a burger and a beer. Or two.

He checked the street before he took the Nova out. It looked clear for a couple of blocks each way. He pulled the car out, closed and locked the shop and drove off towards the bar down the street.

Three blocks behind him, the lights of a Maserati Merak popped on.

Chapter 17

The Buck and Wing was an old-school dive bar that served the aging neighborhood. It was a squat, beige cinderblock building, but the owners kept it spotless outside and in. As he approached, Bolly could see the lot was mostly empty. It was, after all, nearly eleven on a weeknight. He knew the grill closed at ten but figured he could sweet-talk them into making a burger for him.

He was surprised when he cruised right by it without slowing.

"What the …?" muttered Bolly.

You know, said the devil. *We're going where you can get a beer, a burger … and a blowjob.*

Oh no! said the angel. *Not this again. I thought we were past this, Michael.*

"Both of you shut up," said Bolly. He fished a Lothar the Psycho CD from the console and turned it up loud. He meandered through Rivertown and headed across the Iron Bridge into East Fester.

He turned left on Slocum and headed towards Mike's Place.

Oh boy, oh boy, oh boy, said the devil. *This is gonna be great!*

He pulled into the lot and parked behind the tall wooden fence that separated it from the road. *Michael, I'm begging you,* said the angel. *Turn this car around and go home right now.*

"You stay in the car," said Bolly.

Nyah, nyah, said the devil.

"You stay, too," Bolly told him. "The two of you are making me crazy."

He went into Mike's Place. There was another bouncer, but he came from the exact same mold: huge slab of beef, shaved bald with no neck. His skin tone was a couple of shades darker, but that was the only difference. He was even wearing the same type of sunglasses. He went through the rigmarole with ID and seated himself in the part of the main room where he had before, where it was good and dark.

A hostess came by shortly. "What do you want, hon?"

"Is, um, Candy working tonight?" asked Bolly.

"Sure is. Should I send her over?"

"Not yet. First, I'd like a cheeseburger and a beer, please. And a shot of Jäeger."

"Coming up."

She returned a few minutes later with the shot and the beer. Bolly knocked the shot back in short order, hoping it would help take the edge off.

It didn't. Neither did the beer.

The burger came. It was actually pretty good, as were the fries. He demolished the food in less than ten minutes and burped, satiated. At least one part of his hunger was satisfied. He could feel himself coming off the edge of freaking out with some food in his belly at last.

The hostess came by to clear off the dishes. "Sorry, hon, but Candy is currently engaged. Would you like to speak to another of the girls? They're all top-quality and very friendly."

"No, I'll wait for Candy." Bolly still wasn't entirely sure he intended to go through with this. He certainly didn't want to strike up a conversation with a new girl. He felt he already had a connection with Candy. "Could you bring me another porter while I'm waiting?"

"Coming up, hon."

The hostess returned with another beer and Bolly closed out the tab. If Candy hadn't showed up by the time he finished, he would just go home. Maybe that would be for the best.

He nursed his beer, watching an Orioles ball game on one of the big TVs arrayed around the room. The first half of the beer disappeared quickly. He nursed the second half, watching the ball game with feigned interest. He was about to take the last swallow of beer when the hostess came by.

"Sorry, hon, Candy is still engaged, but she should be done real soon. Can

CHAPTER 17

I bring you another beer?"

"Yeah, sure," said Bolly automatically. He was in this to completion, it seemed. If you come to a brothel twice, and leave both times without getting any—well, that was kinda queer, wasn't it? Bolly wasn't sure, but he knew plenty of guys who would probably say so. He may have left the angel and the devil out in the car, but it was pretty clear who had won the argument.

Bolly was halfway through the beer. He was pretty buzzed, he definitely had to pee, and it was getting late. He was on the verge of getting up to go when Candy appeared by the table.

"Mike!" she said with a sexy lilt in her voice. "I'm so glad you *came* back! How are you this evening?" She sat down and took both of his hands in hers.

"Uh, I'm good, Candy." He sounded like an idiot. Her perfume was heady, strong enough to be noticeable without being cloying. It smelled like apple blossoms and honeysuckle. And she *looked* incredible. Viewed through Bolly's beer-enhanced vision, her hazel eyes sparkled like stars, her face glowed with an inner radiance—and, boy howdy, those *tits!* Bolly was hammered, horny, and about to take a plunge.

Candy looked over her shoulder. "Excuse me just a minute, Mike. I'll be right back. Boss is calling." She got up and walked off, leaving Bolly again wondering if he shouldn't just go home.

Before he could give it a second thought, she was back. "So, Mike," she husked. "Are we done with the preliminaries? Past the pep talk? Should we go upstairs and talk turkey? I promise you'll be glad you did." She turned his hands over and lightly stroked the sensitive skin on the inside of his wrists.

Bolly's cock was immediately hard. "Yeah," he said thickly. "I'm gettin' pretty tired of this ball game."

"Oh, we can play ball, all right," she said, then stood up and held out her hands. Numbly, Bolly stood and took her right hand. He didn't look around as she led him to the door in the back of the room. He was vaguely aware of the looks from the other guys at the tables as they passed. He didn't care. His big head had abdicated all of the decision-making to his little one.

They climbed the stairs to the second floor. The stairs opened onto a narrow corridor that ran the length of the building. Doors were arrayed along either side, spaced about every eight feet. The corridor was decorated like a low-rent version of the Playboy Mansion: red shag carpet, maroon wallpaper, gold-painted trim and miniature chandeliers. Candy led them to a door with the letter Q bolted on. She opened it and led him in.

The garish décor continued inside. The space was barely large enough to hold the single bed, which was covered with a crimson duvet and matching pillows. There was a small nightstand by the bed and a tiny sink in the corner. The room was lit by a low-wattage red bulb in a shaded overhead fixture. It was both sexy and lurid.

Candy sat on the bed and patted the space next to her. Bolly sat.

"Okay, sweetheart," she said. "We just have to talk a little business and then we can have a whole lot of fun, okay?"

"Okay."

"Payment's up front, cash or credit card. Remember, the credit charge will look like it was from a hardware store. Prices vary by what you want: straight lay, half and half, around the world, whatever. I don't do the real kinky stuff, so if you're into hardcore S&M or water sports, I'll have to decline. Of course, there are other girls—and a few guys—here who can take care of you in that regard. So what's it going to be, then, Mike? Whatever you choose, I guarantee you'll love it."

"Uh, well," Bolly stammered, now thoroughly blown out. Also, he really had to pee. "I, uh, don't want to go all the way, y'know?" *Did that come out sounding as dumb as I thought it did?*

"Of course, sweetheart, I understand." She put her arm around him, and he felt that thrill shoot down his spine and into his shorts. His cock was on full alert. "You already told me about your, ah, domestic situation. I just want to give you a little of the good stuff you're not getting at home." She gave him a little squeeze.

Bolly took the plunge. "How about a BJ?" he asked.

Candy smiled broadly. "Oh, that's my specialty," she said. "Good choice. That'll be eighty bucks. Do you want to pay cash or charge?"

CHAPTER 17

"Uh, cash." He pulled four twenties from his wallet—between this and the inflated amount he'd paid for his dinner and drinks, it almost cleaned him out. Still, there was no way he was putting it on a credit card. Janie did all the bills and would be sure to have questions.

"Thank you, sir." She tucked the cash into her shorts pocket. "Now that we have the boring business part out of the way, let's have some fun, sweetie!"

"Uh, yeah, I love fun all right," said Bolly. He looked around for a bathroom door, but the only door in the room was the one they'd come in through. "But first, I have some more business to take care of. All the beer I had is really backing up."

"Sure, bathroom's down the hall by the stairs. We passed it coming up."

"Okay, great—I'll be right back."

Out in the hallway, Bolly felt weird. It was different when Candy had been leading him by the hand, but now he was on his own. Hostesses came and went in various states of undress, some with clients, some not. A few single guys roamed the hall, most heading towards the exit. They looked either vaguely ashamed or pie-eyed with pleasure. Bolly kept his head down and headed for the bathroom. It occurred to him again that he could just leave right now and probably save himself a lot of trouble. He pushed the thought away. *No way*, he thought. *I paid for a blowjob and, dammit, I'm gonna get a blowjob.* It would be the first in over a year.

The bathroom was a small, single-use number with just a toilet and a sink. There were breath mints and cologne on the sink with a few other accouterments. Bolly took a long time to pee. His wang was still at half mast, which slowed down the process, but there was a lot of beer backed up behind it. After what seemed like five minutes, the flow subsided.

As he zipped up his pants, he cranked out a tremendous fart. "Damn Keystone," he said. Keystone beer always gave him the toots. And it smelled horrible. Desperately, he looked around for something to cover the smell. *Yeah*, he thought. *It's considered bad form in polite society to stink up the whorehouse crapper.* There was a matchbook with the hot-pink Mike's Place logo sitting on the sink. Bolly grabbed it, ripped off three matches and lit them, then blew them out. He waved around the smoking matches and stuffed the matchbook into his back pocket. He found the switch for the exhaust fan and flicked it on.

Thus relieved, he headed back to room Q. Candy was sprawled seductively on the bed. She hopped up. "Okay, sweet Mike, you just take your pants off and make yourself comfortable right here." She patted the bed.

He awkwardly kicked off his sneakers and dropped his pants. "Uh, should I take my socks off?" he asked.

"Whatever you're comfortable with."

He awkwardly toed off his socks and got on the bed. His cock was rock hard.

Candy giggled. "You must be a good mechanic—your tool is at the ready." She climbed on the bed and knelt down between his legs.

"Hey," said Bolly. "Could I ask you to, uh, take off your top?"

"Sure thing, hon." She shucked her shirt. Her boobs were spectacular—they put Miss October's in the deep shade. He reached out towards them.

"Ah, ah, ah," said Candy. "Touching costs extra." Bolly quickly withdrew his hands. "Just lie back and relax, Mike—I'll take care of all the rest."

She leaned down and went to work.

It was magnificent. Candy had not been exaggerating; she was a real pro. In what seemed like no time, Bolly exploded into her mouth, his toes curling, his hands grasping at the duvet. "Oh ... Jesus ... *Christ!*" he exclaimed.

"I knew you'd like it," said Candy. "Just relax in the glow, hon." He laid back on the bed and enjoyed a long period of thinking about absolutely nothing.

Candy bounced up from the bed and put her top back on. She took a small bottle of mouthwash from the nightstand, took a mouthful, gargled and spat it into the sink. "Do you want me to walk you out, Mike, or can you find your way?"

"Oh, uh," said Bolly, scrambling to get back into his clothes. "I think I can find my way out." He wondered if you were supposed to tip prostitutes. He guessed so; something extra for services well-rendered. He fumbled open his wallet—there was only a ten and two ones left. He plucked out the ten and held it out. "Here ya go."

CHAPTER 17

She took it and stashed it in the bedside table. "Oh, so manly *and* generous. I sure hope I see you again, Mike. Maybe next time we can try something a little more ... adventurous."

"Yeah, sure," said Bolly distractedly. He wasn't thinking about any next time; he just felt incredibly tired and wanted to go to bed. "See ya."

He went back into the hall and down the stairs. He hung his head but could still feel a goofy grin on his face. It was, after all, a pretty amazing blowjob.

He could see the lot had cleared out—it was now nearly 12:30. He wondered if Janie would be pissed at him for coming home late. Probably not—she's undoubtedly been zonked out for hours at this point. He started the car and headed home.

He made it about halfway before the guilt crashed over him like a tidal wave.

Chapter 18

"Auntie, do you know where Ronald is?" Thelma Louise asked.

"I don't," she said. "I think he's taken those dirty monkeys for a ride."

"Good," said Thelma Louise. "Let's have some tea. I think we ought to talk about some things."

"Such as?"

"Let's get the tea first, then we'll talk."

They went down to the kitchen and Thelma Louise started the kettle while Ophelia gathered the tea, milk, and sugar. Not too long ago, there would have been servants to make the tea. Things in the Schmidt household had declined a great deal in the last few years. Many of the servants had simply up and quit, something that always enraged Ronald. The declining local popularity of the Schmidts in general—and Ronald in particular— had made it increasingly difficult to find replacements for the domestic staff. When their last full-time help, a veteran housekeeper named Wilma, retired due to declining health, they hadn't even bothered looking for a replacement. The house was huge, but there were only three of them, so there was no real reason for a live-in domestic staff. Now there was only a Mexican couple who came out four days a week.

After Wilma retired, the three remaining Schmidts had to learn to fend for themselves and acquire skills they had been raised to believe were beneath them. Thelma Louise had taken up the food preparation and found that she rather enjoyed it. The only thing unpleasant about it was Ronald's frequent criticism of her cooking and unfavorable comparisons to meals cooked by the professional chefs who had once been in their employ. Of course, Ronald had no ability to cook himself. On those rare occasions when he had to fend for himself in the kitchen, he usually stuck with Pop-Tarts or canned soup.

Ophelia took care of the laundry, and in fact had been doing so since before Wilma left. She refused Thelma Louise's help, saying it was like meditation for her and reminded her of when she was a child and would sometimes help the housekeepers with the washing. Thelma Louise understood how she felt; cooking and sewing was the same way for her. It was calming and made her feel like she was doing something positive for the family.

A lack of those interested in domestic work wasn't the only challenge to employing staff. After the company had been sold, the family carried on with their profligate spending as if nothing had changed. The problem was that there was no longer any substantial income.

For nearly a decade, there was enough in savings to cover the costs of the household staff, the high-fashion wardrobes, and luxury vacations. Ophelia had raised concerns about their financial situation, but Ronald had written her off as being alarmist. As Ophelia aged and slowed down, Ronald had taken over more control of the family finances. Of course, by then there were fewer finances that needed management.

Eventually, even Ronald had to admit that some measure of austerity was called for. The house staff layoffs had begun then, and one of the wings of the house was mothballed and closed up. Thelma Louise's cash donations to charity had been severely curtailed.

There was one area for which Ronald absolutely refused to scale back expenditures, and that was on the upkeep of the exterior of the house. The mansion was large and old, and required a lot of maintenance. Ronald insisted that it be kept up, and Ophelia and Thelma Louise agreed. After all, exterior appearances *must* be maintained—otherwise, what would the quality people think?

Ophelia finished brewing the tea and poured cups at the small kitchen table. In headier times, it was only the servants who ate at the kitchen table, while the Schmidt family dined in the grand dining room. Tea might be taken in any of several suitable locations—the drawing room, the morning room, the library, from a tray delivered to one's bedchamber—but those days were gone now. At least the kitchen table had a nice view of the garden and the front lawn.

"What's on your mind, Thelma Lou?" asked Ophelia after they had had a few sips of tea.

"Please don't call me that, Auntie. It makes me sound like some sort of hillbilly."

"We certainly don't need any more of them around here."

"I'm worried about Ronald," said Thelma Louise. "His behavior is really getting out of hand. This latest incident with the neighbor was really too much."

"'Too much' is what it cost us, dear," said Ophelia. "Ninety thousand dollars to keep him from pressing charges. That's the problem with picking on people up here in the Heights. They're too expensive. Most of the time when Ronald gets into an altercation in one of the taverns he frequents it is more affordable. *Those* people can be bought off with a hundred dollars or so.

"Fitch was much more expensive—but he could have done much more harm. He claimed he could reveal things that would be damaging to the family."

"What could he possibly have known?" asked Thelma Louise.

"I don't know," said Ophelia. "But the man has been living next to us for ages, and he's quite the nosey parker. Actually, I don't think he knew anything—at least, anything really damaging. It doesn't matter. If he had pressed charges against Ronald, it would have been very problematic. It may have finished us in Fester for good."

Thelma Louise wasn't sure that hadn't already happened. She was acutely aware of the decline of the family fortune and reputation over the last twenty years. She suspected Aunt Ophelia was in denial. There was no point in getting her upset, though. She had led the family through some challenging times back in the nineties. She was owed some peace and respect in her

CHAPTER 18

declining years.

"I'm still worried about Ronald," said Thelma Louise. "We've always known he has a temper. He just seems more, well ... unhinged lately."

"He seems to have gotten into more bar brawls lately."

"It's gotten worse, Auntie. This episode where he locked you in your room and attacked Mr. Fitch is just the latest escalation. I pray it won't get worse, but who can say? I'm worried."

"I'm worried, too, dear," said Ophelia. "It seems like he's spending more time in the monkey house. Although maybe that's for the best."

Ronald had built a zoo-quality enclosure for his monkeys. When he'd first brought home Rondo, Ophelia had put her foot down and had Ronald remove the creature from the house immediately. Rondo had lived in the greenhouse for several weeks while Ronald had paid a premium for the expedited design and construction of the monkey house. As soon as it was built, Ronald had obtained Berryman, a spider monkey, and Peewee, a white-faced capuchin. Ronald had fashioned a den in the monkey house and even equipped it with a cot where he sometimes spent the night.

"Auntie," said Thelma Louise, leaning over conspiratorially. "I'm pretty sure Ronald has a gun."

"Oh, you know he likes collecting those military antiques," said Ophelia. "They're mostly just replicas."

"*Mostly* isn't *all*. The idea of Ronald having a functional firearm makes me very nervous."

"Oh, if he has anything like that, it's probably an ancient blunderbuss that would come apart if he ever tried to fire it."

Thelma Louise couldn't understand why her aunt was so sanguine—especially after the way Ronald had locked her in her room. "I was thinking that maybe there was something we could do," she said. "Some legal injunction, or ..."

"*No!*" Ophelia hissed. "Absolutely not! Thelma Louise, you put such thoughts out of your head right now! Our situation is precarious! This family *built* this town. Karlheinz Schmidt's mill was the basis of the growth of Fester and our fortune. We must protect the family reputation at all costs, especially now. That is the most important thing, Thelma Louise: protect the family reputation."

"Okay, Auntie."

Ophelia drained the dregs of her teacup and sighed. "I had no idea that the new owners were going to lay off so many people. I knew they'd make some changes, but not a wholesale sacking of the workforce. If I'd known they would do that—well, I may not have been so eager to sell." She sighed again. "Or maybe not. We really had no choice at that point, given the way that Cecilia woman had left the company finances."

Thelma Louise didn't remember the company finances being particularly bad when Cecilia had been in charge. If anything, it seemed like it was doing better than before. She couldn't be sure. She'd never paid close attention to the family finances. She didn't have a head for numbers; she'd been an English Lit major at Bryn Mawr.

"So what do we do?" asked Thelma Louise.

"We do nothing," said Ophelia. "Things are good now, with Fitch out of the way. They better be, with what it cost us. Let's pray nothing like that happens again—we won't be able to afford it. We're going to have to raise the rents on the commercial properties again, just to make up for what we had to pay Fitch."

"Oh, Auntie, no!" exclaimed Thelma Louise. "We just raised the rent. The tenants were all very unhappy. Maybe we should try to fix up some of the other rental properties to get more income. We could take out a loan or something."

"Take out a *loan?*" asked Ophelia. "Thelma Louise, we are *Schmidts*. We do not go hat in hand asking for money like common peasants. We simply have to raise the rents. It's either that or sell off some of the furniture and art."

"Oh no, we couldn't possibly do that!" said Thelma Louise. The art collection was the thing that had kept her grounded over the recent difficult years. The idea of selling even a small piece was like selling a child.

"Well, then," said Ophelia primly. "I guess we'll have to raise the rents again then."

CHAPTER 18

"Okay, but please try to not raise them very much. And let the people know as soon as possible, so they can prepare."

"My dear, you've always been too soft-hearted. But very well—I will have Ronald speak to Mr. Nasté about sending a letter to the tenants sooner rather than later. Will that suffice?"

"Yes, Auntie, thank you," said Thelma Louise. She paused before continuing, "Okay, what do we do about Ronald?"

"Again, Thelma Louise, we do nothing."

"What if something ... else happens?"

"Then we will deal with it when it happens. If worse comes to worst, then we will see about sending your brother on an extended 'vacation' at an exclusive resort. A resort with a large medical staff and rooms with doors that lock from the outside."

Thelma Louise nodded and decided it would be a good idea to start researching such resorts immediately. Then again, would they even be able to afford it? Maybe they *would* have to start selling off the art collection if it came to that. Thelma Louise shuddered. It was best not to think about such things.

"Look, there's no problem now," said Ophelia. "Let's not borrow trouble."

"But what about his gun?"

"If he has one—let the baby have his bottle. Besides, do *you* want to try and take it?"

"No. Absolutely not." Thelma Louise didn't care to think how her brother might react if someone tried to take away his gun. Besides, she wasn't even sure where he kept it, or even if he actually had one.

"Remember, Thelma Louise: whatever happens, the most important thing is to protect the family name ... and the family home. Don't forget that."

"I won't, Auntie."

Chapter 19

"You call that a pony ride?" asked an aggrieved Harold Todd. The Hickory Acres Mall Fourth of July Fair was just getting started, and Harold was rushing around the plaza outside the main entrance like a decapitated chicken making sure everything was going to be okay.

"Yeah, I call it a fuckin' pony ride," said Greasy Tony Vaginello. He gestured at the swaybacked creature tethered to a pole with a concrete base that had been set up in the parking lot. "Whaddaya call that?"

"It's a pony ... I think." Harold was no horse trader, but this looked to be a sorry example of horseflesh.

"'Course it's a fuckin' pony," said Greasy Tony. "And what is that little kid doin'?" He waved at a six-year-old girl who was mounted on the mangy pony. The little girl was crying.

"She's riding that sorry-looking beast," said Harold.

"Well, there ya fuckin' go."

"Look, you said I'd get *six* ponies. Like you get at a carnival. Six ponies, in a paddock, attached to one of those rotating dealies with arms that spins around so we can get six kids riding at the same time. We'll never be able to accommodate all the kids with just one damn pony."

"Hey, look, pal—you said you wanted a *pony* ride," said Greasy Tony. He pulled a half-smoked cigar from behind his ear and lit it. It smelled like a yeti's armpit. "There's a pony, and there's a kid ridin' it. You got a pony ride."

Harold looked at Greasy Tony with distaste. He lived up—or down—to the name. He wore a Bon Jovi T-shirt with the sleeves ripped off, a pair

CHAPTER 19

of jeans with the knees blown out, and a pair of rotting Keds sneakers. His hair was down to his shoulders and was, as advertised, greasy. He was mostly bald on top, but the chrome dome was ill-concealed by a horrendous comb-over. He sported a Pancho Villa-style moustache, also greasy. "Also," added Greasy Tony. "I don't think you have to worry about too many kids not gettin' rides. There just ain't that many of 'em here." He gestured at the meager crowd milling around the plaza.

Harold ground his teeth. He'd been worried about turnout all week—he felt like he hadn't slept in days. He'd run two full-page ads in the *Fester Daily Dispatch* over the last week. He'd also spent more money than he'd really wanted trying to blanket the local radio stations with ads. He'd even coughed up for TV ads on one of the TV stations in Weaverville, although he could only afford slots late at night. True to his word, Merle had gotten up a convoy of trucks and cars, and the family had distributed nearly two thousand flyers all over the city. Harold couldn't think of what else he might have done to promote this event.

Yet the turnout had been disappointing so far. Harold checked his phone. The fair had been going on for an hour, and the number of cars in the parking lot were only slightly more numerous than on an average Friday morning. Well, it was still early; there were still six more hours to go. At least the weather was nice.

He turned back to Greasy Tony. "Look, this isn't—" he began. From the other side of the plaza came the sound of a muffled *bang*, followed by the sound of "Pop Goes the Weasel" slowing and slurring. The miniature merry-go-round had blown a fuse again. "Shit!" Harold exclaimed. "I'll deal with you later," he told Greasy Tony, then rushed off to find the handyman who'd promised to be able to supply power to the rides and booths.

That kicked off another bout of rushing around, putting out minor logistical brush fires. He ended up standing by the hand statue, listening to the general manager of Sears gripe about the poor turnout. He was interrupted by a tap on his shoulder.

"Hey, pal," said Greasy Tony. "You owe me some money, and I want it now."

"Excuse me," said Harold to the Sears manager. He led Greasy Tony over to the hand statue.

"Awright, slick—make with the money," Greasy Tony demanded.

"So, what, I gave you twenty percent down?" asked Harold.

"Yeah, and I want the rest."

"You promised me a carnival-grade pony ride with six decent ponies, and all I got was one lousy broke-down nag. I'd say *you* owe *me* some money."

"Why, you cheap motherfucker!" said Greasy Tony. He gave Harold a shove to the chest. "I'm done fucking around with you. You either hold up your end of the bargain, or I'll kick your fuckin' ass."

"What bargain?" demanded Harold. He was pissed. He had worked his ass off putting this damn fair together and it was falling apart at his feet. The fair was shaping up to be a bust, the mall might soon be a bankrupt, and he was arguing with a scumbag who had shorted him. "I ain't paying you jack shit, *pal*. I'm not entirely sure that I won't take you to court!"

"Awright, asshole—you asked for this." Tony reared back and delivered a punch straight to Harold's nose. It folded with a sickening crunch, and blood shot out of Harold's nostrils, down the front of his freshly laundered shirt and onto the ground.

Overhead, thunder rumbled. There was a loud whinny from the vicinity of the pony ride. The clapped out-looking pony was rearing on its hind legs, eyes rolling wildly. Fortunately, there hadn't been a child on the pony. A little girl, who had just gotten off the ride, screamed and grabbed her father's legs. He gathered her up and hurried away.

"Now pay up!" demanded Greasy Tony. "Or I'll give you another."

Harold barely heard him, his nose hurt like hell, he felt like he was going to puke, and blood was running down his front. His hands were clasped to his face. From behind them, Harold managed to choke out a muffled "Fuck you."

Greasy Tony reared back to hit him again, but someone behind him caught his arm. Greasy Tony spun around, saying, "Hey, what the fuck …"

Behind him were Harold's father and his cousins Vince and Ted.

"What the fuck do *you* want, assholes?" demanded Greasy Tony.

CHAPTER 19

"Nice to see you again, too, Mr. Vaginello," said Merle. "Or it would be if I hadn't just seen you punch my son in the face."

"Hey, hey—I didn't know he was your kid, man," stammered Greasy Tony. "This asswipe's tryin' to cheat me!"

"Is this true, Harry?" asked Merle.

"Hell, no," said Harold, still holding his hands over his nose. The gush had subsided a bit but was still flowing. "This guy promised me a carnival pony ride, and all I got was that." He gestured with one bloody hand towards the raggedy pony, where the handler had just managed to get it calmed down.

"That's a pretty sorry excuse for a carnival ride, Anthony. Hell, it's a pretty sorry excuse for a pony. Did you give Anthony here a down payment?"

"Yeah," said Harold. "Two hundred bucks."

Merle snorted. "Shit, that damn broke-ass nag ain't worth two hundred bucks. You came out ahead, Anthony. Let's just call it even, all right?"

Greasy Tony glowered, then said, "Yeah, yeah—you got me over a barrel, ya bastards."

"Okay, good," said Merle pleasantly. "That settles the matter of the pony money. Now there's just the matter of you hitting a Totenkopf. Looks like you broke his nose, too."

"Hey, hey," said Greasy Tony, now thoroughly alarmed. "I'm sorry! I didn't know he was your kid!"

"Doesn't matter," said Merle. "His name might be different, but he's still a Totenkopf. And you attacked him. There's only one thing for that."

He gave Vince a slight nod. Vince stretched his arms up like was he was about to yawn. Then he brought his left elbow rocketing down into Greasy Tony's nose. The nose flattened like a pancake and Greasy Tony went over backwards. Nose gushing blood, he rolled on the ground, wailing.

Thunder pealed again, louder this time. Harold looked at the sky—it was covered horizon to horizon with ominous dark clouds. They had sprung up from nowhere.

"Any real law here, Harry?" asked Vince.

"Nope. Few private security guys, but no constables."

"Good," said Merle. He leaned over Greasy Tony and told him, "Okay, *now* we're even, Mr. Vaginello. If I were you'd I'd want to keep it that way. Now go ahead and collect your sorry-ass pony and get the fuck away from our mall. Boys." He nodded, and Vince and Ted hoisted Greasy Tony to his feet and began hustling him towards the pony, which was in the midst of another thunder-induced freak-out.

"Are you okay, Harry?" asked Merle.

"Yeah, I think so. The bleeding's slowing down. I just need to get to my office. I've got a first-aid kit. Also, I keep a spare shirt there. This one's pretty much shot." He looked down at the huge red stain that now covered the front of his dress shirt. He was glad he had chosen not to wear a tie.

"Do you need help?" asked Merle.

"No, I'm okay. Go make sure that Vince and Ted don't do anything too extreme. Greasy Tony's an asshole, but I think he's learned his lesson. Let's just let things drop."

"I make no promises, but I'll see what I can do," said Merle, and he walked off to where the skittish pony was being loaded into a trailer.

Harold rolled his eyes skyward. The dark clouds were still overhead, but at least it wasn't raining. This weather sure wasn't going to do anything to boost attendance. Holding his hand over his nose, he quickly made his way to the side entrance to his office. He didn't want to alarm people by walking through crowds looking like an axe-murder victim.

Christopher Young was five years old, and he was supremely bored. He had been excited for the Fourth of July Fair all week, after seeing commercials on TV. But now that he was here, he was disappointed. He'd expected a miniature version of Disney World (which the Youngs had visited last Christmas), but instead it was just a lot of junky stuff in a boring old parking lot.

The face-painting booth had refused to give him a full-face Spiderman job and had merely drawn a web on his left cheek. The pony ride had been terrible; the pony smelled bad and slowly limped in a circle. Not at all like a real cowboy horse would have done. The merry-go-round broke down while he was riding it, the ride and the recorded calliope music running down with a scary wheezing sound. By the time the ride got going again, there was a long line, and Christopher had a meltdown waiting to get back on.

He was tired of the fair and wanted nothing more than to go home and play with Legos. He knew that wouldn't happen soon. Mommy had said something about shopping in the mall—super-duper boring—and they hadn't even been inside yet. There was only one thing that really interested him right now.

"Daddy," he said, tugging on his father's sleeve. "Hey, Daddy—I want to climb on the rock."

"Not now, Christopher," said his father distractedly. He was rooting around in a diaper bag while his mother attempted to calm down his little brother, Luke. Luke was crying his head off, and Christopher could smell a boom-boom wafting from Luke's onesie.

Luke was nine months old. At first, Christopher had been excited about being a big brother. Then when Luke came along, Christopher had been disappointed. His little brother didn't *do* anything—he just slept, ate, and pooped. How was Christopher supposed to have adventures with a sidekick like *that*? Even worse, Mommy and Daddy no longer paid as much attention to him. Until Luke came along, he'd been the sole recipient of his parents' affection and attention. Now his little brother got most of the care—and Christopher acted out, a lot.

"*Please* don't tell me you forgot the wipes," said Mrs. Young, who was desperately trying to quiet a screaming Luke.

"They're in here, they're in here, dammit," said Mr. Young, who suspected that he *had* forgotten the wipes, but didn't want to admit it.

"Daddy," whined Christopher. "I wanna ..."

"You want to shut up, or you won't be watching *Paw Patrol* for a month!" snapped Mr. Young.

Christopher knew this wasn't an empty threat, so he shut up. Daddy didn't say he could go climb the rock that looked like a hand. Then again, Daddy hadn't said he *couldn't* climb the rock that looked like a hand. Seeing that his parents were busy, Christopher courteously left them undisturbed and went off on his own to climb the rock that looked like a hand.

He darted away from his parents and ducked under the chain around the rock that looked like a hand. There were conspicuously large signs on the chain in black and red reading: DANGER! DO NOT TOUCH! He couldn't read the words, but he knew the meaning of chains with signs. He ignored them. He was too focused on his goal.

He touched the rock shaped like a hand and an electric thrill ran through him. He was full of energy! It was just like the time at Carl Hogan's birthday party when he'd eaten three slices of double-chocolate cake *and* a handful of bite-sized Snickers. He'd run around for a solid forty-five minutes and had been so out of control that his parents had been called to pick him up early. Well, this was *ten* times better than that. No, a *hundred!*

The rock shaped like a hand was still rough enough to provide plenty of handholds for little hands and feet. The top of the fist was about four feet above the level of the plaza. Christopher quickly surmounted the knuckles and looked around for Mommy and Daddy. There were plenty of people milling around the rock shaped like a hand, but Christoper couldn't spot his parents. A few people regarded him idly, but no one said anything or tried to stop him.

He was still full to the top with energy; the fine hairs on the backs of his arms tingled and stood straight up. There was nowhere to go but up, so Christopher began climbing the index finger.

As he ascended the feeling of being full of energy grew stronger. His hair stood on end. Christopher laughed. He scaled the rocky finger like a monkey going up a vine. He very quickly reached the top.

Then he kept on going.

Christopher Young levitated above the top of the finger of the rock that looked like a hand. His hair (long now—Mommy had wanted to take him to the barber for a month, but Christopher had raised a stink) stood straight out like a fright wig. He felt all tingly and zoom-y. "Look Mommy! Look Daddy!" he shrieked. "I'm flying! I'm flying!"

People were looking at him now. They stood in amazement, jaws hanging half-open. They weren't too amazed to forget to whip out their cell phones—

CHAPTER 19

it was like a convention of quick-draw artists, gunfighters from the old Westerns Daddy like to watch on Saturday afternoons.

"Christopher William Young!" shrieked Mrs. Young. "You come down from there right now!" Christoper could see them now; they were only a few feet away.

"Holy fucking shit," said Mr. Young as he scrabbled for his phone.

"I'm flying!" repeated Christopher. "I'm flying!"

There was a huge peal of thunder and a flash of blue lightning that seemed to come from everywhere. Then Christopher William Young was flung to the ground. He lay on the grass face down, not moving.

His parents were beside him in moments. "Christopher!" wailed Mrs. Young. "Oh my God, Christopher!"

"Don't touch him!" commanded Mr. Young. "Something might be broken. *IS THERE A DOCTOR HERE? MY BOY NEEDS HELP!"*

The crowd milled around, ogling the still form of the boy. Others were already arguing about what they had just witnessed.

"Bullshit—the kid just climbed up and jumped off."

"No bullshit. I was standing right there—I had a perfect view. There was at least a foot of daylight between the bottom of that kid's shoes and the top of the rock."

On the grass by the statue, Christopher stirred, then sat up. He looked around, eyes glassy.

"Oh, thank God!" cried Mrs. Young.

"Are you okay, Pumpkin?" asked Mr. Young.

Christopher shook his head, and his eyes lost the glazed expression. "I wanna go again!" he screeched. *"I wanna go again!"*

Harold Todd emerged just in time to see Christopher fall. He had staunched the flow of blood from his nose with an icepack and had swapped his shirt with the spare he kept in his office. He didn't think his nose was broken, but it was really swollen and it hurt like hell.

After all the hard work he had put into arranging the fair, it hurt to see it was falling apart. His plans for keeping the mall afloat all hinged on this event being a success. All he could do was hope the worst was behind him, and that he could salvage the rest of the fair. The rumbles of thunder he heard from his office didn't give him much optimism.

He did have a brief moment of hope when he saw the crowd around the hand statue. Then he noticed they were all looking up. Then he looked up himself—just in time to see Christopher Young jump off the top of the statue and land face-first in the grass.

Harold whipped out his cell phone and called Jacob, who was heading up the security for the event. He told Jacob to send one of the rent-a-cops with paramedic training to the entrance, pronto.

Harold reached the crowd around the boy the same time the paramedic did. The man looked official: he wore a blue baseball cap with a caduceus logo, mirrored shades and carried a large toolbox with a red cross on it. By this time, the boy was sitting up and screaming that he wanted to go again. As he watched, the boy's parents managed to get him calmed down enough to be examined by the paramedic. The paramedic rummaged in his box, snapped on a pair of latex gloves and removed a stethoscope and reached out to touch the boy. There was an audible *zzzzzt!* and the paramedic hollered "Ow!" and yanked his arm back. This startled the kid and he began screaming again. The parents had to start all over getting him calmed down.

Harold looked around. Most of the crowd were now staring into or pecking furiously on their phones. A man a few feet away was looking around with a dazed expression.

"Did you see what happened?" Harold asked him.

"Oh, yeah, man—I saw it all." The man was in his mid-twenties, wearing a well-worn, oversized green sweater, and had locks of dirty blond hair peeking out from underneath a brown knit cap. "That kid, he fuckin' *flew*, man."

"Did you see him climb the statue?"

"Yeah, man, he came runnin' up and went up that statue like crazy. I mean he was wired, man."

"So you saw him approach the statue?" asked Harold, now acutely aware of the liability ramifications of this situation. "You saw him cross the chain with the warning sign?"

"Yeah, yeah," said the man. "But you're missing the *point*, dude. It wasn't how he started the journey. It was how he finished it."

"What are you talking about?" asked Harold, now thoroughly confused.

"Look, when the kid climbed to the top of that finger, he fuckin' *levitated*, man. He just hung there in the air. Not ten feet away from my face. I swear."

Harold gave him a skeptical look. The guy looked higher than Snoop Dogg at a Dead show. He must have caught Harold's look. "Hey, maybe I *am* a little toasted," he said. "But I *saw* what I *saw*." He gestured at the crowd around them. "You don't have to believe me. There are at least a dozen people who recorded the whole thing on their phones. *You'll* see." He gave Harold a dismissive look then turned and moved away.

By now, the paramedic had completed his examination and was packing up his kit. The little boy was sitting up and happily babbling about flying. Harold sidled over as the paramedic was getting ready to leave. "I'm Mr. Todd, the general manager of Hickory Acres Mall," he said.

"How nice for you!" chirped the paramedic.

"Yes, thank you. I was wondering if you could tell me about the child's condition?"

"Well, it's against my para-Hippocratic oath, but what the hell, here goes: the kid's just fine. They're pretty resilient at that age. It's also a good thing that it had rained and the ground was wet. But no problems with the kid, not so much as a bruise. I told the parents to take him to see his regular doc in a day or so, just to be sure. But otherwise fit as a fiddle." He shrugged and walked off lugging his supply box.

"Excuse me," said an angry voice. Harold turned to confront an angry middle-aged man with cheap glasses and a Steelers cap . "Did I hear you say that you were the general manager of this mall?"

Harold had a sinking feeling in his stomach. "Yes, I am," he said, barely suppressing a sigh.

"In that case, *you* are the one legally responsible for my son's fall. I intend to take legal action."

Harold eyed him. Was it even worth the bother to tell him he had witnesses who had seen his unattended child climb over the chain with the warning sign, and therefore the mall had no liability? No; this man looked too dumb to argue with.

"That is your prerogative," said Harold. "If that is the case, I see no further reason for continuing this discussion without legal representation. Good day, sir." He turned and left the man huffing behind him. He wanted to retreat to his office and call the lawyer. As he crossed the plaza back to the entrance, he noticed a television van from WEVL-TV entering the parking lot, followed by two constabulary cruisers.

He turned and ran for the office. The excrement had hit the air conditioning.

Chapter 20

"Can you believe this shit?" asked Bolly.

"I can believe I need your help with the laundry," said Janie. "Can you turn that off and lend a hand?"

"In a minute, babe—I just want to see this thing. This is freakin' unbelievable."

Bolly was glued to the TV set, watching the video from the Hickory Acres Mall Fourth of July Fair. Bolly and Janie had missed all of the fun. They'd gone to Weaverville and spent some time with Bolly's dad, then had gone to a friend's house for a barbecue. Everyone had gotten hammered and Bolly and Janie ended up spending the night. Now, a full day later, they were watching the heavy coverage of the events at the mall still running on the local news.

As predicted, there were nearly twenty people who had captured cell phone video of Christoper Young's airborne adventure. However, the events had happened so fast that they were almost over by the time anyone had managed to get their phones out and start recording. The best video so far had been from Mrs. Myra Kottmeyer, who had been standing about fifteen feet away.

Mrs. Kottmeyer's video started out jerky, with the sound of Christopher calling, "... Mommy! Look Daddy!" There was an electrical transformer humming sound in the background. The picture finally stabilizes on Christopher as he called out, "I'm flying! I'm flying!" From the video, it really did look like he was flying—or at least hovering. For two and a half seconds, Christopher could clearly be seen hanging motionless in midair.

His feet paddled the air several inches above the top of the hand sculpture's raised index finger. Then there was a bright blue flash that washed out the entire picture. When the flash faded, there was a blur as Christopher's body moved rapidly out of frame. There was a wet *thump* and a gasp from the crowd as Christopher fell to earth. Then the camera swung around to catch the crowd as they gathered around the boy—mostly just backs and backs of heads, then the image cuts off. Mrs. Kottmeyer's cell phone video had been broadcast on news channels across the country and overseas and had received over two million hits on YouTube.

It was the best of the videos but was by no means the only one. Depending on the timing and the angle where the person was recording, it also looked like Christopher just jumped from the top of the statue. This had touched off a firestorm of debates as to what had really happened.

There were those who insisted the event was a true act of God. Supporters of this "Mall Miracle" belief insisted it was a work of the Almighty to give strength to the faithful in these uncertain times. Others insisted a rambunctious boy had climbed up to the top of a statue and simply jumped off. The thought in this camp was that Mrs. Kottmeyer's video had been doctored somehow. An optical engineer from the University of Arizona claimed to have done calculations showing that Christopher's apparent "hovering" was due entirely from the angle from which Mrs. Kottmeyer had shot the video, and the slow descent of gravity's pull merely *looked* like hovering on video.

The argument even extended to ESPN, where little Christopher's amazing hang time was compared to Michael Jordan's. "Don't talk to me about 'hang time!'" yelled Stephen A. Smith. "Jordan's legendary slam duck from the free throw line, his hang time was 0.92 seconds. That's *less than* one second! That kid is hanging in midair for a good two, three seconds! That kid is *levitating!*"

"I'm surprised you're not more interested in this," said Bolly. "Hell, we were at that damn rock on the Night of the Old Mill Fire."

"That thing creeps me out," said Janie, who had plopped down the basket of dirty laundry and joined Bolly on the couch. "You forget I had been out

CHAPTER 20

to that rock before—with Paul. It was raining, and we found a skull. That place is damn *creepy,* Bolly. That's why I don't like shopping there. I'd rather make the drive out to Weaverville than go to Hickory Acres. There's just too much bad history there. Like that old asylum—and that powwower whose house got torched."

Bolly had forgotten Janie had a longer history with the place than he did. She'd even accompanied her father out there when she was a kid, when he had a job surveying the site. Janie seemed to be more worked up than usual lately, and the story about Christopher Young just got her more agitated.

"And just when this story couldn't seem to get any weirder," the CNN anchor said. "It does. New video reveals what appears to be the ghostly image of a person standing behind the rock as Christopher Young is thrown to the ground." The video cut to another shaky cell phone view. The camera is skewed, with a portion of the hand statue and one of Christopher's sneakers appearing in the upper left corner. In the background, the image showed display windows of the Bon Ton department store. There is a sudden blue flash, and a human figure suddenly appears close to the center of the shot. It quickly fades into nothingness along with the blue glare. The cell phone video ended and was replaced by a blurry still showing the figure. It was difficult to say what the image was. It certainly did look like a person, but it also looked like it could have been a person-shaped piece of shrubbery. Even weirder, it seemed to be transparent. In the still, you could clearly see the mullions of the Bon Ton storefront through the figure.

"That's just crazy," said Bolly.

"It's just bullshit," said Janie. *"Fester* bullshit, of which there is no shortage. You can sit here and gawk at it; I've got practical stuff to do."

She got up, grabbed the laundry basket and marched out of the living room. Bolly sighed. It seemed like she'd been in a worse mood ever since he'd had his encounter with Candy. He'd felt enormously guilty about his transgression, and it plagued him constantly. At first, he'd tried to overcompensate by trying to be thoughtful and attentive. He'd even brought home a dozen roses the night after—something he'd never done before. He realized he might be overplaying his hand, and that Janie could become suspicious of Bolly's overly thoughtful behavior. So he started acted sullen and withdrawn, which did absolutely nothing to improve his wife's mood.

On CNN, the optical engineer was explaining the ghostly image behind the hand statue was likely an illusion caused by the lightning flash reflecting off one of the manikins in the department store window.

Bolly heard Janie say from the laundry room, "What the fuck? What the *FUCK*?!"

This did not sound good.

Angry footsteps approached, and Janie marched out of the laundry room, arm extended. "Michael Marcus Bollinger," she said. "I want you to tell me what *this* is doing in your jeans pocket!" In her hand was the matchbook from Mike's Place.

"Um, ah," said Bolly, realizing he was in deep shit. He had two choices: he could either come clean with his wife about what had happened at Mike's Place and face the consequences or lie like hell. He chose the latter. "I got that at work. Someone left it in the crapper, and I used it to cover up a real stinker. I must have shoved it into my pocket and forgotten about it."

She stared at him for a long time without speaking. Bolly fidgeted and foolishly tried to embellish his story. "Yeah, Bob must have left it there. You know Bob, young guy, always up to some sort of crazy shit. I think he goes there sometimes. He says they've got really good burgers there. Big tap selection, too."

Janie's right eyebrow lifted a quarter of an inch. "Burgers? You have to be fucking kidding me! Don't lie to me, Bolly—have you been there?"

Bolly's mouth opened and closed a few times. He decided a half-lie might be more effective than outright bullshit. "Okay, yes, yes," he said. "Bob talked me into going out there with him one time after work. I guess he's really stuck on one of the girls or something. We just had a burger and a couple of brews—nothing more."

Her eyebrow hoisted even farther. "Really," she said flatly. "You expect me to believe you went to the most notorious whorehouse in the county, and you only had a burger and a beer?"

Without thinking, Bolly went on the offensive. "Well, sometimes when

CHAPTER 20

a man isn't getting good cooking at home, he might need to eat out sometimes!" he said hotly.

"Eat out?" shrieked Janie. "*Eat out?!* Just what—or who—did you *eat?*"

"*I ate a fucking hamburger!*" Bolly yelled. "And I looked at the girls! So sue me! I talked to them, and they were nice to me! They showed some interest in me—which is more than I can say about *you* most of the time!"

"Oh, I should have figured!" yelled Janie. "Just because I'm not your damn *fuck toy,* you use that as an excuse to go whoring around! You sneaky, unfaithful *bastard!*"

Bolly cringed. That word "unfaithful" hit him at his core. Because she was right: he *had* been unfaithful, and it had eaten at his conscience ever since he'd driven home from Mike's Place that night. And now he'd compounded the problem by lying about it.

Well, he'd made his choice; now he'd have to live with it. Of course, Janie was not without responsibility. If she had been a little more responsive to his needs, he never would have even *thought* about Mike's Place. *I'm a good dog,* he thought, *but it's hard to keep me on the porch if you don't pet me once in a while.*

"Aw, fuck this!" shouted Bolly. "I don't have to stand here and listen to these bullshit accusations!" Except they weren't bullshit, but Bolly was in full fight-or-flight mode now, and he knew he wasn't going to be able to win the fight. "I'm outta here!"

"Yeah, sure!" yelled Janie through her tears. "Go running off to your *whore!*"

"She's not *my whore!*" shouted Bolly. He was mad at himself – and *furious* with Candy. She had sweet-talked him into the whole misadventure. "Goddamn bitch – I should have killed her!" He couldn't believe the words that were coming from his mouth.

It was enough to silence Janie, who stared at him, open-mouthed.

"You know I didn't mean that," he said, horrified at what he'd said.

Janie just shook her head.

"I'm outta here," he repeated, but with much less energy than before. He spun on his heel, stalked out to the garage and by an almost superhuman feat of will, avoided slamming the door behind him.

He climbed into the Nova and started it. Then he just sat there. His heart was thudding like the bass drum at a Slayer concert. He held his hand out—it was shaking like crazy. He took a few deep breaths, trying to calm his racing pulse. He needed to get himself under control before he took it to the street. Also, he secretly hoped Janie would come out after him, and they could get things worked out—at least a little bit. Deep down, he also knew he could shut off the car, go back inside, and tell Janie everything. That was really the only way this was going to get resolved in any fashion. But he couldn't do it, at least not now. He dropped the Nova into reverse and slowly backed out of the driveway.

But where to go? There was always the Buck and Wing. He could go there and get blitzed, and pour out his woes to Schulzie, the bartender. Then take a cab home to an empty house. Maybe he could just go to the shop. There was an Army-surplus cot stashed away there somewhere.

He looked down at the passenger seat. There was a letter there from Schmidt Properties, Inc., notifying him of yet another rent increase, another hundred bucks a month. It had put him in a bad enough mood when he came home, but the weird story from the mall had made him forget it earlier.

The goddamn Schmidts were shafting him again. He knew what he was going to do now: a fuckin' *epic* zoo run. One the Schmidts would hear—and see—for sure. He'd have to be careful not to lose it around Dead Man's Curve, but that didn't matter. It was going to be the launch that mattered, and Bolly knew how he could smoke out his adversaries.

He stopped at the Food Ape and picked up a gallon of bleach, then continued up to the top of Morningwood Promenade. On the way up, he scanned carefully for constables, but the coast seemed clear. Good. This was going to be his last zoo run, and he wanted to make it a good one.

At the very top of the hill, he turned the Nova around and lined it up on the dividing line. Then he got out and poured half of the bottle of bleach behind each of the rear tires. He climbed back into the car and backed it up a few feet so the tires were standing in the puddles of bleach.

The bleach was for smoke. Back in high school, Bolly had known a guy named Ralph Shoop who drove a bored-out Mustang he called the King of Smoky Burnouts. Shoop had rigged a windshield washer pump in the trunk of the Mustang to spray bleach on the tires; he could burn them for minutes at time, generating huge white clouds of toxic rubber-and-chlorine smoke. Bolly had always wanted to try the bleach burnout trick. Tonight seemed a perfect opportunity.

He popped a Nazareth CD into the player—a bit old-school, but appropriate to the occasion, he felt. As the opening cowbell to "Hair of the Dog" rang out, Bolly cranked the volume, dropped the Nova into first, and punched the gas.

The results were gratifying. The tires spun and shrieked like banshees. A huge cloud of smoke billowed out from underneath the rear end of the car. The smoke looked red in the glow of the taillights. The rear end swung back and forth as the tires tried to find purchase through the slippery bleach. At last, the bleach began to burn off, and the Nova began to move forward, rear tires still spinning madly.

The Nova had just reached the end of the Schmidt property when a figure stepped out from behind a bush, raised a pistol and fired.

Between the roar of the stereo and the screeching of the tires, Bolly almost didn't hear the gun go off. But the muzzle flash was unmistakable, then the windshield starred and there was a burning pain in his left shoulder.

He had been shot!

He needed to get the hell out of here before his assailant could get off another shot, but the tires were still spinning in the residue of the bleach. "Jesus!" he yelled. "C'mon! *C'mon!*" At last, the tires found purchase and the Nova shot forward. Screaming with fear and confusion, Bolly raced down the hill at top speed. Was that another shot? Bolly couldn't tell for sure. He just needed to get off this damn hill full of rich maniacs and never come back.

Once he got down by the country club, he'd regained enough composure to calm down and ease up on the accelerator. It probably saved his life. He was still going at high speed as he went into Dead Man's Curve. "Oh, shiiiiiiiiiit!" he yelled. He tried the bootleggers turn he'd pulled on his first run weeks ago, but it was too little, too late.

The Nova left the road going sideways and slammed into the tree that had caved in Webby Schultz's head. It crushed the passenger side of the Nova and killed the engine. The CD rolled on to the next track: "Miss Misery." It seemed appropriate.

"Oh shit, oh shit, oh shit!" yelled Bolly. His arm hurt like hell. He touched his left shoulder, and his hand came away bloody. He craned his neck, looking around to see if the shooter was pursuing him. He couldn't turn very far—it hurt too much. Panting with pain and fear, he managed to pry his phone from his jeans pocket and dialed 9-1-1.

Chapter 21

Martin was about to get ready for bed and trying to relax by browsing eBay for rare Batman comic books. He clicked around, seeing nothing of interest and feeling guilty that he was spending five minutes attending to his own wants rather than working. He was getting ready to shut off the computer when his phone rang.

"Hey, Chief," said Chief Inspector Blount. "Really sorry to bother you at home, but this one's pretty big."

"Oh, for goodness' sake," said Martin. "What do you have, Dan?"

"Shooting on Snob Knob. Got a car slid sideways off the road at the turn just below the country club. Driver has a bullet wound to his shoulder. Driver's name is Michael Bollinger. He says someone at the top of the Promenade popped a round into him."

"Top of the Promenade?" asked Martin. "Where?"

"Right by the Schmidt house."

"I'm on my way."

Martin arrived at the crash site less than ten minutes later, just as they were getting ready to load Bolly into an ambulance. Martin approached, asking to speak to him before they carted him off to Kerian Memorial.

"How are you doing, sir?" he asked.

"Doin' pretty good now that they gave me a shot for the pain," said Bolly. "Doin' just fine, in fact." His eyes were glazed and his words were slurred.

"Do you mind if I ask you a few questions?"

"Ask away, Chief-a-rooney."

"Where were you when you were shot?"

"Right at the top of the hill, man."

"Were you in the vicinity of the house at the very top? The one owned by the Schmidt family?"

"Right in front on the shit house ... I mean the *Schmidt* house." Bolly began giggling.

"Did you see who shot you?"

"Naw, it was too dark. Fucker popped up from behind a bush and blasted me. I didn't want to stick around, so I just floored it. I was freaked. Kinda overshot it on Dead Man's Curve."

Martin eyed the car that was squashed up against to tree. You typically didn't see forty-year-old Chevys cruising around Morningwood Heights. "Would you mind telling me what you were doing at the top of Morningwood Promenade?"

"Just going' for a ride, man. Tryin' to clear my head. Ain't no law against that, is there?"

"No, certainly not," said Martin. "Now, when this person appeared from behind the bush ..."

"Excuse me, Chief Constable," interrupted the paramedic. "The patient is stable, but he is injured. We need to get him down to the hospital. Please."

"Of course, of course," Martin said. "You're in good hands, Mr. Bollinger. I may have some more questions for you tomorrow."

"Later days, dude," said Bolly, and he closed his eyes.

Martin went to one of the constables who was checking the Nova. "Have you seen Dan Blount?" he asked.

Martin reached for his shoulder-mounted mike, but before he could grab it, Blount called him.

"We need you up here, Chief," said Blount.

"Where's 'here'?"

"The front gate of your favorite Top Hat family's home. Pierre Nasté is already here, and he won't let us in. I have no idea how the bastard got up here so fast."

"He lives nearby," said Martin. "And please watch your language on air, Chief Inspector. There may be citizens listening in."

CHAPTER 21

"Roger, Chief. See you soon."

The ambulance had already pulled away, and the forensics team was going over the Nova, checking for evidence. Martin walked over to see how it was progressing.

"Find the slug yet, boys?" he asked.

"Got it, Chief," said one of the constables. He waved a small evidence baggie with a misshapen lump of metal inside. "It's pretty weird, though."

"Weird how?"

"I'm not sure, Chief. It just doesn't look like any of the bullets I've ever encountered before. Looks like an oddball caliber."

Martin was tempted to take over the analysis. Back when he'd had Blount's job, that sort of forensic analysis had been the best part of the job. No more. He was the chief constable now. Sitting in the big chair meant he had to spend most of his time doing administrative work and practically no time at all doing the fun, Batman-type detection and analysis that appealed to him.

"Carry on, Constable," Martin said. "Please let me know right away when you've got something." He climbed back into his car and proceeded up the hill.

There was a Mexican standoff going on when he got to the front of the Schmidt house. Blount and another constable stood in front of the gate to the property. Behind the gate was the slender, elegant, and slightly sinister figure of Pierre Nasté. Martin approached. "Constables, Counselor," he said. "Dan, would you mind stepping over here?"

He had Dan Blount give him a rundown on what they'd discovered so far. A search of the immediate area had turned up no one hiding or fleeing. There was a patch of shrubbery at the corner of the property showed some signs of disturbance, but there was nothing else. No shell casings had been recovered.

Martin sniffed. Along with the smell of burnt rubber there was an unusual swimming-pool smell. "Chlorine," he said. "Any idea where that came from?" Blount shook his head.

"Okay," said Martin. "Let's get some more warm bodies up here and widen the search. Also, call the staties in Weaverville, see if they can lend us a chopper."

"Is that really necessary, Chief?" asked Blount.

Martin cut a quick glance at Nasté. He appeared to be intently typing something into his phone. Nevertheless, Martin lowered his voice. "No, it is *not* necessary at all. But considering the situation and the persons involved, we have to keep up appearances. How are things with the counselor?"

"Exactly like you'd expect. Stonewalling to beat the band. Wouldn't let us talk to the Schmidts without you here."

"And now that I'm here, it will be something else." He walked back to the gate, where Nasté was finishing up his text.

"So, Pierre," he said. "It looks like we have a situation on our hands. A fairly serious one, from the looks of it. We have a citizen on his way to the hospital with a gunshot wound. He says he was shot right at this property."

"He did?" said Nasté, raising an eyebrow. "And did you speak with him personally?"

"I did, right before I came here."

"Tell me, Chief Constable, what was the, ah, patient's state of mind when he described to you what happened."

Martin sighed. "He had sustained serious bodily trauma. He had been given pain meds when I talked with him."

Nasté's eyebrows shot up. "Pain medication? Powerful narcotics, no doubt, would be administered to a victim of such serious trauma. Utterly justified, in my opinion. However, don't you think that a person under the influence of such strong, mind-altering drugs might not be the world's most reliable witness?"

"Of course, Pierre. We will get his full statement tomorrow, once the docs at Kerian Memorial have taken care of him."

"Do send him my best wishes for a speedy recovery."

"I'll do just that," said Martin. "Regardless, I would like to speak to your clients about what happened here tonight."

"Why?" said Nasté sharply. "Surely you don't think my clients have anything to do with what happened? The Schmidts are one of the oldest

CHAPTER 21

families in Fester, and highly respected. Surely, you're not going to impugn the family name with scurrilous accusations?"

"Surely not," agreed Martin. "That said, we do have a citizen who sustained a gunshot wound somewhere in this vicinity and subsequently crashed his car, presumably while trying to flee his attacker. I'd just like to see if your clients might have seen anything or can otherwise shed light on what happened."

"I'm not sure if that's a good idea," said Nasté. "I detect a distinctly adversarial and accusatory note to your request. I'm afraid I'm going to have to refuse."

"You know, Pierre, I can make a very strong case for probable cause."

"You might be able to do so this evening, but I will rip it to shreds in court tomorrow. I think you know that."

"One of your clients has history of violent behavior. That gives ..."

"Hold on just one second, Chief Constable!" interjected Nasté. "You are making serious accusations here. My clients have no criminal convictions—you know that. There is such a thing as slander."

Martin looked around. He could see flashlight beams sweeping through the bushes at the periphery of the Schmidt property. Farther down the road, others panned back and forth across the road. "Excuse me," he told Nasté.

Martin walked back to where Constable Blount was talking on his car radio. When he was finished, Martin asked, "What's new?"

"Nothing much," replied Blount. "We haven't found anything of note. The staties are sending up a chopper but can't spare it for very long."

"Have any of the neighbors seen anything?" asked Martin.

"What neighbors?" asked Blount. "The house next door is unoccupied. Old Mr. Fitch took off shortly after Ronnie the Rake went after him."

"Constable Blount!" said Martin, alarmed. "You will watch your language and avoid using derogatory nicknames." He cut a quick glance back at Nasté. "Especially in the presence of a litigious defense attorney."

"Oh, right—sorry, Chief. It won't happen again."

"Any other neighbors?" asked Martin.

"None nearby. The next two houses after Fitch's have been unoccupied for some time. The nearest neighbors are a quarter mile away. We've spoken with several, but they heard and saw nothing. You know most of these houses are set back from the road and have large fences and hedges for privacy. They're pretty insulated from the real world."

"I see," said Martin. "Do you have a flashlight handy?"

"Here you go," said Blount as he handed over a heavy Maglite. "We'll make another search up here in the morning when we can see. It's too dark to pick up much of anything right now."

"I'm interested in something that's literally right under our feet," said Martin. He flicked on the flashlight and began playing it over the road surface. "Looks like the tire of someone who peeled out in a hurry. And look at this: they're very distinct here at the edge of the property. Then, as we go back towards the gate, they become much blurrier. I wonder what that's all about."

"I don't know," said Blount. "What should we do now?"

"I'd really like to speak to the Schmidts about what happened here," said Martin. "Especially Ronald. Mr. Nasté, however, appears to be especially stubborn. Might be tough going. We'll see."

He stepped back to the gate where Pierre Nasté was blandly observing the police activity on the other side. "Pierre, it would really ease my mind if I could talk to your clients right now. At the very least, I'd like a few words with Ronald Schmidt."

Nasté shook his head.

"In that case, I think I can make a pretty strong case for a search warrant. I really hate to disturb a judge at home in the evening, but I'm willing to take a chance on it."

"What you really need to be concerned with, Chief Constable, is the terror attack on my clients!"

"Terror attack? What on earth are you talking about, Pierre?"

Nasté sniffed theatrically. "Surely you can smell that? Chlorine! The Schmidt family was the victim of a chemical warfare attack! This is what you should be focusing your attention on rather than baselessly accusing my clients of vague misdeeds. This is a violation of international law! The

CHAPTER 21

Geneva Conventions!"

"The Geneva Conventions?" cried Martin. "Mr. Nasté, you are being rather hyperbolic. All I smell is some swimming pool chemicals. Doesn't this property include a swimming pool?"

"It does, but it was drained three years ago and hasn't been used since."

"Then there must be one nearby."

"I assure you there isn't," said Nasté. "Now why don't you quit prevaricating and start investigating the incident as an assault against my clients!"

Martin resisted the urge to grind his teeth. Pierre Nasté was known to be a tough fighter, and he was living up to his reputation tonight. "I will begin investigating this incident by talking to your clients. If you won't allow that to happen right now, I will call Weaverville for a warrant. I wouldn't expect it to take more than half an hour."

Nasté merely smirked. "You have your job to do, Chief Constable, and I have mine. Let us go, then, and do our jobs." He turned and began walking back to the porch.

Martin was striding back to his car when his phone rang. He was tempted to let the call go through to voice mail, but he changed his mind when he saw that the caller ID was *Thad Lincoln.*

"Hello, Mr. Mayor," said Martin. "How are you this evening?"

"Passing well, Martin, passing well," said Mayor Lincoln. "Look, it seems we have a bit of a situation on our hands up on the Heights."

"You are absolutely correct, sir. We have a gunshot victim now on his way to Kerian Memorial, we have exceedingly little evidence, and we have a number of potential witnesses who refuse to speak with us. I have enough to make a strong probable cause case, and I was getting ready to call over to Weaverville and get a warrant."

"Whoa, now, Martin!" said Lincoln. "Let's not get ahead of ourselves here. This is a very complicated situation, from what I've heard. Let's not complicate it further by barging in on one of the outstanding families of this town."

"Thad, may I speak frankly?"

"Absolutely—you can always talk turkey with me."

"I would really like to speak with Ronald Schmidt about what occurred here. I'd also like to get a copy of the house's security video."

"Well, why don't we take a deep breath and look at the situation from a different perspective. How did the gunshot victim make out? Was it a serious wound?"

"No, fortunately not."

"Good," said the mayor. "Then we don't have that to worry about. Now, the way I see it, the biggest thing on our plate is that there is a dangerous gunman on the loose in the most upscale neighborhood in town. I think that needs to be attended to first, wouldn't you say?" While the Mayor's Residence was close to City Hall, Martin knew Lincoln owned a home nearby.

"Of course, Thad. I have every spare man up here right now. There's a chopper inbound from Weaverville to assist in the search. However, I really would like to speak with the Schmidts immediately. I believe it would help us direct our search."

"Let's just take that off boil, Martin. There are a number of considerations we have to weigh. You know the Schmidts still swing a lot of weight with certain elements in town. *Powerful* elements. I certainly wouldn't want to do anything that might endanger anyone's job—especially mine! Ha ha!"

Martin steamed. He'd had a good relationship with all of the mayors he'd served under—Thad Lincoln was the third. Both were fully aware Martin's position was an appointed one, and the mayor was the one who could appoint and fire the chief constable. Never before had one of them so overtly threatened him with his job.

"Sir, are you preventing me from continuing with my investigation?" asked Martin.

"No, no, no—nothing like that. I wouldn't *think* of interfering in a police investigation. I'm just saying, given the current situation, it would be best for all involved to wait until tomorrow. I will speak with the interested parties, and I'm sure we can arrange to have anyone you like be made available for an interview. There's no need to pester a judge, Martin. Let's wait a few hours and take care of it then. I really think that's the best course

CHAPTER 21

of action, don't you?"

Martin thought nothing of the sort. He paused before continuing. "Honestly, Mr. Mayor, I think the best course of action is for me to interview the Schmidts immediately."

"Why?" demanded the mayor. "Certainly, you don't think one of them is *involved*, do you?"

That was exactly what Martin thought, but again he held his tongue. In the background, he could hear the chopper approaching.

"The idea is preposterous," continued the mayor. "This is one of the oldest and most respected families in town. You cannot go around accusing them of wanton crimes with no evidence!"

"Sir, I would never make such an accusation without adequate evidence."

"Good, then it's agreed. We'll wait until tomorrow and when *everyone* has had a chance to calm down, we deal with matters in a civilized fashion."

"Sir, I rather think ..." Martin had to raise his voice—the helicopter was right overhead now.

"I can't hear you!" shouted the mayor. "The chopper must be there! We'll talk in the morning." Then he hung up.

Martin stared at the phone for half a minute. Never had he encountered such naked political meddling in an investigation. Sure, traffic tickets got fixed and misdemeanors got swept under the rug, but this was a whole new level of interference.

He could go ahead and get the warrant—or try to. No doubt Pierre Nasté could pull some strings in Weaverville and delay the whole process anyway. Even if he did get the warrant, there would be a bad scene at the gates of the Schmidt residence. They might even have to force entry if things really got tough. That would lead to a great number of ugly possibilities.

The Schmidts were on the outs in Fester, but they were still Top Hats. And Martin knew quite well how the Top Hats took care of their own. They would circle the wagons against anyone who dared threaten the old hierarchy. They could easily lobby Mayor Lincoln to fire Martin, even threaten him with a recall campaign if he didn't go along.

"Damn!" said Martin. This was, for him, a very strong oath. He had been skunked by the Powers That Be. Well, he'd go along and play ball—at least for tonight. Tomorrow was another day, and he could deal with matters then as he saw fit. Or so he hoped. He was sure that it would be a busy day.

Chapter 22

When Bolly woke up in his hospital bed, Janie was sitting in a chair beside him. It looked like she'd been crying. He was glad to see her, but also a little surprised. When he'd been brought to the hospital the night before, the nurses had tried to contact her but reported that her cell phone went directly to voice mail. Bolly had thought of trying to call her earlier, but his cell phone had seemed impossibly out of reach. He had fallen asleep before he'd been able to muster up the strength to reach it. He was worried that she'd been out of contact—maybe she'd decided she was done with Michael Bollinger once and for all. Yet here she was in the flesh and red-eyed from weeping.

"Hey, babe," said Bolly weakly.

"Oh, you're awake!" cried Janie. She leapt up and ran over to give him a hug.

"Ow!" said Bolly. "Take it easy, babe! I'm wounded here."

"Oh, I'm so sorry, I'm so sorry—I … I've just been so worried. I hope I didn't hurt you."

"No, really, I hardly felt a thing. They've got me pretty doped up, fortunately. Hell, it's not too bad. I got lucky, babe. Coulda been a lot worse."

"I know," said Janie. "I talked to the nurse while you were asleep. She said that the gunshot wound could have been a lot worse—the bullet only clipped your arm."

"Yeah," said Bolly. "Took out a chunk of meat but didn't hit the bone or anything. Should heal up clean, although I'm probably going to have a divot there for the rest of my life."

"Oh, scarred for life," said Janie with a sob. "But it could have been so much worse! Oh, Bolly—if that bullet had gone a few more inches to the left, you could be d-d-dead!" She burst into tears.

"It's okay, babe, it's okay—I'm still suckin' wind. But the doc says I need to take it real easy. I'll have to be off my feet for a bit—I guess that's going to be a problem at work." His stomach dropped as he said it. How the hell was he going to be able to keep up with work now? He wouldn't be able to do the day-to-day for a while, let alone get back to restoring those back lot cars for extra money. And he was going to have to repair the Nova, too. His mind raced. He was really up shit creek without a paddle now.

"Don't worry about work," said Janie. "I called the shop. They were really worried you weren't there. Larry says he can keep things under control. Him and Bob should be able to keep up with the workload. Larry has a cousin or nephew or something he could bring in to help out if things get too busy. He says the guy is pretty good, and that you can pay him under the table."

"Okay, that's good. One less thing to worry about, anyway."

"What happened to the car?" asked Janie.

"Dunno," said Bolly. "Last time I saw it, it was smashed up against a tree halfway up Snob Knob. I bet the cops towed it somewhere. I guess it's considered evidence now. They'll give it back when they're done analyzing it for evidence and bullets and stuff."

"How long until you'll be able to drive?"

"Not sure. I hope I'll be able to drive and work in a couple of days or so."

"Bolly, you shouldn't rush it. You need to take time to properly recover. Like I said, Larry and Bob can handle the work at the shop."

"Yeah, I'm not worried about that, but I was counting on being able to fix up some of those golden oldies on the back lot and selling them. Money's getting a little tight, babe."

"We can always ask my parents for money if we really need it."

Bolly grunted. The thought of going to his in-laws with hat in hand did not have any appeal. He got on with Janie's parents—at least on the surface.

CHAPTER 22

He always felt they looked down on him, that his family came from a lower social stratum than theirs. He did know they had tried to talk Janie out of the marriage when Bolly proposed. When it became clear they were not going to be able to talk Janie out of the wedding, they had accepted it—albeit grudgingly. Bolly could imagine the look on Mr. and Mrs. Simmons' faces if he and Janie hit them up for money. He wrinkled his nose at the thought of it.

"Look, we don't have to worry about that now," he said. "Things are getting a little tight, but we'll work through it. We always do. It's just that, well, one of the reasons I was in such a shitty mood last night was that I found out the damn Schmidts were jacking up the rent on me. Again."

"Oh, Bolly, I feel so *bad!* After our fight last night, I was so *angry.* I turned off my phone because I didn't want to talk to you. Then when I woke up and found you hadn't come home, I was even angrier. I thought you might have gone to ... that *place* again and spent the night. Finally, I turned my phone on, and it just about blew up with the text messages and missed calls. I came here as soon as a heard. I've been a bad wife."

Bolly squirmed. He was about due for another dose of pain medication, and his shoulder was starting to sing. What was worse was that there was a difficult conversation needing to be had, and it really had to happen now. Well, might as well get it over with before the Demerol came and knocked him back to la-la land.

"You're not a bad wife, babe," he said. "If anything, I've been a shitty husband. I think we need to talk some stuff out. You mean the world to me, Janie. I'm sorry I let things get rocky."

"There's enough blame to go around, I guess," said Janie. "I guess we need to figure some stuff out. Maybe we could get some counseling."

Bolly wasn't sure where they'd get the money to pay for the counseling, but they could worry about that later. "Yeah, that might not be a bad idea."

"There's one thing I have to know right now, though," Janie said. "And I need you to be honest. I need to know what you did ... at *that place.*"

"Mike's Place?"

"Yeah."

Bolly took a deep breath. It hurt. He could try to soft-pedal what he had done with Candy, but that didn't seem like a good idea. The guilt at his infidelity had been gnawing at him like a rabid rat. Best to get it all out in the open right now and deal with the consequences.

"All right," he said. "I've told you the truth—but I didn't tell you the whole truth. Part of me doesn't want to, because I feel so shitty about it. I'm afraid you'll just up and leave—but fuck it—I need to man up and own what I did."

Janie began sobbing lightly and nodded her head. Bolly hoped she'd say she wouldn't leave him no matter what he said, even though he knew he didn't deserve that.

"Okay," he said. "I started going on drives at night, to blow off steam. I was really worried about money when they hiked the rent on me. Do you know what a zoo run is?"

She nodded, sniffling. "Yeah. I rode with Paul on one once. I didn't see what the big deal was."

Bolly nodded. "Paul probably didn't go fast enough to make it real. Anyway, that's what I was doing. I'd go up to the top of Morningwood Heights and peel out right in front of the Schmidt house and haul ass down the hill.

"One night, I came down off the hill, and I almost lost it coming around Dead Man's. I had a huge adrenaline dump and didn't want to come home. There was a shop on the east side I was thinking about renting, and I wanted to take another look at. I'm not exactly sure why." Bolly still didn't know why he'd gone back to that shop. He knew from the first time he saw it that it was too small. Maybe subconsciously, he was just looking for a reason to head over to the east side.

"The shop is on Slocum. So is Mike's Place. It's the only place that's open at night up through there. I went up to the shop, took another look at it, and when I was coming back down Slocum, I pulled into the parking lot. Just to get a beer. I was still pretty jacked from the zoo run and the near miss on the curve."

"'Just to get a beer,' huh?" said Janie.

"Yeah, really," said Bolly. "And that's what I did. Paid eight-fifty for a draft,

CHAPTER 22

then split."

"And that's *all* you did?"

"No, I talked with one of the, um, girls."

"Just talked?"

"Yeah, just talked. She was a pretty, um, persuasive salesperson."

"I bet," said Janie. "I'm sure it's a hard sell talking horny, drunk guys into sex. No pun intended."

Bolly snorted. At least Janie still had a sense of humor. Maybe his marriage wasn't totally on the rocks. He considered just cutting off his story right there, claim he'd picked up the matchbook on his way out and he never went back. Tempting, but self-defeating. He had to pull the band-aid all the way off.

"I paid for my beer and left," he said, then took a deep breath. "That time."

Janie sobbed again. "So, you went back. And I bet you had more than a beer that time, too."

"Yeah, I had a burger," said Bolly with a lame laugh. "Okay, not funny, I know. I did have a burger, though."

"And then?" Janie was sniffling a little harder now, and tears were running from her eyes. Bolly grabbed a box of tissues from the bedside table and handed them to his wife.

He sighed again. "And then I went upstairs with the girl I'd talked to the first time"

Janie broke into loud sobs. A nurse stuck her head in the door, saw Janie crying and withdrew.

Finally, Janie's' sobs tapered off. "Did you fuh-fuh-fuck her?" she asked.

"No."

"What did you do then?"

Bolly turned his head away. "I got a blowjob."

Janie was silent for a long time. "That was it? Nothing else?"

"No, just a BJ."

"Did you kiss her?"

"No."

"Hug her?"

"No. Look, I took off my pants, laid down on a bed, and she sucked me off. Wham, bam, *etcetera*."

"And you grabbed matchbook as a souvenir on your way out?"

"No," said Bolly, cursing the matchbook for causing all this trouble. "I went to the bathroom, cranked a nasty fart and lit a match to cover the smell. I don't even remember putting the matches in my pocket."

"It's nice that you were so concerned about covering up your farts in a whorehouse," said Janie. "Too bad you can't be bothered to show the same courtesy at *our* house."

Bolly thought there might be a tiny bit of humor in that last statement. He looked over at Janie. She was staring at him steadily, but she had stopped crying. "Is there anything else?"

"No, that's it, babe—I swear," said Bolly. "I was a total dumbass and I'm sorry. I'll do whatever you want to make it up to you. Can you ever forgive me?"

Janie frowned. "If I told you I'd given someone a blowjob, would you be able to forgive me?"

Bolly risked a small joke of his own. "Depends on whether you kissed him."

Janie cracked a small smile. "Don't push your luck, buster."

"OK, sorry. Yes, of course I'd forgive you. I love you, babe. Please, I'm so sorry. I'll make it up to you, just let me know how."

"Maybe now *I* get to blow someone, eh? How's that for making it up?"

Bolly wasn't sure if she was joking or not. He had a hard time imagining her going down on some other guy, but if that's what it took to square things with her, he'd accept it. "If that's what it takes, then okay. I just don't want to know any of the details."

She snatched a tissue, gave her nose a good honk and tossed it in the trash. "I'm not going to blow anybody, Bolly. But we're definitely going to have to get some couples counseling."

"I'm perfectly okay with that," said Bolly. He didn't like the idea of spilling his guts to some marriage counselor. It would probably be a woman, and she would probably take Janie's side. Then again, Bolly probably deserved it. He had a lot to own up to. "Yeah, totally okay with that," he repeated. "Maybe we should have done something like that earlier. Like, right after we found out we weren't going to be able to have kids."

"That hit me hard," said Janie. "I'd always wanted to have a big family, just like mine."

"I know." Janie had two brothers and two sisters. Bolly had wanted one or two kids at the most. The thought of five rugrats tearing around the house was enough to make him go pale.

"I knew it was going to be hit or miss," said Janie. "My mom cranked out the babies no problem. I have four aunts and three of them tried really hard to have kids, but no dice. I guess I got the no-baby gene." She sniffed again and helped herself to another tissue.

"It's not all your fault, babe," said Bolly. "I was firing blanks, too, remember? Guess I still am."

"Yeah, I remember. I remember it made me mad at you, too. I know that sounds stupid, but that's the way I felt. I guess that's also part of the reason I became less interested in, y'know, the bedroom."

This was a lot to process. They were going to have to work it all out, but at least it didn't seem like Janie was going to walk out on him. He closed his eyes and took a deep breath. The last day had been insane and there was a lot on his plate: he was short on cash, his car was smashed, his wife had caught him cheating on her, and somebody had tried to kill him.

Abruptly, Janie burst into loud sobs again. *Uh-oh,* thought Bolly. "What's the matter, babe?"

"It's muh-muh-my fault. I knew that I wasn't, y'know, holding up my end of the bargain in the marriage bed. I *knew* it. I just figured all of the porn in that old toolbox would be enough to, y'know, make up for it."

"You know about the toolbox porn stash?"

"I hope you take better care of the toolboxes at the shop than the ones at home. I can think of at least two times I came into the garage and found that toolbox with the lid up, and *Big Bouncy Asses: Volume 8* sitting right there for the world to see."

"Ah, jeez," said Bolly, feeling like a pretty big ass himself.

"It's okay, babe," said Janie, smiling for real now. "I think we both fucked up on this one. Just remember that you fucked up *more*. A lot more."

"Oh, yeah, I did."

"And I did too," she said, sniffling again. "I should have known better." She reached out and stroked Bolly's arm. "How are you feeling, babe? Is the pain bad?"

"No, not too bad." His arm radiated ugly jolts of pain up his shoulder. "I think I'm supposed to get another shot soon."

"Good," she said, and slid her chair closer to the bed. "Does it hurt when I do this?" She slid her hand under the sheet and began massaging his cock.

"Uh, no," said Bolly, his penis instantly erect. "Doesn't hurt at all."

"Good, good," she said.

"Um, what are you doing?" asked Bolly. "Is the door closed?"

"Yes, the door is closed. As to what I am doing, I should think that would be perfectly obvious." She began stroking faster. "I am taking care of my man. If I had done a little more a little sooner, we wouldn't have had this problem."

"Oh," said Bolly. "Okay ."

"All right, all right," said Janie, mostly to herself. Her right hand was stroking Bolly's penis; he could see her left hand busily at work underneath her skirt. "Yeah, that's good, isn't it, babe?"

"Quite good, yes," said Bolly. He had never really seen Janie behave like this, at least not since they were first dating. He'd forgotten how delightfully dirty she could be. He kept shifting his eyes towards the closed door. What would happen if a nurse happened to come in? Well, what's the worst that could happen? They'd both be embarrassed for a bit. It's not like they were going to kick Bolly out of the hospital—although they might ask Janie to leave.

"Ohhh, yeah, yeah," said Janie. "You feeling good, babe? I'm feeling good. Ohhh, yeah, *real* good!"

Before Bolly could internalize what was happening, Janie stood up, dropped her panties, flipped up Bolly's bedsheet and climbed up on the bed. In a moment, she lowered herself onto his straining erection.

CHAPTER 22

"Oh, that's what we've been missing," she purred, grinding up and down.

"Holy shit!" said Bolly.

"I'm not hurting you, am I?"

"No, no—not at all." Actually, it was making his arm bark a little, but the sex felt too damn good to say anything about it. If a nurse came in now, she'd sure get an eyeful. He could always claim he was just a helpless invalid, completely at the mercy of this wanton woman.

She increased the pace and soon she was bouncing up and down on Bolly like a piledriver. They both attempted to stifle their groans, with limited success. Bolly couldn't help worrying about someone walking in on them; at the same time, the danger of being discovered was also a turn-on. Before he knew it, he was ready to launch his load.

"Ohhh, *shit!*" cried Bolly, his back arching as he ejaculated.

"Eeeee-*yahhh!*" exclaimed Janie loudly and clapped her hands over her mouth.

There was a scrabbling at the door and Janie hopped off Bolly just as quickly as she had jumped on. Bolly pulled up his sheet just as a nurse walked into the room. Janie was back on the chair, where she demurely arranged her skirt and kicked her panties under the bed.

"Is everything all right?" asked the nurse. "I thought I heard someone cry out."

"Oh, I, uh, bumped my arm," said Bolly.

"You *do* look a little flushed," said the nurse. "Well, I've got some Demerol for you." She uncapped a syringe and injected the contents into Bolly's IV. Is there anything else I can get for you?"

"No, I'm good, thanks," said Bolly. Janie, who was still panting lightly, just shook her head.

"Well, ring the call button if you need anything," said the nurse, who then left—but not without casting a final glance over her shoulder.

"Do you think she knew?" asked Janie with a giggle.

"Probably, but what the hell? She didn't say anything—but maybe she put a note in my chart. Jesus that was good." Bolly exhaled. He could feel the pain meds coursing through him, spreading a muzzy warmth throughout his body. "So, babe, I've got to ask—are we all made up now?"

"Not quite," said Janie. "There's two more things. First is that we get counseling to make sure we work through everything, okay?"

"Okay, I'm good with that. What's the second?"

"I still reserve the right to give somebody else a blowjob."

Chapter 23

In Room 323 of Kerian Memorial Hospital, an interrogation was taking place. "Just tell me what you remember," Martin Prieboy said. "You are not in any trouble. There are no wrong answers. Just be truthful."

"Yeah, okay," said Bolly. He was still too buzzed from the Demerol and the sex to care. "I went out for a drive and ended up at the top of Morningwood Promenade. I turned the car around and was just starting to come back down the hill when this guy pops up from behind a bush and fuck... freakin' shoots me! Naturally, I floored it to get away. I guess I coulda slowed down after I was, y'know, out of range but I was pretty wigged out. I lost it coming around Dead Man's Curve, and, well, you saw what happened then."

"Indeed," said Martin. "You were lucky to escape with only minor injuries from the crash. The bullet wound is bad enough. How are you feeling?"

"I don't feel that lucky, although I guess I should. The bullet didn't do much damage, thank God—but it still hurts like a bitch, 'scuse my language. The pain meds help a bit, but only so much."

"I'm sorry about that. I wish you a speedy recovery." Martin checked his notebook. "You said a 'guy' popped up from the bushes—did you get a good look at him?"

"No, it was pretty dark, and the car was moving."

"The location of the shooter—where was it, exactly?"

"That I remember," said Bolly. "That house at the top of the hill..."

"The Schmidt residence?"

"Yeah, right. So there's this big fence that runs along the front of the property, right? And there's a row of bushes in front of the fence on either side of the main gate, right? Well, whoever shot me popped up from the last bush at the corner of the fence. On the downhill side."

"And you're sure of that?" asked Martin. "Is there any possibility it happened in front of another house?"

"No," said Bolly decisively. "It was the last bush at the corner of the Schmidt property, no doubt."

"Okay, that's good to know. Now, I've got a few more questions for you, if you don't mind. Are you still feeling okay? You're not too tired?"

"No, I'm doin' good," said Bolly. "Ask away."

"I'm just very curious about why you were up at the top of Morningwood Promenade in the first place. It seems an odd place to wind up if you were …" Martin consulted his notebook. "… just 'driving around to clear your head.'"

"Okay, do you know what a zoo run is?"

"Yes, although I haven't heard the term in a long time," said Martin. "It's when someone—usually a teenager—goes to the top of Morningwood Promenade, then drives back down into the city at a dangerous speed. Are you saying that's what you were doing up there?"

"Yeah," sighed Bolly. "I've been under a lot of pressure lately—problems with my business and some, uh, problems at home, too. It just seemed like a good way to blow off some steam. And it worked, too—at least at first."

"Uh huh," said Martin. "So this was not the first time you've gone to the top of the Promenade and made a 'zoo run'?"

"Yeah, okay, I've done it three or four times in the last couple of weeks. I started when they jacked the rent up on my shop."

Martin flipped back through his notebook. "And you are the proprietor of Bollinger Automotive?"

"Yeah."

"And your financial problems began when your landlord announced a rent increase on your place of business."

"Yeah," said Bolly. "And before you ask, it's the damn Schmidts who own the property. You'd figure that out on your own soon enough, so I'll just get it out up front."

CHAPTER 23

"I appreciate that," said Martin. He jotted a few lines in the notebook. "I noticed some patches of rubber on the road in front of the Schmidt residence. Did you do that as well?"

"Yeah. Hey, if you're gonna do a proper zoo run, you need to get off to a fast start, okay?"

"Of course, and if you're going to 'blow off some steam,' why not do it with a loud, obnoxious burnout right in front of the house of the people who are causing you stress?"

Bolly sank into the hospital bed. "Yeah, that's pretty much it, man."

Martin jotted in his notebook, then said, "I have one last question, then I will leave you to your recuperation. There was a noticeable smell of chlorine in the air when I went up there last night. Do you know anything about that?"

Bolly sank farther into the bed. "Yeah, I do. Look, you gotta understand that they'd just jacked up the rent on me *again*. That's twice in like a month! I was pissed."

"What does that have to do with chlorine?"

"Y'know, if you dump bleach on tires before doing a burnout, it makes it really loud and smoky. Didn't you ever do that when you were a teenager?"

"No, I did not," said Martin. "I had a rather unconventional upbringing, in an orphanage in Hershey." Certainly, there had been no opportunities to do smoky burnouts at the Holy Jesus Christ Almighty Home for Unfortunate Boys.

"Well, it does," said Bolly. "Those bastards are driving me out of business! I wanted to give them a good, loud, smoky burnout. That was going to be my last one. I guess it was."

"I most certainly hope so. Mr. Bollinger, did it ever occur to you that such smoke could be toxic? Chlorine gas is poisonous." He thought of Pierre Nasté's complaint about chemical warfare.

Bolly closed his eyes and shook his head. "No, I never even thought of that. I guess it was pretty stupid. Am I in trouble now?"

Martin shook his head. "No, this isn't about what you did, Mr. Bollinger. Of course, you did engage in a number of citable offenses, but nothing worth bothering with."

"Thanks, man."

Martin paused. "I'm sorry to Columbo you, Mr. Bollinger," he said. "But I *do* have one more question. You seem familiar to me. Have we ever met before?"

Bolly chuckled. "Yeah, sort of. I was there in Mill Park the night of the fire. I watched you come hopping out of that burning mill in your Batman costume."

Martin felt himself flushing. That was an event he felt was best left forgotten. After being unfairly suspended from the constabulary, he had continued his crime-fighting efforts as a masked superhero called the Fliedermaus. He wondered what he had been thinking. Running around town dressed as a superhero and trying to take the law into his own hands. He shook his head, amazed at the clarity of hindsight. He'd been a fool to act like that, but then again, he still clearly remembered the burning desire for justice that had driven him to those extremes. How different things seemed now.

"Well, that was quite a strange time for me," said Martin. "It must have been for you as well, if you were one of those 'meddling kids' who got caught up in that."

"It wasn't me so much, but my wife and a buddy called Paul Plummer were into it. They're the ones who found those bones in the Wizard's Woods."

"Oh, yes," said Martin. "I remember now. Those were strange times, Mr. Bollinger."

"In Fester, they never seem to end," said Bolly. "Do they?"

"It sure seems that way. Thank you for your time. I imagine we'll be speaking again before too long."

Martin looked at his watch. He needed to get back to headquarters soon. Pierre Nasté would soon be there with his clients to provide what Martin expected to be utterly meaningless interviews.

He was absolutely correct. Pierre Nasté had shown up with Ophelia, Thelma Louise and Ronald in tow. Martin had spoken with each in private and had

CHAPTER 23

gotten almost identical answers: they had spent a quiet evening at home. No, they hadn't heard a car squealing its tires. No, they hadn't heard a gunshot. They claimed minimal knowledge of the injured driver, other than he was one of their many commercial tenants in town. He paid his rent on time, other than that, they knew nothing.

"I hope you're satisfied," said Nasté. "I will not have my clients treated as common suspects!"

"I'm just doing my job," said Martin "Trying to be thorough."

"As a citizen of Fester, I appreciate your dedication," said Nasté. "Nevertheless, as an attorney, I cannot permit your zeal to impugn the sterling reputation of my clients."

"Of course not," said Martin. "And it's quite unfortunate that the security system malfunctioned last night. Nothing at all got recorded?"

"Not a single thing," said Nasté, shaking his head sadly. "The DVR that records the video feed had apparently been out for three days. It's a shame nobody noticed."

"Shameful indeed. That video would be invaluable for learning what happened last night."

"Undoubtedly, it would show that my clients had absolutely nothing to do with this unfortunate incident. I am very sorry we can't show you the video."

"Don't be too despondent, Pierre," said Martin. "As I'm sure you know, all security systems must be registered and licensed by the Fester Constabulary. We got in touch with the Electro Security Agency, who handles the Schmidt security systems. Fortunately, they keep backup copies of all of their clients' security feeds to their servers. I've already gotten a subpoena for the video from the Schmidt residence from last night. We expect to have a copy shortly."

"Oh, ah, well," stammered Nasté. "How very fortunate. I would never have thought of that. Oh yes, very good, Chief Constable." Nasté seemed rattled, but only for a moment. "Well, I must be off now to accompany my clients back to their home." He bowed slightly and departed in a hurry.

Martin sat back in his chair and exhaled slowly. The deal with the backup video had been Blount's discovery and it had probably salvaged the case. Now it was just a matter of waiting for the data from Electro. Of course, it would take some time—Electro would certainly fight the subpoena. They would have to. Nobody would want to hire a security company that rolled over and gave information to the cops at the drop of a hat. Electro would make a lot of bad noise, but in the end, they would get the video from the Schmidt residence.

Martin was very interested in what it would tell him.

Chapter 24

Harold Todd was distraught.

He had spent the rest of the Saturday of the fair managing damage control. He spoke with the constables as little as possible, saying he'd seen Christopher Young jump off the top of the hand statue. He also pointed out the statue had a chain and warning signs all around it, and that the child had been left unsupervised. This seemed to mollify the cops, who didn't see any reason to continue their involvement.

A lot of the crowd had drifted off after the incident, further adding to Harold's despondency. He'd put his heart and soul into the fair, and it had been a spectacular bust. The crew from WEVL-TV had hung around interviewing eyewitnesses, but the looming threat of rain—and the strange blue lightning—had convinced most of the crowd to go home.

Harold wished he could do the same. Nothing doing—he had to clean up the larger portions of the mess before he could leave. The first thing he did was put in a call to Flint and Yates, Attorneys at Law. Darryl Flint at least eased Harold's mind in one respect: there was no way the Youngs had a valid case if their unattended child had crossed a barrier with warning signs. That made Harold feel a little bit better.

After he got off the phone with the lawyer, he'd gone back outside to check on the situation. It was dismal. The clouds were lower and darker, and the crowd was even more sparse. As he'd come out the main entrance, the rent-a-cops were in the process of pulling a college student off of the hand statue. Apparently, that had been the third person after Christopher Young to try to climb it.

Harold had hustled back inside and managed to contact a contractor he knew. After some wrangling (and the promise to pay double rate for weekend work), Harold had arranged for an eight-foot chain-link fence to be erected around the hand statue. Just to be safe, he'd arranged for the fence to be topped with strands of razor wire. No point in encouraging behavior that might result in a frivolous lawsuit. Frivolous lawsuits still cost money to defend, and after this weekend, the mall's financial cushion had been worn thin.

At six o'clock, he'd supervised the loadout of the last vestiges of the fair. The balky mini-carousel had been the last thing to go. As soon as it had been loaded onto the flatbed and driven away, Harold locked up his office and made a beeline for his car.

He'd spent the rest of the holiday weekend hiding in his condo. He had already made arrangements for his assistant to deal with running the mall. His assistant called him at ten a.m. on Sunday to tell him that the fencing had gone up. Then she'd called back at eleven to say someone had attempted to scale the fence, had cut their hand on the razor wire, and was threatening to sue. Harold told his assistant that anyone else who wanted to sue should take a number. He'd also told her not to call him again unless someone died or the mall was on fire.

He'd spent the rest of Sunday licking his wounds, lying in bed, vainly trying to get back to sleep. Around noon, he'd given up and ordered pizza. The rest of the day was spent eating pizza, drinking Scotch, and watching old James Bond movies on Netflix. He went to bed early with a stomachache.

Monday morning came around as it unfortunately does, and Harold reluctantly got up and got ready for work. It was time to face the mess that had come from the Fourth of July Fair. His head and his stomach were both complaining about his Scotch-and-pizza diet. Dumping a load of black coffee on top of that had not helped much, but Harold didn't care—he needed the caffeine boost.

He drove to the mall lost in dark thoughts. He parked as usual, not really noticing the cars in the parking lot. There were actually quite a few of them for a Monday morning. He stopped to check out the fencing around the

CHAPTER 24

hand statue. It was imposing; looked like something that would surround a prison. Sure enough, there were some smears of blood around the razor wire at the top.

He went into his office through the service entrance, not wanting to deal with the shoppers or any of the store owners who would doubtless be disappointed by the poor turnout and overall weirdness of the fair.

"Good morning, Mr. Todd," said his secretary, Stella. She was always at work early and always cheerful. Excessive cheerfulness was the last thing Harold wanted to deal with this morning.

"It's morning, I'll give you that," groused Harold. "Not sure there's anything good about it."

"Of course it's a good morning!" chirped Stella. "The sun's out, the birds are singing..."

"And the mall is doomed!" finished Harold.

"Doomed? What on earth are you talking about?"

"The fair. It was an unmitigated disaster! I don't know how we're ever going to come back from that mess."

Stella looked confused. "I don't know how you can say that," she said, optimism going full tilt. "I brought the kids, and they had a blast. Jenny got flowers painted on her face, and her and Jason rode on that cute little carousel three times! It's a shame they packed up the pony ride early."

"The kids didn't miss much there," muttered Harold.

"Well, I'd say it was a great success."

"Did you not see that child fall off the hand statue? And all the weird stuff people are saying about it?" He'd spent the weekend carefully avoiding the news. He knew there was a hue and cry about the Young boy supposedly flying, and there was even more talk about people seeing a ghost. When he'd heard this, he'd tuned into the local news, which was running regular loops of the kid and the supposed ghost. This last one gave him a start—it looked very similar to the man he'd seen by the hand statue the month before. He hadn't paid much attention to the details. He had a business to save; the supernatural could wait.

"Mr. Todd, what happened on Saturday was a flat-out miracle. We've been blessed!"

Harold stared at Stella in disbelief. Her pervasive upbeat nature could be trying at times, but this mindless sunniness was verging on lunacy. He worked his mouth a few times, trying to formulate an appropriate response. None sprang to mind.

"Before you say anything, go take a walk around the mall," said Stella. "You'll see. Just go, Mr. Grumpyface."

Harold removed his coat and quickly walked to the door that led to the mall interior. He wasn't so much interested in following Stella's advice as he was in getting away from her infuriating optimism before he said something he'd regret later. His stomach hurt, his temper was short, and he knew he was about two heartbeats away from saying something mean to her. He'd done it before and she'd bawled like a scalded toddler. He'd promised himself that he'd never let it happen again.

He pushed his way into the main part of the mall, right in front of the entrance to the Bon Ton. There seemed to be a lot of people for a Monday morning. He looked into the Bon Ton. There was a healthy line by the perfume counter cash register, and he could see a lot of other people browsing elsewhere in the department store.

He turned to head towards the other end of the mall. He noticed there were a lot of people with selfie sticks. The were recording themselves and gesturing around at the mall. Nearby was a twenty-something man with long hair and a beard. He wore a T-shirt that showed a sasquatch smoking a pipe and was jabbering animatedly into the iPhone at the end of his stick. Harold sidled up to listen to what he was saying.

"... proof positive of supernatural intervention!" the man enthused. "We have at last evidence—*hard* evidence—of otherworldly influence on the material plane! Dozens of eyewitnesses and multiple video recordings, attest to the undisputed *fact* that young Christopher Young ..." He stopped. "Oh, shit, that sounds dumb. Have to cut that part. Try again. Dozens of eyewitnesses and multiple video recordings, attest to the undisputed *fact* that young Christopher actually levitated, hanging motionless in midair for several seconds. And what of the apparition some are calling the 'ghost

CHAPTER 24

punk?' Some think..."

Harold moved away, shaking his head in disbelief. If it had been just one person, it would be easy to dismiss, but there were at least a half dozen ghost hunters and supernatural believers visible from where he was standing. He began walking slowly towards the Sears at the other end of the mall. The stores all seemed to be doing an uncharacteristically brisk business for a Monday. The food court was jammed with vloggers picking up a snack or a drink to quench throats tired by talking.

Not all of the videographers were on board with the idea of supernatural intervention. Past the food court was a semi-professional looking crew: a girl with a shoulder-mounted camera, a guy with a boom mic and an older, professorial-looking gentleman who was holding forth. They all wore black T-shirts with a jagged logo that read *Skepticizer!* The professor wore a sport jacket with leather elbow patches over his T-shirt.

"... just so much nonsense," the professor said. "The National Weather Service had reported a number of high-pressure anomalies in the Fester area that day. These really could be called micro-super-cells, and while they are not common, they are not unheard of, especially in the Allegheny region this time of year. It's clear that a sudden, strong updraft from one of these micro-super-cells is responsible for the boy's so-called levitation, and not any of these ridiculous notions of spirits and ghosts."

Harold walked on in disbelief. He'd thought the incident at the fair would have given the mall a bad reputation. People in Fester were very superstitious, and given what Pap had told him of the area's history, he figured they would avoid the mall like a plague pit after what had happened at the fair. It appeared that, happily, he was wrong.

He quickstepped back to his office, where Stella beamed at him. "Not so bad, is it, Mr. Todd?" she said. "And you have some messages you ought to check, too."

In a daze, Harold floated back to his office and began checking his voicemail.

"Hello, this is Diana DiVolo, regional vice-president of Skank Brands. We've rethought our position on our distribution of Fashion Bitch locations in south-central Pennsylvania, and we've decided to re-up our lease at Hickory Acres Mall. Please call me ASAP to discuss the details."

Harold was flabbergasted. The next several messages were all from media outlets requesting interviews and information. It would take a lot of his time to address it all, but it was more than worth the free publicity that would be generated. He got up and went back into the reception area of the office where Stella sat.

"See, Mr. Todd—I knew things would work out."

"You were right, Stella, and I'm awful glad of it. It looks like our little fair did the job."

"I told you it was a miracle," said Stella with a beatific grin.

"You were absolutely right," said Harold. "And to show my appreciation for your optimism, I am going to buy you lunch today. And *not* at the food court."

Chapter 25

The call came in as Billy sat down to watch *America's Most Wanted*. He had just come in from his evening run and had cracked a can of Coors when the phone on the wall rang. Slightly annoyed, he snatched it up. "Snyder," he said.

The voice on the other end was hoarse and muffled. "It's J," the voice said. "I've got some information you might be interested in."

Billy knew that "J" was Joseph Schultz, one of his contacts at the constabulary. Schultz had retired three years ago but still had interaction with a lot of current constables. He and Billy went way back. Billy still sparked loyalty from the old-school constables who had served under him when he was chief. It was always a good idea to have an intelligence network, and he was able to maintain his by buying a few beers here or slipping someone a twenty there.

"What do you have, Joe?" asked Billy.

"Don't use my name!" hissed Joe. "This line might be bugged!"

"Just get rid of the handkerchief and talk in your normal voice, okay? I can hardly hear you with your snot-rag over the mouthpiece and you growling like that."

"But the line..."

"Are you calling from a pay phone?"

"Yeah, I am. Do you know how hard it is to find a pay phone anymore? I'm using one at a Grab 'n' Gulp in Rivertown."

"Don't worry, then. *This* line isn't bugged. I've got a box of high-tech gear on it. If it was bugged, I'd know about it. So lose the hanky and talk normally." He wondered at the attention Joe was attracting by talking on a public pay phone with a handkerchief over the mouthpiece.

"Okay, fine," said Joe. "Here's the skinny: there was a shooting up at the Schmidt place last night. They haven't charged anybody yet, but the chief's pretty sure it was Ronald Schmidt. I think it's just a matter of time before they bring him in. I hear Schmidt's been acting pretty wild lately. Apparently, he attacked a neighbor with a rake not long ago. The Schmidts paid the guy off so he wouldn't press charges, and he up and moved out of town. Can't say I blame him. If I lived next to a looney-tune like Ronald Schmidt, I'd be looking to move, too."

Billy let Joe's blather wash over him; he was too busy processing the real news he had imparted: that Ronald Schmidt was suspected of having shot someone. "Okay, thanks," said Billy when Joe's diatribe wound down. "I owe you for this."

"Yes, you sure do. I might need your help with something soon. We'll talk later."

"Okay, great. I appreciate the call. You'll let me know what happens next, right?"

"Will do, Billy. Talk to you soon."

Billy hung up the phone and yelled "SHIT!" at the top of his voice. He *knew* that selling Ronald a functioning firearm had been a dangerous move. Of course, Ronald might have shot the person with another gun, but Billy wasn't willing to make that assumption. *Expect the worst and hope for the best,* he thought.

The special project was of paramount importance now. If the law started snooping around Billy's place, he could be in serious trouble. Billy had undertaken the special project to mend fences with his own past—specifically, his service in Vietnam. But there was also an undertone to the special project, a word fully internalized but never really spoken out loud. That word was *revenge.* Billy had never processed these thoughts, but they were always there, lurking just below the surface of his consciousness.

But now, Billy had work to do—a lot of it. First was to move the really troublesome items out of his workshop and hide them. After that, he could

CHAPTER 25

more leisurely take care of aboveboard stuff—and perhaps relax a little. It was best not to take chances.

He hurried out to the workshop and took inventory. He'd have to get the recoilless rifles taken care of immediately. And the ammo. Those were the things that would really get him in trouble. He knew he was on the sheriff's radar. He longed for the good old days, when the sheriff of Kerian County could be bought off simply by intentionally losing a few hands of five-card stud at his hunting cabin in Kugels. Well, those days were long gone. Time to deal with the reality of the here and now.

First, he would have to get a few supplies—basic hardware stuff. He didn't want to pick them up in Fester—that would be like strolling into the belly of the beast. Weaverville offered anonymity and plenty of shopping choices, but it was too far away. He wanted to have those rifles stashed by early afternoon at the latest. He wouldn't even be able to make the round trip to Weaverville and back by then. The best bet was Mellonville. It was close, and it had a small True Value. Nothing fancy, but it would have almost all of the stuff he'd need. Also, the owner was an old-school Pennsylvania German, suspicious of government authority in general and cops in particular. Billy hopped in his car, a huge old Ford Crown Victoria, and took off for Mellonville at top speed.

He was back less than an hour later with what he thought of as body disposal tools: pick, shovel, plastic sheeting, tarps, rope, duct tape, and a few other odds and ends. He stopped at the end of the driveway and locked the gate.

Billy knew the Schmidts would have Pierre Nasté and his team of legal vultures running interference for them. In fact, there was a good chance that Nasté could stonewall the entire investigation. That would be great, but it was not a given. Billy had to proceed under the assumption the law would sooner or later show up at his place and start asking questions. Probably sooner. A locked gate wouldn't slow them down for long, especially if they showed up with a warrant.

Time was wasting. He hurried back up to the workshop.

He transferred the purchases from the Crown Vic to the Land Rover and loaded on the recoilless rifles and a few other items. Soon, the heavily laden Land Rover was charging up the hill.

Four hours later he was done and could breathe a sigh of relief. All of the really illegal shit had been wrapped in plastic, taped up, swaddled in tarps, and buried in a trench not far from where he'd test-fired the recoilless rifle. Along with the M40 rifles, there were the boxes of ammo and a couple of not-quite-legal assault rifles Billy had bought at a discount, no questions asked.

Billy stretched and tried to loosen up his back. He'd had to dig a pretty big trench to hold all of the contraband, and hefting the rifles and boxes of ammo hadn't exactly been a picnic. He looked at his watch. It would be getting dark soon. He got back into the Land Rover—now considerably lighter—and was soon rocketing back down the hill. He allowed himself a slight smile, knowing that his immediate concerns were addressed. He also just loved the roller-coaster thrill of the ride.

He parked the Land Rover in a clump of trees to the side of the house. Then he moved the Crown Vic behind the workshop. With the vehicles concealed, he made a brief stop in the house to take a leak, check his answering machine for messages (none), and grab a beer. He considered heating up a can of something for dinner but dismissed it. He was too amped up and had too much to do. Dinner could wait; the beer would sustain him for now.

He locked up the house and stuffed the beer into his back pocket. There was one more thing to do before he could get to work. Sticking to the tree line to stay out of sight, Billy crept down to the gate at the end of the driveway. He half-expected to see a sheriff's patrol car parked there, but it was vacant. He crept through the bushes until he could see the road in both directions, then waited for ten minutes. There was nothing. Satisfied he wasn't being observed, he checked the mailbox (empty) and went back to the workshop.

With the contraband out of the way, the special project was perfectly legal. Billy was just an aficionado of military hardware and history, undertaking a simple restoration job. No different than rebuilding a '57 Chevy, really.

CHAPTER 25

Billy was good with his hands, good with gadgets. He'd started as a child by disassembling and reassembling the telephone. His pop had caught him at it once and had whaled the tar out him, but that didn't stop him. He'd bought a busted radio at a flea market for a dime, fixed it up and sold it the following week for a dollar. As he grew older, he graduated to grander gizmos: cars and motorcycles. When he was sixteen, he used the money he'd accumulated to buy a broken-down '41 Dodge pickup. It took him a year to restore, but eventually he got it purring. He still thought about that truck sometimes; it would probably be worth a bundle now.

Billy never really cared about the money; he'd just liked working on things, fixing them up, getting them working again. He loved the feeling of mastery it gave him. No broken widget was going to outsmart Billy Snyder.

When he'd volunteered for the Marines, he'd scored through the roof on his aptitude tests for mechanical and electrical skills. The Marines had been more than happy to have him and had pushed hard to assign him to aircraft maintenance. While the idea of tinkering with something as awesome as a warplane had a definite appeal, Billy had balked. He hadn't joined the Marines to fix stuff; he could have stayed home and done that. He wanted some action.

A suitable compromise was reached and Billy had become a driver on an M50 crew—and the driver typically acted as a field mechanic. As such, he'd be able to aid the Corps with his top-flight mechanical skills and still get to ride out into battle. Billy had gotten what he'd wanted. He just never realized what the cost would be.

Now here he was, elbows-deep in the same type of equipment he'd worked on, ridden in, and bled over in Vietnam. He wanted to get this puppy running and get it stashed in the woods quickly. Fortunately, all the pieces were there, and many of them were already bolted tight. Right now, he just had to get the engine to play nice with the transmission. Easy peasy.

Billy cracked his beer, opened the toolbox, and got to work.

Chapter 26

Dan Blount poked his head in Martin's office and said, "I got good news and bad news, Chief. Which do you want first?"

"Might as well give me the bad news," sighed Martin.

"Electro's really digging their heels in about the subpoena. Their lawyers filed about half a dozen motions yesterday against it."

"For goodness' sake! Every day that we have to wait, the case gets more stale. How long do the legal people think it will take to resolve?"

"Two, three weeks," said Blount. He shrugged. "Fiddle-dee-dee."

"*Fiddle-dee-dee*? You seem pretty nonchalant about this, Chief Inspector. I'm concerned you're not treating the situation with the proper respect."

"Perhaps not," said Blount. "But maybe you can respect *this*." He reached into his pocket and pulled out a thumb drive.

"What's that?" asked Martin.

"That's the good news," said Blount. "I wrangled a copy of the video, anyway. Don't ask how, and I know it's not admissible as evidence, but it can at least tell us if we're on the right track."

"Well, that is a surprise I can respect!" said Martin. "Take a look at it and let me know what we've got."

"Very good, Chief," said Blount, and went off to study the video.

It took Blount about two hours to piece together the segments they needed. "I think we've got him," he told Martin. "I really think we have the bastard this time!"

"Very good," said Martin. "Show me."

CHAPTER 26

"Here we go," said Blount. "This will be a little choppy as I switch feeds. I can edit it down to something smoother later."

"Smoother can wait," said Martin. "Right now, I just need evidence."

"Right. First feed is from the front porch." Blount clicked a window showing a top-down view of a wide porch, a foreshortened view of the front yard, the gate and the street beyond it. In the lower right corner of the image was the date, time, and a number associated with the camera that was being viewed.

"And at 20:02, the star of our show appears," said Blount. The door beneath the camera opened and out stepped a man wearing a red windbreaker. He looked to his left, giving a three-quarters profile. It was very clearly Ronald Schmidt. He spent a few moments scanning the street, then descended the front stairs and went around the left side of the house.

"Just a mo'," said Blount. "Switching to the camera on the south side." He made a few clicks, and the image switched to a view of the side of the house. Beyond the house were an expanse of open lawn, a few trees, and the shadows of some buildings beyond them. The side of the house was well-lit, but it was almost sunset, and the rest of the yard drew long with summer shadows. The time stamp read 20:04 when Ronald came around the side. He was nearly facing the camera in this shot—his identity was very clear. He walked past the camera, across the yard and disappeared through the trees.

"Do we know what's back there?" asked Blount.

"I've checked images from Google Earth," said Martin. "They appear to be some outbuildings. There's also a good-sized house in the far corner of the property. It's the other direction from where he went, though."

"I'll just speed things up again," said Blount. The image jittered and jounced, then Ronald could be seen walking back from the way he came. He walked past the camera and disappeared.

"Does it look like he's carrying something?" asked Blount. "Like he might have picked something up from one of those sheds?"

"If he did, it was something pretty small. Looks pretty much the same to me."

"Back to the front porch," said Blount as he switched the feed again. "Unfortunately, this is the best shot of the front yard. The camera angle makes everything look squished down the farther away it is." Ronald walked into the frame and down to the end of the driveway where the massive iron gates stood open. He stepped through the gate, then closed it. He looked up and down the street.

"Now we go to the gate camera," said Blount. "Here's where it gets a little dicey. There's a pretty big gap in coverage, since the camera is pointed down the hill. We can't really see anything uphill of the gate except on the front door camera, and that's partially obscured by the fence. Shouldn't be too much of a problem, though. The real action is on the downhill side." He clicked another window to show Ronald walking down the road in front of the house. A row of waist-high shrubs stood between the road and the fence. Ronald reached the end of the fence, took a step to his left, and disappeared behind a shrub. The time stamp read 20:16 .

"That's all we'll see for a while," said Blount. "Let me fast forward." He let the feed from the gate camera run forward, stopping at 20:44. A pair of headlights appeared in the distance. Blount resumed playback at normal speed, and the image of a dark Chevy Nova approached then passed the camera. Blount switched back to the porch camera, which showed the Nova pass the front gate, then turn around at the cul-de-sac at the end of the property. The car stopped, then the driver got out. It was clearly Michael Bollinger, and he was holding a white plastic jug. He walked around to the back of the car and began dumping the contents of the bottle on the road.

"I still can't figure out what he'd doing here," said Blount. "Maybe he's dumping out some beer he doesn't want to be caught with."

"No, it's bleach," said Martin. "He told me about it earlier. He wanted to do a burnout to annoy the Schmidts. The bleach makes it smoke more."

On screen, the driver got back into the Nova, then backed it up a few feet. There was a pause, then the rear wheels of the Nova began spinning wildly. A huge plume of smoke shot from the tires and wafted back from the car.

"It worked as promised," observed Blount. "Now we switch back to the gate camera." He switched back. The time stamp was now 20:46. At first

CHAPTER 26

there was nothing visible but the twin cones of light thrown off by the car's headlights. The beams juddered back and forth like searchlights. The front end of the Nova slowly came into view, still slewing back and forth as the tires tried to find purchase.

"Now it gets interesting," said Blount. The front half of the Nova was now on the screen, and it was moving forward quickly now. From behind the last shrub in front of the fence, a dark figure rose up. It held out both hands in front of its body, and there was a bright flash. The Nova seemed to jerk at the same time, then moved forward faster and faster away from the camera, weaving as it picked up speed. The dark figure behind the bush dropped out of sight, and in moments the Nova was just a pair of diminishing red taillights.

Martin and Blount looked at each other for a moment. "Stop and run it back to the point where the shooter pops up, then pause it." Blount did exactly that. "It's too dark to really get a good look," said Martin. "The shooter is standing just outside the beam of the headlights. See if you can pause it right as the gun is going off."

"The muzzle flash?" asked Blount.

Martin nodded.

It took three tries, but Blount was able to freeze the feed at the exact moment when the gun went off. The shooter's face was illuminated much better than it had been.

"Well, what do you think?" asked Blount. "Is it Ronald?"

"It's hard to tell," said Martin. "The image is too small and blurry. Zoom in and enhance."

Blount shot him a funny look. "This isn't *Blade Runner*, Chief. Best I can do is to grab a screenshot and maybe run it through a couple of Photoshop filters.

"Okay, then do that," said Martin, feeling slightly foolish. He loved high-tech crime tools, but sometimes forgot the ones he really liked didn't yet exist, exactly. He sat back and watched as Blount used Photoshop to open a screenshot of the shooter. He fiddled with contrast, color curves, and sharpening filters . The final result was striking. Half of the shooter's face was clearly visible, as was the shoulder of his red jacket. He was a dead ringer for Ronald Schmidt.

"Looks like Ronald to me," said Blount.

"Yes, me too," agreed Martin. "One final but important question: do we see Ronald or anyone else come back up the road and go through the gate?"

"No. I sat and watched the next twenty minutes of the video, and nothing happens. The next thing we see is the arrival of the first cruiser. I come up a few minutes later."

"What do we have here?' asked Martin, mostly to himself. "We see Ronald Schmidt leave through the front door of the house. He walks to one of the outbuildings on the back of the property, then returns a few minutes later. What he did while off camera is not apparent. He then goes to the road in front of the house and closes the gate. He walks a short distance down the road in front of the house and disappears behind a bush at the end of the property. Half an hour later, Bollinger arrives in his car. He gets lined up to do a burnout, and as he does, a shadowy shooter pops up from behind the same bush where Ronald Schmidt was last seen. An enhancement of the view in the muzzle flash shows that the shooter bears a similarity to Ronald Schmidt. Am I missing anything?"

"That about covers the fuckin' waterfront," said Blount. "Pardon my language. It's a shame we can't arrest him right now, Chief.'"

"Don't worry. We're going to arrest him," said Martin. "We just have to wait for the legal process to take its due course. Besides, what I'd really like to know is what happened to Ronald after the shot was fired. It'd be a cinch if we'd seen him walking back to the gate."

"He must have another way to get back on the property. Either he climbed over, went under or squeezed through. He's lived his whole life in that house. He must know every secret there is about that property."

"I want you to go up there and find out how he got back in," said Martin.

"I wish we could go nail the bastard now," said Blount. "After all the headaches that asshole's caused me…"

"Patience, Dan. Let the system work."

"I hope that weasel doesn't slip away while it's working."

CHAPTER 26

"We'll get him," said Martin. "Now go see if you can figure out where Ronald went immediately after the shooting."

"Will do, boss." Dan Blount nodded and stepped out of the office.

Chapter 27

"I'm impressed, Chief Inspector," said Martin Prieboy. "I'm really very impressed. I thought it would take weeks to get that subpoena through. Somehow, you managed to get it through in five days."

"I had to call in some favors," said Blount. "A *lot* of favors. I even had to make a few promises of my own. One of which I will not be proud of later."

Martin raised an eyebrow. "Such as?"

Blount looked from side to side, as if making sure no one was hiding in Martin's office. "Well, to seal the deal, I had to promise to be in the Weaverville Jaycees annual talent show fundraiser."

"That doesn't sound too bad."

"Uh, yeah, well, I had to agree to do a ballet dance. Me and a bunch of guys from the DA's office. In tutus."

"A ballet dance?" Martin had a hard time imagining his hard-nosed inspector in a tutu.

"Yeah," said Blount. *"Swan Lake.* 'The Dance of the Little Swans.'"

"You'll be sure to tell me when the tickets for this event go on sale."

"Oh, you bet I will."

Martin made a mental note to check the Weaverville Jaycees website—he suspected Blount would "forget" to remind him. "You really took one for the team, Dan. I appreciate it."

"Oh, it wasn't for the team—it was for me. Ronnie the Rake's been a thorn in my side for years. I want to see him perp walk just once."

"Please don't use that nickname for the suspect. I appreciate your frustration, but we can't give Nasté the slightest opening. If he hears 'Ronnie

CHAPTER 27

the Rake,' we'll be hearing about police prejudice and official malfeasance before you know it."

"Gotcha, Chief. Won't happen again."

"Very good."

"Okay, since I've promised to be a good boy, when can we go nail that upstanding citizen, Ronald Schmidt, Esquire?"

"Let me check something," said Martin. "He leaned over his desk and tapped a few keys on the computer. "Yes, good. We just got back the enhanced image from the lab in Wrightsville. They were able to grab a frame from the video and enhance it. Good thing we were able to tell them exactly where to look."

He tapped a few more keys and stared at the screen, "Chief Inspector Blount, this image is of the assailant who shot Michael Bollinger. It appears to me to be one Ronald Schmidt. Who do you think this looks like?" He turned the monitor around.

"I think it looks like probable cause," said Blount.

"Indeed. I will start things moving. Please return to your office and await further instructions. I want to get this taken care of right away."

Blount nodded and left, almost at a run. Martin shut the door to his office and dialed the mayor's personal cell. "Hello, Thad," he said. "A quick courtesy call to let you know that I intend to charge Ronald Schmidt with attempted murder in the shooting on Morningwood Promenade."

"Jesus, you can't be serious!" exclaimed the mayor. "What evidence do you have?"

"We have the video from the security system. It clearly shows Ronald Schmidt exiting the house, hiding in the bushes out front, then rising and shooting Mr. Bollinger as he drove by."

There was a long pause. "I ... see. Well, if you feel you have enough evidence, then it's your call. I just ask that you be discreet. Please."

"I will," said Martin. "I will call Pierre Nasté and have him bring Ronald in for booking. Then it will be off to Weaverville for the arraignment. As it is a weekday, I expect it to happen very quickly—Nasté will see to that, I'm certain."

"What if you can't get in touch with Nasté? Will you go up and arrest Schmidt at home?"

"I won't need to," said Martin. "I'm sure I'll be able to get in touch with Mr. Nasté." He was certain that Nasté had been expecting his call ever since Electro handed over the video.

"Well, okay," said the mayor. "You do what you feel you have to do Chief Constable. I'd appreciate it if you can provide me with an update as things unfold. And remember, do try to keep it discreet."

"I will do my best, Mr. Mayor," said Martin.

As expected, Pierre Nasté picked up Martin's call on the first ring. He didn't seem to be at all surprised that Martin was going to charge his client and agreed to arrive with Ronald Schmidt at the back door of headquarters in exactly one hour. Martin expected Nasté to spend at least forty-five minutes of that hour making calls to Weaverville about the arraignment. Martin spent those forty-five minutes catching up some other work, then went down to receive his guests.

There was an unwelcomed visitor in the bullpen: Walter Herr, veteran reporter for the *Fester Daily Dispatch*. "Mr. Herr," said Martin, when he spotted the reporter mooching around. "To what do we owe the pleasure of your visit today?"

"I'd heard that you caught the Fishtown Flasher," said Herr. "I was just following up a tip." The Fishtown Flasher was a notorious self-exposure artist who had been reported in the Rivertown district of downtown. The *Fester Daily Dispatch* had coined the term "Fishtown Flasher" for alliterative purposes.

"Sorry, Walter," said Martin. "Your tip must have been mistaken. We've made no arrests in that case. I think you're wasting your time."

"Are you sure?" asked Herr. "My sources are usually correct. Oh well, since I'm here, I might as well grab a cup of coffee and make my rounds, see what's new and exciting in the world of Fester law enforcement."

Martin considered how he could get Herr out of the building before Nasté and Ronald Schmidt arrived. He watched Herr wander the bullpen with a cup of toxic constabulary coffee, chatting amicably with constables and

CHAPTER 27

other staff. It was probably impossible to run Herr off without arousing his suspicion now.

Martin waited until Herr was occupied, then slipped out the back door to the parking lot. He checked his watch; Nasté should be arriving any moment now. The lawyer's Mercedes arrived right on the hour. Nasté and Ronald Schmidt stepped out of the rear; one of Nasté's clerks was driving. Martin shook hands with Nasté. He didn't offer his hand to Ronald.

"Gentlemen," Martin said. "Let's go ahead and take care of this."

"This is ridiculous!" shouted Ronald. "I am innocent! I can't believe this travesty of justice!"

Martin ignored him and addressed Nasté. "Please see what you can do to have your client keep his composure," he said. "I am trying my best to maintain discretion, but there are reporters in the building. We will go to my office to handle the details privately."

Nasté pulled Ronald aside and spoke with him. It calmed Ronald down slightly. Unfortunately, it didn't last. As soon as they had stepped through the door and walked across the back of the bullpen, Ronald shouted, "I'm the victim! This is bullshit!"

Every head in the bullpen turned to watch—including Walter Herr's. Immediately he was on his feet, waving his cell phone—which was undoubtedly recording every word.

"Mr. Schmidt! Mr. Schmidt!" Herr called, rushing over to where Martin was leading the two men to the stairwell. "What is 'bullshit,' Mr. Schmidt? Why are you here?"

"I'm being persecuted!" shouted Ronald. "I'm being arrested for a crime I didn't commit!"

Martin shot a dark look at Nasté, who leaned into Ronald and told him to remain silent. It was too late—the office was in an uproar and the town's pit-bull reporter was on to a story that would undoubtedly take up the front page of the next edition. The cat was out of the bag.

Chapter 28

RONALD SCHMIDT ARRESTED FOR ATTEMPTED MURDER
by Walter Herr
Fester Daily Dispatch

Ronald Klaus Schmidt was arrested and charged yesterday with attempted murder in connection with the July 5 shooting of Michael Bollinger outside of Schmidt's home on Morningwood Promenade. Schmidt surrendered at the Fester Constabulary Headquarters, accompanied by his lawyer, Pierre Nasté.

The shooting took place after Bollinger had driven to the top of Morningwood Promenade to "take in a view of the city" according to the constabulary. Constabulary sources state Schmidt ambushed Bollinger, firing through the windshield of Bollinger's car and striking him in the shoulder. Bollinger was able to drive away from the scene of the assault, but lost control of his car which impacted with a tree at the intersection of Highland Avenue and Morningwood Promenade, an area of roadway popularly known as "Dead Man's Curve." Bollinger was transported by ambulance to Kerian Memorial hospital, where his injuries were determined to be non-life-threatening. He sustained a gunshot wound to the upper left arm and suffered minor injuries in the vehicular collision.

No information on the motive for the shooting has been released.

According to reliable sources, Bollinger, the owner of Bollinger Automotive, is the tenant of a commercial property at 505 Jefferson Street in Fester owned by the Schmidt Properties, Inc.

CHAPTER 28

Ronald Klaus Schmidt, 54, is the scion of the Schmidt family, which traces its roots to the founders of Fester. Best known as the former owners of the Schmidt Pretzel Bakery, the family's generations of community and philanthropic efforts are notable.

Although no charges have ever been filed, various sources allege Ronald Schmidt has been involved in a number of altercations at local drinking establishments. According to constabulary records, Schmidt was also allegedly involved in a recent attack on a neighbor with a garden rake.

Shortly after his arrest, Ronald Schmidt was transported to the Kerian County Courthouse in Weaverville where he was arraigned and posted a $750,000 bond. He returned to his residence on Morningwood Promenade within hours.

When reached for details on the case, Schmidt's lawyer Pierre X. Nasté said, "My client, Mr. Schmidt, is innocent of the charges against him. This is an incredibly flimsy case, and I have no doubt the so-called case will fall apart like wet tissue paper once the evidence is presented in court."

Fester Chief Constable Martin Prieboy had no comment.

ABOUT THE SCHMIDT FAMILY

Karlheinz Schmidt constructed the region's first grist mill in 1764 along the Mill Creek by the Black River at the current site of Mill Park. A replica of the mill was burned down in an arson attack in 1994.

The Schmidt family grew the original mill into the Schmidt Pretzel Bakery, Fester's largest employer. The business was relocated in 1933 to the opposite side of the Black River from the original site, where it remains to this day. The Schmidt Pretzel Bakery, at its peak in the mid-1980s, employed over 8,000 citizens of Fester and Kerian County. Increased competition led to a downturn in the bakery's fortunes.

There was a brief reversal of those fortunes in the 1990s, when Cecilia Schmidt, widow of Emile Schmidt, became CEO after her husband's death. Under Ms. Schmidt's management, the ailing company was revived. Ms. Schmidt's interest in the company was bought out by the rest of the family in 1995. Thereafter, she was no longer associated in any way with Schmidt family business interests.

In 1996, the Schmidt Pretzel Bakery was sold to Zut Brands, Inc. of Hanover, PA. Zut added the bakery to its portfolio of snack food holdings. In 1997, Zut undertook major upgrades to the factory, including extensive automation, and reduced the bakery's workforce of 5,000 by nearly half. A serious blow to the area's economy resulted.

Chapter 29

"Wooo-*hooo!*" yelled Vince Totenkopf. "That sure is some fine hooch you got there, Uncle Merle. I mean, God*damn!*"

"It tastes good," said his cousin, Ted. "Makes my belly feel happy."

"That there is some special stuff, boys," said Merle. "It's the Poppi Totenkopf Special Recipe. This recipe is handed down directly to the head of the Totenkopf clan from his predecessor, and only the *jefe* can cook it up. It's a secret formulation brewed up by the very first Totenkopf in Fester."

"Is that the one who witnessed the Indian mass—" started Harold.

"Yeah, yeah, yeah," said Merle, dismissively flapping his hand. "We don't need to talk about that now."

"Right, Pap," said Harold. He was already half bagged. He, his father and his cousins Vince and Ted were celebrating the mall's surprising rebound following the fair. This month's numbers were up—way up. He was a hero to the entire family now. The threat of losing the income from the mall evidently made them realize how much Harold had done for the family.

"Well, we can't just sit here and get all liquored up," said Vince.

"Yeah, we can," said Ted.

"We do that all the time," said Merle. "It's time to celebrate Harry's skill in keeping our bacon out of the fire. You boys should go out and have a good time."

"Ain't you coming, Pap?" asked Harold.

"Nope. I've already used up plenty of fun tickets whooping it up in the big city. Besides, I'd just hold you back. You boys go on and have your fun."

They crammed into Vince's F-150 and took off. He drove like a bat out of hell and got to Weaverville in about twenty minutes. Deciding they should take on some ballast to sustain them through a night's serious drinking, they hit up a steakhouse called Stoneman's. There they enjoyed the house's finest T-bone steaks and several rounds of top-shelf Scotch.

They then proceeded to work their way through a series of sports bars. They kept getting thrown out because of the fights Vince started. The third time it happened, Ted bonked Vince on the top of the head and told him to quit being an asshole. Ted was generally docile and rather slow (hence the townie nickname "Inbred Ted"), but he was also strong. Vince had to sit down on the curb for a few minutes to clear his head afterwards.

"I'll tell you what," said Vince once he could see straight. "Whyn't we go to the Pitiful Princess?"

"What, that strip club?" asked Harold. "I've never been there, have you?"

"Yeah, I went about two, three years ago with some buddies. I really don't remember it all that well—I was pretty wasted."

Harold wondered how much he'd be able to remember—he was feeling pretty wasted already. He was tired of sports bars, and the idea of having some pretty women take their clothes off in front of him had a definite appeal. "Yeah, sure," he said. Let's go."

"How about you, Teddy?" asked Vince. "You in?"

"There's gonna be pretty women there?" asked Ted. "Yuh, sure thing."

"You sure you're okay to drive, Vince?" asked Harold.

"Yeah, sure—I'm sober as a judge. I'm not a lightweight like you."

Vince managed to drive fairly straight, but he had a hard time remembering how to find the bar. He got pissed when Harold attempted to navigate with his cell phone. "I'll find it, dammit, I'll find it," he kept saying. It took almost an hour of wrong turns and backtracking before they pulled into the parking lot on the far side of town.

Vince's mood was further soured when he was denied entry to the strip club. "You can't come in with that jacket," said the gorilla-like bouncer. "No colors." He tapped a sign by the door that said, "No weapons/No colors/No bare feet/No attitude."

CHAPTER 29

"Waddaya mean colors?" asked Vince. He was wearing an unadorned black leather jacket.

"Leather jacket is colors," said the bouncer. "You gotta leave it in the truck." He stood back, as if expecting Vince to give him lip. Harold almost hoped he would—he was starting to feel tired. To his surprise, Vince just nodded, stripped off his jacket and tossed it in the truck. The bouncer collected the three-dollar cover charge and let them in.

Surprisingly, Vince was well-behaved and seemed to be enjoying himself. They got a table with a good view of the stage and settled in. Vince ordered a pitcher and three tequila shooters.

"Aw, no, Vince," objected Harold. "I think I've had enough for one night."

"Aw, don't be such a pussy," said Vince. "Shoot it! Shoot it! Shoot it!"

In for a penny, in for a pound, thought Harold. He threw back the tequila. So did Ted, but Vince just watched.

"Good boy," said Vince. "Just for being a pussy, though, you gotta do another." He shoved his tequila in front of Harold and hollered, "Shoot it! Shoot it! Shoot it!" People at adjacent tables took up the chant, and Harold downed the shot just to shut them up. His stomach hitched once, then settled.

"Jesus," said Harold. "No more fuckin' tequila, okay? That shit goes straight to my head." He pulled his beer mug in front of him and grasped it defensively. He was well beyond drunk. Fortunately, Vince was absorbed in his beer and ogling the dancers.

"Waddaya think of this one, Ted?" said Vince, nodding at the buxom brunette who was spinning on the pole onstage.

"Oh, yuh, I like her," said Ted, a goofy grin plastered across his face.

"Then check this out." said Vince. He got up, stood by the stage, and when the dancer noticed him, he stuck a dollar bill in her G-string. She leaned over, shook her boobs in his face for a few seconds, then moved off to another admirer.

"Wow," said Ted. "Can I do that?" He began rummaging in his pocket for dollar bills.

"Anyone with a dollar can do that," said Vince. "Just don't touch the girl.

You touch her, that asshole bouncer is going to toss us out of here sooner than you can say boo."

Ted nodded and got up. He was soon stuffing singles into the dancers' G-strings like he was posting bail. Harold was so absorbed watching Ted throwing away money he didn't notice that three more tequila shots had materialized at the table.

"Oh, Christ, Vince," said Harold. "I really can't ..."

"Shoot it!" cried Vince. "Shoot it! Shoot it!" This time, the entire bar took up the chant. Even the dancer on the stage was chanting "Shoot it! Shoot it!"

"Oh, all right you fuckers!" yelled Harold. He downed the shot to cheers and applause from the entire house. "That's it, though, Vince. I mean it."

Vince just nodded.

Harold was really drunk now. He could barely focus on the stage and was having trouble holding his head up.

Ted had run out of dollar bills and returned to the table to down his shot. "That was fun," he said. "Only costs a dollar to have some big ol' titties shook in my face. I wanna come back here for my birthday."

Amazingly, Vince seemed sober—at least to Harold, who was definitely nine sheets to the wind. "Yeah, I guess it's okay," he said. "Still, Pennsylvania sucks when it comes to titty bars. Ya can't do anything here. I hear that up in Canada, the strippers get completely naked *and* they can rub up on you. There's a thing called a lap dance where you give 'em a ten spot and they sit right down and wiggle around in your lap! Guy I know went there said he practically bust a nut!"

"How far away's Canada, Vince?" asked Ted. He, too, seemed amazingly sober.

"Too far to go tonight," laughed Vince. "But ..."

"What, Vince?"

"I just had an idea ..."

"Uhh, blarglep," said Harold. He's had enough of Vince's ideas for the evening. He was having trouble communicating his concerns, however. "I un noodlup gowwa homsun."

CHAPTER 29

"I agree," said Vince. "This place is beat. I know a place we can go where we can actually get some tail for a price. It's back in Fester, too. It's called Mike's Place. You guys heard of it?"

"No," said Ted. "What's it like?"

"Glurrm," said Harold. Consciousness was fading in and out now, like a lightbulb when the power's about to go out.

"It's kinda like Hooters, but if you like one of the girls you can take her upstairs."

"And then what?" asked Ted.

"Then you have sex with her, you big lug!"

It took Ted nearly a minute to process this, but when it had finally landed, his face lit up. "Oh, yeah, Vince—let's go! Let's go! Do we have enough money for ficky-fick?"

"Yeah, I got plenty. Waddaya say, Harry? Wanna go to Mike's Place for some ficky-fick?"

"Shlurt," said Harold. He wasn't entirely sure where he was now.

"Sounds like a 'yes' to me," said Vince. "C'mon, Teddy, let's help the man of the hour out to the truck."

Vince settled up the tab. He and Ted flanked Harold and helped him stumble out to the parking lot. Harold made it all the way to the truck before he puked. Forty dollars' worth of overpriced strip club drinks splashed on the side of Vince's F-150. "Now it's a party!" he declared. "Better put Mr. Liquid Laughter by the window, just in case he erupts again."

They loaded into the truck and took off on Route 17, going fast. Harold still felt like hell. Throwing up had helped clear his head somewhat, but he was still foggy on the details of what was going on. He hoped they were heading home.

Amazingly, Vince wasn't done with party mode. He pulled a joint from his shirt pocket and sparked it with the truck's cigarette lighter. He took a hit and passed it to Ted. Ted took a hit and held it up in front of Harold's face.

"Huhhh?" said Harold.

"Just smoke it, okay?" said Vince.

"Yuh, Harry, just smoke it," agreed Ted.

Too wasted to resist, Harold took a hit. Ted passed it back to Vince, who passed it back to Ted, who passed it back to Harold. Amazingly, Harold managed to roll down the window and toss the joint out.

"Oh, major party foul, cousin!" said Vince with a laugh.

"Pollowa!" said Harold.

"What?"

"Pollowa!" repeated Harold. "Pollowa! PULL OVAH!"

Vince stood on the brake and guided the truck to the side of the road. Harold opened the door just in time to unleash another torrent of vomit. When he was done, he sat there for a minute, panting. Taking a toke off that joint had been a horrible idea. His head spun like a top, and he just wanted to lie down.

"C'mon, c'mon," said Vince. "We're not getting any younger, you know." Harold pulled the door closed and Vince took off with a spray of gravel. He rooted around in the ashtray and came up with a small silver cylinder that he dropped in Harold's lap.

"Whazzis?" asked Harold.

"Breath mints. You don't wanna be meeting the girlies at Mike's with puke breath do ya?"

"Don' wanna go Mike," said Harold. "Wanna go home."

"No way!" said Vince. "Got too much invested in this evening to bail now. We need to see it to its natural conclusion. Besides, you don't want to disappoint Ted, do you?"

"Yeah, do yuh?" repeated Ted.

"Fush yoogize," said Harold.

"Sounds like a yes to me," said Vince. "Too bad I didn't get a little blow before we headed out. That would help take care of things."

"Shit," said Harold. His head was really spinning now, and it seemed like he really couldn't see out of his left eye. He wondered what the symptoms of alcohol poisoning were.

The truck was really hauling ass. Vince seemed hell bent on getting to Mike's Place, and Harold knew there was no chance of talking him out of it.

CHAPTER 29

Outside, the darkened scenery rushed by.

Amazingly, Harold began to rally. He no longer felt like he was about to go to sleep, and he could hold his head up better—but he was still beyond wasted. He had no idea it was possible to be this torn up and still be able to maintain cognition. Fuck it. They were going to a whorehouse. Whoopee ding dong. Harold didn't think he'd be able to get it up if the Dallas Cowboys Cheerleaders were tickling his junk with ostrich feathers.

He became aware that there were more lights flashing by outside; they were coming into Fester. They drove through a darkened part of town then turned into a parking lot and stopped.

"Here we are, boys!" crowed Vince. "Let's get at 'em!"

"Hooray for boobies!" said Ted.

The three of them stumbled out of the truck and began weaving their way to the entrance. About halfway between the truck and the front door, Harold blacked out.

But he kept walking.

Chapter 30

Billy Snyder was back in the bush.

When the might of Commonwealth of Pennsylvania law enforcement hadn't immediately fallen upon him after Ronald Schmidt's arrest, he'd used the time to work on the special project. The work had gone quite smoothly, and he now felt confident enough to take the old girl out for a spin.

When he wasn't working on the special project, he made preparations to hole up. He'd made several supply runs to Weaverville, always after dark. He made sure there weren't any cars lurking nearby before he took off. It took him a long time to get to Weaverville as he stuck to rural routes and county roads as much as possible.

One time he'd passed a sheriff's patrol car, and Billy's asshole had tightened up so quickly he thought he could hear it squeak shut. He looked in his rearview mirror for the telltale flash of brake lights, but the deputy just kept going. That didn't stop Billy's paranoia. Maybe the deputy had hung back and was following from a distance.

Fortunately, Billy was almost back from a supply run when this happened. He hurried home as fast as he dared, stashed the Crown Vic behind the workshop and slunk back down to the front gate (padlocked, of course) and spent the next two hours monitoring the traffic on the road. It consisted of two pickup trucks and a minivan blasting Jason Aldean at top volume.

Billy began shifting his supplies up the hill to where he had buried the recoilless rifles and ammo. He'd started thinking of it as "Camp Vengeance." He would be living there pretty soon.

CHAPTER 30

To that end, he had set up two tents. One was a medium-sized canvas frame tent, big enough for him to stand up in. This he furnished with a cot, a table, a chair, and a small propane stove. The other tent was similar, but much larger. Once he was finished with the special project, he intended to bring it up here. He planned on stringing up camo netting above the tents—he'd already picked up quite a bit of it at a military surplus store in Weaverville.

He'd also picked up a small generator. The thing was noisy as hell, though. Billy had rigged up a small housing out of two-by-fours and plywood, then lined it with some pink batt insulation left over from when he had weatherproofed the house. It did a pretty good job of keeping the noise down. He'd also located the generator a good fifty yards away from the tents.

The surplus store had furnished quite a bit of Camp Vengeance. Billy hadn't frequented the surplus place before, which was probably for the best. He didn't want anyone to recognize him and tip off the cops.

In fact, Billy had no idea whether law enforcement was looking for him at all. He assumed that it was only a matter of time before he was fingered as the one who sold Ronnie the Rake the gun used in the shooting. Of course, Billy didn't know for sure that was the gun Ronald used, but it would be foolish to assume otherwise. Likewise, Billy had to figure that Ronald's greasy lawyer would give Billy up as part of a bargaining process to get his client off the hook. Perhaps the cops wouldn't care—after all, private gun sales were legal. But at the very least, there would be deputies who would come around with questions—and there'd be a lot more questions if they discovered the special project. The recoilless rifles and their ammo would definitely mean prosecution.

He hadn't heard from any of his contacts for the last few days. He still kept his cell phone off—but that was going to have to change if he was going to quit living in the house entirely. He'd have to keep in touch with the outside world somehow, and the cell phone was the only option. Actually, he realized he should have thought to get a burner phone when he was in Weaverville. He could give the number out to Joe and one or two other well-trusted confidantes. He figured to pick one up the next time he left the property—whenever that might be. He imagined he'd probably make one more major supply run once he'd got the special project secured at Camp Vengeance.

Which would be soon. He took a quick look around, making sure everything was secure. He didn't expect anyone to come nosing around this isolated part of the property, but you never knew. The sheriff's deputies—or worse, the state police—might come calling if things went south.

He'd had his reservations about digging in on his own property, regardless of how isolated it was. If any sort of decent search was put on, he was sure to be discovered. If he was smart, he'd just decamp to somewhere far away. He owned a hunting cabin up in the Poconos that was suitably isolated, but relocating there—especially with the special project—would be expensive and logistically difficult.

Not that money was a problem. He had wet his beak and lined his pockets well during his tenure as chief constable. That ill-gotten money had been ratholed away in dozens of banks and safe deposit boxes all over the northeast. Of course, he'd blown a big chunk of his money on lawyers' fees at his trial and spent another wad of cash when he'd bought this property. At least he hadn't had to part with any of the off-the-books money when he divorced.

He just didn't want to spend it to run away. His life had been a roller coaster over the last few years, and as unpleasant as it might seem compared to his glory days as chief constable, it sure beat the hell out of prison. It was, relatively speaking, a peaceful life, and one that had allowed him to do a lot of thinking. He spent a lot of time thinking about the past—and a lot of time thinking about people who had wronged him.

No, he was not going to run away. Sure, he'd done some bad things in his life, but in the grand scheme of things, Billy's transgressions seemed minor. Certainly, selling an antique pistol to a rich lunatic was penny-ante stuff. People sold guns to lunatics every day in this country. Why should Billy have to suffer just because he dealt with the wrong lunatic?

The Schmidt family. The more Billy thought about them, the more he

CHAPTER 30

ground his teeth. First, his career as chief constable was upended by that bitch Cecilia Schmidt. She was one of *them*. She'd borne the name and run the family company. And while the circumstances that led to the Mill Fire and his arrest were complicated, he still blamed Cecilia.

Once again, the Schmidts seemed poised to upend the meager life he'd made for himself. Damn, that family had crushed him once, and now they were about to finish the job. Well, he had a few ideas about what he could do to even the score. There'd be plenty of time to think about that later—right now he still had work to do.

Camp Vengeance was tight. Billy walked the perimeter and saw everything was buttoned up and secure, then climbed into the Land Rover and went careening back down the ridge to the house. He stashed the truck in the trees and made his way along the tree line to the front gate. He needed to make absolutely sure the coast was clear before his next move. Satisfied it was safe, he hurried back to the workshop.

After a great deal of time and a whole lot of money, Billy's special project was practically done. Any late-stage adjustments and fine tuning could be taken care of at Camp Vengeance. Feeling like a little kid on Christmas morning, he raised the door to the workshop, stood back and admired his handiwork.

Inside the shop was a restored M50A1 Ontos. The Ontos (which was Greek for "thing") was a tank—and a very strange-looking one. Billy had served as the driver on one in Vietnam. He had been working on this Ontos—which he had come to think of as the *Thing*—on and off for several years. Over the last six months, a number of previously hard-to-find components had become available. Billy had snapped them up and ramped up his restoration project. Except for a few final touches (like mounting the recoilless rifles), he was done.

Billy Snyder had built himself a tank.

For a relatively small armored vehicle, it packed a punch with its six recoilless rifles that were accurate to over a thousand yards. The high-explosive rounds could knock a huge hole in a masonry wall. One Ontos could flatten a medium-sized building in less than two minutes.

The Ontos had a fearsome reputation for the carnage it wreaked on the battlefield. Also, it just *looked* scary. The main body looked like a light tank, but the six recoilless rifle barrels arrayed around the turret gave it an ominous, insectile appearance. It looked like an alien tank from a sci-fi movie. The North Vietnamese and the Viet Cong never stuck around when an Ontos showed up on the battlefield.

Right now, Billy's Thing was missing the rifles. It made it look naked to Billy's eye. It was like a huge buck with its antlers removed—still imposing but greatly diminished. That would be easy enough to fix once it was relocated to Camp Vengeance.

The Thing was quick, but lightly armored. Billy doubted, though, whether any firepower of sufficient power would be brought to bear in Kerian County. In a worst-case scenario, the State Police Special Emergency Response Team might bring in some high-caliber sniper rifles, but Billy didn't think they'd pierce the armor. Once Billy had the Thing fully operational, they would have to bring in the National Guard to take it out.

It was time to give it the test. He had installed the engine and hooked it up to the transmission. The engine was easy to get. The Chrysler 461 cubic inch V-8 had been produced for twenty years, and it had been easy to find a good rebuilt model. The transmission was another story, and Billy had had to rebuild much of it himself. He'd connected the two the other night, now it was time to see if the tranny and engine would actually play together.

He climbed into the driver's seat and started the engine. It turned over easily. He shifted it into low gear and pushed on the steering yoke. There was a loud *clank* from the transmission, but no further clamor from the engine compartment. Billy opened the hatch and poked his head out, then gave it a little gas. The Ontos moved forward and out the wide door easily. He steered it around the workshop giving the building and nearby trees wide berth, It had been a long time since he'd driven one of these, and the steering yoke took some getting used to. He drove it once around the workshop building, then again. It felt *good.* He'd put a lot of work into it, and it was gratifying that it had all paid off.

CHAPTER 30

Be a shame if something happened to it, he thought. A bubble of paranoia burst in his mind: *they* might be coming for him right now. If they found the Thing, he'd be up shit creek for sure. It was running and running well. There was no reason why he couldn't take it up to Camp Vengeance right now.

He resisted the urge to immediately charge up the hill. Instead, he backed into the workshop and spent some time loading up the crew compartment with tools and some odd supplies he might need, then securing them for the ride up. It was time to move out.

He pulled the Ontos out and locked the workshop. In moments, he was climbing the hill. *Damn,* thought Billy. *I'd forgotten how this thing can move out* . He felt exultant as he charged up the hill. The Land Rover was sure-footed enough, but this Ontos was large and in charge. It was exhilarating.

When he got to the flat part at the top of the hill, he stopped and got out. The daylight was fading fast. Behind him, he could see the twin tracks of the treads pressed deeply into the earth behind him. That would never do—it was a dead giveaway that he had taken a tracked vehicle up the ridge and would lead pursuers directly to Camp Vengeance.

Fortunately, he already had a solution. He'd purchased a large landscaping rake meant for a tractor and welded on a hitch that would attach it to the Land Rover. It was basically just a huge metal rake with dozens of sturdy metal tines. In the morning, he'd walk back down to the house, attach the rake and drive the Land Rover back up the ridge. It would obliterate the tread marks, although it would still show a pretty obvious path up the hill. Well, there was nothing to do for that but hope the weather would help smooth things down. There was some rain forecast for the weekend; that would help. He would have to find a less-obvious route for future trips with the Land Rover. The Thing would stay up at Camp Vengeance for the time being.

Billy climbed back into the Thing and maneuvered it through the trees to Camp Vengeance and parked it in the large tent. He secured the flaps and walked the perimeter of the camp. Satisfied it was secure, Billy went to his cot in the other tent, where he slept a deep and dreamless sleep.

Chapter 31

Harold Todd woke up and immediately regretted it. His head pounded and his stomach roiled. His face felt like it had been hit with a cinderblock. It was only slightly more painful than the rest of his head. Also, his back hurt and he felt like he was twisted into an uncomfortably confined space. He opened his eyes briefly and snapped them shut again. The light in the room—wherever it was—was bright and painful. It felt like he'd been crammed into a metal coffin. His clothes were stiff and tacky. He tried to shift into a less uncomfortable position and failed. He'd have to try opening his eyes again.

He counted to three, then gave the whole vision thing another try. It took a few moments for the achy image to register: he was lying in a bathtub—and he was about to puke. Somehow, he scrambled out of the tub and positioned himself in front of the toilet before he let go. His stomach spasmed repeatedly, although there wasn't much left to come up. When the heaving subsided, he decided the bathtub was still the best choice for his immediate resting needs, so he climbed back in and fell asleep.

When he opened his eyes again his headache had taken about 20 percent off the top. His stomach was sore from heaving, but the sick nugget of nausea that had lodged in his gut seemed to have shrunk. He carefully sat up and managed to get himself to a sitting position on the side of the tub. His eyes were swollen half shut, but there seemed to be an awful lot of red in his extremely blurred field of vision. He placed his hands on his thighs, pushed, and managed to shakily get to his feet. He leaned heavily on the sink, willing himself not to heave. He looked into the mirror and gasped.

CHAPTER 31

His shirt was soaked through with dried blood. The entire shirtfront was a red-brown mess. It ran in a huge streak down the front of his shirt and had splattered on his pants as well. There were spots of blood on his face, too. He looked over in the tub, and it too had streaks and splotches of drying blood.

His head spun and he sat back down on the edge of the bathtub, trying to get his bearings. He searched in his pants pockets for his phone, but his pockets were empty. His wallet and keys were gone, too.

He realized that he must have had his keys, otherwise he wouldn't have been able to get into the condo. He staggered to his feet again, now thoroughly alarmed. A jolt of fear-adrenaline shot through him, giving him the energy to make it to the bedroom.

The bedroom was untouched; the bed was made and nothing was out of place. There was no sign of his phone, wallet, or keys.

He stumbled into the living room. It wasn't exactly trashed, but it was in rough shape. The glass-topped coffee table was tipped over and the top had a huge crack in it. The cushions from the couch had been scattered around the room and the vertical blinds on the patio window had been torn down. He searched all over but couldn't find any of his stuff.

Finally, he noticed that the front door was slightly ajar. He got up and opened it—his keys were still in the keyhole. He stuck his head out the door. His next-door neighbor Bev was just coming out of her unit. A look of alarm crossed her face as she noticed Harold's battered and bloody face. He snatched the keys, slammed the door and staggered over to the couch, where he dropped onto its cushionless surface with a sob.

He took a series of deep breaths, trying to calm himself. What had happened last night? He remembered going to Weaverville with Vince and Ted, the dinner at the steakhouse, then visiting a number of bars where Vince kept getting into fights. He remembered driving aimlessly around the east side of Weaverville and winding up at a crummy strip club. He recalled how Vince kept pressuring him to do tequila shots, then throwing up in the parking lot afterwards. The ride back was even hazier. A joint had been passed around. After that, Harold's memories faded in and out, like the reception on their pre-cable TV when a storm was coming. There was a vague memory of leaning out of Vince's truck and throwing up. After that—nothing.

One thing, however, was abundantly clear: the rest of the night had gone horribly wrong.

Chapter 32

It was a slow Monday night at the Wise Owl Café. The grumpy man in the paper hat wiped down the counter as a creaky wooden fan made an attempt to stir the stale air. At the end of the counter, the old couple huddled together eating soup. Only two of the booths had customers.

Martin Prieboy was at his regular booth in the back. It was once again date night, and he was wearing a brand-new cardigan that he thought Charlene would like: a dark red cable-knit. But tonight his date was late. He checked his phone again. It was quarter past eight. It was very unlike Charlene to be late. She was very punctual and usually came swinging through the door a few minutes early.

Well, who knows? Maybe she had car trouble, maybe she'd got caught up in her application for the nursing program at Prosser College. She was sure to turn up any moment now. Martin decided to wait. He took a listless slurp on his Pepsi and surveyed his surroundings. The man in the paper cap continued to swipe at the counter. The couple at the end of the counter kept spooning up their soup. Outside, a pickup truck raced by, loud and fast.

Martin checked the phone again—it was nearly eight-thirty. Enough—she was officially late. He scrolled through the contacts list to the Ts and dialed the number for Charlene Troutman. It rang and went to voice mail. Martin hung up, then changed his mind and redialed. This time he left a message, "Charlene, it's me, um, Marty. I'm waiting for you at our usual place and I'm concerned that you're late. I just wanted to make sure you were okay. Please give me a call when you can, although I hope to see you coming through the door soon. Goodbye."

He toyed with his Pepsi some more. The man with the paper cap came over to his booth. "So your frien' ain't shown up?"

"Afraid not," said Martin, not really wanting to talk to him.

"You want me to get ya a burger goin'?"

"No, I'm not hungry. Maybe in a bit."

"'Nother Pepsi?"

"No!"

"Okay, okay, no need to get snippy now." The man in the paper hat moved away, casting a mistrustful look over his shoulder.

Martin felt bad—for snapping at the man in the paper hat, but mostly because of Charlene. Something was wrong. She was normally so reliable. He spent the next twenty minutes fidgeting and checking his phone. At ten till nine he tried calling Charlene again. Still no answer.

He opened up the browser on his phone and did a search for *mike's place fester*. It was peppered with cheesecake photos of the Mike's Place hostesses in various tawdry poses. He got the phone number from the top of the page and dialed it.

After nine rings, it picked up. "Mike's Place," said a bored male voice. "How can we service you?"

"I'd like to speak to Mr. Solheim, please."

There was a snort at the end of the line. "He's not here."

Martin waited for an offer to leave a message, but none was forthcoming. Martin suspected the man was lying. Mike Solheim was always at his place during working hours. Supposedly, he'd once had a mild heart attack but refused to go to the hospital until the place had closed for the night.

"Listen up," said Martin. "This is Chief Constable Martin Prieboy, and if Mike Solheim isn't on the phone in thirty seconds I'm going to grab six of my meanest constables and come down there and start asking a lot of hard questions. Do you want that? More importantly—do you think your boss wants that?"

"N-no."

"Right. Go get him. Now!"

CHAPTER 32

There was a long silence, and just as Martin was getting ready to hang up and go down there in person, someone picked up. "This is Mike Solheim," he said pleasantly. "How may I help you?"

"This is Chief Constable Martin Prieboy, Mr. Solheim. I have to say you have some very rude people answering your telephone."

"I'm sorry about that, Chief. I'll have a word with my staff. Now what can I do for you?"

"I'm trying to get in touch with Charlene Troutman. Her, ah, stage name is Candy Floss. When was the last time you saw her?"

"What's the matter? Is she in some sort of trouble?"

"I'll ask the questions, Mr. Solheim. When was the last time you saw her?"

"She worked Saturday night, we exchanged pleasantries, nothing more. Just a moment, please." There was the sound of shuffling paper. "She's not scheduled to work tonight but is supposed to be in tomorrow."

"What time?"

"She is supposed to be in at 6:30 tomorrow evening."

"Okay, Solheim, if she's even fifteen minutes late, I want you to call me immediately. Heck, if she shows up on time, I want you to call me." He read off the digits to his personal cell phone.

"Okay, sure thing, Chief," said Solheim. "She's a good kid, that one. Did you know she's going to be a nurse?"

"Yes, I'd heard. I hope she's not in any trouble. One way or another, I want to hear from you by 6:30 tomorrow evening. If I don't, I *will* pay your establishment a visit with a couple of my men, and we will not be happy. Do you understand?"

"Yes, Chief, sure. You'll hear from me for certain, probably before six. Candy's almost always early."

"I sure hope so. I'll talk to you soon, Mr. Solheim." He hung up without waiting for a response.

Maybe he was being too protective. Her absence could have a completely innocent explanation. Maybe she had just broken her phone. That would make sense—she busted her phone and was now desperately trying to replace it. Martin knew smart phones were like life support systems for young people—they practically couldn't live without them. It was probably something simple like that.

Or maybe not.

Chapter 33

The next evening, Martin Prieboy drove over to Charlene's apartment complex. He was in uniform, but driving his personal vehicle, a nine-year-old Chevy Malibu. He hadn't wanted to attract attention by pulling up in a cruiser. It was early evening, and the parking lot was full. Most of the residents were home from work or school.

The apartment complex was relatively new but starting to look a little run-down. Martin had never been there before. He tried to respect Charlene's privacy and hadn't ever visited her at work or home. Charlene was a big girl and could take care of herself, but Martin thought it wouldn't hurt to make sure she was okay—for no other reason that his own peace of mind.

His peace of mind had been eroded when he talked to Mike Solheim and learned Charlene had missed work. "Normally, I don't worry about it that much when a girl flakes on me," Solheim had said. "But I'm worried about Candy. She's got a good head on her shoulders. I wouldn't have expected her to just take off without saying anything. I'm glad you're looking into it, Chief. You let me know what you find out, okay?"

Martin assured him that he would. As much as he hated what she did for a living, he felt an almost fatherly affection for her. He'd always liked Charlene, and in the year since Sam had been gone, he'd begun feeling more protective of her.

Martin had never really thought about having kids. Reproduction just wasn't on his radar. However, he felt he'd really come to know Charlene over the years they had worked together, and felt a great deal of affection for her. He'd never thought about what it would be like to have a daughter, but if he'd had one, he would have liked her to be someone like Charlene. Although preferably with a different job.

He pulled into the parking lot of the Vista Meadows Apartments. It didn't have much of a vista—the apartment block was hemmed in by other cheap apartment houses and tired-looking duplexes. There were no meadows within miles. He got out of his car and scoped the parking lot. Charlene's blue Camry was present and accounted for. He hoped that he'd find Charlene at home, sleeping off a bad cold or a bender or something with a safe and sane explanation.

A plastic sign with a red arrow pointing towards a ground-floor unit read OFFICE. Martin pushed through the door. A small brass bell rang as he entered. The office featured two mismatched chairs by the door and a Formica counter that ran nearly the entire length of the room. Behind the counter sat a bored-looking young man in an oversized sweater and paisley scarf.

"Are you the manager?" asked Martin.

The young man sighed deeply. "Yes, I guess I am now," he said. "Normally, my mom runs the show, but she's in the hospital, so I'm left holding the bag. Her bursitis is acting up again. There's no telling when she'll be back." He heaved another enormous sigh.

Martin squinted at the young man; he seemed familiar. He was part of Fester's gay community, Martin was sure. The young man regarded him with suspicion. As far as he was concerned, Martin was just another cop in a town where queer-bashing went unreported and unpunished.

"Do you know who I am?" asked Martin.

"No." Short and sullen.

"My name's Martin. I'm the chief constable." He smiled and held out his hand.

The young man squinted, as if some rusty memory machinery was turning over. Suddenly, his eyes opened wide. "Oh!" he exclaimed. "Oh, yeah! I know you!"

Martin nodded. "Good. What's your name, son?" Martin had only recently picked up the habit of addressing young men as "son." It still

CHAPTER 33

felt a little forced, but he'd found a lot of kids responded to it.

"John," said the young man. "My friends call me Johnny."

"Nice to meet you, Johnny. I have a question about one of your tenants." He pulled out his phone and swiped to a picture of Charlene. "This is Charlene Troutman. Do you know her?"

Johnny briefly glanced at the phone and shrugged. "It's my mom who knows stuff like that. She's in the hospital." He shrugged again. "I mean, I guess I've seen her around, but I dunno."

"Have you seen her around since your mother went into the hospital?"

"I dunno. I don't think so, but I can't say for sure."

"Look," said Martin. "Charlene is a friend of mine, and I think she's in trouble. I've been trying to get in touch with her, without success. I'm very worried about her. Can you help me out?"

"What do you want me to do?" said Johnny uneasily. He clearly didn't want to have to do anything.

"I would like you to let me into her apartment," said Martin. "It's unit 208."

"I dunno. I should probably call my mom first. She might get mad if I let you into one of the apartments. Aren't you supposed to have a warrant or something?"

Martin was beginning to lose his patience. He resisted the urge to lean on the young man and instead plastered on a friendly smile. "Look, Johnny, I'm not asking you to do anything wrong. If you want to call your mom, that's fine. If you really want me to get a warrant, I guess I can do that, too. Johnny, I'm just trying to find out what happened to a friend who nobody has seen in a couple of days. I'm really worried about her, and it would mean a whole lot to me if we could just stop messing around here. Please open up her place so I can take a quick look and make sure everything's okay. Can you do that for me?"

Johnny took a long time thinking this over. Martin thought about slipping the lock. These apartments didn't look too sturdy; he could probably get inside the apartment with a credit card. Finally, Johnny said, "What the hell—what Mom doesn't know won't hurt her. Let's do it."

"Thanks, Johnny."

They went up to the second tier where the apartment was located. "Hold on," said Martin. "Let me knock first." He laid into the small brass knocker that was screwed to the door. It was cheap; Martin could feel the door flex as he knocked. "Charlene?" he called. "It's Martin Prieboy. If you're there, please come to the door. It's important!" He waited, then pressed his ear to the door. A bad feeling uncoiled in his gut. Something was off here; something was wrong, and his cop intuition was clanging a mad alarm.

Martin gave Johnny a nod, and the young man fished through an enormous keyring until he found the right key. He went to unlock the door, but Martin stopped him. "Please let me handle that," he said as he pulled a handkerchief from his pocket. He unlocked the door and used the handkerchief to turn the knob.

"Wow," said Johnny. "Do you think this is a crime scene or something?"

"I sincerely hope not, but it's best to play it safe. Why don't you go back down to the office, Johnny? I really appreciate your help—thank you."

"Sure, uh, Chief. Hey, you've been to The Embers before, right?"

"Yes, I have. My, um, partner owned it."

"Oh, yeah—I forgot," said Johnny. "Wow, bummer. I'm sorry for your, uh, loss. Look, if you ever want to meet up there or anything, that'd be cool. You know, just to talk."

Martin looked at Johnny. He seemed like a nice kid, but Martin was not in the least bit interested. Johnny wasn't even half Martin's age, and even if he were older, Martin would think thrice before involving himself. It wasn't uncommon for younger men to be attracted to him—or to the uniform—but there was no way he was going to get involved with someone like Johnny. Hell, there was no way he was going to get involved with *anybody*. The wound of Sam's death was still raw and weeping.

"I think I'll take a pass on that, Johnny," said Martin. "You seem like a good guy, but I'm too busy for anything resembling a social life right now." *And I'm worried that it's about to become a lot busier,* he mentally added.

"Oh. Okay."

"Go on back to the office now," said Martin. "This should only take a few

CHAPTER 33

minutes, I hope. I'll stop by before I leave, okay?"

"Okay," said Johnny, and he left looking a little disappointed.

Once he was out of sight, Martin used the handkerchief to turn the knob. He stepped inside the apartment, his heart pounding. "Charlene?" he called. "Are you here? It's Martin Prieboy."

There was no answer. Martin stood just inside the front door. It opened on the living room, which had a shabby, oatmeal-colored wall-to-wall carpet. There was a small galley kitchen with a breakfast bar and chairs to the right of the living room. Everything looked to be in order. The apartment was small, but Charlene kept it neat.

This should have eased his fears, but for some reason it didn't. Carefully, he moved through the living room, scanning to see if there was anything suspicious or out of place. At the back of the living room was a short hallway that presumably led to the bedroom and bathroom.

There was a spot of blood on the carpet right in front of the hallway.

Martin unsnapped the strap holding his sidearm in place. "Charlene!" he called, unable to keep a quaver from his voice. "CHARLENE! Can you hear me?"

Okay, calm down, he thought. Just a small splotch of blood. Maybe she'd cut herself in the kitchen or stubbed her toe. Domestic accidents abounded—that's why they made band-aids.

He squatted down to take a closer look. It was definitely blood. "CHARLENE!" he called again and moved into the hallway. At the far end, the door stood open, revealing the bedroom. The bed was made, and from what Martin could see, it was just as neat as the living room.

Halfway along the hall, there was a closed door; presumably this was the bathroom. There was another small drop of blood right in front of the door.

Martin' stomach clenched and he felt his heart racing. He was afraid that his awful intuition had been right. Gingerly, he reached out with the handkerchief and opened the bathroom door.

Her body was in the bathtub.

"Oh, no," whispered Martin. "Oh, Charlene."

She had clearly been in there for a day or two; her skin was going a mottled blue-gray. Nevertheless, Martin knelt down and felt for a pulse. There was none. Charlene Troutman was obviously and irreparably dead.

"I'm so sorry, honey," he said, then reached over and closed her eyes. Her face was so cold.

He called in homicide and told Dan Blount that he would be taking charge of the case personally. Then he carefully retraced his steps to the front door, stepped outside and waited for his colleagues to arrive.

Chapter 34

Harold Todd was miserable. After his big night out with his cousins, he'd been nonfunctional all the next day. He'd called in sick on Monday, still feeling massively ill and hungover. He'd managed to drag his ass into work on Tuesday, but locked the office door, turned out the lights and told Stella to hold all his calls.

The problem wasn't just the physical effects of the hangover—although they were plenty bad. It was the blood. Harold had no idea whose it was or how it had gotten there. He felt sure, though, that something horrible had happened that Saturday night. Something that *he* was responsible for.

He eventually remembered Vince had decided they would go to Mike's Place. There was a blurry recollection of driving back from Weaverville, pulling into the parking lot at Mike's Place, and getting out of the truck. After that, nothing until he had regained consciousness ("woke up" was just too much of a stretch) in the bathtub at his condo. Covered in blood.

He spent Monday in fear of an accusatory phone call, until he realized that he couldn't find his phone. He had ventured into the basement garage to find his Lexus parked across three reserved spots, none of which were his. He cleared the nastygrams out from under his windshield wiper and moved his car back to its rightful spot. A quick search of the car turned up his wallet. All the credit cards were there, but he was down to three singles in cash (after leaving the house with nearly $300). A thorough search failed to turn up the phone.

His great achievement on Tuesday was to go down to the far end of the mall, purchase a new phone, and spend half the afternoon on the line with a Verizon customer service representative getting his account transferred. Figuring that was the most he could be expected to achieve for the day, he left early and went home.

There, he plopped onto the couch, fired up the browser on his new phone, and pulled up the WEVL-TV website. He wondered if there was anything in the local news that might be able to shed some light on what had happened Saturday night.

There was.

HOOKER HOMICIDE! blared the headline. Harold read with mounting terror about the murder of Charlene Troutman, a/k/a Candy Floss, a hostess at Mike's Place, whose body had been discovered earlier that evening. He didn't get past the first two paragraphs, but they told him all he needed to know. Then the world grayed out and he leaned over and hyperventilated.

It was clear what had happened: blackout drunk, Harold had gone to Mike's Place, then gone home with one of the girls and had brutally murdered her (the article said that she had been found at her apartment). He must have left his phone at the scene of the crime. If that were the case, the constables would be around soon to arrest him. They could be on their way *right now.*

Now in a blind animal panic, Harold bolted. He pulled the front door shut behind him, sprinted down the hallway, clattered down the stairwell and ran for his car.

Only when he was in the car with the doors locked did his mind start to unclench. He took a series of deep breaths, willing himself to calm down enough to drive. *You should turn yourself in,* he thought. *Explain that your damn cousin got you wasted and made you go to Mike's Place. Confess and maybe they'll go easy on you.*

Harold shook his head. He really didn't know *what* had happened. That girl's death and his coming home covered in blood could be a coincidence. But it might not be. There was only one thing to do now: go home. The family had always been there when he'd needed them and boy did he need them now. Maybe Vince or Ted would be around and could tell him what happened after they got to Mike's Place. And if they weren't around, Pap

CHAPTER 34

definitely would be. He would know what to do. With that comforting thought, Harold put the car in gear and headed home.

Chapter 35

Ronald Schmidt enjoyed spending time with his three best friends. He really didn't have any friends other than Rondo, Berryman, and Peewee, and that suited him just fine. Generally, he thought monkeys were superior company to people.

They were all in what Ronald called the Monktorium, but his sister and aunt called the "stinky monkey house." It was a specially built enclosure that he had commissioned shortly after he had brought home Rondo. He had originally planned on keeping Rondo in his room, but Aunt Ophelia had been quite emphatic she would not share a house with a smelly monkey. That was back when Ophelia still had a little steel in her spine; still had some of the moxie that had allowed her to deal with Cecilia. Now, Ronald figured he could move all three of the monkeys back into the house and Ophelia wouldn't say boo.

He wouldn't, though, because he liked spending time in the Monktorium. For one, his sister and aunt never came out here, and he could be assured of privacy. Mostly, though, Ronald liked to spend time here because it was the only place he really felt like he could be his true self. He had mostly designed the building himself and had hired a design-build firm that specialized in zoo enclosures. They had fleshed out Ronald's design and built the Monktorium in a matter of weeks, after being enticed with a bonus that was twice their normal fee.

The Monktorium was a long, low building with thick walls and wire-reinforced windows. The builders claimed it could contain a troupe of mountain gorillas. Originally, it was open, with a small, caged foyer just

CHAPTER 35

inside the entry door. The cage had a gate that led to the rest of the open area, which was where Ronald's three pals spent their time. Later, Ronald had had to add another barred wall so he could separate Rondo from Berryman and Peewee. Rondo had been a sweetheart when he was a youngster but had become a great deal more difficult as he'd gotten older. He sometimes didn't get along with Berryman and Peewee, so Ronald had to keep him separate from the other two when he left them unattended.

That hadn't happened much lately. Ever since the shooting, Ronald spent almost all of his time in the Monktorium. He only went to the house to shower and change clothes (which was occurring at longer and longer intervals), and to get some food. He'd tried to get Thelma Louise to bring his meals out to him, but she refused, citing the smell.

Ronald growled. There was a time, and it seemed not so long ago, that there were dozens of obedient servants who would do exactly as Ronald demanded, without question. Those days were gone, alas, and Ronald often wondered what could be done to bring them back. He himself had no idea. He had started taking business courses at the University of Pennsylvania, but then an Unfortunate Incident had occurred and he'd had to leave.

His personal history was festooned with a long string of Unfortunate Incidents; minor speedbumps in the meandering mess that was Ronald Schmidt's life. They were problems for someone else to fix—usually Pierre Nasté or one of his associates.

This latest Incident was probably the most Unfortunate since the one at Penn. Ronald had actually been arrested! The ignominy of it was almost too much to bear. He tried explaining this to the constables and later to the judge. Nasté had struggled to keep Ronald from expressing himself, but in the end convinced him that this Incident might end up being a great deal more Unfortunate if Ronald didn't keep his mouth shut. So Ronald had; he endured the booking, the fingerprinting, the mugshotting, and the arraignment without making his situation worse.

Usually, Ronald's Unfortunate Incidents occurred when he went down to what he thought of as the "Low Town" to kick up his heels in one of the Low Town's many sleazy watering holes. Often, once he had announced his identity, there was someone there who had lost their job after the Zut buyout. These miscreants typically voiced their uninformed opinion that the Schmidts had sold out the town and were nothing but a pack of greedy, rich scumbags. This inevitably resulted in fisticuffs unless the person apologized immediately. That almost never happened, and Ronald almost never lost the fight. He was a big man and had avidly studied a number of martial arts disciplines: judo, aikido, and tai kwan leap. Ronald usually ended the fights by giving the miscreant a boot to the head.

This was where Mr. Nasté usually got involved. He would approach the miscreant, offer to pay for their medical bills, with a few hundred dollars thrown in to sweeten the deal. This was usually enough to get them to drop the charges. Occasionally, Nasté would find that the miscreant had an outstanding warrant, in which case things were forgotten immediately.

The Unfortunate Incident with Mr. Fitch, formerly of next door, had been largely the same. Of course, the price tag had been a little higher given that Fitch was a higher quality of person.

None of these events were Ronald's fault, really—they were just Unfortunate Incidents. They never would have happened if people would have let him be and let him have what he wanted. Was that so wrong? Ronald Schmidt was a child of wealth and privilege, and deserved the best, always. If other people couldn't understand that, then it was they who were to blame.

Ronald sighed and sat down on his Monktorium cot. Now that he spent his nights sleeping there, maybe he could get a nicer cot, or have a small bed brought out here. There was a handyman and cleaner—a husband and wife team—who came out several times a week to make sure the place didn't fall apart entirely. Ronald could have the handyman/gardener husband—he thought his name might be Rafael—haul a bed from the house out to replace the cot. It might make things a little cramped, though. The caged-in alcove was pretty small, to allow for more room in the monkeys' living space.

Ronald looked around. Things in the Monktorium were quiet. Rondo was in his sequestered area, swinging idly in his tire and looking half-asleep. Berryman was swinging back and forth on a swing and climbing the jungle

CHAPTER 35

gym that was in the area he shared with Peewee. Peewee herself was curled up in Ronald's lap asleep and making little monkey snores. It was peaceful. Ronald wished it could be like this all the time. Monkeys were much better to spend time with than people. They weren't as troublesome or deceitful. You always knew where you stood with a monkey.

Ronald's problem was that he didn't know where he stood right now. The damn constables had gotten their hands on the estate's security video. Mr. Nasté had told him not to worry, that the security video had provided enough probable cause to make an arrest, but it wouldn't hold up during a trial. Ronald had gone cold at mention of the word "trial"—he'd never had to think about that before. Aunt Ophelia and Thelma Louise had been similarly aghast. What would a trial do to the family name? Mr. Nasté had told them not to worry; he would make every effort to see to it that the case never came to trial. He had a lot of connections in Weaverville.

That still didn't sit well with Ronald—in fact, it made him rather angry. He'd been on a slow burn ever since he'd gotten back from the arraignment. He suspected Aunt Ophelia and Thelma Louise didn't mind his spending all of his time in the Monktorium. They didn't like having him around, and he didn't want to be around them, either.

People were dangerous morons. Just look at that Bollinger idiot. How dare he come up to Ronald's own house and make a ruckus—and a stink—with his miserable old car? Peons like him shouldn't even be allowed up on Morningwood Promenade, yet every serf in Low Town was free to drive his jalopy right up to the front of the Schmidt family estate and cause trouble. It was a ridiculous situation.

The first time it had happened, Ronald had chalked it up as a random occurrence. Kids used to do it all the time fifteen or twenty years ago. But none of them had the audacity to come right up to the Schmidts' front gate and squeal their crummy retread tires. The second time it had happened, Ronald got very angry. He reviewed the security video and was sure he had seen that car before—down at Bollinger's armpit of a repair shop. The last time he'd driven Aunt Ophelia and Thelma Louise there to collect the rent the car hadn't been there. Thelma Louise had actually had the nerve to take

Bollinger's side and support his argument there were a lot of cars that came and went at the place.

Ronald noticed the beginning of Bollinger's criminal trespasses coincided with the rent raises. If Bollinger couldn't afford the increased rent, that was his problem. Those properties were the last vestige of the Schmidts' once-mighty business holdings in Fester. They had to produce income.

When the Unfortunate Incident with Mr. Fitch had happened, they'd had to pay out a lot of money to get him to shut up and move away. (Worth every cent, in Ronald's opinion.) Aunt Ophelia said that they would need to raise the rent again to help make up for the loss. Thelma Louise had argued strenuously against it, saying it was unfair to raise the rent again after so recently having hiked it. That was typical Thelma Louise—she was a total bleeding heart, always fretting about people she didn't even know. It was that college education she'd gotten that turned her weak and foolish. Or rather, weaker and more foolish.

When the subject of the second rent raise had come up, Ronald had supported it wholeheartedly. First, it was always good to have more money—that went without saying. More importantly, he knew another rent raise notice would bring Bollinger back up the hill. And this time, Ronald would be ready for him.

So Ronald had gotten his gun, hidden in the bushes outside the house and waited. Sure enough, Bollinger came back that very night. The lowbrow types of Low Town were predictable. Ronald had only meant to scare Bollinger; he didn't really want to hurt him. Well, not much. The thing was that when the crappy old junker had turned around at the end of the road, Bollinger had gotten out to pour poison on his tires, Ronald had been overcome with rage. His hands had been shaking so hard he really couldn't aim the gun properly. So, yes, perhaps he'd been aiming directly at Bollinger's head, or maybe he'd only been aiming for the radiator. Ronald didn't remember. All he remembered was a fierce sense of satisfaction when the jalopy's windshield shattered. Later, he'd ditched the gun—tossing it off the middle of the Iron Bridge the night after the shooting.

He figured Bollinger couldn't have been hurt too badly—he'd managed to

CHAPTER 35

get his junkheap down the hill and out of sight. Ronald vaguely remembered hearing Bollinger had run his car into a tree down by the country club. It didn't concern him, though. It wasn't his fault that Bollinger couldn't drive.

Besides, he was *glad* that Bollinger was hurt. It was all his damn fault that Ronald was having to deal with another Unfortunate Incident. If Bollinger hadn't taken it into his head to come up to Morningwood Heights where he didn't belong, if he hadn't started disrespecting his social and intellectual betters, none of this would have happened. Just thinking about it made Ronald furious.

Well, he wasn't done with Bollinger yet. He had come up with a way to get back. Soon that Bollinger lowlife would regret he'd ever heard the name Schmidt.

"Don't worry, Peewee," he said, stroking the sleeping monkey in his lap. "I've fixed his little red wagon. It won't be long. Just wait and see."

Chapter 36

"Don't be a fool, boy!" exclaimed Merle Totenkopf. "You don't just go to the law and confess. Even if you *are* guilty. *Especially* then. Jesus!"

"Besides, you don't even know if you done anything," said Vince. "None of us do. Right, Teddy?"

"Ayuh," agreed Ted.

Merle took a pull on his jug, but none of the others had an interest in taking a swig. Merle shook his head. *These boys must have really tied one on*, he thought. He took another hefty knock and said, "Okay, let's go over it again, boys. You went out to Weaverville and raised a little hell, then decided to cap off the night with a trip to the cathouse. What happened then?"

"I don't remember!" exclaimed Harold. "Vince kept pouring those damn tequila shooters into me, then made me take a hit off a joint. I don't remember anything!"

"Hey, I didn't *make* you do anything, ya fuckin' lightweight. You did all that yourself. Don't blame me if you can't handle your high."

"All right, knock it off you knuckleheads!" shouted Merle. "Let's quit pointin' fingers and try to figure out what the fuck actually *happened*."

"I sure as hell don't remember," said Harold. "I vaguely remember coming back into town and pulling into a parking lot. It might have been Food Ape for all I know."

"It weren't no Food Ape," said Vince. "And party boy Harry here actually didn't seem to be in very bad shape, either. He puked it all out on the way back from Weaverville. By the time we got to Mike's Place, he was walkin' and talkin' pretty good. For a lightweight."

"I don't remember any of it!" said Harold. "I must have completely blacked out."

"You're startin' to sound like a broken record, boy," said Merle. "Since you don't remember shit, why don't you let these boys tell it?"

"Thanks, Uncle Merle," said Vince. "Like I was sayin', we were all pretty tore up, but we were gettin' by. We behaved ourselfs well enough for the bouncer to let us in. We got a table and were checkin' out the girlies."

"They were pretty," said Ted with a sappy smile. "I was gonna play with some boobies."

"Sorry it didn't work out for ya, Teddy," said Vince.

"Vince is mad 'cause he got thrown out again," said Ted. "He said somethin' to a girl that she didn't like, and the bouncer threw him out. Me too."

"That sounds about right," said Merle. "So where was Harry when all this was goin' on?"

"Not sure," said Vince. "He'd lit off by then."

"Lit off?" said Merle. "To where? Did he go off with a girl?"

"Don't know," said Vince. "He said he was goin' to take a piss and never came back."

"How long was he gone before you got thrown out?"

"Don't remember," admitted Vince. "I was pretty wasted, too. Can't be sure, but I'd guess he'd been gone for at least ten minutes. Maybe fifteen."

"That's a long time to take a piss," said Merle. "So then what happened when you go thrown out?"

"We went back to the truck and waited for Harry," said Vince. "But he never showed up. We musta waited for at least an hour."

"Nuh-uh" said Ted. "We didn't wait for no more'n ten minutes. I kept checking my watch." He held up the cheap Timex on his left wrist. "I knew I'd never been out that late before, so I kept lookin'. It was ten past one when we got throwed outta the bar, and twenty past when Vince said we're goin' home."

"Awright, awright," said Vince. "Maybe we didn't stick around too long.

If Sweaty Teddy there says it was ten minutes—and you trust him to read a watch right—then I guess it was. Like I said, I was pretty wasted."

"Aw, Vince," said Merle sadly. "You never leave a man behind—especially if they're kin. You were taught better'n that." Merle sighed. "What happened next?"

"I know what happened next," said Harold. "I went home with that poor girl and I killed her! That had to be what happened!"

"You don't know that, boy," said Merle. "You said the next thing you remember was you wakin' up at your place. And your car was there?"

"Yeah, that's right."

"But you left your car up here when you three stooges took off for Weaverville?"

"Yeah."

"So after you got done 'murdering' this girl, you somehow got a ride back up here, then drove yourself home, is that it?"

"I must've got a cab or something," said Harry. "It's the only thing that makes sense."

"If you got a cab," said Ted. "Whyn't the cabbie notice you were covered in blood? Wouldn't he say somethin'?"

Merle looked sharply at Ted. Sometimes he thought his "slow" nephew wasn't as dull as he was made out to be. "That's a good point, Teddy," he said. "Although, in Fester on Saturday night, a cabbie picking up a blood-covered guy might not be all that unusual."

"So where does that leave us?" asked Harold. He was wracked with guilt, compounded by the lingering effects of his overindulgence. He couldn't remember what happened but felt sure he was guilty. Of something. Maybe just taking one toke over the line, maybe murder. Probably murder.

"It leaves us pretty much where we started," said Merle. "You don't know that you did anything besides get fucked up with your cousins and take three steps inside the front door of a whorehouse."

"I've got to tell the constables," said Harold. "They'll figure out what happened."

"They'll figure that out one way or the other," said Merle. "No reason for you to go helpin' them. The law around here's never helped the Totenkopfs. There's no goddamn reason why we should go helpin' them."

"But… " said Harold.

"But me no buts, boy," said Merle. "You ain't goin' to the law. If they decide that you mighta had somethin' to do with this mess, well—that's another story. You can spill your guts then if you want. Until then, there's no point in doin' their job for them. Understood?" He glared at all three of the younger men. They all looked down and nodded.

"Good," said Merle. "Now that that's settled, let's just get some goddamn rest, awright? Harry, maybe you should stay here tonight. The bed in the attic room's made up." The attic room was also the farthest from any of the house telephones, just in case Harold had an attack of conscience in the middle of the night. He'd have to tell Sassy to make sure Harold didn't do something stupid.

"Okay, Pap," said Harold. "I'm gonna go up right now."

"Yeah, that sounds like a good idea," said Vince. "I'm pretty beat."

"You boys really tied one on," said Merle. "Go rest up. Things will look a lot better in the morning."

"I sure hope so," said Harold, and he dragged himself off to the bed in the attic.

"You don't think he did it, do ya Uncle Merle?" asked Ted. His normally open face was scrunched up in concern.

"Aw, hell no. That boy wouldn't say boo to a chinabird, much less commit a murder. We just gotta make sure he don't blow a fuse and go runnin' to the constables with that fairy tale. Now you'n Vince git on outta here. Your bullshit is makin' me tired."

Chapter 37

The main floor was jumping at Mike's Place. It was a busy Saturday night. Every table was occupied and the booze was flowing like tap water. Hostesses shuttled back and forth between tables, then upstairs and downstairs. A lot of the men who accompanied them came right back down for more drinks and food. There were two bouncers working tonight, but so far there hadn't been any trouble.

Mike Solheim was in his office behind the bar, checking the receipts. He was pushing seventy, but tried to keep himself fit and was always fashionably dressed. "Clothes make the man," his father had always said, and Mike had taken that to heart. Especially when a well-tailored suit could conceal an old-guy paunch. And Mike was able to afford all of the well-tailored suits he wanted. Sex sells, and Mike Solheim knew how to sell it at a premium.

From the next room a voice called, "Uh, Boss?" It was Irving Senft, his technical guy and general gopher. Mike found Irving mildly annoying, but the young college dropout was too damn useful to get rid of.

"What is it?" snapped Mike. He was trying to straighten out a snarl in the books. "Jesus, can this wait?"

"I don't think so. You really need to come now." There was a note of alarm in Irving's voice that made Mike forget all about receipts.

He hurried into the next room—a big closet, really—where Irving had his computers and security monitors. Irving's normally pale face was now chalk-white, which made Mike's stomach do a quick barrel-roll. Something was definitely wrong. "What the fuck is it?" he demanded.

"Camera one," said Irving, pointing at one of the dozen video monitors

CHAPTER 37

in the array.

Mike hurried over and squinted at the screen. Camera one showed a view of the entrance from Slocum Street. It currently showed a convoy of constabulary cruisers speeding into the parking lot. As he watched, a half dozen cruisers slid in, followed by a line of police trucks.

"Oh, *fuck!*" exclaimed Mike. He bolted from the tech closet and rushed into the main room, yelling, *"Raid!* Lock the door! *Lock the fucking d—"*

He was too late. A phalanx of constables in riot gear slammed through the door. One of them grabbed Jerry, the bouncer who was on the front door, spun him around and cuffed him. The rest fanned out across the main room.

Panic descended on Mike's Place. Most of the patrons were too shocked to react and soon found themselves up against the wall with their zip-tied hands behind their backs. The hostesses were savvy enough to bolt for the back door the moment the constables burst in, and a number of the customers were sharp enough to follow the hostesses. A flying wedge of constables in riot gear peeled off from the main group and made a beeline for the back door.

In the front door came Martin Prieboy. Dan Blount followed close behind. He surveyed the interior of Mike's Place with grim satisfaction. From the corner of his eye, he spotted Mike Solheim attempting to run back to the office behind the bar. "Stop that man!" commanded Martin, pointing at Solheim. Two constables grabbed him by the shoulders and hauled him over to where Martin stood.

"What the hell, Prieboy?" asked Solheim. "What's going on?"

"I think you know what's going on," said Martin. "We have received reports that your bar is a front for illegal activity. I intend to put a stop to it."

"Aw, Jesus," whined Solheim. "You know we—"

"Shut up!" commanded Martin. "We'll discuss this in your office. That is, unless you want to go down to headquarters right now."

"No, no," said Solheim, shaking his head. "The office is fine." Martin gave the nod and the constables let him go.

"Let's go, then," said Martin. "Inspector Blount, you keep an eye on things in here."

Solheim led Martin to the back rooms. When he got to the tech closet, he was gratified to see there was a red light flashing on the wall. That meant Irving had managed to hit the panic button that alerted the girls upstairs there was trouble. Irving was nowhere in sight. There was a small window open at the top of the room and a dirty footprint on the table below it.

When they arrived in Solheim's office, he flopped down behind his desk and wearily indicated that Martin should have a seat across from him.

"I'll stand," said Martin, shutting the door behind him.

"I repeat," said Solheim. "What the hell, Prieboy? We had a deal."

"*Had* being the operative word," said Martin. "The deal was that I left you alone if nobody was coerced or got hurt. Well, Charlene Troutman is *dead*, so the deal's off."

"Hey, hey, hey!" said Solheim. "That had nothing to do with me or my place. It didn't even happen here!"

"Oh, for the love of Jesus!" said Martin, barely able to keep the rage out of his voice. "Don't try to tell me that it wasn't one of your scumbag customers who killed her."

"You can't prove anything!" said Solheim. He was now wishing that instead of trying to warn the bouncer, that he had locked himself in his office and called his lawyer.

"Not yet," said Martin. "But I intend to." He jerked his chin back at the tech closet. "What's that flashing light on the wall mean?"

"Radon detector," said Solheim, who was determined to be uncooperative. "The safety of my employees is of paramount importance.

"Except for the ones who get murdered," said Martin. "Looks like someone made it out the window. Who was it?"

"That was me. I cranked a nasty fart and stood on the table to open the window."

"Look, Solheim, you're in some serious trouble here, do you realize that? You're looking at another, I don't know, five years in Camp Hill. Maybe more, since you're a repeat offender."

CHAPTER 37

"Yeah, if you can make it stick. Which you can't." Solheim had a quaver in his voice now. His previous time in prison had not made him eager to repeat the experience. He had barely made it through his stretch before, and he had been twenty years younger then. He'd never last in lockup now, no matter how much money he spread around to grease his way.

"We can make it stick," said Martin. "I'm sure some of the fine citizens out there would provide some corroborating evidence if it meant keeping their name out of the paper."

"The *fine citizens* out there were doing nothing more than enjoying a drink and watching a Pirates game on TV. Nothing illegal there. In fact, I wouldn't be surprised if you were hit with a raft of lawsuits for false arrest."

"Well, perhaps not the ones out there, but the ones upstairs," said Martin.

"Upstairs? What would be going on upstairs?" said Solheim with mock innocence.

Martin remembered the flashing light on the wall. "So, one of your peons sounded the alarm and climbed out the window? Well, we'll see how fast he really was." He put his fingers in his mouth and gave a sharp whistle. Almost immediately, a constable was in the room. "Constable Sitler, keep an eye on this man until I return. No phone calls and no computer use, understood?" The constable nodded and Martin went back out to the bar room.

He found Blount questioning one of the girls. "Step over here, Inspector Blount," Martin said. When they had a bit of privacy, Martin asked. "How did things go upstairs?"

"Not so good, Chief. There were two back exits. We had one of them covered, the one on the ground floor. But there was another—a fire escape on the second floor on the other side of the building. A lot of the people who were upstairs went out that way. There's a hole in the fence to that junkyard next door. Do you want me to call Weaverville for chopper support?"

"Good lord, no," said Martin. "We don't need to involve any outside agencies here. Just get a couple of cars patrolling the neighborhood. Maybe some of them ran off naked—we can pick them up for public indecency. At the very least, we need to make sure they're okay. Running around half-naked in a junkyard in the dark can't be very safe. Dan, at least tell me you got *some* of the ones upstairs."

"Yeah, a few," Blount admitted. "Some of them were too, uh, engaged to make a timely getaway," he said with a smirk. "Got three of the girls and two of the johns."

"Any of them known to us, good, bad, or indifferent?" Martin was hoping to have bagged someone higher up on the social scale; someone who'd be willing to provide evidence in return for having the charges dropped.

Blount shook his head. "Couple of nobodies: some redneck from out by Kugels and a college boy from Prosser."

"Okay, not the grand haul we had hoped, but it's better than nothing. Take the ones you caught upstairs down to headquarters for questioning."

"Will do, Chief. What about these guys?" he indicated the men and women who were still up against the wall with plastic cuffs.

"Cut them loose," said Martin. "Let them go."

"Won't some of them be pissed? They might make a fuss—start hollering about police harassment and false arrest."

"I doubt it," said Martin. "I'm sure they were informed they were just being detained, not arrested. Most of them will be so relieved to be off the hook, they'll slink off into the night. Make sure the entrance to the parking lot is clear—let's allow them to get out of here. The ones you bagged upstairs—take them downtown. Get some cars patrolling for the runaways. I will figure out what to do with Mr. Solheim."

He left Blount to do the mopping up and went back to Solheim's office. "Well, Mr. Solheim," he said. "Your snake might have sounded the alarm and wriggled out, but he wasn't fast enough for all the fornicators upstairs to get away. We caught enough to make your life interesting. Five years in Camp Hill, easy."

"You don't want to mess with me, Prieboy," sneered Solheim. "I've got important friends in Fester. I have friends in the Top Hat families—*all* of them."

Martin shrugged. "I don't give a hoot if you're friends with the president or friends with the pope." The Top Hats didn't quite swing the same weight

CHAPTER 37

as they once did. On the other hand, even a dissipated family like the Schmidts still had enough influence to interfere with a serious criminal investigation—that much had been made clear. "You're right," said Martin. "I don't want to mess with you."

"Huh?"

"What I want, Mr. Solheim, is to find out who killed Charlene Troutman. And you are going to help me."

"What? How? Look, it didn't even happen here—it was at her place. I can't believe she was freelancing like that. She knew it was against the rules."

Martin resisted the urge to belt the man. He couldn't believe a pimp was lecturing him about following rules. "I'm convinced Charlene was murdered by a customer from your place." Solheim started to object but Martin held up his hand to silence him. "Ah, I don't want to hear it, Solheim. I want to know every customer that Charlene was with over the last week."

"What? You have to be kidding! I don't have that information! Besides, I could never give it out even if I did. My customers' privacy is of—"

"Don't hand me that crap!" snapped Martin. "Don't act like there's some sort of Pimp's Code protecting your johns! The Pimp's Code is all about protecting your own butt, and yours is in a sling right now. I've already seen your TV studio in there; don't try and tell me it's for watching all of your favorite streaming series."

Martin sat down across from Solheim and leaned in. "Listen, Mike," he said. "Your choice is simple. You can provide me with the information I want. If that happens, things will settle down pretty quickly. You stay closed for a week or so, then very quietly open back up. We're back to our original arrangement and nobody needs to be concerned about what happened this evening.

"The alternative is that you dig in your heels and make my life difficult. If that's the case, I will do everything I can to make sure you go back to prison. Maybe you'll be convicted and maybe you won't. Either way, it's going to be a lot of bad publicity and lawyer's fees. And you with no income, since this place will stay closed. *And* I'll get the information I need one way or another, so you'd be stupid to not play ball. *Really* stupid."

Solheim stuck his jaw out and looked truculent, but Martin knew he'd beaten him. After a moment, he slumped and said, "Okay, fine. I'll get you the video from Candy's crib for the past week and all this goes away, all right?"

"That's the deal."

"I don't know if we keep the video for a whole week. Might not be more than a day or two. I'll have to get my IT guy in to retrieve the files. I don't know how to do all that fancy computer stuff."

"Is he the snake who slithered through the window?" asked Martin. Solheim rolled his eyes to the ceiling. "Just get him in here, Solheim. The faster you get me those files, the faster you can go home. I'll also call down to headquarters and release the ones we hauled off from upstairs."

"You don't leave me much of choice, Prieboy. I guess I'll have to go along."

"You won't get a better deal, Solheim. Count on it. Now make the call."

Chapter 38

At his desk the next morning, Martin shuffled through a stack of paperwork. He wanted to get all the administrative busywork out of the way as soon as possible, so he could get going on the real police work. He still had some involvement with the Schmidt case, but that was now largely the problem of the DA in Weaverville.

The Schmidt mess was of minor importance next to the Troutman murder case. It consumed Martin's thoughts. He had spent most of the night tossing and turning. Of the dozens of jumbled thoughts that tumbled through his mind, this was the loudest: was he too close to this case?

Charlene's death had hit him hard. He didn't want to say it felt to him like losing a child—he didn't want to cheapen the experience of parents who have had to go through such a horror. Yet losing Charlene was the closest thing he could imagine to that. Charlene Troutman was funny, smart, and empathetic, and Martin had cared for her very much.

Martin saw now that he had in some sense transferred the protectiveness he'd had for Sam onto Charlene. They were paternal feelings; good-cop feelings—to protect and serve. He hadn't been able to protect Sam, but should have been able to protect Charlene. He hadn't, and his failure was tearing at him.

Over the course of four decades in law enforcement, Martin had encountered hundreds of extremely nasty crime scenes. Yet nothing was so deeply disturbing as finding Charlene's body in the bathtub of her apartment. It still upset him a great deal—and it made him question his own judgment.

His raid on Mike's Place was the most obvious example of this. Martin had been so *angry*—looking for someone at whom to lash out. Mike Solheim was an easy target. Martin had rushed the raid, just wanting to grab Solheim and shake him for what had happened to Charlene. Not checking the place out, not covering all of the exits properly—that was just sloppy. If one of his subordinates had performed like that, they would have been lucky to have gotten away with only a reprimand.

No, he *had* gotten too close to the case. The next mistake he made might be more consequential. It might allow the killer to go undetected or escape justice. Martin couldn't let that happen. He owed it to Charlene to make sure her case was handled with the utmost skill and care. And he wasn't sure that he could do that right now.

He shook his head. He'd turn the case over to Dan Blount. He hated to do it but felt it was right for Charlene. Martin would still be involved, of course—*closely* involved. But it would be Blount's show. He was reaching for the phone when the intercom buzzed.

"Sorry to bother you, Chief," said the duty sergeant. "There's a guy here who says he knows who killed the Troutman girl."

Martin sighed. Whenever there was a high-profile case like this—and especially when it was a murder case—the weirdos came out of the woodwork. "Get a name and number," he said. "And tell them a detective will get back to them."

"No, I don't think you understand, Chief—the guy's here at the front desk. He seems pretty agitated. He doesn't seem like a run-of-the-mill crazy, either."

"Okay," said Martin. "I'll come down." He really didn't have time for this nonsense, but he needed to step away from talking himself in circles. He'd take a few minutes to humor this person then call Blount and hand the case over to him.

When he arrived at the front desk, the duty sergeant nodded at a man sitting in one of the uncomfortable chairs in the waiting area. The man looked innocuous—late twenties, well-groomed, well-dressed. Looked like a professional, not one of the usual street whackos or retired busybodies

CHAPTER 38

who injected themselves into big police cases. Martin presented himself to the man and held out his hand. "I'm Chief Constable Martin Prieboy. I understand you have some information that might be of use to us."

"Uh, yeah, hi," said the man. He stood up and shook Martin's hand. "I'm Harold Todd. Is there somewhere we can go to talk?"

"Certainly," said Martin. "We can go to an interview room." The man was clearly very nervous—he was pale, his hands shook slightly and there was a sheen of perspiration on his forehead.

Martin led Harold Todd to Room #3, the nicest of the interview rooms. It was still pretty stark, with cinderblock walls and small, wire-reinforced windows set high in the walls. The furniture was from Ikea, though, and it was relatively clean and well-lit.

When they were seated across from each other at the Skogsta table, Martin repeated, "So you say you have some information pursuant to one of our cases?"

"Yes," said Harold. "I think I know who killed that poor Charlene Troutman."

"You do? Who?"

"Well, I uh, I ... I think it was me!" blurted Harold.

Martin leaned back. So, it was another false confession. It just went to show that the looney tunes came in all shapes and sizes—especially in Fester. Harold was sobbing now and holding his hands out in front of him.

"Why are you doing that?" asked Martin.

"So you can arrest me!" wailed Harold. "I'm under arrest, aren't I?"

"Nobody's under arrest, Mr. Todd," said Martin. "You look familiar—do I know you?" Most people looked familiar to Martin—he was always mentally snapping pictures and filing them away. Martin had been in Fester a long time, long enough to have encountered many of the town's residents once or twice—and some many more times than that.

"I don't know that we've met before," said Harold. "I was on TV last week, though—on the news. Maybe you saw me there."

"You can put your hands down, Mr. Todd. So why were you on the news, if you don't mind me asking."

"I am the general manager of the Hickory Acres Mall. We had a Fourth of July Fair, and some people thought they saw something weird. It made the news."

"Does this have anything to do with the Troutman case?"

"No, not really. Only tangentially, I guess."

"Please explain."

Harold ran through the whole story of his celebration with his cousins that caused Harold to black out. When he finished, he slumped back in his chair and held his hands out again.

"No cuffs, Mr. Todd. Your name wasn't originally Todd, though, was it? You're one of the Totenkopfs, aren't you? That's where I know you from."

Harold kept his hands held out. "Yes, that's right—I'm one of the terrible Totenkopfs. The town's original no-goodnik clan of hillbillies and troublemakers. I guess you really want to cuff me now, huh?"

Martin resisted the urge to grind his teeth. All Todd knew for sure was that he'd gotten wasted with some of his cousins and blacked out. Martin pointed that out to him.

"But don't you see? I was *at* Mike's Place. Where that girl worked. It had to be me!"

"Because you woke up covered in blood?"

"Yes, that's right. I must have stabbed that poor girl. I was out of my mind! It was that damn Vince and his tequila shots!"

"I see." Charlene Troutman hadn't been stabbed; she'd been strangled. The coroner reported contusions and small cuts around her face—she had been hit shortly before being strangled. The coroner suggested the assailant had been wearing a heavy ring on his right hand that had opened up the cut. That accounted for the small blood spots Martin had found on the carpet. It certainly wouldn't have been enough to soak through this man's shirt. It was, after all, another bogus confession. Yet this man—who otherwise seemed respectable—seemed like he *wanted* to be responsible for this horrible crime. He definitely wanted to be handcuffed. Well, that was something that this guy needed to work out with his therapist.

"You say that you arrived at Mike's Place at what time last Saturday?"

CHAPTER 38

asked Martin.

"I was too blotto to remember," said Harold. "But my cousin says that he and Vince got thrown out about one. We probably hadn't been there that long—Vince usually gets us thrown out of places pretty quick—so I'd guess we got there around twelve-thirty."

"Maybe we can clear things up and shed some light on what went on once you arrived at Mike's Place. Excuse me, won't you? This should only take a few minutes." He got up and went to the door.

"Don't you want to shackle me to the table or something?" asked Harold.

Martin shook his head. Harold Todd must be some sort of latent bondage enthusiast. "No, Mr. Todd, you are not under arrest. I will leave the door unlocked. You are free to leave any time." He closed the door behind him, hoping Todd would take him up on his offer.

Martin went back to his office and spent fifteen minutes reviewing the security video from Saturday night. Mike Solheim had had his tech guy provide Martin with all of the recorded feeds from the previous two weeks. Martin couldn't bring himself to view the feed of Charlene with her customers. He'd had Dan Blount review it and get good screen grabs of the customers' faces. There was no need for any of the salacious video now. He got all he needed from the cameras in the main room.

He returned to the interview room. Todd was still there. "Well, Mr. Todd, I think we can put your mind at ease about this matter." He put the laptop down in front of Harold, then pulled the other chair around the table so he was sitting next to him.

"What's this?" asked Harold.

"Video from Mike's Place from last Saturday night. Let's watch." He opened a window for the feed from the main entrance and hit the space bar. It showed the bouncer checking the IDs of Harold, Vince, and Ted then waving them in. The time stamp was 00:34. The three then weaved their way off camera.

"Probably shouldn't have let you in," said Martin. "Being that you were visibly intoxicated. I won't even comment on your cousin driving while imbibing." He switched cameras to one in the main room. It showed Harold and his cousins being ushered to a table and sitting. Martin hit the fast forward button: at high speed, a pitcher of beer arrived, was poured out, consumed. There was much hilarity and handwaving. Occasionally, a hostess would come by but wouldn't stay long. Suddenly, Harold stood up from the table and walked off. Martin froze the playback. "Where did you go?" he asked.

"I think I went to take a leak."

"You did. There's video from the men's room, but I think we can skip that. Let's keep watching what went on at the table." He fast forwarded ten minutes. Vince and Ted sat at the table, continued to drink and laugh. Another hostess came by and Martin slowed the feed down to normal speed.

The video showed the hostess and Vince talking. He must have said something she didn't like, because she leaned over Vince and started yelling at him. Vince reached out and tweaked her nipple through her tight-fitting top. She turned and yelled, and almost immediately a bouncer appeared at the table. The bouncer picked Vince up by his hair and frog-marched him towards the front door. Ted followed closely behind.

Martin fast forwarded a few more minutes and Harold came wobbling back into the view. He looked at the table, then looked around in confusion, then wobbled out of view.

"For a few more minutes, you wander around the room looking for your cousins."

"Yes, but where was I after I left the table?" asked Harold. He sounded like a defense lawyer who had just spotted a hole in the prosecution's case. "Maybe I went up and found—"

"Since you asked," said Martin. He switched to another feed showing the interior of the men's room. Harold was leaning up against the wall in front of a urinal. His pants and underpants were around his knees. He appeared to be snoring. "You were taking a nap while relieving yourself, it appears," said Martin. "Would you like to see more?"

"No, that will do," said Harold hurriedly.

Martin skipped to another view, that showing a closeup of the bar. Harold could be seen staggering back and forth through the frame, then hauling

CHAPTER 38

himself up to the bar and making a grand pronouncement to the bartender. The bartender seemed to demur and Harold shook his head, holding up three fingers. The bartender shrugged, laid out three shot glasses, and filled them from a square green bottle.

"Dear God," said Harold, staring lividly at the laptop. "Did I order three shots of Jägermeister?"

"That bartender should feel lucky I don't arrest him for serving a clearly intoxicated person," said Martin.

"*I* should feel lucky I'm still alive!" exclaimed Harold. "Three shots of Jäger on top of the crap I'd already had. Dear Christ!"

"Not quite three," said Martin. "Watch now."

On the video feed, Harold tossed back the first two shots quickly, then picked up the third and gestured grandly with the shot glass. He seemed to be making a toast. Then, before he could bring the glass to his lips, he spun and keeled over. He fell against the bar, where his face made solid contact with the thick wooden nosing of the bar. A huge gout of blood shot out of his nose and splashed down the front of his shirt. On screen, Harold opened his mouth and yelled while those around him shrank away from the blood which was splashing all around him.

"It goes on like this for a bit," said Martin, nodding at the screen where Harold was vainly trying to staunch the flow of blood with a handful of cocktail napkins. He switched the feed again. "Here's the finale," he said.

The view cut to an exterior shot of the entrance. One of the bouncers was supporting a shaky Harold as a yellow cab pulled up. The bouncer bundled Harold into the back seat and walked away, wiping his hands on the seat of his pants. The cab pulled away into the night.

"There you have it, Mr. Todd," said Martin. "You're off the hook. No murder—you didn't even talk to one of the girls from what I can see. Just a bit too much to drink and a fall on the face."

"'A bit'?" said Harold. "I'm lucky I didn't end up in the ICU after all that shit. Three shots of Jägermeister! I should give up drinking entirely."

"That's your choice," said Martin, who hardly ever touched the stuff himself. "You would certainly avoid further such incidents if you did."

Harold looked around the interview room as if he were seeing it for the first time. "Jesus," he said, and ran a hand through his already-mussed hair. "Jesus, what a relief! I really thought I'd hurt that poor girl. Oh, God!"

"You seemed pretty convinced you were responsible," said Martin. "It's really not all that uncommon."

"Christ, I don't know why I was so sure I had done it," said Harold. "I've been under a lot of stress at work lately. I guess it's just taken its toll."

"That's quite all right, Mr. Todd—I understand, believe me," said Martin. "I appreciate your willingness to cooperate." *Now please get out of here so we can get to work finding the real killer,* he mentally added.

"Okay, fine, thank you," said Harold, rising unsteadily to his feet. "I'll just get out of your hair, then."

"I'll show you to the door," said Martin.

When he had ushered Mr. Todd to the front door, Martin returned to his office. Todd had provided him with nothing other than an unwanted distraction. He thumbed through the case folders on his desk, still uncertain of what to do. He hated to give up the case. He felt an acute responsibility to Charlene. If he had insisted she get out of her line of work earlier, if he had lent her money to pay for college last year. A chain of *ifs* could lead him around the bend. No, for Charlene's sake—and the sake of his own mental health—he would let Dan Blount take over the investigation.

There was a knock at the door.

"What?" called out Martin. He did not want another distraction right now.

It was one of the crime scene techs, a young man named Hamberger. "Sorry to bother you, Chief," said Hamberger. "I thought you'd want to see this right away."

Martin's head snapped up. "Yes, Constable Hamberger, what do you have?"

"We decided to make a secondary search of the Troutman crime scene. As you know, there wasn't a lot to start with."

Martin nodded. The perp had done an amazing job of covering his tracks. They had vacuumed every square inch of the carpet and swabbed down the

CHAPTER 38

entire bathroom and found very little forensic evidence that couldn't be directly connected with Charlene or her friends.

"Well, we went back and did another sweep of the apartment, focusing on secondary evidential locations. We discovered this behind the stove." He held up a small evidence bag containing a credit card. There were several splotches of blood on it.

Martin leaned up and squinted at the card. The name of the owner was known to him. His pulse sped up. This was the first real break in the case.

"What about the bloodstains on the card?" asked Martin.

"We've already tested it," said Hamberger. "It's a match with the victim."

"Very good, Constable, thank you. You are dismissed."

"Should I leave this with you, Chief?"

"No, take it back to the evidence locker. Make sure all of the blood evidence is well-preserved. That is all."

Hamberger opened his mouth to say something more but must have caught the dark look on Martin's face. He turned on his heel and left.

Martin sat for several minutes, thinking. This was a very strange turn of events—he had not expected to see the name on the card. Something twitched in his memory. The johns—he had casually flipped though the stills that Blount had made of the feed from Charlene's crib. Martin really hadn't liked looking at them—there were just so *many*. But maybe he had seen the credit card owner.

He pulled the folder from the stack on his desk and began flipping through the stills, scrutinizing each one. There were several faces he recognized but had no interest in lingering on. About two thirds of the way through the stack, he found the one he was looking for. It was the man whose name was on the credit card.

Martin closed the folder and replaced it in the stack. There was no question of handing the case over to Blount now. He was going to take care of this himself.

Chapter 39

At Bollinger Automotive, Bolly was confined to the office. His arm was starting to heal but he still hadn't regained full use. He had gotten tired of hanging around the house, loopy on painkillers and not really accomplishing anything. It had been okay at first, and he had been content to pop pills and watch shows about World War II on the History Channel. That had grown stale very quickly, and he soon became restless.

He was still worried about the garage's finances. Despite the fact his landlord had shot him—or so the constables alleged—Bolly was still on the hook for the rent. He'd received a formal letter from the law firm of Nasté, Brutus, and Shore informing him that in the future, his rent should be remitted directly to their office. That was fine with Bolly. It meant no more creepy late-night handoffs to an old Cadillac full of weirdos.

Bolly had been interviewed again by Chief Constable Prieboy and twice by an investigator for the DA's office in Weaverville. He hadn't even *seen* the person who shot him. The shooter could have been a sasquatch in a green neon track suit for all Bolly knew.

The idea that Ronald Schmidt had shot him—perhaps intending to kill him—was surreal. Of course, there had been plenty of rumors about Ronnie the Rake, like how he had attacked his next-door neighbor and run him out of town. There had always been stories about Ronald tearing up some dive bar in a brawl he started, then getting off scot-free. The Schmidts, however diminished, still had enough pull to keep one of their own from having to be accountable for his misbehavior.

CHAPTER 39

Bolly figured that was probably going to happen again this time. There were already mutterings around town about how Ronnie the Rake had been handled with kid gloves—spent no time in a cell, was arraigned and posted bail almost immediately, and was back at his mansion in time for afternoon tea. Everyone figured he'd managed to wriggle off the hook for the attempted murder charge, too. Money talked and bullshit walked in Fester as with anywhere else.

Bolly resented the idea—or at least he had until Janie had pointed out that one of the ways the Schmidts and people like them had managed to weasel out of their legal transgressions was by forking over cash to the victims. It was rumored Alexander Fitch had financed his relocation to Boca Raton with the payout he'd received after the rake attack.

Bolly was of two minds about this. On one hand, a big lump sum of cash would not be unwelcomed. It would definitely take care of the rent problem, perhaps indefinitely. If it was big enough, Bolly might be able to buy his own place outright. He and Janie had discussed it extensively, but for now it was all just wishing and speculation. Besides, Bolly would be just as happy to see Ronald Schmidt spend time in jail, even if it meant missing a big payout.

Either way, Bolly still had bills to pay, and the business's cushion was quickly evaporating. He had insisted on coming to the shop for no other reason than to try to feel useful. Janie had strenuously objected, and made Bolly's mechanics, Larry and Bob, promise they wouldn't let Bolly work on any of the cars, and would make him stay in the office. They had done that so far, but Bolly thought he might go in the back lot and poke around on an old AMC Javelin. He thought he might start fixing it up once he was done with the Firebird.

He dug through a stack of invoices, trying to triage the ones that had to be paid right away and which ones could wait. The phone rang. It was Janie.

"What's up, babe?" he asked.

"Oh, I don't know, Bolly. That Chief Prieboy was here, h-he just left." Bolly could hear her voice shaking.

"He came to your office? What did he want? I thought that the DA's inspector was taking care of all this shooting business."

"That's just it," said Janie. "He didn't ask *anything* a-about the shooting. He was asking about that damned M-m-mike's Place. He wanted to know if you ever w-went there, and if we ever fought about it."

Bolly felt his stomach drop. He didn't know why Prieboy would be asking questions about his visits to Mike's Place, but he didn't think that it was a good thing. What on Earth did that have to do with Ronald Schmidt trying to kill him?

"What did you tell him?" asked Bolly.

"I don't know," said Janie, who was now on the verge of tears. "I guess I told him the truth. I just said you'd gone there, and I found out about it. I told him about our fight. I was so surprised, I didn't know what else to do!" She broke down sobbing.

"It's okay, babe, it's okay," he soothed. "I'm sure it's nothing."

"O-okay," she sobbed. "I'm sorry if I did anything wrong. I'm going home, Bolly—this really upset me. Janice is letting me take the rest of the day as sick time."

"It's okay," he repeated. "Look, how about if I just head home? I'm done sorting through invoices, anyway."

"Y-yeah, I'd like that. Please."

"Be right there, babe," said Bolly, and he hung up.

He was putting on his jacket when Larry called from the garage, "Hey Boss, there's a law dog here says he needs to talk to you."

Bolly walked out to the garage. Chief Constable Prieboy was there with another constable standing just behind him. Larry and Bob were on the far side of the bay, casting dark glances at the cops.

"Hello, Chief Prieboy," said Bolly with a friendly self-confidence that was entirely feigned. "What can I do for you today?"

"I was wondering if you could tell me," said Prieboy, "if you've ever patronized an establishment called Mike's Place."

Despite the heads-up from Janie, Bolly was flabbergasted. He hemmed and hawed, unsure of what to say.

"Maybe this will help refresh your memory," said Prieboy. He shoved a

CHAPTER 39

piece of computer paper in Bolly's face. On it was a screen grab showing Bolly walking down the upper hallway at Mike's Place with Candy.

"Okay, yeah, that's me," he muttered, deeply embarrassed and now becoming slightly scared. What was this all about?

"So you admit that you patronized Mike's Place and engaged the services of one Charlene Troutman, working name Candy?"

"Uh, I think I should have a lawyer or some—"

"Where were you last Saturday evening, the night of the 2nd?"

Fear blazed in Bolly's gut. Whatever was going on was *serious*. "Uh, I, um, was working at the shop," he said. He was pretty sure he'd been dinking around with the Firebird, getting it ready to sell.

"Can anybody verify this?" asked Prieboy. "Was anyone here with you?"

"Uh, no."

"How unfortunate," said Prieboy. "Mr. Bollinger, did you not tell your wife that you 'should have killed' Charlene 'Candy' Troutman?"

Bolly's eyes widened. He had heard something about a murder, and that it might have been connected to Mike's Place. He'd been too gakked out on pain meds to pay it much attention. He hadn't realized that it had been Candy who had been murdered—and now the constables suspected *him!*

"I...I didn't..." Bolly huffed. "I might have said something like that, but I didn't *mean* it! We were fighting! I wouldn't hurt Candy, or Charlene or whatever her real name is. I haven't seen her in over a month!"

"I see," said Prieboy. "I was wondering if you might be able to identify this." He held up a small plastic bag with an evidence label stuck to it.

Bolly squinted at the bag. "What the fuck? That's my credit card!" How had the cops gotten his credit card? He hardly ever used the thing—it was for emergencies only. He couldn't remember the last time he'd used it.

Instinctively, his hand went to his rear pocket to check his wallet, but before it got there, a handcuff was slapped on it.

"Michael Bollinger," intoned Prieboy. "You are under arrest for the murder of Charlene Troutman."

Chapter 40

In his cell in Kerian County Jail, Bolly felt like he was losing his mind. He struggled to make sense of what had occurred. He'd thought his spat with Janie—and the whole mess at Mike's Place—as the worst thing that had happened to him. Things couldn't have possibly gotten worse.

Then he'd been shot and wrapped his car around a tree. Things couldn't possibly get worse after *that*.

Then he'd been arrested for murder.

It seemed like he'd been thrown into a horror movie. He didn't understand what was happening or why. The ride in the back of the cruiser to the jail in Weaverville had been surreal. Another constable was driving, and Prieboy rode shotgun. It seemed an appropriate description, as Prieboy peppered him with questions the whole ride—a buckshot blast of recrimination. Bolly had seen enough cop shows to know to keep his mouth shut. He'd have to get a lawyer—or there would be one appointed for him. How would that happen? He guessed he'd be allowed to call Janie. She could get some money from her folks to hire a lawyer. Of course, that would just reinforce their opinion of Bolly as a lowlife who had stolen their sweet baby away and condemned her to the drudgery of the wife of an auto mechanic.

The opinion of his in-laws was of minor import. He had bigger things to worry about now: *murder*.

The notion was insane. Bolly was no murderer. He was no tough guy. Sure, he had gotten in a few fights when he was young, dumb, and full of malarkey. He was big enough that he'd usually won them. But he'd never

CHAPTER 40

started any and hadn't thrown a punch in decades. He certainly hadn't killed anyone. He couldn't imagine why anyone would think he had.

During the course of Prieboy's rapid-fire questioning, Bolly came to understand they thought he'd killed Candy because she had seduced him into cheating on Janie. That Bolly held her responsible for ruining his marriage and had killed her out of revenge. It was ludicrous. Sure, Bolly had fucked up by patronizing Candy, but he'd made that decision of his own free will.

Then there was the matter of his Visa card. Prieboy had said it had been found at the crime scene, and that it had the victim's blood on it. If that was true, Bolly had no idea how it had gotten there. He couldn't even remember the last time he had used it—or even seen it. Bolly was a mostly cash-only guy—a fact that drove Janie nuts.

His arrival at the Kerian County lockup was a bad dream. They gave him an orange jumpsuit and plastic sandals and bagged his personal possessions. Then they stuck him in an isolation cell—"to make sure you sober up," said the guard. There he sat for several hours. Bolly had no idea of the time, but it seemed like someone slid the observation door to the cell open every half-hour to check on him.

They finally took him out and gave him the standard treatment. First was the booking mugshot, then the fingerprints. Then he was given his phone call—from an ancient wall-mounted rotary phone. Of course he called Janie.

"Hello?" she said. This was followed by a recorded announcement saying the call was coming from the county jail. "What?" she said. "What is this? If this is supposed to be a joke, it isn't funny!"

"It's me, babe," said Bolly. "No joke. I've been arrested."

"Arrested! For what?"

Bolly could barely get the word out: "Murder."

There was a long silence. "You *are* joking. You *have to* be joking."

Bolly could hear the desperation in her voice, and it broke his heart. "No, they think I killed that woman from Mike's Place."

"Oh no!" she wailed. *"Oh no!* When I told the cop that you had ... been with her, and that we fought about it. Well—*oh God, I'm so sorry, Bolly!* I thought he was just, y'know, gathering information to bust that place. I didn't think they'd arrest you for *murder!*"

Yeah, well they did, Chatty Cathy, thought Bolly, then immediately regretted it. It wasn't her fault—she'd just told the truth. "It's true. I'm in jail in Weaverville."

"What do I do? *What do I do?*" He could hear the panic in her voice.

"First thing, Janie, is to stay calm, okay? I need you to keep your head on straight. Take a deep breath, okay?"

"Okay."

"Good. Okay, I'm gonna need a lawyer. As soon as possible."

"Okay, okay," said Janie. She sounded calmer now. "Do we have enough money for one?"

"Probably not," said Bolly. "You can check the savings account, but I don't think there's enough for a decent lawyer." *Probably not even enough for an indecent one,* Bolly thought.

"That's okay. I'll call Daddy. He'll be able to help out."

Bolly sighed. At least Mr. Simmons wasn't as condescending as his wife—but they were both sure to hate him now. Especially when it comes out that he'd fooled around with a prostitute. Well, fuck it. He could deal with the social niceties with the in-laws later. If there was a later.

Bolly felt a rising tide of panic. He'd been trying to keep cool to keep Janie cool, but he could feel his control slipping.

"Okay, time's up," said a guard. "Cut it short or I will." He moved towards the phone.

"Oh, shit," said Bolly. "I guess I gotta go now."

"Okay, Babe—I ... I don't know what to say. I love ..."

The guard's hand came down on the cradle, cutting the call. "C'mon, loverboy," he said. "Time to meet your new bunkies."

Bolly's stomach dropped. Here it was—the ultimate in fear. He didn't care about the insane murder charge—he just wanted to survive the next few hours. There were two things he was sure of: he was going to be in a fight, and someone was going to try to buttfuck him. He wasn't worried

CHAPTER 40

about the former. He may not have been in a fight in ages, but he was sure he could hold his own. He'd stayed in shape by hoisting car parts around all day.

As for being sexually assaulted—what could he do other than fight like hell? He figured he could hold off one or two guys, but if more than two came at him, he was toast. Either way, he'd fight like hell. Cause enough damage so they'd think twice about trying to cornhole him again.

"Where's this one going?" the guard asked another guard behind a desk.

"Ward C," came the reply.

"Ward C? Really?" asked the guard. The guard behind the desk just shrugged.

"Come on, precious," said the guard, giving Bolly's shoulder a shove. "You must have a guardian angel or somethin.'"

"Huh?" said Bolly. "Why's that?"

The guard pulled his billy club from its holster and smacked it lightly in his hand. "Ward C's for good little boys. You look like a fuckin' troublemaker to me. Tell you what, precious—you fuck up or cause any trouble, you're goin' to Ward A with the *real* hard boys. I guar-on-tee it!" He punctuated this threat by jabbing the billy into Bolly's kidney.

"No trouble from me," gasped Bolly. At least they weren't putting him in with the real bad dudes. Still, there was no telling what he would encounter in Ward C.

The guard led him to an elevator which opened onto an alcove with yet another heavy Plexiglas-shielded desk. Another bored-looking guard sat at the desk. "Who we got?" asked the desk guard without looking up.

"Bollinger, Michael," said Bolly's guard. "Going into Ward C."

The desk guard checked something on his computer terminal and stood up. "All right—let's go." He used a key card to open a door at the end of the alcove. The door opened onto a large open area painted a dull battleship gray. The space was empty. On the far wall were three heavy steel doors with the letters A, B, and C painted on them. The guards led Bolly to the door marked C.

This was it. Shit was about to get real. Bolly tried to cop the proper attitude. He didn't want to come off as super-aggressive—that would just cause trouble. At the same time, he didn't want to be perceived as a pussy or an easy mark. He stood up straight, squared his shoulders and scowled at the floor.

The desk guard unlocked the door to Ward C and swung it open. Behind it was a large day room with doors on either side and tiny slit windows at the far end. A number of inmates in orange jumpsuits looked up as they walked it. Bolly continued to scowl at the floor and avoided making eye contact with anyone. His heart was racing.

"All right," said the desk guard. "Put him in Cell 8, with Bugfuck Bob."

Unfortunately, Bolly misheard the name as "Buttfuck Bob." *They're putting me in with an ass-bandit!* he thought wildly. He opened his mouth to protest, then abruptly shut it again. He was just going to have to deal with the situation as it was. Maybe he should pick a fight with Buttfuck Bob as soon as the guards were gone, just to establish he was not someone who could be messed with.

The guard opened the door to Cell 8. Inside was another man in orange. He was short, rotund, and appeared to be in his late fifties. *I could take him,* thought Bolly. His tension eased back half a notch. Still, he hesitated at the threshold of the cell. "Have fun getting acquainted, precious," said the guard, who jabbed him again in the kidney. Bolly jumped into the cell and the door slammed behind him.

The cell consisted of a pair of metal bunkbeds and a unitized metal toilet/sink combo. Bob sat on the lower bunk, regarding Bolly warily. "Hello," he said.

"Uh, yeah, hi," said Bolly. He decided to take the initiative and assert himself—an easier task now that he saw his cellmate wasn't a muscle-bound bruiser. "Look, I don't know why they call you 'Buttfuck Bob,' but I've gotta tell you that if—"

"Wait—what?" said Bob. "Why they call me *what?*" He made a strange face and his head jerked to the side, like he was trying to bite his own ear.

"'Buttfuck Bob,'" repeated Bolly. "I don't go in for any of that shit, and if you try any bullshit…"

CHAPTER 40

Bob did that weird ear-biting twitch again and made a sound that sounded like *nnyarllh*. Then he broke into a grin and started laughing. "Ha! You got it all wrong, roomie! You musta misheard. It's 'Bugfuck Bob.' *Bug*, not *butt*, okay? They call me 'Bugfuck Bob'—I'm not sure why. *Nnyarllh*."

Bolly let out an explosive breath of relief. Okay, so maybe his cellmate wasn't going to try to rape him—but he couldn't be sure of anything. He'd have to be careful; this guy seemed more than a little off. There had to be some reason for the nickname.

"Look, how about if I just call you 'Bob'?" said Bolly. "I'm Bolly." He reflexively held his hand out to shake.

Bob looked at the outstretched hand for a moment, then stood up and shook it. "Well met, Bolly," he said. "Given the circumstances. What are you in for?"

"Uh, I've been accused of murder," said Bolly. It felt bizarre to say such a thing. "I didn't do it, though. I'm innocent."

Bob laughed. "Yeah, you and every other guy in here. Nobody did anything. Except me, of course."

"You? What did you do?"

"Passed some bad checks," said Bob. "It's so damn easy. This is my sixth time in for that—no, seventh. I'm starting to lose track. When they let me out, I'm gonna do it again, too. Fuck 'em."

Suddenly, Bolly felt exhausted. The day had been hyper-traumatic. He'd had adrenaline pumping into his system nonstop for the last several hours. Now he felt like he was going to crash. "Jesus, I'm tired," he said. "I guess I got the top bunk, huh?" He didn't mind that too much; he would be harder to get at if Bob—or anyone else—decided to mess with him.

Bob scrunched up his face and made that ear-biting motion again. "Uh, no," he said. "No. I got the bottom bunk. My stuff's on the top bunk. You sleep on the floor." He pointed at the floor by the toilet where a ratty gray blanket lay folded. A thin pillow was on top of it.

Bolly goggled at him. There was no way he was sleeping on the fucking floor. He glanced at the top bunk. There were small piles of jailhouse goods arranged in neat rows: carefully folded T-shirts, balled up socks, small bars of soap, a toothbrush and tube of toothpaste, and various small packages of snacks. It looked like Bolly was going to have to assert himself after all.

"Look, man—I'm not sleeping on the fuckin' *floor!*" he growled. "Now move your shit from *my* bunk!"

Bob looked distraught and made three ear-biting gestures in quick succession. "No," he said. "No. Can't do it. They're in a very specific configuration. Can't move them."

Glowering, Bolly pulled a neatly folded white T-shirt and threw it on the floor. Bob cringed.

"Look, man," said Bolly. "I don't want to be a dick or anything, but I'm not sleeping on the fucking *floor* so your shit can have its own fucking bunk. This is your last chance. Move your shit, or it's goin' in the toilet!" He grabbed a rolled-up pair of socks and moved to toss it in the metal toilet bowl.

"Okay, okay!" cried Bob. "I'll take care of it! No need to be an asshole about it!" He jumped up and grabbed the socks from Bolly's hand. He then spent a very long time removing the items from the top bunk and arranging them at the base of his own bunk.

Bolly watched wearily. What a hell of a day it had been. He'd gotten up thinking of little more than limping into work and trying to get something accomplished. Now, he was in jail on a murder charge and arguing with his demented cellmate about where his socks would live. It was utterly insane.

At last Bugfuck Bob finished relocating his stuff to his own bunk. "There, it's done," he said truculently. "I'll have to sleep curled up in the fetal position to be able to fit. I hope you're happy."

"I'm not happy at all," said Bolly. "But if you don't like the bunk arrangements, you can sleep on the floor."

He picked up the blanket and pillow from the floor, climbed up on the top bunk and tried to make himself comfortable. He couldn't. Instead, he lay there with his hands behind his head, staring at the cracked ceiling and wondering how his life had gone so spectacularly wrong.

Chapter 41

The incoming call was from an unidentified number. Normally, Martin would screen calls like that. This was his personal phone. Unidentified callers were usually telemarketers or scammers. However, something made him answer this call—intuition told him it might be important.

"Martin Prieboy speaking," he said brightly, preparing to fend off whatever huckster might be calling.

"Bollinger is innocent," said an electronically altered voice. "I know how he lost his credit card. I know who took it and why. I don't know for sure who killed the Troutman woman, but I can take one hell of a guess."

"What?" Martin began. "Who is—"

"I can tell you that later," said the voice. "It's not safe for me right now."

"Look," said Martin, "I'm going to need more to go on than just this."

"Sorry, that's all I can give you right now. There's more—a *lot* more. I will be ..." There was a loud thump and some unidentifiable sounds on the line. Martin couldn't tell for sure what it was. The scrambler effectively masked the background noise. The voice said, "Gotta go," then the line went dead.

Martin sat and stared at his phone. There was an uneasy feeling in the pit of his stomach. He'd hoped that Charlene's murder case had been resolved with the arrest of Michael Bollinger, but here it was still lurching along like a zombie.

Martin put the phone down and stared into space. The longer he sat there, the more the uncomfortable feeling in his stomach grew. It took him a while to recognize it. It was a feeling he hadn't had in quite a long time.

He had close familiarity with it at the Holy Jesus Christ Almighty Home for Unfortunate Boys—in fact, it was the default emotion at that place.

It was guilt.

From the moment he had placed the handcuffs on Bollinger, there had been a nagging voice in his head telling Martin he had gotten the wrong man. Martin had ignored it. Just like the twitch that told him to take the call from the unknown caller, Martin had built his career on following his intuition. Why had it been so silent on this case?

Martin thought he knew the answer to that question: his feelings for Charlene Troutman had clouded his judgment, had forced him to rush to make an arrest when he should have been slower and more methodical.

Martin remembered the feeling of impotent rage he'd felt when he discovered her body in the bathtub. She'd seemed so vulnerable then, so *unprotected.* And it had been his job to protect her—protect her in a way that he couldn't do with Sam. And he'd failed miserably. She'd been so close to finally getting away from her abhorrent lifestyle. Then he had let his guard down and she'd gotten killed.

That the perpetrator was Michael Bollinger seemed pretty straightforward. Bollinger had visited Mike's Place and had engaged Charlene's services. (Just the thought made Martin's blood pressure rise.) This had caused conflict with Bollinger's wife. Bollinger had blamed Charlene for the marital rift, had felt she had somehow tricked him into infidelity—and he had threatened her life.

This seemed pretty farfetched at first, but interviews with other hostesses at Mike's Place had let him know that Charlene specialized in bringing in new or wavering first-timers and getting them to commit to engaging in Mike's Place's special services. When he'd learned that, Martin had felt alternately proud and ashamed. He knew Charlene was smart as a whip, but he felt awful she was using that intelligence to convince others to engage in illegal practices.

Then there was the matter of the credit card. That had been the final straw—and what an amazingly large straw it was. Martin could see of no other way that Michael Bollinger's credit card had turned up at the crime

CHAPTER 41

scene other than he'd been there and committed the crime. Enraged by what he saw as her fault in his own infidelity, he'd either followed her home or had made a private appointment in order to get her away from the safety of Mike's Place.

Martin had a little trouble believing that Charlene would be so foolish to bring one of her johns into her own home—especially since she had already charted a course out of her life of iniquity. But the evidence was there.

Or was it?

Now he had to face the possibility he'd made a dreadful mistake. Had he arrested the wrong person? In a nearly forty-year career, Martin had never, to the best of his knowledge, arrested an innocent person. Sure, some of the perps had gotten off in court due to procedural missteps (but never his) or prosecutorial incompetence, but never because he had brought in the wrong man.

Until, perhaps, now.

Martin pushed the thought away. He had too much on his mind right now to chew over something as big and potentially indigestible as this. He knew he'd be revisiting the idea soon enough, probably late tonight.

Besides, it may have been a crank call. There was no way to tell for sure. If the caller was serious, they would get back in touch.

With that marginally comforting thought, Martin turned and attacked the mound of paperwork on his desk.

Chapter 42

In Ward C, an ancient TV with bad color was bolted high in one corner of the day room. A carefully negotiated viewing schedule had been worked out to ensure the various Ward C factions got to see their favorite programming—usually game shows in the morning and soap operas in the afternoons. It was the Rojos who insisted on the soap operas—particularly *The Young and the Restless.*

The Rojos were Ward C's jailhouse gang. They were a group of young Puerto Rican men who were related in convoluted ways. It was hard to tell, since they only spoke Spanish to each other, and minimal English to anyone else. They were definitely a gang and acted aggressively gay. Bugfuck Bob said the belligerent homo attitude was just an act to intimidate the Anglos, but they were still dangerous and to be avoided.

Bugfuck Bob turned out to be a lifesaver. He had been in and out of the Kerian County jail so many times that he was a regular. The guards regarded him as almost a colleague and most of the other jailbirds treated him with respect. Even the Rojos showed grudging deference to Bugfuck Bob—he was a county lockup OG.

Having Bugfuck Bob as a cellmate had made Bolly's introduction to jail life much easier than it might otherwise have been. After Bolly had forced Bugfuck Bob to move his stuff so he could claim the top bunk, he was worried his cellmate would have it in for him. Bugfuck Bob, though, had actually shown Bolly more respect after the incident. Also, since Bolly refrained from commenting on any of Bugfuck Bob's weird tics and mannerisms, the OG had taken Bolly under his wing and put the word out

CHAPTER 42

that Bolly was a good dude and shouldn't be messed with.

Despite vouching for him, Bob still warned Bolly the Rojos would try to test him. It didn't take long. A Rojo named Jorge had gotten in Bolly's face, accusing him of looking him in the eye and disrespecting him. Bolly had tried to de-escalate the encounter, but it soon became obvious Jorge was going to keep pushing Bolly until he reacted. So Bolly did, ranting and peacocking and generally acting like a pro wrestler on meth. Bolly couldn't believe some of the shit that came out of his mouth. He claimed to be "the king of the nighttime world" and that he "kicked Superman in the balls for breakfast—and twice after dinner." After a couple of minutes of insane shit-talking and chest-thumping, Jorge had said something nasty-sounding in Spanish and retreated to the back corner of the day room which was the Rojos' turf. After that, they left Bolly alone, although he had caught Jorge giving him the hairy eyeball from time to time. Bolly let it slide.

On the morning of his second day of incarceration, he was hauled to a courtroom for his first appearance. He was given the option of a court-appointed attorney, representing himself, and hiring a lawyer. He told the judge that his family was in the process of hiring a lawyer. The judge set the bail at $500,000 and went on to the next case. It was quick and impersonal.

Soon he was back in the day room, where the typical chat- and game-show TV schedule was in full swing. A guard came in and barked, "Bollinger! Your lawyer's here!" The day room erupted in hoots and catcalls as Bolly got up and followed the guard to the visiting rooms. Bolly's heart sped up—maybe a lawyer would be able to untangle this whole unbelievable mess.

The guard ushered him into the visiting room. Sitting in one of the chairs was a man in his late thirties, with thinning dirty-blond hair that was starting to gray at the temples. He had a pinched, worried face and deep-set eyes framed by thin metal-rimmed spectacles. He looked vaguely familiar to Bolly.

"Peter Minnick," said the man. He extended his hand but didn't stand up. "Sorry it's taken me so long to get in to see you. I had all sorts of stuff going on in court yesterday, and it went way late."

Bolly squinted. "Peter Minnick?" he asked. "Did you go to Fillmore Elementary?"

"Uh, yeah. For a while."

"I think I remember you," said Bolly uncertainly. He remembered there being a kid named Peter Minnick who was in second grade when Bolly was in third. For reasons he couldn't remember, Bolly had made it his life's work to torment Peter Minnick at every opportunity. He had mostly forgotten about it over the summer between third and fourth grade and was only vaguely disappointed when Peter Minnick hadn't shown up for school the next year.

"Yeah, I remember you, too," said Minnick. He shot Bolly a look that was half distrustful and half smug. *Yeah, figures a kid like you would end up in a place like this.*

"Yeah, look," said Bolly. "Sorry about all that shit back on the playground and stuff. That was really mean and stupid of me. I'm really sorry, man." And he was—especially given the possibility the only thing standing between him and a life sentence was a person he had given atomic wedgies to on multiple occasions.

"It's okay," said Minnick, cutting away his eyes. "We were kids. Kids do stupid things. It was no big deal. I just had to start going to a child psychiatrist. My parents pulled me out of public school and sent me to Kerian Country Day. Hour-long bus ride, each way."

Bolly winced. "Sorry," he said.

Minnick frowned into the distance for a moment, then opened his briefcase. "Okay, let's get to business. Murder in the third degree. This is quite a case." If this guy could litigate like he could understate, Bolly would be home free. Minnick pulled out a case file, flipped through a few pages, and placed it on the stainless-steel table.

"This is a pretty weak case on the surface," said Minnick. "There's a lot of circumstantial evidence here. The only real piece is the credit card. Their whole case hinges on it."

"Is there anything you can do to get me out of here?" Bolly asked. That was the only thing that mattered. He looked back on his life of just four

CHAPTER 42

weeks ago with a bitter nostalgia. He'd had no idea how good things had been. He'd give anything to get it back now. With just a couple of poor choices and a run of incredibly bad luck, everything had gone to shit.

"Well, I will petition to have the charges dropped," said Minnick. "But that doesn't stand a snowball's chance in hell. The judges in this county are a bunch of hard-asses. Our best bet would be to try to have your bail reduced . That's more likely."

Minnick flipped through the pages again. "Yes, very good. You're certainly no flight risk, Mr. Bollinger. Local businessman, no major stains on your legal record, just some stupid kid stuff when you were in school." He shot Bolly a hurtful look. "You've got a lot of family ties to the area. Your father lives here in Weaverville, doesn't he?"

His father! Bolly hadn't even thought about him. Certainly, he'd heard about his only son being arrested for murder. All he did all day at the assisted living facility was watch TV news and curse humanity in general. He'd have to have Janie give the old man a call and try to explain it was all a huge, ugly mistake.

"How much do you think you can get the bail reduced?" asked Bolly. He was still in shock at the half-million dollar price tag.

"I might be able to get it down to two hundred thousand ," said Minnick. "Maybe even one-fifty if the judge is feeling generous that day."

Bolly slumped. Even if Minnick wheedled the bail down to $150,000, that meant they'd have to come up with fifteen grand for a bail bondsman. Bolly wasn't sure he had fifteen thousand pennies to rub together. Maybe Janie's parents could come up with that kind of money, but he hated the thought of his in-laws posting his bail. They'd already coughed up some dough to pay for this lawyer, but Bolly hoped they hadn't paid much. Peter Minnick was not filling him with confidence—and not just because Bolly thought he bore him a grudge for all those grade-school wedgies.

"We need to start thinking about the probable cause hearing," said Minnick. "The probable cause here is very weak. As I see it, the credit card is the thing we need to hammer on." He checked his notes. "You said you hadn't used or even seen your credit card in months."

"Over a year, probably," said Bolly. He'd had plenty of time to think about this now. "I'm pretty sure last time I used it was last spring. I was doing some handy work around the house and had to go to the hardware store for nails. I'd forgotten to get cash, so I used the card. I usually carry cash—the card was only for emergencies."

"Good, good," said Minnick, who began scribbling furiously. "I'll go online and get the records from the credit card company. We should be able to show the last time you used the credit card. If it was as long ago as you said, that's over a year between when you last saw it and when it turned up at the victim's apartment. That's a long time. Anything could have happened to it."

"Like what?" asked Bolly, who was still having trouble imagining how the card had gotten out of his wallet in the first place. Why would someone steal just one credit card and leave everything else, especially the cash that he almost always carried.

"Who knows?" said Minnick. "Maybe your wife took it."

"What? Are you suggesting my wife set me up?" Now Bolly was mad—whatever their differences, Janie would never play him foul like that. He started to get up—he'd see if he could still give Peter Minnick an atomic wedgie.

"No, no! nothing like that!" Minnick objected. "I'm talking something completely innocent. Maybe she saw something she wanted to buy on Amazon, but her card was maxed out. Maybe your wallet was sitting out and she took your card—with *every* intention of telling you about it afterwards, of course. Maybe she stuck it in her pocket, meaning to return it, and got distracted. Maybe the card went through the wash, maybe she just plain lost it. These things happen. Maybe it was so long ago that she doesn't even remember it. Or won't remember it—unless you remind her, Mr. Bollinger. Think you can do that?"

Bolly wasn't sure. That was a hell of a lot of maybes in that scenario. Minnick must have sensed his hesitance. "I shouldn't have to remind you, Mr. Bollinger, that you are facing *very* serious charges. I suggest you follow my instructions closely." He flashed Bolly a wicked smile, to show him

CHAPTER 42

which of them was in the driver's seat and which of them was going back to Ward C.

"Look, I would never ask anyone to *lie*," said Minnick. "I'm just saying that a year is a long time, and people can forget things that happen. *Important things.* I'm not even asking you to talk to her about it. I will talk to her and take a deposition You might want to suggest to her, the next time you speak with her, that she should assist me in helping her search her memory. Is that acceptable?"

"Yes, of course. I'll tell her." He wasn't even sure the next time he'd be able to call her.

"Very good," said Minnick, stuffing the file back into his briefcase. "I'll let you know about any bail reduction I can wrangle. I'll file to have the charges dismissed, too, but that's a long shot. Talk to you soon. Guard!"

When Bolly got back to Ward C, they were still avidly following the adventures of Ian Ward and Nikki Newman, but Bolly couldn't care less. He went back to his cell, climbed onto his bunk and collapsed.

Chapter 43

Up at Camp Vengeance, Billy dug.

First, he had dug a shallow trench around the perimeter of the camp, about twenty feet away from the tents. Then he had deepened it—at least six feet deep. Then he had widened the trench at strategic locations. He had constructed a roof of logs and dirt at these points, creating a system of interconnected bunkers.

Then he'd gone out and dug *another* trench, about thirty yards out from the first one. This he kept about knee-deep. It was much longer and he couldn't make it as deep as the first. Maybe later he'd go back and deepen it—if he had time before the attack came.

He was glad he'd held onto the assault rifles. He'd created stashes of food, ammo, and an assault rifle in each bunker; one he kept in his tent. He didn't sleep in his tent every night. Some nights he hauled a thin air mattress and sleeping bag to one of the bunkers and spent the night there. He'd also taken to wearing a .45 pistol strapped to his thigh wherever he went. He had to be prepared.

He had no doubt that an attack was coming. That lunatic Ronald Schmidt had probably thrown Billy under the bus the first opportunity he'd gotten. Soon, the county sheriff's deputies—hell, maybe even the staties—would be looking all over for him. They'd be here before long, Billy was sure.

At least as sure as he could be. The problem was that he had totally isolated himself from the world and had severely throttled his source of information. He had a small TV set that was hooked up to the generator, but the reception was notoriously lousy in western Kerian County. Besides, the local TV news

CHAPTER 43

was just propaganda, anyway. He also had a commercial police scanner, which he listened too continually, but that too was of limited value. Billy knew that the super-cops who were after him had secret communication frequencies unavailable to the great unwashed. Billy wished he still had some of the comm gear he'd had in his old office when he was chief constable. That had been top-shelf spook stuff, obtained via an old buddy in Navy intel. Well, it was long gone now—doubtless thrown in a dumpster when Billy had been removed as chief constable.

Billy also had his cell phone, but he was only going to use it for emergencies. Several times, he'd been tempted to call one of his contacts to get the low-down on how the investigation against him was proceeding. He hadn't dared, though. There was no telling who they'd gotten to; his whole network might be compromised at this point. He didn't dare use the cell phone—that would be like firing up a beacon the super-cops could pinpoint from a hundred miles away. Billy had removed the battery from the phone, put them both in an old ammo box and stashed it in a hollow tree about a hundred yards away from the outer trench line of Camp Vengeance.

You just couldn't be too careful.

About the closest Billy came to contact with the outside world was the surveillance he performed on his own property. Every other day or so, usually just before sunrise or right after sunset, Billy would creep down the hill far enough to see the back of the house and the workshop. He was very careful to approach and return a different way each time. When in place, he'd sit motionless with a pair of binoculars, scanning the property, looking for signs of intrusion or imminent attack.

It was hard to be sure. The super-cops were clever and stealthy. At one point, Billy thought he had caught them out. He noticed an old shovel leaning against the back of the workshop that he could have *sworn* had been at least two feet farther away a day earlier. Yesterday, Billy had spent eighteen hours keeping an eye on that shovel, but it hadn't moved again. He reluctantly conceded he may have made a mistake.

When Billy wasn't digging trenches or spying on his own house, he was working on the Thing. It was pretty much all together now. He'd dug up the recoilless rifles and, with the help of the Land Rover and a heavy-duty block and tackle, had gotten the guns mounted on the turret. It had been backbreaking and difficult—the guns were monstrously heavy—but Billy was driven. The Thing just didn't look right without the guns. Now that the Thing was complete, Billy felt slightly calmer.

Even with all the big parts together on the Thing, there were always plenty of bits to work on. After all, the vehicle was nearly sixty years old. There was a lot of maintenance to be done. Billy spent many afternoons and evenings in the garage tent, listening to the police scanner as he tinkered with the engine or the drive train. He wanted to make sure that the Thing was in proper working order and would not seize up when time came to use it.

That time was coming, Billy knew. He wasn't exactly sure how things would unfold, but he knew it was coming soon, one way or another. Billy would know when the time came, and he also knew he could handle the situation, however it unfolded. He had been there before, first at Hue and then during the mess at Khe Sanh. He could handle it now, just as he had before.

Chapter 44

Lance Corporal William J. Snyder arrived in Vietnam in January of 1968. He was nineteen years old. He was assigned to the First Armored Battalion of the United States Marine Corps. He was the driver/commander of an M50A1 Ontos, along with a gunner named Mopey Mike and a loader called Speedy. Billy didn't have a nickname; he was always just "Snyder."

Shortly after his arrival, Billy's unit was attached to the 2nd Battalion, 5th Regiment, the 2/5 Marines, which was going up to a city called Hue to "clear out a few snipers." The commies had just mounted a country-wide offensive over the Tet holiday, surprising everybody but causing little damage. With the exception of Saigon, most of the gains were minor and short-lived—and even Saigon was cleared out after a couple of days. Apparently, there were still a few troublemakers lurking around in Hue, but the 2/5 Marines would clear them out in short order.

This assignment was thought to be a boondoggle. Hue was an international city and had once been the capital of imperial Vietnam. Better yet, it had been largely untouched by the war. It was a relatively modern city, full of good food, strong drink, and pretty women. Billy and his crew were looking forward to the visit.

What the U.S. command was incapable of understanding was that the North Vietnamese and Viet Cong had completely overrun Hue and were heavily dug in. Instead of a paid vacation to a flashy city, Billy had gotten an express ticket to a hellish urban warscape.

Billy's baptism by fire came on the trip from the big Marine base at Phu

Bai to Hue. There had been a few random potshots at the convoy as they had rolled through the countryside, but it had really gotten heavy as they'd gotten to the southern outskirts of the city. The highway passed between rows of two-story masonry houses that were jammed to the rafters with snipers and rocket launch teams.

The convoy reached the MACV compound in Hue with moderate casualties. The headquarters of the Military Assistance Command Vietnam was never meant to be a fortress. MACV was the organization that coordinated the disposition of American military advisors with their South Vietnamese advisees. The building had originally been a hotel—good enough for MACV, which was essentially a jumped-up military personnel bureau. Now, it was one of two allied military positions in Hue that hadn't been completely overrun by the commies.

The MACV compound had been quickly but efficiently reinforced with whatever materials were on hand. Billy had gotten his first lesson in the fine art of trench-digging as soon as he arrived, as all able-bodied men were put to work reinforcing the perimeter. It was mostly Marines, but there were plenty of Army grunts and a handful of Air Force intel weenies. As he dug, Billy absorbed the wisdom of those who had been there. *Whew, you think this is bad? You shoulda been here* yesterday. *Day before that was even worse!*

It sounded bad. A couple of companies from the 1/1 Marines had shown up earlier and gotten chewed up badly. The brass at Phu Bai refused to believe the North Vietnamese Army was there in force, and had sent the 1/1 companies on suicide missions, attempting to link up with an isolated South Vietnamese regiment. They had been brutally used and retreated, some platoons with over 60 percent casualties.

The medical bay at the MACV compound was constantly busy, and it was impossible to ignore the stacks of body bags that accumulated outside when the convoys couldn't get through to run the dead and wounded back to Phu Bai.

There were corpses in the streets, too. Billy hadn't really noticed them on the trip in; he was too concerned with not getting his ass shot off. But he

CHAPTER 44

could see—and smell—them now. Mostly, they seemed to be NVA soldiers and some Viet Cong, but there were plenty of civilians as well. About thirty yards past the bunker where Billy was wielding his entrenching tool, a little girl of about eight sprawled face-down in the dirt. It looked like she had been there awhile. Nobody had come for her. Nobody could; anybody who set foot in the street became a bullet sponge. The little girl stayed there for days. It bothered Billy, at first.

What really bothered him was the stack of body bags outside the medical bay. It had never really occurred to Billy that he might die here. The notion was ridiculous. He was going to ride into battle on wings of eagles, kick ass repeatedly, be decorated extensively, and return home a hero, honored by men and lusted after by women.

But that's not how it had happened.

The horrors kept coming as the 2/5 Marines slowly made their way across the southern part of Hue, engaged in brutal house-to-house fighting. At last, the brass at Phu Bai had gotten it into their heads that there were a *lot* of enemy soldiers in Hue. Due to the historical and cultural importance of the city, the American forces weren't allowed to use heavy weaponry such as artillery or aircraft assaults in the city. Fortunately, Colonel Cheatham had thought of that and stockpiled a bunch of heavy rocket launchers and recoilless rifles.

Big Ernie Cheatham was the battalion commander of the 2/5 Marines, and it was his unenviable job to clear the enemy from the portion of Hue south of the Perfume River. After the bloody first days of the fight, the Marines had extended the perimeter around the MACV compound, securing the surrounding buildings and a route to the LZ by the riverside.

The next step was to sweep east along the river and secure the provincial and municipal buildings that occupied that piece of real estate. The area was especially hot, as the NVA were dug in like ticks and putting up a fierce resistance. Most of the buildings were solidly built masonry structures, constructed during the French colonial era. The walls were strong enough to stop most rifle and machine gun fire, and even the heavy rockets didn't do much more than gouge divots in the façades.

In addition to the rockets, recoilless rifles, and Ontos, Big Ernie had scrounged up a couple of "real" tanks, heavily armored M-48 Pattons. The Ontos wasn't considered a tank, and its crew weren't considered tankers. They were just jarheads who rode around in a crazy-looking bullet magnet. The Pattons' crews never failed to rag Billy and his crew about this whenever they had a chance. Which wasn't often as the Patton crews rarely left their tanks, not even to sleep. Being larger and more powerful, the Pattons attracted much more fire.

After some trial and error, Big Ernie figured out the best way to flush out the enemy and blow away the bunkered building the commies were using as cover. He would first send one of the Pattons forward to draw enemy fire. When a nest of NVA exposed itself by shooting at the big tank, it would fire a round from its cannon. Then, while the enemy had their heads down, an Ontos would rush forward, fire a bunch of high-explosive rounds at the building, then rush back before the commies could launch an RPG or mortar round that would easily pierce the Ontos' thin armor.

Big Ernie was big, loud, and—apparently—bulletproof. He would stand in the street watching the Patton draw fire, then bang on the top of the Ontos and direct Billy where to go: "That house halfway down the block with the dead zip hanging over the fence. Tear it up, boys!" Then Billy would haul ass to the target and Mopey Mike would fire a round or two. Then Billy would haul ass backwards just as fast, hoping he wouldn't run over Big Ernie in the process. Fortunately, the back blast from the recoilless rifles kicked up so much dust and debris that it provided effective cover for the Ontos' retreat.

Billy became numb to the horrors that unfolded around him. He couldn't sleep and barely ate. On their second week in Hue, Mopey Mike had popped his head through the gunner's hatch at the wrong moment and had taken a machine-gun round to the head, killing him instantly. Shortly afterwards, Speedy, the loader, had copped some shrapnel that had gotten through his flak jacket and unzipped his guts.

The loader's job was the worst on the Ontos. The recoilless rifles had to be loaded from outside the vehicle, making it a perilous undertaking. Speedy

CHAPTER 44

was good—he was fast, which, along with his penchant for amphetamines, had led to his nickname. On that day, he wasn't fast enough. He had just finished loading the guns when a mortar attack hit. At first, Speedy had seemed unfazed. He ran back to the rear of the vehicle and had yanked open one of the doors. Billy turned to see him with a crazy grin on his face. Then Speedy's face went slack and he keeled over backwards, blood running out from underneath him like it had been poured from a pitcher. Wilson— Mopey Mike's replacement as gunner—had hopped out to render aid. When he'd opened up Speedy's flak jacket to find the wound, Speedy's midsection had just come apart, leaving a glistening mound of viscera spilling over his pants and into the dirt of the street.

Something inside Billy began to wither. He had to wall off the feelings threatening to overwhelm him as horror after horror confronted him. It was the only way he could function; the only way he could keep from being a complete basket case.

The final straw came weeks later, farther north. Hue had been reclaimed by the combined U.S. and ARVN forces, destroying 80 percent of the city in the process. Billy's unit was sent north as part of an effort to break the siege of the remote Khe Sanh combat base. Billy's Ontos had been at the rear of the column, and the loader—Speedy's replacement, whose name Billy had never bothered to learn—had just loaded all six guns with beehive anti-personnel rounds. These were filled with thousands of wickedly sharp steel darts. Billy's Ontos was towards the rear of the column. The poorly armored Ontos were usually kept to the rear—to allow the thick-armored Patton tanks to take the brunt of the RPGs.

They weren't expecting much trouble. Both Billy and Wilson were riding with their heads out of their hatches. It was a decent enough day—at least for central Vietnam. It was warm going on hot and humid as hell, but at least it wasn't raining—that would surely come later in the day.

Billy was pushing the Ontos a little faster, trying to catch up with the elements in front of them that had pulled out of sight. Suddenly, a man in black pajamas darted across the road. Billy and Wilson had both screamed "Zip!" at the same time, and Wilson had dropped back through his hatch and slammed it shut. Billy felt hypnotized. He knew he should drop back down and close the hatch, but his arms were reaching for the hatch in slow motion.

As he watched, the man in the black pajamas—a VC fighter—reached the far side of the road, then noticed Billy gaping at him from the front of the tank.

The VC took two quick steps into the road and raised his rifle. Billy still couldn't move. *This is it,* he thought. *My next trip is going to be in a black plastic bag.* There was a whir, then a blinding white flash, and then the world went silent. Wilson had swiveled the turret and loosed a beehive round at the VC at point blank range.

In total and serene silence, Billy watched as the VC soldier's upper half vanished, along with his pants. It was like some sort of diabolical magic trick. For a quarter of a second, all was still. The man's naked lower half stood perfectly motionless and unbloodied in the road. Billy could see the VC's penis resting limply in a thatch of pubic hair. Then blood overtopped the legs and poured onto the dirt. The legs slowly toppled over backwards.

Something left Billy then, something that had been trying to get out ever since he'd seen the little girl lying in the street in Hue. Deep inside, a door slammed shut with a shuddering finality. It was like he'd rid himself of something dangerous. He was glad to be shut of it.

Billy dropped back into the driver's compartment and pulled the hatch closed after him. He shoved the yoke, throwing the Ontos forward so quickly that Wilson and the new loader cursed him. Billy didn't care, nor did he care when he ran over the VC's legs in his hurry to catch up with the rest of the convoy.

Chapter 45

At the Hickory Acres Mall, things had resumed a regular cadence following the strange events of the Fourth of July Fair. There had been no more "supernatural interventions," and there was still a raging debate online about whether the levitation and ghostly apparition had been something genuinely otherworldly or merely misperception.

Now, more than a month after the fair, the number of shoppers at the Hickory Acres Mall was running a little higher, but a lot of that was due to the normal back-to-school rush. Harold Todd was relieved but still worried. The numbers were nowhere near their heyday; the uptick following the fair had been just a glitch. The Golden Age of Shopping Malls was in the rearview mirror.

In the meantime, there was maintenance to be performed, rents to be collected, repairs to be made. The mall was not getting any newer, and had been constructed as inexpensively as possible, so there was always plenty of infrastructure improvement needed.

There was a renovation going on in the loading dock area: replacing some walls and installing a new sprinkler system. This was good in that it minimally impacted the public areas of the mall, so there were no tenants complaining about inconvenient access or throttled foot traffic. The only impact on the public shopping areas was a wall that had been demolished where the loading dock holding space met the main mall promenade.

It was just past sundown when a shopper named Irma Postlethwaite came out of the Mittens 4 Less store and began strolling back towards the entrance. She had scored a pair of rabbit fur-lined leather numbers that would drive her best friend Janet mad with envy. Irma was passing the demolished wall when she noticed someone standing back in the construction zone. This wasn't right; there were sawhorses blocking the area that clearly read *Construction Area—KEEP OUT!*

Irma turned to admonish the person who wasn't following the rules but paused. Something was weird—it looked like the person was floating rather than standing. Irma snatched her rhinestone-studded glasses from the rhinestone-studded cord that hung around her neck and jammed them on her face. The person violating the construction area rules appeared to be a woman. She was staring down, her long, red hair concealing her face. She wore what looked to be a tattered black floor-length robe with long sleeves.

And she was definitely *floating*. Irma could see a pair of black-stockinged feet extending below the robe—they were a good two feet above the floor. Also, the woman was transparent. Irma could clearly see the scaffolding and construction equipment stacked up on the wall behind the woman.

Irma hadn't been at the mall for the fair, but like everyone else in Fester she had heard about the strange events that day. Reverend Eyler had said that it was the work of the Devil. Then again, he said that about everything he didn't like. Irma had thought it was all a bunch of superstitious nonsense. But here ... here was something that was very much out of the ordinary.

"Bosh," Irma muttered under her breath.

Immediately, the floating figure looked up, tossing her hair back to expose a haggard, corpse-like face. The figure now appeared to glow red, and her eyes shone with an unearthly crimson light.

Irma grasped for her rhinestone-studded glasses, took a step backwards and screamed before getting her feet tangled up and falling over backwards.

Even though it was a weekday night, there were still a fair number of shoppers in the Hickory Acres Mall. Irma's scream attracted the attention of everyone browsing on that side of the mall. A few people even stuck their heads out of the stores to see what was going on.

A young couple, Dale and Amy Marks, were the first to reach the stricken Irma Postlethwaite. "All you all right?" asked Dale. "Did you hurt yourself? Can you show me where you are injured?" Amy knelt down, fumbling in

CHAPTER 45

her purse for a first aid kit, and trying to remember how to perform CPR, just in case the situation deteriorated.

Irma tried to speak but could only produce kittenish huffing sounds.

"I can't understand you!" said Dale loudly. "Can you be more clear?"

Amy had found the first aid kit and was quickly flipping through the accompanying booklet. "She may be having a stroke!" Amy reported. "Check to see if her pupils are different sizes!"

Annoyed, Irma shook her head. She pointed at the floating apparition. "Look ... *hwaa* ... you dopes!"

"Now there's no need for talk like that," said Amy sternly. "We're just trying to help you."

Dale actually looked where Irma's finger was pointing. "Ho-lee *shit!*" he exclaimed.

This was enough to get Amy's attention. Dale *never* swore. She turned to behold the malign phantasm and uttered an ear-piercing shriek. Immediately, the entire mall was alerted that something heavy was going down outside the Mittens 4 Less.

Through it all, the floating figure just hovered and glowered, flashing red eyes flicking back and forth over the gathering crowd.

In no time, a throng had assembled around Irma and the Marks. *It's back! It's happening again! No shit, this place really is haunted!* In moments, the cell phones were out and recording the ghostly, ghastly woman.

"Murder!" intoned the woman. Her voice was horrid, creaking and clotted with dead leaves and grave dirt. "Bloody murder!" She raised her arms and blood poured out from a dozen wounds on her body, where it splashed and puddled on the floor.

The crowd gasped.

The woman disappeared.

There was a moment of stunned silence, then everyone started talking at once. Those who had the presence of mind to record the supernatural scene began typing furiously on their phones, rushing to be the first one to post video of the latest haunting at the Hickory Acres Mall.

Many of the onlookers shrank back from the hole in the wall where the visitation had occurred. A few of the braver ones—mostly young men—pushed forward towards the hole, determined to investigate.

Jacob Zook, the head security man, and a part-time security guard came running up to the scene. They had been at the far end of the mall and had missed almost everything. "Hold on here! Hold on here!" yelled Jacob. "You can't go back there! It's restricted."

This prompted a loud argument, that kept getting more heated until Jacob and the other security guard unholstered their flashlights and threatened to bop anyone who didn't shut up and step back. "We'll investigate this!" announced Jacob. "We're authorized!"

Jacob and the other guard carefully stepped around the sawhorses and into the space beyond. The crowd pushed right up to the barriers as the two security men shined their lights around. There was no huge puddle of blood on the floor where it had been just moments ago and no other evidence of anything otherworldly. Eventually, Jacob had the presence of mind to turn on the work lights, which revealed an ordinary-looking construction area. No blood, no ghosts, nothing.

It didn't matter that there wasn't any physical evidence—there was *video*. Already, it was circling the globe at the speed of light and in no time the Haunting of Hickory Acres was again worldwide news.

Chapter 46

While the news of the latest apparition at the Hickory Acres Mall was making the rounds, life went on in Fester. On the far east edge of town, Paolo Fandango eased his pickup truck up the winding driveway of a large house. It was fancy—modeled after the White House, in fact—and located in a rural neighborhood near the town line. It wasn't so much a neighborhood as it was a collection of properties of varying sizes and with varying qualities of buildings. This was a twenty-acre spread with a huge house and an unused stable. Just down the road was a scrubby half acre dotted with several mobile homes and a few barely standing outbuildings.

Mike Solheim lived alone in the big house. His wife had divorced him shortly after his conviction on prostitution charges. Since then, he had lived with a frequently rotating cast of live-in girlfriends and casual playthings. He had recently been between relationships and was living the life of a happy bachelor.

Paolo and his landscaping crew had shown up promptly at nine this morning for their twice-weekly trim and clean. Paolo was worried about getting paid. Solheim was once again late with his payment, and Fandango worried he wouldn't be able to pay his crew if Solheim didn't settle up. This had happened before. Solheim wasn't negligent, just forgetful. He usually paid up—with profuse apologies—once he was reminded of his obligation.

Paolo went to the front door and rung the bell, even though the front door stood open a crack. After three rings and no response, he gingerly eased the door open and called out, "Hello? Mr. Solheim? It's Paolo from

Superbush Landscaping. Hello?"

Fandango felt a burst of unease wash over him. Mr. Solheim was almost always home during the day and, forgetful or not, it was very unlike him to leave the front door open. He had given Fandango a rundown of all of the property's security measures and showed him how to turn the outside sensors and alarms off from a control box by the garage. The man was serious about security.

Despite his misgivings, Fandango stepped inside and continued calling out. He continued to get no response. He knew the smart thing to do would be to call the cops, but Mr. Solheim had made his intense dislike for law enforcement very clear. Besides, Solheim owed him nearly a thousand bucks, and Fandango really needed it. He wasn't going to blow it just because the boss man was taking a nap.

The house was darkened, but there was a door standing open at the end of a hallway that led from the entry foyer. Light spilled from the room into the hallway. All else was dark. He crept down the hall calling, "Mr. Solheim? Mr. Solheim? It's Paolo Fandango. Mr. Solheim?" When he got to the door, he looked in, screamed like a woman and rushed back outside to call the police and take a stiff drink from the flask of rye he kept in his glove box—not necessarily in that order.

The homicide guys called Martin as soon as they realized the victim's identity. He dropped what he was doing to get to the crime scene. Another homicide would be a big enough problem by itself, but this case indicated to Martin that there may be worse problems waiting.

Martin stepped out the front door and leaned against the fiberglass Corinthian column. It was a warm morning, but Martin felt cold. Things looked like they could be bad. On the broad, semi-circular driveway two constabulary cruisers, the crime scene van, an ambulance, and Martin's car were parked haphazardly. There was a commotion from inside the front door and Martin stepped aside as the sheeted corpse of Mike Solheim was wheeled out.

Solheim had been found in an unhappily familiar scene: in a bathtub, dead from strangulation. Just like Charlene Troutman. This was going to

CHAPTER 46

keep Martin up tonight. It certainly was the same MO, and it was hard to keep from wondering if it was the same perpetrator. Of course, it could be a macabre coincidence—but Martin didn't think so. He'd consult with the coroner to see if there was any way to match the marks on the necks of the victims.

Now there was the possibility of a serial killer prowling Fester. That was far from certain, but Martin could easily see the *Fester Daily Dispatch* connecting the dots and whipping up a frenzy. Martin could guess how the citizens of Fester would overreact to the news there was a modern Boston Strangler stalking them. Armed vigilante groups would take to the streets, drinking, hassling innocent citizens, and getting into fights with each other. Then there would be the inevitable avalanche of recrimination against the constabulary for letting the killer strike again. And God help them if there were further murders! The problems would increase exponentially.

At least as bad as these ideas—perhaps even worse—was the growing certainty he had arrested the wrong man. If the same perp had killed Troutman and Solheim, then it couldn't possibly be Michael Bollinger—he was safely locked away in the county jail. Martin had a terrible feeling in the pit of his stomach. He may have perpetrated a gross injustice.

There'd be plenty of time to worry over that later. Right now, he had things to do. He left the crime scene team to their work and headed back to headquarters. There he stayed just long enough to clear his schedule for the rest of the day. Then he was on his way to Weaverville to attend Solheim's autopsy and talk with the coroner. He had to find out if there was any tangible connection between the two killings.

Chapter 47

The following Monday, Martin Prieboy was going through the case files at his desk when the intercom buzzed. "What is it now?" he snapped. He was tired, frustrated and the last thing he needed right now was another distraction.

"It's a lawyer named Ellis Howe," said the duty officer. "He says he has something very important for you. Says it's urgent. Something to do with Michael Solheim."

Martin's head snapped up. It was the Solheim case—along with the Troutman murder—that had him pensive and on edge. This was an interesting coincidence. Martin had learned long ago to pay close attention to interesting coincidences when investigating, because they often became a good deal more interesting upon further examination.

"Send him in."

Ellis Howe was in his early forties, dressed in a high-end off-the-rack suit and had an expensive-looking gelled haircut that made him look slightly greasy. He seemed like just the sort of person Mike Solheim would choose for legal representation.

"Good afternoon, Chief," said Howe. He looked around Martin's office nervously, as if someone might slap cuffs on him at any moment.

"Please, have a seat, Mr. Howe," said Martin, indicating one of the chairs opposite his desk.

"Oh, no, no, thank you," said Howe. "I'm afraid I can't stay long." He opened his massive leather portmanteau and began rummaging around in one of the compartments.

CHAPTER 47

"You are here representing Mr. Solheim?"

"Yes, yes, that's right." Howe continued rummaging in his voluminous briefcase.

"I was very sorry to hear about the demise of you client," Martin offered.

"What? Oh, yes, yes—a terrible tragedy, that. Ah! Here we go!" He held up a large manila envelope triumphantly.

"What is this?" asked Martin.

"It's an envelope," said Howe. "It was given to me just last month by my client, Michael Solheim. Along with it came these specific instructions: I was to hand deliver this envelope to you, the Chief Constable, in the event of Mr. Solheim's 'untimely death.' Those were his exact words. Given the circumstances, I would deem his death to have been untimely. Therefore, I am discharging my duty." He handed the envelope over with a flourish and began redoing the straps on his monster briefcase.

Martin took the envelope. It was a standard manila mailer with a metal clasp. On the front the words "Chief Constable Martin Prieboy" were written in a clumsy longhand. "Is there anything else, Mr. Howe?" he asked.

"Nope," said the lawyer as he straightened his tie. "Please excuse me, but I must be off. If you have any further questions, here's my card." He did a neat about-face and marched quickly out of the office.

Martin watched the door close. He hefted the envelope, then flipped it over and tore it open. Inside was a single sheet of lined notebook paper, written on both sides with the same loosey-goosey handwriting as the envelope. Martin read through it twice, then sat it on his desk while he stared out the window for a couple of minutes, then picked it up and read it again.

"Damn," he said in a small voice, the one he always used when he swore. He reached for the phone. His first call was to tell Inspector Blount to get his keister to headquarters as quickly as he could.

Then he called the District Attorney's office in Weaverville. The DA, Johnson Smith, was holding a press conference at the moment, but Martin said he would hold. He needed to speak with the DA as quickly as he could. After nearly thirty minutes, Smith got on the line. "What do you have,

Chief?" he asked.

"I have a sinking feeling that we—I—got the wrong guy," said Martin. "The Troutman case. I-I've made a terrible mistake. Bollinger is innocent."

Chapter 48

"If you want me to do it again, it's going to cost you," said the young lady. "Triple."

"Jesus!" exclaimed Harold Todd. *"Triple?* You've got to be joking!"

"No joke. Last time was too close. Those rednecks almost caught me."

"God, you're bleeding me dry here," complained Harold. "Think of the exposure you're getting!"

"Consider it hazard pay. Look, I barely had time to clean up and clear out before those mall guards came rushing in. That blood was a mistake—too messy, too much trouble."

"Okay, tell you what: a repeat performance and I'll pay you double what I did last time. No blood—but see if your boyfriend can think up something equally dramatic."

"Okay, deal," said the young lady. Her name was Libby Schenker, and she was a theater major at Shippensburg University. Her boyfriend was also a theater major at Ship, focusing on the technical end of things—particularly special effects. They had been responsible for the ghostly apparition that had so frightened Mrs. Postlethwaite and electrified the country.

The boost in business after the Fourth of July Fair had been great, but it was short-lived. After two or three weeks, foot traffic had dropped back to what it had been before the fair. It was better than nothing, but to Harold it seemed like he was right back where he started. It was only a matter of time before something bad happened—Fashion Bitch could change their minds again and pull out or one of the anchors could get nervous and close up shop—then the Hickory Acres Mall would be royally screwed.

Unless Harold did something.

The answer seemed obvious. The supernatural had brought an enormous boost in attention to the mall, along with the attendant increase in business. Harold really didn't know if something supernatural had happened. Sure, there had been the thing with the stones, and that blue guy he'd seen by the hand statue. And *sure*, the weird stuff at the fair might have had something to do with those events too. Maybe his pap was right, and there *was* some ancient, occult weirdness going on. It really didn't matter. What mattered was that it brought shoppers to the mall. If they wanted ghosts and goblins rather than rides and games, well, then Harold Todd would give them what they wanted. That was his job.

He figured some theater students would be able to help him gin up a haunting. They'd be skilled enough to put on something credible looking, but as college students they'd be dirt poor and would work cheap. Harold knew better than to use students at Prosser College—it was too close to home. Shippensburg University, however, was only forty miles away and had a better theater department.

Harold had put an ad in the student newspaper and was soon connected with Libby and her boyfriend Gunther. Harold explained the project and soon Libby and Gunther came out to take a look at the mall to see what they could do to create a good ghost illusion. They seemed nonplussed until they got to the construction area.

"Wow," said Gunther, who was tall, skinny, and wore a purple vest. "Wow. You thinking what I'm thinking?"

"Pepper's?" asked Libby.

"Yes!" said Gunther. "Absolutely perfect shape for Pepper's!"

"What are you talking about?" asked Harold. "What's 'Pepper's?'"

"It's an illusion called 'Pepper's Ghost,'" said Gunther. "It's been around for hundreds of years. You ever been to Disney World?"

"No," said Harold. When he was growing up, a trip to Disney World seemed as likely as a trip to the moon.

"Oh," said Gunther. "Well, they use the Pepper's Ghost illusion on the Haunted Mansion ride. It makes it look like there's a ghost riding in the car

CHAPTER 48

with you."

"I see," said Harold. "How does it work?"

"Well, you need an L-shaped space for it to work properly," said Gunther.

"Just like the space here for your loading docks," added Libby.

"Right," said Gunther. "Perfect set-up. From the shopper's side, they can only see one leg of the L. We'll have Libby standing off at the end of the other leg where the shoppers can't see."

"Then how will she appear to be a ghost?" asked Harold.

"Ideally, a sheet of glass is placed at an angle where the two legs meet," said Gunther, who was clearly getting excited at the idea. "The glass semi-reflects the 'ghost's' image where the audience can see it. By changing the lighting on the 'ghost,' it will seem to materialize and dematerialize."

"And be transparent!" said Libby.

"That all sounds great," said Harold. "But this space must be close to fifteen feet high. How are we going to get a sheet of glass that big?"

"Fortunately, it doesn't have to be glass," said Gunther. "It just has to be something transparent. I've got some heat-shrink plastic sheeting that we can attach to the scaffolding. When we heat it up with a hairdryer, it will tighten up very nicely and behave like a sheet of glass. Then we do the bit and swing the scaffolding with the plastic out of the way, and no one will be any wiser. Got me?"

Harold got him and had approved the stunt, which had gone off perfectly. Perhaps *too* perfectly. Now there was clamor for more ghosts at the Hickory Acres Mall. Harold had been inundated with requests for interviews and permission to videotape at the mall.

"So you agree to pay double?" asked Libby.

"Yeah, okay," said Harold. "And no blood, either. But it has to happen Friday night."

There was muffled discussion on the line as Libby conferred with Gunther. "Three days is pretty tight," she reported. "But we can make it work. Gunther says he has a great effect—my hair will catch fire! But it'll take some time to get ready. Shouldn't be a problem, though."

"Great!" said Harold. "See you Friday night."

Chapter 49

Bolly observed Libby's first performance from the day room in Ward C. The typical TV schedule was replaced by the local news, which was running nonstop coverage of the ghostly apparition at the Hickory Acres Mall. It wasn't often that events in Kerian County made national news, but some of the video of the fiery-eyed phantom had made it onto CNN, *Good Morning America,* and *Today.* The residents of Ward C sat glued to the set, with none of the usual petty bickering and day room drama. They were all trying to spot people they knew in the crowd shots.

WEVL-TV cut from a commercial with a dramatic update. The cookie-cutter blond anchor led off with, "We have here in the studio Mrs. Carolyn Adenauer, who claims to know the identity of the Hickory Acres Ghost."

The camera cut to an aged woman wearing a lace collar and a headscarf. "I worked for the Schmidt Pretzel Bakery for forty years as an executive assistant," said Mrs. Adenauer. "And I'd recognize that face anywhere. That is clearly the ghost of Ms. Cecilia Schmidt!"

The TV cut to a still from one of the recent videos from the mall set side-by-side with a publicity shot of Cecilia Schmidt from the early nineties. This sparked a heated debate in the Ward C day room about whether the two images were similar.

"Hey, Bollinger," said McCullough, who was in for his seventeenth DUI. "You're from Fester. Whaddaya think about that shit?"

"I dunno," Bolly shrugged. "I never go to the fuckin' mall." This non-answer seemed to satisfy McCullough. Actually, he didn't think the two pictures looked alike at all. He didn't volunteer this opinion to the Ward C day room at large, of course. He was trying to keep a low profile and keep his mouth shut.

He was also starting to smell ripe. He'd been in jail for twelve days and had only showered twice. Both times, Bugfuck Bob had surreptitiously stood guard while Bolly was in the shower room. Bob was taking a nap now, and Bolly didn't want to wake him up. He grabbed his sliver of soap and scrap of washcloth from his bunk, wrapped a towel around himself and slid into the shower room.

The shower room was a space the size of one of the cells, tucked into the corner of the ward. It was creepy, and Bolly briefly considered going back to wake up Bugfuck Bob. He decided against it; he could handle this himself.

When he stepped into the shower room, Jorge and another Rojo called Ramon were waiting for him.

"Hey there, *mamabicho*," said Jorge. Ramon hung back at the entrance, keeping an eye out for the guards.

Bolly froze. He was trapped, vulnerable, and Bugfuck Bob was nowhere around. His initial impulse was to try to talk his way out of the situation. He bit down on the impulse, hard. He knew these guys would only see it as weakness. Instead, he unloaded his entire inventory of Spanish curses: "*Chinga tu madre, cabron!*"

Jorge's eyes grew wide and Ramon looked back over his shoulder, laughed and said something in Spanish. Jorge turned dark red. "What did you say about my mother, you cheap *lambón?*"

"You heard me, Whore-Hay!" spat Bolly.

"Okay, that's it, *puta*. Get ready to go!" He shoved up his sleeves and took a menacing step towards Bolly.

Bolly could only think of one thing to do: he ripped off the towel. He remembered reading in a Stephen King novel that fighting in the nude was a move that usually threw the enemy off guard.

It worked, at least for a moment. Jorge stopped in his tracks, nonplussed by the sight of Bolly standing naked with the end of a towel in his hand. After a few tense moments, he said, "Yeah, I always figured you for a *maricón*.

Don't matter to me. I'll beat up a faggot even worse than a regular guy. Prepare to die, *puta!*"

Bolly reacted instinctively with a move he'd perfected in the eighth grade gym locker room. He twirled his wrist twice, twisting the towel into a long rope, then reached out quickly and snapped his wrist, hard. The towel lashed out and connected solidly with the front of Jorge's tight orange jail pants. He went down, grasping his crotch and squealing.

Ramon was trying to keep an eye out for the guards while monitoring the situation in the shower room, so he didn't see immediately that Jorge had gone down. Bolly knew he had to act if he didn't want to be bottled up in here. He put his head down and charged Ramon.

The denizens of the Ward C day room were amazed by the sight of Ramon stumbling out of the shower room, followed by a butt-naked Bolly, who was followed by Jorge, who limped out bent over and holding his crotch. He said in a comically strangled and high-pitched voice, "I'm gonna get you, *puta!*" Most of the rest of the day room laughed at this, but the other Rojos came boiling out of their corner to defend their cousins.

"What the *fuck* is this all about?" Two guards had just pushed through the door to Ward C and were staring in amazement at the scene there.

"Never mind," said the lead guard. "I don't want to know what the fuck this is about. Bollinger! Get dressed and get your stuff."

"What?" asked Bolly. "Why?" He feared that he was being put into solitary for fighting.

"You're out of here," said the lead guard. "You're being released."

A wave of cheers and catcalls washed through the day room. Bolly stuffed himself into his clothes as quickly as possible and returned to the day room, where the lead guard was admonishing Jorge. "Looks like you got what you deserved, Garcia," said the guard. "You fuck up one more time, you're going straight to Ward A, got me, little goat?"

Bolly didn't care about Jorge. He just cared about getting out. He followed the guards back the way he had come in. Janie and Peter Minnick were waiting for him in the foyer.

"Oh, babe, babe!" cried Janie. "I'm so glad to see you! Oh, my God! I've

CHAPTER 49

missed you so much!"

Bolly ran to her and hugged her for a long time. "Oh, I've missed you, too—you don't know how much. I know we've still got some stuff to work out, but we can do it. I'll work hard for you."

Minnick gave him a firm handshake. "They're going to drop the charges," he reported. "There will be some perfunctory paperwork to take care of, Ts to cross and Is to dot, but I can take care of that. Congratulations! You're a free man."

"Oh, thank God," said Bolly. "Now let's get out of here and go home. I really want to take a shower."

Chapter 50

Ronald Schmidt hung up the phone. He felt cold—very cold. He had just spoken to a man at constabulary headquarters, a man whom Ronald paid two hundred dollars a month for any information that might be of interest. He had gotten his money's worth tonight: he'd been informed he was the lead suspect in two homicides.

"Ronald, what's wrong?" Aunt Ophelia had been watching him sit silently with the phone in his hand for the last two minutes. "You look like you've seen a ghost."

"Not quite," said Ronald. His lips felt numb. "We need to go, Auntie. All of us. Tonight. As soon as possible."

"This isn't about that silly affair at the mall is it?" asked Ophelia. "That's all just nonsense. There's no way that's the ghost of Cecilia…"

"No, it's not that," said Ronald. "There have been, um, a number of Unfortunate Incidents. Bad ones. *Very* bad ones."

Ophelia froze. *"Very* bad? Worse that what happened at Penn?"

"Yes. Much worse."

"Oh, dear."

"We need to start packing," said Ronald. "I'll go tell Thelma Louise."

That didn't go over very well—Thelma Louise just didn't understand.

"Why, Ronald?" she exclaimed. "Why do we have to go?"

"We just do!" he snapped. "There's no time for explanations now, but there will be plenty of time later on. For now, we need to get the car packed and on the road. We're getting out of here as soon as it gets dark.

"You get two suitcases. Pack like you're going on a vacation but pack

CHAPTER 50

for any type of weather. It'll be an adventure!" He tried to inject this last statement with a note of optimism, but it fell flat. Thelma Louise bustled off, casting a mistrustful look over her shoulder.

"I'm going to call Nasté," said Ronald.

"Why don't you let me do that?" said Ophelia. "I've been dealing with him for a long time—I know how to finesse him."

"Fine by me," said Ronald, who no longer trusted the family lawyer. He hadn't been able to keep Ronald from being arrested. The man was becoming incompetent in his old age.

Ophelia, on the other hand, seemed to have regained some of her old edge. Ronald listened in on the extension as Ophelia called Nasté. He was impressed with how his aunt handled him.

"I assume you are calling about this nonsense out at the mall?" said Nasté.

"Indeed, I am," replied Ophelia with disgruntled hauteur. "I do not know what this is all about, but I do know that this family has had quite enough harassment. It is *persecution*, Pierre! First these asinine charges against poor Ronald and now this! You must put a stop to it!"

"Yes, ma'am," said Nasté. "I will take all appropriate measures to make sure you are not inconvenienced and the Schmidt name isn't associated with whatever may be going on at that shopping mall."

"See that you do, Pierre. We have enough to contend with. Speaking of which, have you made any progress with Ronald's case? I certainly hope he won't have to be in that terrible courtroom again anytime soon."

"You shouldn't fear about that, Ophelia dear. I have three petitions before the court now, and it will take at least nine months to get those untangled. When that happens, I will petition for a change of venue."

"Quite right," said Ophelia. "The whole community is biased against us. A Schmidt can't get a fair hearing in this county."

"I will take care of it."

"Very good," said Ophelia. "See to it. Goodbye, Pierre."

"Goodbye, ma'am."

"Oh, and one more thing."

"Yes, ma'am?"

"This awful persecution has exacerbated my adenoiditis. I will be going down to Palm Beach at the end of the week to take the sea air. I may need you to wire me funds on short notice. Make all of the necessary arrangements."

"Very good, ma'am."

"Good job, Auntie," said Ronald after Ophelia hung up. *This* was the old Ophelia, one with steel in her spine. That was good—the family was going to need all the fortitude it could muster now.

They spent the afternoon rushing around, packing, unpacking, repacking, and arguing over what was necessary and what was frivolity. At one point, Ophelia descended into the basement to find Ronald digging through the contents of a pair of mildewed duffel bags. He was throwing some items on the floor and stuffing others into a plastic trash bag.

"What are you doing?" asked Ophelia.

"I put these bug-out bags together twenty years ago, when, y'know…" He jerked his head towards the freezer in the corner.

"Why are you sorting through them? What's in them?"

"You'll see," he said. "There's some stuff in here that we'll need. Ah-ha!" He pulled out a tightly wrapped sleeping bag, hefted it and shoved it into the garbage sack, followed by two more.

"Why are you hanging onto those sleeping bags?" asked Ophelia. "Surely, we're not going to have to rough it?"

"Because of these sleeping bags, we shouldn't have to. There's five thousand dollars in hundreds sewn into each of them. We need to bring as much cash as we have on hand, plus whatever other valuables we might be able to exchange for cash. We won't be able to use our credit cards, you know."

"In other words, we're going to be fugitives."

"Yes, we are," said Ronald. "And it's best if we started to internalize that fact. It certainly beats the alternative." He dumped out the contents of another of the duffel bags and began pawing through the pile on the floor.

"Ronald? Do you happen to have any, ah, alternate forms of identification?"

"Yes, I do," said Ronald. "It cost me a pretty penny, but it was worth it. A

CHAPTER 50

New York driver's license, a passport and three credit cards in the name of Walter Royer, all with $20,000 credit limits."

"Good, good," said Ophelia. "That makes me feel a little better."

"We'll see about getting you and Thel some fake passports once we get to Cleveland. I have a friend there who can help us."

"Is that where we're going?"

"First stop is Pittsburgh. I've got a place where we can stash the Caddy and get a less conspicuous vehicle. We should be able to get there tonight. After that, Cleveland. I know another guy in Reno who might be able to put us up in a cabin in the hills for a while longer. After that, who knows?"

"Ronald, I'm scared!" said Ophelia.

"We're in a tight spot, Auntie, but we'll get out of it. We always do—we're Schmidts! Now go make sure Thelma Louise is packing light. We're going to need to get new wardrobes anyway."

"Oh, Ronald, how did it come to this?"

"This shouldn't be happening," he said, mostly to himself. "That's why I had that whore steal his card. So they wouldn't know it was me."

"What are you talking about?"

"Nothing."

"Ronald?"

"What?"

"What about the, um, the artifact? Should we take it with us?"

"Good lord, no! Can you imagine what would happen if we got pulled over and searched with that thing in the car!"

"Well, maybe we should bury it in the yard."

"Don't be ridiculous! A patch of freshly dug-up soil would be investigated immediately. Leave it where it is—it's been there for twenty years; it will be fine to stay there. I'll stack some boxes and junk on top, no one will notice. And if they ever do, we'll be far away. Now go see to Thel."

Ophelia went upstairs and began wrangling with Thelma Louise over the jewelry they were going to take.

"Just take all of it, dear," said Ophelia

"*All* of it?" asked Thelma Louise. "But they're precious family heirlooms.

I don't want to take them in the car—something might happen to them. Where are we going, anyway? And when will we be back?"

"Thelma Louise, the family is in trouble. *Serious* trouble. We need to pull together to get through it. I don't know exactly how that is going to work out, or when. All I know is that we need to gather up our valuables, get in the car and go. We can't delay. If we do, your brother or me—or even *you*—may wind up in jail. You don't want that, do you?"

"Jail? *Me?* Why would I end up in jail, Auntie?"

"Because you're a Schmidt, and the Schmidt name is very low right now. *Very* low. We will rebuild that name to its former glory, and quite soon, but for now, we have to *go!*"

"But, Auntie ..."

"No buts, no questions, Thelma Louise. There will be plenty of time for explanations on the road. Now go get your jewelry and get in the car!"

In the next room, Ronald listened with approval. Ophelia was bearing up well. Ronald was impressed with his aunt, but was worried about his sister. She had never really understood the ruthlessness required to keep the family afloat, especially in these perilous times. He briefly considered leaving Thelma Louise behind, but that wouldn't do at all. They couldn't leave the *naif* here to face the music alone, even if she was completely innocent. It wouldn't be right to abandon family like that.

Finally, the sun had set and the last of the luggage had been loaded into the Cadillac. Ronald was about to climb in, then he stopped and gave himself an anguished smack on the forehead. "The monkeys!" he exclaimed. "I forgot all about Rondo, Berryman, and Peewee! How could I do that? I need to go get them!"

"Ronald, no!" Ophelia cried. "There is no way we are traveling with those dirty monkeys in the car!"

"Then I'll take them in my car!" he said. "Thelma Louise can drive the Caddy and I'll follow behind."

Ophelia shook her head. "No, Ronald, I don't think that will work. We're trying to be sly, and I can think of nothing more obvious than driving a vintage Italian sports car with three monkeys inside. You'll be pulled over

CHAPTER 50

by the first policeman we see once we're out of town. Besides, what would you do with them once we got to wherever we're going?"

Ronald paused for a long time. The thought of leaving his three best friends was crushing. He knew Ophelia was right—and he hated her for it. Desperately, he wracked his mind for another way, but couldn't think of one.

"I understand how much Peewee and Rondo and Berryman mean to you," said Ophelia. "This must be very hard—"

"Zip it, Auntie," snarled Ronald. "I'm going to go let them out. I can't just leave them locked up to starve."

"Yes, of course, dear. You go do what you need to do."

Ronald turned and disappeared around the corner of the house. Ophelia sighed and climbed back into the Cadillac. "Where's he going, Aunt Ophelia?" asked Thelma Louise. "He's not going to fetch the monkeys, is he?"

"No, he's just going to unlock the cages and leave them some food."

After what seemed like an hour, Ronald returned and climbed behind the wheel without a word. It was full dark now. He drove the car past the gate, then stopped and got out. He opened the trunk and removed a length of anchor chain, a heavy-duty padlock and a tube of superglue. He chained the front gate shut, padlocked the chain and shot a wad of superglue into the lock. If anyone wanted to get into the grounds, he wasn't going to make it easy for them.

When he was finished, he climbed back into the car without another look at the house. Then the Schmidts' Cadillac slipped silently into the dark unknown of night.

Chapter 51

"Are you ready yet?" asked Harold Todd. He checked the clock on his office wall again.

"Yes, soon," muttered Gunther. "You can't rush the creative process." His long hair was in a ponytail, and he was wearing a bright paisley waistcoat over a puffy-sleeved poet blouse with rawhide laces halfway down the front. If let loose to wander the mall, he would have caused nearly as much comment as the ghost illusion he was preparing.

"You're sure this is going to be safe?" asked Harold.

"Of course," said Libby. She had on a bald wig, which Gunther had blended into her skin. "We did a couple of trial runs earlier this week in Gunther's studio. It worked perfectly."

"Yes," said Gunther. "Check it out—the *pièce de resistance*." He reached into a shopping bag and pulled out a red fright wig. The hairs were loose and wiry, and stuck up in random profusion. "This is a special chemically impregnated fiber. It burns bright red but doesn't throw off that much heat—very safe."

"Yeah, I couldn't even really feel it earlier," said Libby.

Gunther reached into the shopping bag and pulled out a large bottle of Astroglide. "What's that for?" asked Harold, eyeing the bottle of lube skeptically.

"Just a little insurance," said Gunther. He squirted a huge blob of lube into his hand and began smearing it on Libby's chrome dome. "Water-based, right? It provides an insulating layer between Lib's head and the pyrotechnic wig. And if all else fails, I have this." He reached into the bag

CHAPTER 51

and pulled out a small fire extinguisher.

"Well, I sure hope you don't need to use *that*," said Harold. "How much more time will this take?"

"Look, we'll need, ah, fifteen minutes of *uninterrupted* time to finish setting up and to do some exercises prior to the performance," said Gunther. "Why don't you go take a walk or something. Try to relax."

"Yeah, yeah, right," said Harold. He was pretty wound up. He was much more nervous about this stunt than he had been last week when Libby had made her bloody debut. There were more people around, for starters. It was a Friday night, so people weren't so worried about getting home for school or work the next day.

Also, there were still a lot of ghost-hunters lurking around. They had come back in droves right after Libby's first performance, but the numbers had dwindled over the week. There were still a few diehards hanging around; some had been camping out in the parking lot.

Harold questioned whether this was a good idea at all. He certainly couldn't keep up this promotional hoaxing—sooner or later, it would blow up in his face. Maybe he'd call it quits after tonight. No more fake haunts to drum up publicity. Screw the mall. It had quit being fun to run it a long time ago, anyway. Maybe Harold would start discreetly looking around for a buyer—cash out entirely.

Still fretting, he did a lap of the mall, hoping a little exercise would help him relax. It didn't.

By the time he got back to his office, Gunther and Libby were ready to go. "Showtime?" asked Harold. They both nodded, Libby's wiry wig bobbing maniacally.

"Okay," said Harold. "I'll go unlock the loading dock door and make sure the coast is clear." He slipped out the employee's entrance to the office suite, across a breezeway and onto the loading dock. There was an array of construction gear and warning signs around the dock. He unlocked the door by the loading bay and poked his head in. A sparse light came from the emergency lights overhead. A reflected glow from the main shopping area came from around the corner.

Harold peeked his head around the corner. Shoppers walked back and forth beyond the barriers that blocked the opening to the construction area. There was a small knot of podcasters and looky-loos clustered on the benches on the opposite wall.

Harold looked up. The space was dark, but he was still nervous about being seen. He crept to the scaffolding and swung the frame with the plastic film into place and tied it off. He went back to the door and poked his head out—the coast was clear. He quick-walked back to the employee entrance, looking all around for stray shoppers. There weren't any—it was too far from the main entrances. He saw Libby and Gunther peering at him through the glass door and he frantically waved them over.

When they were in the loading dock, Gunther took a penlight from his ridiculous vest and began checking a rack of stage lights that had been mounted on the wall. Libby got on her mark and adjusted her black, reedy-looking dress. Gunther finished setting up the lights, then scuttled over to Libby. "Final thing," he said. "The squib that ignites the pyrotechnic."

"You still have that fire extinguisher, right?" asked Harold.

"Yeah, it's right over there," said Gunther. His hands were buried in the frizzy mass of the wig. He withdrew them and handed Libby a switch connected to a wire than ran into the back of the wig. "Okay, honey, when you're ready to rock, just hit the switch and—hellfire!"

"Okay, great," said Harold. "This time, I've gotta watch. Give me five minutes to get back into the mall, then start the show. Good luck!"

"Never say that to an actor!" said Libby. "It's bad luck. Say 'break a leg.'"

"Oh. Okay. Break a leg," said Harold. He turned back to the door and slithered into the night.

Gunther waited five minutes for the Todd guy to shag his polyester-clad ass to his preferred viewing spot. "Ready, honey?" he stage-whispered. In front of him, Libby nodded and gave him as thumbs-up behind her back.

"Here goes," he said to himself, and brought up the red lights that highlighted the wiry-haired "ghost." He couldn't see the audience in the mall, but the effect was instantaneous: a yelp, a rumbling murmur, then

CHAPTER 51

shouts of alarm and excitement.

Gunther felt the hair on his arms standing up. There was an almost sub-audible hum that quickly grew in volume. In the space between where Gunther was manning the lighting controls and where Libby was waving her arms, a blue light popped into view. It grew into a large electric-turquoise lozenge that quickly resolved itself into the form of a man. The man had long hair on one side of his head and was shaved to the scalp on the other.

The blue man must have been visible to the crowd in the mall—the hubbub increased exponentially.

"What the fuck?" cried Gunther. The blue man began pacing towards Libby. "Honey, watch out!"

Libby turned to see the ominous blue figure pacing towards her. Her angry mien dissolved into a look of confusion, then alarm. Startled, she squeezed the switch that triggered the pyrotechnic wig. She didn't realize her hair was on fire—only that something was very wrong and some glowing weirdo was coming straight for her. She stumbled backwards and fell into the giant plastic sheeting stretched on the scaffolding frame. The blazing wig ignited the plastic, and a sheet of flame rocketed up the scaffolding.

The blue man stepped through the sheet of flame, seemingly unfazed. Behind him, Gunther rushed up with his fire extinguisher. He first turned it on Libby, making sure the wig was out and that it hadn't spread to her dress. Then he turned the spray on the flames on the scaffolding, but the small canister gave out quickly.

"Come on, Lib!" he cried, hauling his smoldering girlfriend to her feet. "Let's get the fuck outta this madhouse!" The two ran to the door in the back of the loading space and had just tumbled through when the fire alarm and sprinklers began going off all over the mall.

The glowing blue man paid no attention. He stepped forward, almost to the barrier that separated the construction space from the rest of the mall. In the mall, it was utter pandemonium—people fled, bumping into those steadfastly recording the glowing man on their phones, fire alarm or no fire alarm.

The glowing man looked around, raised his arm and uttered one word:

"Down!" A blue bolt shot from his upraised hand, then the man was himself enveloped in a blue glow that flashed blindingly bright and disappeared into nothingness.

Chapter 52

High over central Pennsylvania, flight Whiskey Echo-11 increased its speed. Piloted by Major Dan Thompson of the 112th Fighter Squadron, Whiskey Echo-11 had taken off twenty minutes earlier from the Toledo Air National Guard base, bound for the aerial bombing range at Fort Indiantown Gap, Pennsylvania..

Major Thompson piloted an F-16C Viper, and he was loaded for bear. There were four Mark 84 bombs—the big boys—mounted on the underside. He was to drop them on the FITG range and return to base.

This was just fine with Major Thompson. Live fire exercises were few and far between, and he relished the chance to put the F-16 through her paces with live ordnance. Major Thompson had learned to fly before he'd learned to drive, and he loved to fly the Viper—it handled like a dream.

Major Thompson also had another reason to relish this early-evening bombing run. His wife, Vera, was fooling around with a guy she'd met at the gym. Major Thompson had met the douchebag once—he and Vera had been strolling around the Franklin Park Mall and bumped into him. His name was Rex, and he and Vera seemed *way* more friendly than seemed called for, given an allegedly casual gym relationship. Rex was a weenie, and Major Thompson figured he could take him in a straight fight, but Rex had the advantage of being twenty years younger. Vera had always had an eye for the young guys.

Major Thompson didn't *know* that Vera and Rex were having an affair, but he had his suspicions. The late night "workouts" that sometimes ran until nearly midnight, the strange phone calls, and the long hug the two had exchanged at the mall had all raised his suspicions. And Rex was from Pittsburgh, so Major Dan Thompson was gratified at the prospect of blowing up some of that asshole's home state.

Air traffic control was nagging him about his ETA, so he pushed the throttle forward and the Viper surged ahead. Flight Whiskey Echo-11 had been late taking off. There was supposed to have been a second plane in the flight, but the wingman, Captain Tommy Mantell, had been stricken with an incapacitating bout of the Hershey squirts and had to scrub. Rather than lose a valuable opportunity for live bombing training, command had opted to go without Captain Mantell, and Major Thompson was flying solo.

He had just passed within view of Pittsburgh and was idly contemplating the consequences of "accidentally" releasing his bomb payload onto Rex's childhood home. Major Thompson shook his head—whatever his domestic problems were, he had taken an oath to defend the citizens of the United States of America, even if they were wife-stealing gym-rats. Besides, the paperwork for such an event would be a nightmare.

He had just had this sobering realization when there was a blinding blue flash and every instrument in the cockpit went dead. Later, when recounting this story to Captain Mantell, he swore that immediately before everything crapped out, he saw the image of a man in the blue flash. The man had long hair on one side of his head and was shaved to the scalp on the other side. Of course, *that* hadn't gone into the official report.

Major Thompson wasn't concerned about reports now—he had bigger problems to contend with. The first was to regain control of a $20 million piece of hardware that had an almost-full load of fuel and four tons of high explosive on board.

It was hopeless. The engine was still running—albeit with greatly reduced thrust—but none of the controls in the cockpit were functioning. The control stick was unresponsive and all of the displays and gauges were dead. The throttle had no effect on the sputtering engine.

Major Thompson keyed his headset and said, as calmly as he could manage, "Mayday, mayday. This is Whiskey Echo-11 declaring an emergency. Can anyone read me? Over." There was no response.

CHAPTER 52

There was nothing he could do but bail out. He looked all around through the bubble canopy. He was over an unpopulated area—good. Before he ejected, he wanted to make sure the F-16 would not crash where there were people. It didn't seem to be a problem; the jet was nosed down and was on a trajectory to land on a wooded hillside. Major Thompson gave the control stick one more hard shake, but nothing happened. He had no control of the aircraft.

He took another look around but could see nothing but the wooded Allegheny foothills rushing up to meet him. The F-16 was headed for the middle of nowhere and there was nothing he could do to control it. It was time to blow this clambake.

He reached down between his legs and yanked the ejector seat handle. For a moment, nothing happened. Major Thompson had just enough time to contemplate his own fiery death, then there was a loud bang as the canopy blew upwards. There was a microsecond of howling wind, then the ejector seat dragged Major Thompson backwards out of the cockpit at eighteen times the force of gravity.

He blacked out for a moment, but it wasn't for very long. When he came to, he could still see the now-canopyless F-16. It was bathed in a blue glow that faded quickly. The F-16 seemed to be flying more level now; it was no longer nosediving for the hills. As he watched with mounting horror, the unmanned fighter plane began to turn—and was soon heading right back at him!

Desperately, Major Thompson yanked on the rudimentary controls that gave him a small measure of ability to control his descent. It didn't really matter; his ability to steer was minimal, but the jet passed him with a good five miles to spare. He got the ejector seat turned so he could follow the jet, and when he had, he could see the F-16 headed back towards him again!

Again, it passed him with miles to spare, then again began looping back. Major Thompson realized the stricken jet was spiraling downward in the same general trajectory as his own. It didn't matter now—it was descending faster than he was and was now at least two thousand feet below him. The winds were carrying him in an easterly direction; the fighter was heading that way as well.

The fighter dropped through a layer of cloud cover below and was lost from sight. When Major Thompson broke through the clouds, he was horrified to see he was over a populated area. To his left were the lights of a small city. A broad river ran through it, with more lights diminishing to the east and south.

He scanned for signs of the runaway jet but couldn't see it. Maybe it had crashed already. But, no—he would have been able to see the fire and the cloud of smoke. The sun was beginning to set behind him, but there was still plenty of daylight left.

He drifted lower and would soon be on the ground. Just ahead, there was a large V-shaped building with an even larger parking lot in a great wooded area. As he drifted closer, he saw the building was a mall or shopping center. Oddly, people seemed to be streaming out of the building. Over his shoulder, he could see a line of flashing red lights coming down a road that led to the city center. There must be a fire or emergency going on there. Well, it was too late for him to safely navigate to any place else. Whatever excitement was going on, he figured, it was about to get a lot more exciting.

He was proved right just moments later. There was a quick blur in the corner of his vision, and he jerked around to see the wayward F-16 fighter zooming in from over the river. It screamed across the parking lot at treetop height and slammed into the middle of the mall at approximately four hundred miles an hour. There was an enormous explosion as the remaining fuel and four one-ton bombs detonated.

The updraft from the explosion lofted Major Thompson skyward and over the river, where he came down in a cornfield. *The paperwork on this is going to be a bitch,* he thought.

Chapter 53

A column of official vehicles snaked its way up Morningwood Promenade. Martin's personal car was in the lead, followed by three marked constabulary cruisers and a SWAT van. Martin was loaded for bear. They were finally going to arrest Ronald Schmidt.

The letter from Solheim had alleged that Ronald had paid him five grand to have Candy swipe Bolly's credit card, no questions asked. Candy had done so and gotten a cool grand for her effort. She'd handed the card to Mike who had given it to Ronald. No questions were asked.

There were some smudged and partial prints on the card that they had assumed came from some long-forgotten merchants. Martin had gotten the fingerprint team to do a closer inspection and compare any partials with Ronald Schmidt's prints. A match had come back, and Martin had gotten a warrant. There'd be no mistakes this time, no interference from the mayor or from Pierre Nasté, no weaselly bullpoop like that. Martin had made a mistake already in this case. He wasn't about to do it again. He was going to go by the book.

The idea brought Martin no sense of vindictive pleasure. He had nothing against Ronald Schmidt personally, but he had been breaking the law for years and getting away with it. Now he had broken the most taboo law of all, and Martin was going to arrest him. He was going to set right what he had done wrong to Michael Bollinger. And he had learned an important lesson about not letting your emotions interfere with objective police work. It was a lesson he should have learned a long time ago.

The Schmidt mansion looked vacant. There was also a stout chain wrapped around the front gate.

"Oh, for goodness' sake!" said Martin. "Stay here while I check this out," he told Dan Blount, who was riding shotgun.

Martin got out and stalked over to the gate. The heavy chain was shut with a padlock the size of a man's fist. Martin examined the lock. Epoxy or glue had been injected into the lock mechanism. Whoever had put up this chain wanted to make sure no one got in—or out.

"Absolutely not," fumed Martin to himself as he fast-walked back to the car. He'd get a front-loader up here to knock the gate down, if it came to that. He was just about to instruct Blount to get one from the city motor pool, when the inspector rolled down the window and stuck out his head. "Chief, you better check this…" he said.

"Oh, for goodness' sake, what now?" asked Martin, exasperated. He took two more steps and could hear the radio: "…10-33. Repeat, 10-33. Fire and explosion at the Hickory Acres Mall. Possible mass casualties. All units respond. Repeat, all units respond."

"What are we gonna do, Chief?" asked Blount.

"What else?" asked Martin. "We respond. Let's go!"

Chapter 54

It was quiet in the foothills outside of Fester. As the sun lowered in the west, the shadows had begun to lengthen on Billy Snyder's property. A close observer would notice an indistinct air of neglect around the house and workshop. The windows weren't broken, but they were grimy. The lawn wasn't overgrown, but it was shaggy. The place looked like it had been recently abandoned.

A sound rose from the woods behind the house. It was faint at first, but it resolved to a roaring, clanking grind—the sound of aging mechanical parts and a poorly muffled engine.

The Thing emerged from the tree line, about a hundred yards up the hill from the house and workshop. Its engine roared, the treads churning up the recently concealed track on the hillside. It reached the bottom of the hill and thundered down the driveway. It slowed a bit when it reached the gate at the bottom of the drive, then accelerated and knocked it flat. The Thing came to rest in the middle of Dockstock Mountain Road.

The front hatch popped open and Billy Snyder stuck his head out. He sported a motorcycle helmet with internal headphones and mic, plugged into a digital radio that picked up police frequencies. There was a lot of *very* interesting chatter right now. At first, Billy had picked up transmissions between the cop cars that were heading up to the top of Morningwood Heights to arrest Ronald Schmidt. He knew his time was short when he heard that. He had briefly contemplated abandoning Camp Vengeance and just making a run for it. But no, the idea was unacceptable. He'd put too much effort into the Thing to give up now. He knew he just had to hang tough and look for an opening. Something would eventually present itself. And it had.

Something big had happened at the Hickory Acres Mall. Billy didn't understand the details, but they really didn't matter. All that mattered now was that every emergency vehicle in the area had been ordered to go to the mall to respond. Billy saw his chance. He'd take the Thing to the damn Schmidts house and blow the front of their fancy mansion off. It would be just like Hue. With luck, he'd be able to destroy the gun he'd sold Ronald. At the very least, he'd inflict some damage on the old-money family that had ruined his career and his life. If Billy Snyder was going down, he was going as hard as he could. And he intended to take the Schmidts with him.

Billy turned the rest of the way onto the road and headed downhill towards civilization. He decided to keep driving with his head sticking out of the hatch. He didn't anticipate a lot of sniper fire, and it was a nice evening. The air was warm, but he could feel a little edge as the sun slipped behind the hills. Without thinking, he reached down and turned on the Thing's headlights. "Safety first," said Billy to himself, then drove his tank into Fester.

Chapter 55

"I'm gonna need a joint to deal with this," said Janie.

"Better roll one for me, too," replied Bolly.

"Serious?"

"Hell, yes! Wouldja look at this shit?" He gestured at the TV, which was blasting WEVL-TV's nonstop coverage of the madness at the mall.

"... now reporting that an explosion caused by a crashed Air National Guard F-16 jet fighter. Other reports indicate a fire alarm in the mall was activated five minutes *before* radar lost contact with the F-16. We are now getting preliminary reports that the pilot of the F-16 has been recovered from a cornfield in east Fester. He has been transported to Lakeside Hospital in Weaverville and is expected to make a full recovery. We'll be right back after these messages." The channel cut to a Food Ape commercial advertising rump roasts.

Janie expertly twisted up a pair of joints, stuck them both in her mouth, lit them and handed one over to Bolly.

"Thanks, babe," he said, and took a hit. It was the first time he had smoked since the night he first went to Mike's Place. It made him feel a little guilty. Still, this was some exciting stuff. And *weird*—even by Fester standards. "Jeez, I never thought this town could get any stranger, but here ya go!" He gestured grandly at the TV.

Janie furiously pecked at her phone, bomber joint dangling insouciantly from her lip. "You think the news is weird?" she said. "You should see some of the stuff flying around Twitter. Somebody said they saw a freaking *tank* driving through downtown!"

"Ah, what a load!" said Bolly. "I bet there's a completely ordinary explanation for this."

Janie took a huge hit and shot a plume of blue smoke before replying. "Man, this weed must've gotten right on top of you," she said. "You gotta be stoned to be saying stuff like that. You've lived here all your life—you *know* how fuckin' weird this place is. I stood right beside you watching the chief constable come hopping out of a burning building in a homemade Batman costume. Escaping a fire set by suburban Satanists led by your best friend's mom."

"He wasn't chief constable at the time," Bolly pointed out.

"Oh, and that makes it *normal?*"

"Normal in Fester and normal everywhere else are two different things. Okay, I'll admit that this shit is weird, even by local standards. I was just hoping there was some more rational explanation. My life's been plenty weird enough lately, without crashing jets and tanks rolling through town, thank you very much. I just want the weirdness to end."

Bolly wasn't going to get his wish.

A Dairy Ferret commercial featuring a pair of cartoon weasels capering around with ice cream cones ended, and the news coverage resumed.

"Another twist in the already bizarre story coming out of the Hickory Acres Mall in Fester. WEVL-TV has learned that immediately prior to the fire and explosion, there was another alleged supernatural visitation, similar to ones reported there earlier this month." The anchor tossed her hair and laughed in a isn't-it-all-too-ridiculous sort of way. "This time, there were *two* ghosts who appeared to be fighting. I ... I don't know what else to say about this, so we're just going to roll the video obtained exclusively by WEVL-TV."

The view cut to shaky handheld phone video, showing a red translucent figure of a woman. She is gesturing angrily towards the crowd. There was sound, but it was entirely of people in the crowd gasping and talking excitedly about the apparition. Then the figure looks around and draws back, seemingly surprised. There is a shout of excitement as the ghostly figure's hair goes up in flames.

CHAPTER 55

Another ghostly form appeared, this one a blue, bare-chested man. He strides past the flaming-haired ghost, who staggers back out of the blue man's way. The fire suddenly jumps up, racing across the opening like a sheet of flame. The red figure disappears, shrinking back from the wall of fire. The blue man walks unhindered though the flames. The sheet of flames dissipates quickly, but small fires could still be seen burning at the top of the space.

The blue man begins gesturing and talking. A loud, deep voice can be heard over the rising murmur of the crowd. Bolts of blue lightning flash behind the man as he continues to wave his arms and intone. Then the fire alarm goes off. The picture jerks, then goes dark.

"What the actual fuck?" said Bolly, open-mouthed.

Janie just shook her head and tapped wildly on her phone. "The latest meme on Twitter is even crazier," she said. "Now they're saying that Arab terrorists used black magic to conjure up evil spirits to cause an explosion. The fighter jet and the tank were sent by the army to stop them, but the evil terrorist spirits were too powerful and overcame them."

"Whew," said Bolly. "That's just nuts. And people are *buying* it?"

"Yeah, it's getting re-tweeted like crazy."

"Besides, we don't know anything about a tank. There hasn't been anything on the news about it."

Janie shrugged. "There were pictures posted. It sure looked like a tank going up Highland."

On the TV, the coverage continued. "...timestamp from the video provided matches the time the fire alarm was relayed to Emergency Services. It seems as if the impact of the F-16 occurred approximately eight minutes later. This was actually good luck, as nearly the entire mall had been evacuated by the time of the jet impact and explosion. As of now, there are three confirmed dead and forty-four injured, although those numbers are expected to rise. Firefighting and rescue operations are ongoing..."

"I don't know if I can handle much more of this," said Bolly. His mind felt fragile. The events of the last few weeks had been jarring enough on their own. This latest sideshow was seriously testing his composure. "I'm starting to get the Fear."

"Don't worry, babe," said Janie. "I've got the cure." She pulled out the weed tray and began rolling two more joints. "Besides, you don't really want to bail now that things are starting to get interesting?"

Chapter 56

In the confusion surrounding the events at the mall, few people paid attention to the unusual sight of a large armored vehicle rolling through downtown Fester. Billy had been apprehensive about riding with the hatch open and was prepared to drop back into the driver's compartment and navigate with the periscope. However, people only gave him a passing glance; a few honked and waved. Billy realized that most of the people thought that he was responding to whatever the hell was going on at the mall. In fact, most of the traffic seemed to be headed towards the mall (despite official exhortations to stay away), and once he had turned off River Road to head up the hill, there was practically no traffic at all. This was especially true when he got onto Morningwood Promenade—it seemed like all of the townies were heading to the site of the disaster while all of the rich folks on the hill had hunkered down.

Billy roared to the top of Morningwood Promenade unimpeded and soon brought the Thing to a stop outside the gate of the Schmidt mansion. He was surprised to see that the gate had been padlocked shut. Had the Schmidts barricaded themselves inside? Or had they fled, locking the gate behind them. No matter. Billy had a tank.

He considered using one of the rounds from the recoilless rifles to take out the gate. He had loaded up the Thing with ammo: six rounds in the recoilless rifles, another six in the rack inside and five more slung underneath the hull. Billy had been a little nervous driving with all of that ammo on board. It was probably fifty years old and possibly unstable. Billy had winced hearing the big shells chattering in their racks as he raced the Thing through Fester and up Morningwood Promenade.

He decided against expending a round on the gate—he wanted to retain as many good rounds for the house as he could. He ducked into the driver's compartment, pulling the hatch after him, then surged forward. The Thing knocked the gate down like it was made of balsa wood.

He popped back out of the hatch, holding a megaphone. "SCHMIDTS!" he broadcast. "COME OUT OF THE HOUSE! YOU HAVE EXACTLY TWO MINUTES BEFORE I BEGIN FIRING! IT'S TIME YOU PAID FOR YOUR CRIMES! TWO MINUTES!"

Billy checked his watch. When ninety seconds had passed, he spoke into the megaphone again. "SCHMIDTS! YOU'VE RUINED MY LIFE AND NOW I'M GOING TO RUIN YOURS! IN THIRTY SECONDS, I'M GOING TO START TAKING YOUR MANSION APART IN BIG FUCKIN' CHUNKS! IF YOU'RE IN THERE COME OUT NOW! I DON'T WANT ANYONE TO GET HURT!" *But wouldn't care too much if someone does,* he mentally added.

He checked his watch. Time was up. "LAST CHANCE, YOU MANIPULATIVE BASTARDS! COME OUT NOW!"

Nothing. Just because he was a nice guy, he waited another thirty seconds. No one came out of the house; there was no movement at all inside that he could discern. "Fuck it," he muttered. "They've been warned."

He clambered back from the driver's compartment and into the gunner's seat. He popped open the hatch and stuck his head out. Aiming would be simple—the façade of the house was huge, and he was only fifty feet away. He made a slight change to the position of the turret to center the guns. Then he armed all six of the recoilless rifles. He sure wasn't going to fire all six at once—they were meant to be fired sequentially. The blast from just one was devastating. In the Marines, he'd heard they'd test-fired all six at once at the Aberdeen Proving Ground. The resulting blast and aftershock had blown out all the windows in a half-mile radius.

Billy hovered his thumb over the button that would fire Gun #1. He wondered if it would fire; there was still no telling how many of the old rounds were still good. He was about to find out.

CHAPTER 56

A small figure darted across the front of the house, followed shortly by another.

"What the *fuck?*" said Billy. Were there kids running around up here? He didn't think that Ronald or Thelma Louise had kids. Maybe there were some nephews and nieces visiting. But why were the gates padlocked shut if there were visitors? Billy boosted himself through the gunner's hatch and slid to the ground to investigate.

"Hey!" he shouted. He had forgotten to grab the megaphone. "Hey, kids! You need to get outta here!" He walked cautiously in the direction that the two small figures had gone.

"Come here, kids! You need to get out of here now! Demolition begins shortly. Hey! Where the hell are you?" He stalked past a huge Japanese maple tree, looking around for the kids who had run past him. There was a screech from above, and Billy was driven to the ground as two hairy bodies dropped on him from the tree.

Rondo, Berryman, and Peewee had been enjoying themselves for the last few days. They had free run over the entire grounds since the Schmidts departed. There was plenty of food and water left in the Monktorium, and there was even more exotic fare available in the main house. It had only taken Rondo a day to discover a way into the house, and the three monkeys had a blast exploring it from top to bottom. Berryman had eaten nearly two gallons of ice cream he had discovered in the kitchen freezer. The gastric results had been catastrophic—both to Berryman and the living room. He managed to sleep it off over the next day and was soon back to exploring his new environment.

The monkeys mostly stuck to the grounds of the estate. They had a strong sense of territoriality, and they instinctively knew the high fence around the property was the boundary of their territory. They sometimes ventured outside it, but never for very long. At night, they returned to their familiar beds in the Monktorium.

They barely missed Ronald, and they were having quite a good time roaming the grounds and rearranging the contents of the house. So they were quite upset when a loud, clanking machine came up the street. That was bad enough, but then the machine barged into their territory and knocked down part of the barrier!

Rondo and Berryman screeched and scuttled to their new favorite tree to hide and await further developments. Peewee—the rebel of the group—took the opportunity to scale the fence and check out the machine, which had ceased its irritating noise. In short order, Peewee was swinging merrily from barrel to barrel of the guns.

Billy was not having such a merry time. He didn't know what the fuck had dropped on him, only that they had sharp teeth and smelled horrible. He desperately tried to unholster his .45 while simultaneously trying to protect his face and his crotch.

Rondo and Berryman continued to scratch and bite Billy, who was screaming with fear and frustration. The screams just further agitated the monkeys. The three of them rolled around the lawn like a cartoon dogfight, shrieking and cursing and kicking up clods of earth.

Over at the Thing, Peewee had discovered the open gunner's hatch and had dropped down to the seat. He amused himself by popping up and down out of the hatch like a jack-in-the-box.

Suddenly, there was a loud report. Billy had managed to get out his .45 and had loosed a wild shot into the air. Startled, Peewee leapt back in the gunner's seat, where his butt hit a bank of buttons and simultaneously fired all six guns.

There were two enormous explosions: the first as all six of the recoilless rifles fired their rounds, and another a fraction of a second later as the high-explosive rounds slammed into the façade of the Schmidt mansion. The powerful blast of the guns caused the Thing to flip over backwards and go sailing into a ravine on the other side of the road. Peewee was flung from the gunner's turret and went soaring into the high branches of an oak at the edge of the ravine.

The Thing tumbled end over end, spilling extra rounds from the rack underneath. Several of the high-explosive rounds dropped onto the boulders in the ravine, then the Thing dropped on top of them. One of the

CHAPTER 56

rounds detonated, igniting all of the rest, including the half-dozen inside the hull. There was yet one more astounding explosion in Fester. The Thing came apart like a soda can with an M80 inside.

Billy's ears rang. He had been unconscious, but he had no idea for how long. The monsters that had attacked him had taken off as soon as he had fired his wild shot. He saw as they raced away they were monkeys. He had no idea why there were monkeys up here, but that was typical of the insane shit these Top Hats got up to.

He knew he didn't have much time before the law showed up. Regardless of whatever was going on down at the mall, a report of three large explosions at the top of Morningwood Promenade was going to bring first responders in a hurry.

Billy stood up. He felt shaky, but generally okay. He took a few tentative steps, and that worked out okay, too. He was covered with bruises and monkey bites, but he could still walk.

He realized he really hadn't thought out his end game very well. He'd been so focused on getting the Thing up here unimpeded—and he really hadn't been sure that he'd even be able to do *that*—that he hadn't thought about what came after. Maybe eat his gun, maybe make a run for it.

He was going to run now. Or crawl, if need be. He had to get off this hill and his only chance would be to go overland. With any luck, the constables would think that the driver of the Thing had been vaporized along with the vehicle.

It was a shame the Thing was gone, but it had served its purpose. Billy surveyed his handiwork. The porch and the front section of the Schmidt mansion was just plain gone. Half of the grand staircase hung suspended from the second-floor landing. Everything in front of it had been turned to matchwood.

Billy nodded and walked stiffly through the twisted remains of the gate and onto the road. All that was left of the Thing was a fifteen-foot-wide crater scattered with shiny bits of metal. He shrugged and plunged into the brush. He had a lot of ground to cover, but if he was lucky, he could be back to Camp Vengeance by sunrise. After that, it was bug-out time. He was more than ready to bid *adieu* to Kerian County.

High in the oak tree, Peewee clung to a branch and shivered. He felt terrible and frightened. He clung to the branch for a long time, until at last he felt okay to move. Very slowly, he climbed down from the tree, then made his way back across the road and towards the Monktorium. He wanted to see if there were any more dried apple slices left.

Chapter 57

"The cadaver dog has found something, Chief," said Inspector Blount.

"One of the Schmidts?" asked Martin.

"Don't exactly know. It's kind of strange. Maybe you'd better come look. Be careful, though. There are still some monkeys running around loose around here."

"What?" Martin had heard rumors about Ronald's pets, had never paid them much mind.

"Yeah, there's a building out back with cages and stuff. Don't worry, animal control's on their way."

Martin suppressed a sigh and turned to follow Blount. It had been a hell of a day. Just as things had started to come under control at the mall, the report had come in of multiple explosions on Morningwood Promenade. Martin had been glad to leave the scene at the mall. Since it had involved the military, the feds were all over the place, and the staties and county-mounties had to stick their oar in as well. Martin had been relieved to have an excuse to leave. But now he had to deal with a bigger crisis.

The front of the Schmidt mansion had been blown away, and there was a huge crater across the road from the flattened front gate. There had been reports of a tank seen coming down River Road earlier, but in the confusion following the fire and crash at the mall it had been overlooked.

This investigation would take time. Martin had already requested help from the State Police; crime scene units were already on their way from the mall. The important thing now was to ascertain the extent of the casualties. It seemed that there was at least one.

"We'll have to go around the back," said Blount. That seemed pretty obvious—the entire front of the house was gone. Martin could see the stone walls of the basement yawning below. They went around to the back and descended into the basement through the servants' entrance. There was no power, but a number of lanterns had been set up to guide people through the morass of junk.

As they threaded their way through the junk, they passed an abandoned dumbwaiter. The door hung from one hinge. Inside, Berryman screeched and thrashed around.

"What is that monkey doing?" asked Martin.

"Masturbating, sir."

"Ugh."

"Indeed," said Blount. "Animal control will be here in twenty minutes. In the meantime, probably best to keep out of his way."

"Right," said Martin. "Where's this find?"

"Just over here," said Blount, indicating a corner of the basement.

Three men with flashlights stood clustered around a chest freezer. In the far corner, a uniformed sheriff's deputy held a whining German Shepard on a leash.

"What's all this, then?" asked Martin. He didn't understand what would be going on in this back corner of the basement; surely, any casualties would have been at the front of the building.

Constable Hurley said, "The dog got a hit at this freezer. We had to cut off the lock." He nodded at the broken padlock on the floor. "Take a look." He lifted the freezer lid.

Martin looked in to see a mummified corpse. All of the hair had fallen from the leathery skull, but it was wearing a dress with a black-and-white houndstooth pattern that would have been the height of fashion twenty years earlier. A smell like moldy leaves wafted up from the freezer—and another scent, an undertone, but unmistakable nonetheless—Chanel No. 5.

"It's been here a while, I think," said Blount. "I wonder who it could be?"

"Oh, I have a pretty good idea," said Martin. "I think testing will confirm that these are the remains of Cecilia Schmidt. It's that Chanel No. 5—it was her signature scent."

"Oh, right, I remember!" said Blount. "I was guarding the mayor one time when I was a rookie. Cecilia Schmidt was hizzoner's guest, and man, it was like she had taken a bath in it."

"Indeed," said Martin. "But we're not here to discuss the deceased's grooming habits. We need to get a line to the FBI. We want a BOLO for Ronald Schmidt, Thelma Louise Schmidt, and Ophelia Schmidt. Quickly."

"On it, Chief," said Blount.

"Good," said Martin. "And be sure to do something about those consarned monkeys!"

III

Part Three

May 2015

Chapter 58

Ralph Wallace was a retired detective from Tucson, and he was tired of Astoria. He and his wife were in Oregon to visit his wife's sister and idiot husband. Fortunately, the sister and idiot husband's house was small and couldn't accommodate sleep-over guests, so Ralph and his wife had gotten a large room at the Hampton Inn on the riverfront. It provided a good base of operations when he wasn't visiting Carol's relatives—something he hadn't done in three days. He'd seen enough of them on the first day and would be just as happy to avoid them for the rest of their two-week visit.

He was getting pretty tired of Astoria, though. It had been charming at first, with its nineteenth-century houses and Art Deco downtown. There was an old cannery on pilings out in the river just past the hotel. It had been converted into a tourist trap full of boutique shops and brewpubs. In Ralph's opinion, its only redeeming feature was that it had a good coffee place.

Ralph had worked out a routine: he'd rise early and wander up to the cannery and get a cup of black coffee to go. He'd drink it on his way back to the hotel, where he'd pick up the local paper, the *Astorian,* and the *Oregonian* from Portland. They were both horrible bleeding-heart rags, but Ralph was smart enough to read between the lines. He'd spend a leisurely hour or two in the lobby, combing through the papers and fuming at their blatant liberal bias. Then he'd wander to a park up the hill from the hotel that provided a panoramic view of the Astoria waterfront and watch the ships for an hour or so. Then he went for lunch at the Bowpicker, which sold fish and chips from a converted fishing boat. Afterwards, he'd go back to the hotel to take a nap or watch movies in the room.

Ralph Wallace had been there about a week when he noticed the tall man. Ralph was in the lobby, silently sputtering over an article about Portland tree-huggers trying to block the construction of a liquid natural gas terminal. As if their houses were heated with moonbeams and good karma! He'd just put down the paper when the tall man walked by him, close to the back wall of the lobby. He had a slight limp. It caught Ralph's attention. He squinted. He thought he might have seen the man a few nights ago as he and Carol were heading out for dinner. Ralph wasn't sure because he and Carol had been arguing about something stupid.

He watched the man as he limped up the hallway past the reception desk and pulled open the door to the stairwell. Strange. Who takes the stairs when there's an elevator available—especially if he's having trouble walking? Someone who was trying to avoid attention, in Ralph's experience. His cop-radar was going crazy. This guy was up to something. He'd have to find out more.

The next morning, Ralph bought a John Grisham novel in the hotel's sundries store and spent most of the morning reading it in the lobby. He wasn't staking the place out—not exactly. All he would admit to himself was that he was interested in the tall man. There was something just *off* about him.

Ralph didn't see him that morning. He made a trip to the Bowpicker for his now-daily fish and chips, then resumed his reading in the lobby. He was about to go see if he could scare up an old Clint Eastwood movie in the room when the tall man reappeared. This time, he came down on the elevator and didn't seem to be limping as badly. Ralph got a good look at him. The guy was tall—six-five at least, maybe more. He had a goofy box haircut and the eyes beneath the cut-rate spectacles were deep-set and sullen. With a start, Ralph realized who he looked like: just add a molester 'stache, and the guy was a dead ringer for Edmund Kemper, the serial killer who had chopped off his mother's head and thrown darts at it.

The Kemper look-alike went out to the parking lot. Ralph counted to

CHAPTER 58

ten, then rose and followed him. He stood under the portico and attempted to look intently interested in the weather as Kemper started up a car and backed out of the slot. Black Chevy Impala, four-door, late nineties or early oughts. He noted the Wisconsin license plate, then hurried back inside to write it down.

He called Deke, who had been his chief of detectives, and was even more retired than Ralph. Deke was still wired into the Tucson PD *and* he was still in Tucson, so he had access to resources unavailable to Ralph at the end of the great Columbia River.

Deke called back an hour later to report the tags were clean, and were registered to a 1999 Ford Escort wagon, owned by Mrs. Emily Wanatka of Bohemia, Wisconsin. The car they were on now was definitely not a 1999 Ford Escort Wagon. Ralph started to get excited. He asked Deke to have the chief of the Tucson PD to call the main cop here in Astoria and get him an in.

"Aw, for fuck's sake," said Deke. "You're retired now, Ralph. This ain't your *job* anymore. Let it go."

"Fuck, no!" said Ralph. "There's something *off* about this guy. I can feel it. You know when I get one of my feelings, Deke. You have for thirty fuckin' years, right?"

"Okay, okay," sighed Deke. "I'll see what I can do. But this is the last time, pally. Next time you wanna play Batman, you're doing it on your own dime."

"Thanks, Deke. You're the best."

"Fuckin'-A, right, I am."

Ralph spent the night in apprehension, afraid that Kemper would slip away. The car with the bogus Wisconsin tags was still there in the morning, and Ralph made a beeline to the police headquarters downtown.

It took him half an hour on their computer to make the identity. "That's him!" crowed Ralph to the desk sergeant. "Ronald Schmidt, from Pennsylvania. Wanted for murder, attempted murder, and unauthorized harboring of primates. Wow, sounds like a real creep."

The sergeant came around the desk and looked at the terminal. "Huh," he grunted. "You sure?"

"Hell, yeah! Positive ident!"

"How about these other two?" He pointed at pictures of Ophelia and Thelma Louise. "Didja see 'em?"

"No, no—don't know about either. But that was definitely Ronald Schmidt. As far as I know, he's back at the hotel now."

"Ah, shit," said the sergeant. "Better tell the chief."

Forty minutes later, three unmarked cars slid from behind police headquarters and made the short journey to the Hampton Inn. "You'd better stay here, Mr. Wallace," said the chief.

"Two things there," said Ralph. "First, it's *Detective* Wallace, and second: hell no! I bagged him. I can ID him. You have to let me go, Chief!"

The chief sighed. "Jesus, okay. But remember: you are not a member of law enforcement, you are not deputized, you are not carrying a firearm. You are merely a good citizen helping the police with an investigation. Got it?"

"Got it."

"Let's go," said the chief. "A-team, cover the exits, B-team with me. Rooms 217 and 219—up the stairs, quietly. Let's go."

The B-team split into two groups and ganged up behind the two doors. They had room keys furnished by the very nervous manager. Ralph was in the group of three men in front of 219. What the chief had said wasn't entirely accurate: Ralph *was* armed. He had a Remington .380 auto in an ankle holster. He took it with him everywhere he went; he felt naked without it. When he was sure the other cops weren't looking, he reached down and slipped it in his jacket pocket.

The chief counted to three and the teams rushed through the doors. Ralph waited for the other two to go in first, like a good little boy—but was close behind them. Room 219 was empty. One of the other cops had just poked his head into the bathroom when a shout and a clamor came from Room 217. The two Astoria cops looked at each other and rushed out of the room to see what the fuss was about.

Ralph was alone in the room. He pulled the gun from his pocket. If the

CHAPTER 58

Astoria cops didn't like it, they could go pound sand. Something was off here—he could feel it. The door to the room swung silently shut.

Ralph looked over at the bathroom door. It was standing partway open, and Ralph was pretty sure that neither of the Astoria cops had gone in. Leveling his gun, he moved quickly to the bathroom. He shouldered the door the rest of the way open and swung the gun from left to right, covering the room.

There was a loud *zzzip* sound as the shower curtain was yanked aside. Ronald Schmidt stood in the bathtub. To Ralph, it seemed like Ronald wasn't there at one moment and was there the next. He pivoted to get off a shot, but Ronald reached out with surprising speed and batted the little automatic out of his hand like it was a child's toy. Ralph dove for the gun, but Ronald moved quickly, leaping from the bathtub and shoving Ralph hard in the chest, then scooping up the gun.

Ralph sprawled backwards, the backs of his legs hit the edge of the bed, and he fell over onto the hideous chain hotel bedspread. He panted heavily. Ronald eyed him blankly. He was holding the gun but pointing it at the floor. *Oh shit,* thought Ralph. *Here I am supposed to be retired and I'm gonna get iced by some guy that looks like Boris Fuckin' Karloff. Carol's gonna kill me!*

Ralph could hear a voice in the hall. It was the chief. "... yeah, Mr. Wallace, you might want to see this, if you're of a mind. I mean, you seem like a guy with a pretty strong stomach, so it prolly won't bother you too bad..." He pushed the door open and came into the room, saw Ralph looking in the bathroom, saw what Ralph was looking at. He went for his gun, but in a flash Ronald had the gun up. "Uh-uh," he said.

The chief froze and stayed silent. That was strange enough in itself for three more Astoria policemen to pile into the room to see what was happening. They all froze. All of the police had their hands on the butts of their guns. Out in the hallway, others were calling, "What's the sitrep? Hey! What the fuck's going on in there?"

Ronald's eyes flicked back and forth across the cops, doing the math in his head. It must have added up wrong. He raised the muzzle of the .380 to the underside of his chin and fired. His head jerked, his eyes clouded over red and he dropped in a boneless heap, where a puddle of blood spread on the atrocious chain hotel carpeting.

They estimated that Ophelia had been dead for two weeks. Ronald had just piled a couple of comforters over her, cranked up the air conditioning and put a *Do Not Disturb* sign on the door.

They backtracked the Schmidts' journey across the country. They mostly stayed in small towns along US 30, using credit cards and ID under the name of Walter Royer and family. They had headed west from Pennsylvania, and Astoria was the end of the line.

Thelma Louise had disappeared somewhere in the Midwest. She was last seen with her brother and aunt in Ames, Iowa. After that—nothing. It was speculated that Ronald and Ophelia had eliminated Thelma Louise, fearing she would expose them. Or maybe Thelma Louise decided to get away from her batty relatives and strike out on her own. Either way, she was never found.

After the investigation had been completed, the remains of Ronald and Ophelia were shipped back to Fester, courtesy of Nasté, Brutus, and Shore, Attorneys at Law. The same oversaw their burial in the Schmidt family plot at Rosewater Hill Cemetery. They were interred right next to the plot where Cecilia Schmidt had been buried a few months earlier, following an autopsy that concluded she had been poisoned.

Chapter 59

Janie held back a corner of the hurricane fence, and the two men slipped through. She ducked through quickly and let it spring back into place behind her. They pushed past the scrubby perimeter and soon were in open ground. The demolition at Hickory Acres Mall had been going on for nine months now, and it was mostly complete. There was no activity here on a Sunday morning.

"Good old Janie," said Bolly. "Always knows the back ways in."

"It's no big deal," said Janie. "The service road has been there since they built the mall. It's where all the trucks and stuff used to come in."

The other man laughed. "Just like the Fester cops to blockade the front door and leave the back door wide open!" The man was about forty and wore a brown serape with an intricate pattern of intertwining reds and golds. His graying hair was pulled back in a long ponytail. He wore round, rimless glasses and had deep laugh lines.

"Paul Freakin' Plummer," said Bolly. "Can't believe you're back here, man."

"So glad you are, though!" piped Janie.

"Man, I can't believe I *am* back," said Paul. "Just wish I had come a little sooner."

"Why did you come at all?" asked Janie. "I'm sorry if that sounded snotty, but you just sort of showed up out of the blue."

Paul laughed. "Been keeping tabs on you—Fester's been all over the news. Besides, I've been an online subscriber to the *Fester Daily Dispatch* for years. Much better than the *Weekly World News* or *American Investigator* when it comes to high weirdness."

"Yeah," said Bolly. "For what it's worth, I've been meaning to call you for a while, but, never, y'know…"

"Yeah, I know. Don't we all."

"Here we are," announced Janie. They stood about twenty feet away—a respectful distance—from the hand statue that had graced the plaza of the Hickory Acres Mall. Statue no more, the explosion had returned it to its original status as a hand-shaped rock.

"I remember when we found this place," said Janie. "Nothing but woods around here then."

"Starting to grow back already," said Paul. "Mother Nature overcomes all obstacles." He stared hard at the rock.

After a long time, he said, "Do you guys remember me talking about Chief Tonto?"

Bolly and Janie gave each other a quick look. "Yeah," said Bolly. "Wasn't he, like, that Native American that you hallucinated after you took your mom's crazy pills?"

"Bolly!" hissed Janie and elbowed him in the ribs.

"Sorry, man," said Bolly.

"No worries, brother," said Paul. "Those pills sure did a number on my mom, but she took a lot more than I did."

"We're so sorry about what happened to your mom, Paul," said Janie. Bolly nodded hard.

"Thanks, guys. The drugs that Dr. Ziffer gave her messed her up bad, but at least she was well cared-for at Johns Hopkins. Her death was painful for a long time, but I can come at it from a place of love and compassion now."

"That's great," said Bolly, marveling at his old friend's hippy vibe. Paul had never been the same after he'd taken the experimental drugs his mother had been given. It may have been an improvement—Paul seemed more relaxed and less self-centered after his impromptu trip.

"It opened up my third eye, really," said Paul. Bolly started. It was almost as if Paul had heard his thoughts. Maybe he had.

"It was Chief Tonto," Paul continued. "That 'ghost' in the videos. Believe me, I watched them obsessively. It was *him*. I didn't hallucinate him; I *visited*

CHAPTER 59

him. Like, I sideslipped into the reality where he lives for a while."

Bolly and Janie gave each other another quick look.

Paul shook his head. "Chief Tonto's gone now. I don't sense him."

"Maybe just as well," said Janie.

"The equilibrium has been restored," said Paul.

"So, the destruction of the mall brought balance to the Force?" asked Janie.

"Exactly!" said Paul. "I just felt like I had to come back to, y'know, bear witness."

"Amen, Brother Ben!" said Bolly.

"So what now?" asked Janie.

"I'm hungry," announced Bolly. "How about lunch?"

"Gonna have to take a raincheck on that lunch, Boll-meister," said Paul. "I'm heading up to Harrisburg for a few days to spend time with my cousins, then back to the Land of Enchantment. Hey, you guys should come out!"

"Yeah, that'd be great!" said Janie.

"Yeah," echoed Bolly, knowing that it would never happen.

They began walking back to where they had parked, by the section of fence with the loose chain-link.

"Hey, we need good mechanics in New Mexico, too," said Paul. "Guy like you could make bank."

"Yeah, maybe," allowed Bolly. "But I want to stick near to my old man in Weaverville, and I've got a lot of long-time customers at the shop. It'd be hard to …"

Paul held up his hand, "I know, old friend, I know. But if you ever have a yen to visit the Great Southwest, my door is always open to you. Always. The treasures of Loomis, New Mexico are yours to discover!"

"We'll see."

"I know."

"Yeah, we all know."

Paul stepped to Bolly and gave him a bear hug. There was a delicate but no-less-heartfelt one for Janie. "Later days, my dear friends," he said, then climbed into his rental Kia and drove off.

"Still want some lunch?" asked Janie.

"Do we still have any of that roast beef?" asked Bolly.

"Yeah."

"Good. Let's go home, make sandwiches and binge-watch *Game of Thrones*."

"You're on!"

And life was again good in Fester, at least for a while.

About the Author

Crawford Smith claims to rise every morning at 4:30 to meditate, exercise and eat a breakfast of free-range, fair-trade, organic oat bran husks. He makes many dubious claims.

What *is* known is that he can quote an unsettling amount of material from Monty Python and *The Simpsons*. He is also the author of *Jackrabbit* (2019), a speculative retelling of the career of gangster John Dillinger. This was followed by *Powwows* (2021) and *Fester* (2021) – tales of the strange and hilarious goings-on in the town of Fester, Pennsylvania. In 2024, he released *Laughingstock*, a story of the weird underbelly of stand-up comedy. *Fester Descent,* a sequel to *Fester,* was published in 2026, and there was much rejoicing.

He hangs out in Portland, Oregon.

You can connect with me on:
- http://sweetweaselwords.com
- https://www.facebook.com/CrawfordSmithAuthor

Subscribe to my newsletter:
- http://sweetweaselwords.com/contact

Also by Crawford Smith

To join Crawford's e-mail list, please visit sweetweaselwords.com/contact/

Fester

Inspector Martin Prieboy has a lot on his plate, and when two high-profile cases land on his desk, he soon finds himself entangled in an ancient mystery that Fester's leading citizens want to keep buried. Soon, a chance discovery in the woods unleashes a volatile mixture of history, mystery and greed, threatening the future of Fester. Will Martin stop the absurd dark forces that have been unleashed and keep the town from being torn apart?

Laughingstock

Chuck Marshall has the stand-up comedy world in the palm of his hand – big-time gigs, streaming specials and his own network TV show.

Then he mysteriously disappears.

Duckie Dunne, Chuck's original comedy partner, sets out to locate his old friend. To help his search, Duckie enlists the aid of Cheryl, daughter of the late comedy legend Mickey Gross. However, Mickey may not be quite as dead as everyone thinks. At the end of their long, strange trip is a secret comics' retreat and an explosive comedy showdown!

Powwows

Deep in the woods lives a wizard called the Professor. In the depths of the Depression, the residents of Fester, Pennsylvania call on "powwowers" such as the Professor to heal ailments, tell fortunes . . . and exact revenge. When an upstart powwower threatens to horn in on the Professor's business, he starts making plans for his own revenge. The sinister forces he sets in motion spiral out of control, and soon threaten to consume the leading citizens of the town.

Jackrabbit

What really happened to John Dillinger? It's 1934, and America is in the middle of a crime wave. John Dillinger, a.k.a. the Jackrabbit, has become America's first celebrity criminal. Now desperate to escape the perilous life that he's created, the Jackrabbit concocts a daring plan to disappear. As the FBI draws the noose tighter, the Jackrabbit knows that time is running out. Will his audacious scheme work, or will he go down in a thunderstorm of lead?

www.ingramcontent.com/pod-product-compliance
Lightning Source LLC
LaVergne TN
LVHW041744060526
838201LV00046B/902